Maureen Child e line and can't imagine for a prestigious Roma ward, Maureen is an au nance novels. Her book s and have won severa rd, a National Readers' Choice Award, a Colorado Romance Writers Award of Excellence and a Golden Quill Award. She is a native Californian but has recently moved to the mountains of Utah.

Karen Booth is a Midwestern girl transplanted to the South, raised on '80s music, Judy Blume and the films of John Hughes. She writes sexy big-city love stories. When she takes a break from the art of romance, she's teaching her kids about good music, honing her Southern cooking skills or sweet-talking her husband into whipping up a batch of cocktails. Find out more about Karen at www.karenbooth.net.

RICH RANCHER'S REDEMPTION

MAUREEN CHILD

BETWEEN MARRIAGE AND MERGER

KAREN BOOTH

MILLS & BOON

First Published in Great Britain 2018
by Mills & Boon, an imprint of HarperCollinsPublishers,
1 London Bridge Street, London, SE1 9GF

Rich Rancher's Redemption © 2018 Harlequin Books S.A.
Between Marriage and Merger © 2018 Karen Booth

Special thanks and acknowledgement are given to Maureen Child for her contribution to the Texas Cattleman's Club: The Impostor series.

ISBN: 978-0-263-93590-5

51-0218

MIX
Paper from
responsible sources
FSC® C007454

This book is produced from independently certified FSC™
paper to ensure responsible forest management.

For more information visit: www.harpercollins.co.uk/green

Printed and bound in Spain
by CPI, Barcelona

RICH RANCHER'S REDEMPTION

MAUREEN CHILD

To all of my wonderful readers
for their support over the years.
It's because of you that I'm able
to tell the stories I love to write.

One

It had been two weeks since the funeral that…wasn't. Jesse Navarro still felt like the world had shifted beneath his feet. But, he assured himself silently, that was probably the normal thing that happened when your brother walked into his own damn funeral.

He frowned into the afternoon sun and told himself it wasn't easy to hold a fancy funeral when the guest of honor shows up. Alive. He pushed one hand through his hair and muttered, "Just be grateful, for God's sake."

And Jesse was. Grateful. Hell, he had his brother back. But he also had a damn mystery to solve. And Jesse didn't like mysteries.

If Will Sanders was alive and just now showing up in Royal, Texas, then whose ashes had been in the urn they'd believed was Will's? And who the hell was the guy who'd pretended to be Will for all those long months? And why did he do it?

"No," Jesse said aloud, "I know why he did it. The money." Hell, the Sanders name carried a lot of weight and not just in Texas. So the bastard had tried to cash in on Will's name and had done a damn fine job of it, too. It wasn't just Will's name he'd stolen. He'd had Will's face. Had his movements, his smile, down cold. He'd fooled Will's family.

Hell. He'd fooled *Jesse*.

That was a hard pill to swallow. Somehow, Jesse felt disloyal for not spotting the damn imposter the minute he'd shown up at the family ranch. How had he been duped? In his own defense, Jesse could admit that "Will" hadn't spent much time with the family. He'd avoided too much closeness and at the time, Jesse had just figured his brother had a lot on his mind.

Which, of course, he *had*. Or, the impostor had. The man had worked nonstop to keep up the illusion.

Jesse shifted his gaze to the main ranch house. A sprawling white mansion, it looked nothing like what you'd expect a ranch house to be. It was massive, elegant. All white but for the black shutters at the windows, the house boasted a wide, columned front porch and dormers on the second floor, and at night, the lights made it shine like heaven.

And somewhere inside that massive house, was the *real* Will Sanders. There were a couple of cars out front, and Jesse's gaze narrowed on one of them. It was a beat-up, faded green Honda with Nevada plates, and the woman who'd driven it was inside. With Will.

The woman, Jillian Norris, didn't fit her car. A

woman like that belonged in a Porsche. Or at the very least a classic Mustang convertible. During all the chaos since Will's return, Jillian had somehow become a friend of Jesse and Will's sister Lucy, so she'd been at the ranch a few times. And every damn time, Jesse was slapped with an instant blast of heat that nearly swamped him. He'd spoken to her a few times, and her low, sultry voice had seemed to thrum in his blood, making it steam and sizzle in his veins.

He scowled at the distant horizon, telling himself that if he had any sense at all, he'd steer clear of Jillian Norris. Apparently though, common sense had nothing to do with what his body was demanding. Instantly, Jesse's mind drew up an image of Jillian and everything in him tightened. Shaking his head, he could admit to himself, at least, that it had been that way from the first minute he'd seen her at the funeral.

Drop dead gorgeous, with curves that could bring a strong man to his knees, Jillian Norris had mile-long legs and bright hazel eyes that looked both wounded and defiant. An interesting mix that had drawn Jesse in from the beginning. At the memorial service, she'd stood at the back with her baby girl. Yes, she had a daughter, about two. A miniature version of herself, with big hazel eyes, white-blond hair and a wide smile.

Jesse'd wondered, of course, who the hell the woman was and why she was at Will's memorial service. But then Will had strolled in, asked *What the hell is going on?* And suddenly there were much bigger questions that needed answering.

"And two weeks later, I've still got questions." Jesse shook his head, slapped one hand on the top bar of the corral fence, then squeezed the plank of wood hard enough it should have snapped in two.

His little brother was back from the dead and he was grateful for it. But there were gaps in Will's memories, leaving the family wondering exactly what had happened to him while he was missing. Naturally, Will wondered too, Jesse reminded himself, but somehow, it was harder to be on the sidelines. Hell, it was making Jesse crazy knowing there was nothing he could do to fix this situation. He was the older brother and he was used to riding to the rescue.

This time, though, no one had known a rescue was required and there had been nowhere to ride.

Chaos had erupted at the funeral, with Jesse's mother shrieking Will's name and flinging herself, followed closely by Lucy, into the man's arms. Will had looked at Jesse for an explanation, but he'd been too glad to see his brother to find the words—and didn't know if the right words had existed anyway.

Shaking his head, Jesse remembered that it hadn't been until long after the confusion caused by Will's arrival had settled down some that he'd found out who Jillian was. Some lawyer had told her to come to Texas and claim a part of Will's estate on behalf of the child they'd made together. That little girl was a heartbreaker, but as it turned out, Mac wasn't Will's daughter after all. That had become clear the minute Jillian admitted that she'd never met the "real" Will before. Now she knew that like everyone in Royal, Texas, she'd met and been fooled by the impostor.

To give her her due, Jillian had been ready to leave once she found out the truth. But Will had convinced her to stay for a bit until this was all figured out.

Jesse had quietly kept tabs on her and knew she and her daughter Mackenzie had been staying in a cheap motel outside Royal, and he imagined that being cooped up with a small child couldn't be easy.

Now she was here, meeting with Will, and Jesse told himself *he* should be in there, too. He gritted his teeth in frustration. But Will was as stubborn as he ever was and had insisted that this was *his* mess and he'd clean it up.

Still, that wasn't exactly true, was it? *Will* hadn't done any of this. The impostor was the man to blame and if Jesse knew where he could find the guy—probably better he didn't know.

Still, he wasn't going to stand back and let Will try to untangle this wildly complicated situation on his own whether the man liked it or not. Jesse was and always would be Will's big brother. And damned if he'd let Will forget it.

He settled his black hat firmly on his head again and pushed away from the corral fence. He started for the main ranch house, his long-legged stride eating up the distance. His gaze swept across the palatial white home and as always, he felt that quick tug of gratitude.

He'd grown up here. From the moment his mother, Cora Lee, had married Will's father, Roy, the Ace In the Hole ranch had been home. Hell, Jesse could still remember his first glimpse of the ranch and the house that had, to a six-year-old boy, looked like a castle. All it had been missing were a few turrets, a drawbridge and a dragon or two, waiting to be slain.

And Roy had made sure Jesse and his younger sister knew, from that first day, that this was their house as much as it was Will's. That they were, all of them, *family*. And nothing was more important than that.

Family came first. One of the first life lessons drummed into Jesse, Will and Lucy as they grew up. And the one lesson that never changed or shifted. Jesse would do anything for the people he loved, which was why he wasn't going to leave Will swinging without support.

He'd already screwed things up pretty well with Lucy—but he wasn't going to think about that right now. Instead, as he climbed the steps to the wide, wraparound front porch, another life lesson popped into his head. His mother, Cora Lee Sanders, was hell on tidy, and living on a ranch had meant that she was constantly at war with dirt, dust and God-knew-what-else being traipsed into her house.

Wipe those feet before you drag a mess into this house.

In spite of everything, he smiled as his mother's stern warning echoed in his mind. But dutifully, Jesse scraped the bottoms of his boots on the wiry mat set out for that purpose, then opened the door and stepped inside. Instantly, the quiet wrapped itself around him and made him a little twitchy. Usually, this house was bustling.

Lucy and her young son, Brody, lived in the east wing, but four-year-old Brody had the run of the place and had never known a silent moment. Lucy was a single mom, and again Jesse had to struggle past twin pangs of guilt and regret at the thought. But his sister also had everyone on this ranch helping her out with the boy that kept all of them on their toes.

Jesse headed for the study, Roy's old office. Since

his death, the whole family used it since Jesse hadn't been able to stake his own claim on the room in spite of being in charge of the ranch now. His boot heels hit the shining, hardwood floor in a series of taps that reminded him of a heartbeat, fast and hard.

The double doors were open, so he walked inside, subconsciously taking in the familiar room. Deep, maroon leather chairs, heavy tables and sturdy brass floor lamps. A thick rug with a map of the Ace In the Hole emblazoned across it, walls filled with books, and a bar where crystal decanters filled with whiskey, brandy and vodka glinted in the light. A river stone hearth simmered with a low-burning fire, and at the wide, broad desk sat Will, looking uneasy.

Opposite him, in one of the leather chairs, was Jillian Norris.

The instant Jesse's gaze landed on her, he felt a jolt of something hot and fierce slam into the center of his chest. The woman made a hell of a picture. She was tall, at least five foot ten without high heels. Her long, wavy blond hair was pale enough to look like spun gold, even caught up in the ponytail he'd rarely seen her without. Those huge hazel eyes of hers looked both wounded and defiant. An interesting mix that had drawn Jesse in from the beginning. The few times he'd seen her, Jesse had noticed the stubborn tilt to her chin and the light of devotion in her eyes when she looked at her daughter.

Will looked up at him. "Jesse?"

"Go ahead. Don't let me interrupt." He ignored the flash of irritation on his little brother's face as he moved farther into the room and took a seat in one of the chairs.

Will's frown only lasted an instant, probably because he knew it wouldn't have the slightest effect on Jesse. He focused on Jillian again. "If I could make this easier on you, I'd like to."

Jesse watched the woman. She looked…embarrassed, and he wondered if she'd had that expression *before* he'd intruded on this meeting. He should probably regret coming in here, but he didn't.

"And I appreciate it," Jillian said, her voice soft enough that Jesse had to strain to hear her. "But I've told you. You don't owe me anything. Mac's not your daughter." She took a breath, then sighed a little. "I know that now."

Will got up from behind the desk and walked around it. Leaning back against the front edge, he said, "I'm not her father, no. But the man who is was pretending to be me and that hits close enough to home for me that I can't ignore it."

She stiffened in her chair and folded her hands tightly in her lap. "Look, I don't need your help. Mac and I will get along fine—"

Jesse heard the pride in her voice and knew Will did, too, when his brother spoke next.

"This isn't charity, okay?" He flicked an impatient glance at Jesse, as if silently trying to tell him to go away.

Jesse shook his head.

Sighing, Will turned back to the woman who was saying, "What else would it be?"

"A favor," Will said. "To me."

She laughed, and even in this weird situation, Jesse's insides responded to that low, throaty chuckle. He shifted uncomfortably.

"You want a favor. From me." Disbelief rang loudly in her tone.

"Absolutely." Will laid his hands on his thighs and leaned toward her. "The bastard—excuse me."

She laughed. "I've heard worse and I think we can agree whoever the man was, pretending to be you, he deserves that description and more."

Jesse admired that. She had her pride, but she was also willing to look at a situation and see it for what it was, not what she'd like it to be.

"Well," Will said, "my mom would have a fit if she heard me cussing in front of a lady, so excuse me anyway."

She nodded.

"As I was saying, the man who stole my identity stole more than my name. He took my reputation, too, and ran it into the ground."

Jesse scowled, seeing the look of frustration on his brother's features. He knew Will was having a hard time with all of this, but he hated seeing evidence of it.

"You didn't do anything to me," Jillian said softly.

"I know that, but as I said, it was done in my name and I'm going to feel terrible about that unless you help me out."

A second or two passed before Jillian shook her head and smiled wryly. "Oh, you're good at this, aren't you? Getting people to do what you want, I mean."

"Used to be," Will admitted.

"Still are," Jesse said quietly.

Jillian turned her head to look at him, and their eyes locked. Even on opposite sides of the room, there was a thread of connection that snapped and crack-led between them. And Jesse saw by the flash of ac-knowledgment in her eyes that she felt it, too. Not that he cared.

"My big brother over there knows how hard-headed I am," Will said and Jillian shifted her gaze back to him. "What I'm trying to say is, it's impor-tant to me to rebuild my good name. So let me help. If I'm worried about you and your daughter, it'll take time away from me getting back to my own life."

Jesse watched for her reaction and he could see in her eyes that she wasn't buying it. That was the only reason he spoke up when he did. "He's not lying."

She turned her head to look at him again and that electrical pulse between them erupted. Her gaze fixed on his and Jesse could have sworn even the air be-tween them burned. He wasn't interested in this. Had no time for the distraction of a woman—and *this* woman would be the Queen of all distractions. So he pushed away any sense of attraction he was feeling and focused on making his point known. "Will's got a lot going on right now."

She laughed shortly, but her eyes remained cool and flat. "Yeah. I know."

"Then you should know he's not going to rest until you and your daughter are taken care of."

"I'm not a problem to be solved and neither is my daughter."

"He didn't mean—" Will said.

"That's not what I said," Jesse interrupted, cutting his brother off. "And I think you know it. So don't go looking to be offended when there's no intent."

Will fired a hard look at him that Jesse ignored.

He never took his gaze off Jillian, so he recognized when she accepted his words.

She nodded briefly. "Okay, you're right. I was doing that."

"I'm also right about you letting Will off the hook—"

"He's not *on* a hook," Jillian snapped. "I just said so."

"I never thought I was—"

Jesse cut Will off again. "There you go. Offense where none's meant. I'm trying to tell you that if you don't let Will do what he thinks is fair and right here, you're going to punish him for something that wasn't his fault."

"Jesse, why don't you let me—"

"I told him it's not his fault," Jillian argued, and this time *she* cut Will off.

"He won't believe you," Jesse said.

"Yes, I would."

"Well, he should," Jillian said.

"He won't." Jesse waved one hand at his brother. "He'll wallow in guilt or some other nonsense if you don't let him help."

"I don't wallow," Will pointed out.

"And if I let him help," Jillian countered, "then I feel guilty for taking advantage of a man who owes me nothing."

"No, you won't," Jesse said, shaking his head. "You're too smart for that. You're a mother. You have your kid to think of. So you'll do the smart thing and take a helping hand when it's offered."

She tipped her head to study him. "Oh, will I?"

Her long, blond ponytail swung forward to lie over

her shoulder and across her breast. His hands itched to do the same. Hell. He was jealous of her *hair*. How sad was that?

"Yeah," Jesse said, his gaze locked with hers. "You will."

"You two just let me know when it's my turn to talk," Will muttered.

"He's not going to let this go until you let him help," Jesse said.

"He's right about that anyway," Will broke in, grabbing his chance to get a few words in.

"Why do you care what I do or don't?" Jillian asked, but the question was for Jesse, not Will.

Truthfully, he wasn't entirely sure why her welfare mattered to him one way or the other. He shrugged. "Maybe it's because my mom was a single mother when she married Will's daddy. Because I remember how hard it was for her before we came to live here at the ranch."

Her gaze lowered briefly before she looked at him again. In her eyes, he saw acceptance. She gave him an almost imperceptible nod before looking at Will. "Okay, then. I'll take your help and thank you for it."

Will smiled. "You don't have to thank me. Like my brother said, you're helping me out of a sea of guilt just by saying yes."

Jesse watched her and knew she was still a little uneasy with her decision, but for her daughter's sake, she was clearly willing to swallow a bit of her pride.

"You were living and working in Vegas," Will said. "Is that right?"

Jillian's shoulders squared and her spine snapped straight as a plank. As if just the word *Vegas* invited judgment that she was prepared to defend herself against. "That's right."

"I can send you back there," Will was saying, "You probably gave up your apartment when you came to Texas, so I could help you get a new one, if you like. Or if you prefer, I'll find you a nice place here in Royal."

She chewed at her bottom lip and Jesse's groin went rock-hard in a flash of heat. Damn.

"I'd rather stay here in Royal," Jillian finally said, then added, "if you don't mind any gossip that might spring up. People will know why I came here—thinking you were Mackenzie's father and all."

"Doesn't bother me," Will assured her. "There's always gossip about one thing or another and it'll fade. But this is up to you. Are you sure you wouldn't rather go home?"

Now a sad smile briefly curved her wide, fantastic mouth. "Vegas was never *home*. Just a place to live and work. I came here for a fresh start. For Mac and for me. I'd still like that."

"Then that's what we'll do," Will said, and walked back around to the chair behind the desk. "We own a lot of property in Royal. I'm sure we've got an apartment—"

"It doesn't have to be anything big. Or fancy," Jillian added quickly. "Just clean and safe. Somewhere we can be until I find a job and get a place of my own."

"But—"

Will was going to argue, but Jesse knew what the woman meant. She was willing to take help but didn't want to feel beholden as she would if Will tried to give her some extravagant apartment.

"There's a place off Main." Both Will and Jillian looked at him. "Good building. Safe. Clean. They're studio apartments, but big enough for you and a baby."

Relief shone in her eyes and she nodded even as Will sputtered, "We can do better than a studio. A place with more room. A yard, maybe—"

"No." Jillian shook her head, looked at Will and said, "This one sounds perfect. We'll take it." Then she turned her gaze back to Jesse. She looked at him for a long moment, then said simply, "Thank you."

Those eyes of hers met his steadily, and he felt that swift tug of something hot again. He didn't let her know that, though. "You're welcome."

"How'd it go?"

Jillian walked into the large, plush living room of Lucy Navarro Bradshaw's suite at the Ace In the Hole ranch. The room was huge and airy, with floor-to-ceiling windows along the front wall, displaying a wide view of the ranch the Sanders family called home. The furniture was feminine without being frilly. Overstuffed couches and chairs covered in cream fabric splashed with blue and yellow flowers. Heavy, pale oak tables held stacks of books and brass lamps with amber shades. Rugs in pale, subtle colors dotted the gleaming wood floors and to make it all seem less like a photo shoot layout, toys, trucks and coloring books were scattered everywhere.

Ordinarily, Jillian would have felt completely out of place in such an elegant, old-money kind of home. But Lucy made the difference here.

At five feet six inches, Lucy was much shorter than Jillian's five foot ten. She had layered brown hair, big blue eyes and a friendly smile that had welcomed Jillian from the first. Thanks to Lucy, even with everything that had been going on for the last two weeks, Jillian hadn't felt so *alone* in Royal.

She didn't know why Lucy had befriended her, but she was grateful. Jillian had left behind everything she'd ever known when she came to Royal, Texas, hoping for some sort of settlement from the estate of the man she'd thought was her baby girl's father. Will Sanders. It wasn't until the service for Will, when the man himself had walked through the door, that Jillian had realized she'd been duped. A damn impostor, posing as the rich, successful Will Sanders, had gotten past Jillian's defenses and left her pregnant. Now she had no home, no job, very little money and a daughter to provide for.

Thinking of her little girl had Jillian's gaze sliding to Baby Mac, playing with Lucy's son, Brody. The tiny girl had soft blond hair, big hazel eyes and a dimple in her right cheek that never failed to tug at Jillian's heart. Mackenzie Norris, closing in on two years old, and the light of her mommy's life.

There was *nothing* Jillian wouldn't do for her daughter.

"Jillian?" Lucy asked. "Earth to Jillian..."

"What?" She gave herself a shake and smiled a little. "Sorry. Mental wandering."

"Don't worry. Happens to me all the time," Lucy assured her.

"Mommy!" Mac's face lit up. "I color."

"I can see that," Jillian said, taking a spot on the floor beside Lucy and her son, the small, sandy-haired boy with eyes the color of root beer.

Brody, in his four-year-old wisdom, tried to whisper, "She goes outside the lines."

Lucy laughed and skimmed one hand down her son's head. "She's still little."

Yes, that was the reason, Jillian thought, but a part of her hoped that Mac *always* went outside the lines. She wanted her little girl to push envelopes, to reach for stars and every other heartwarming cliché on the books.

"Why don't you take Mac to your room and show her your books," Lucy suggested.

"Okay." Brody stood up and held one hand down to the toddler already scrambling to go with him.

When the kids were out of the room, Lucy gathered up the crayons and tucked them into a wide, plastic box. "So," she asked, slanting Jillian a look. "How'd it go?"

Jillian gathered up the coloring books, stacked them neatly, then laid them down beside the box of colors. "Pretty well, all things considered."

"That's called answering without answering," Lucy chided. "My mom used to do it all the time to us. Now I do it to Brody."

Jillian laughed a little. "You're right. Sorry."

"What did Will have to say?"

"Everything," she said after a second or two. Jillian thought back over their meeting and couldn't fault the man at all. He'd been kind, understanding and generous, considering that Jillian and Mac weren't his problem to deal with at all. Sighing, she leaned back against the closest chair and stretched her legs out in front of her. "He's a really nice man. Much nicer than the 'Will' I knew."

Lucy reached out and took her hand, giving it a squeeze of solidarity. "He's a good guy."

"Yeah," Jillian agreed. "He is. He offered to pay our way home to Vegas and set us up in a new apartment."

"Oh." One word of disappointment.

She glanced at Lucy and the other woman shrugged.

"I was sort of hoping you'd stay here in Texas," Lucy said. "I mean, I don't have that many close friends and, well, we just clicked, you know? So I'd miss you."

Surprised as much by Lucy as she had been by the woman's brother, Jillian asked, "Why?"

A short laugh shot from Lucy's throat. "Well, come on. Do you have so many friends that you wouldn't miss one if they moved away?"

"No," Jillian said after a moment or two. "I don't. I'd miss you, too."

"Glad to hear it," Lucy admitted.

"But I won't have to miss you."

"What?" Lucy asked. "What do you mean?"

"I'm not leaving Texas," Jillian said, then shrugged when the other woman gave her a grin. "There's nothing to go back to in Vegas and I think maybe Royal is a good place to get a fresh start."

"It's a terrific place," Lucy agreed, leaning over to give her a one-armed hug. "I'm so glad you're staying. But *where* are you staying?" She paused, then brightened. "Oh. You and Mac could move into the east wing here with me and Brody. This place is huge—there's more than enough room. Brody would love having his new friend here and frankly," she added, "so would I."

Tempting. Jillian hadn't had a friend like Lucy in

well…*ever*. For some reason, the two of them had clicked almost from the start and Brody and Mac had already formed a strong friendship, too.

But staying here on Will Sanders's ranch would just be way too awkward.

Besides, Jesse would be here, too.

And she didn't think it was a good idea to spend too much time around that particular man. He made her want things she had no business wanting.

Two

Jillian took a deep breath and realized that not even Will Sanders had made her feel so jumpy and excited and eager all at once. No, she amended silently, *not* Will. Impostor Will. Back then, the impostor had swept her off her feet so fast that Jillian had forgotten all about protecting herself.

And now that she had not only herself but Mac to worry about, Jillian had to be more careful than ever. Especially since Jesse made her want to *not* be.

"Thank you," she said. "Really, thank you for offering, but we can't stay here. It would be…weird, with Will here and—"

"Okay," Lucy replied, "I get that. But you can't stay in the motel forever, either."

"We're not going to." Jillian pushed a strand of hair back from her face and tucked it behind her ear.

"You and Brody have been so nice. He's so good to Mac…"

Lucy sighed a little. "He's got his daddy's disposition, thank goodness."

"I don't know, I think his mom's pretty great, too."

Lucy grinned. "But she's got a terrible temper."

Jillian laughed. "All the best of us do."

From Brody's room came the sound of laughter and the high-pitched whistle of a toy train. Jillian gave a little sigh. Brody had completely taken Mac under his very tiny wing. Only four years old himself, Jillian had the impression that he liked being the "big" kid in the eyes of nearly two-year-old Mac.

Jillian knew she was doing the right thing, staying here in Texas. Mac was happy, even in that crappy little motel they'd been staying in. There were parks to play in, ice cream shops to get treats from and there was Brody. It would work out, she told herself. She'd make sure of it.

"What are you thinking?" Lucy asked. "I can practically hear the wheels in your brain turning from here."

Jillian leaned back against the couch next to her friend. Her *friend*. And wasn't that a gift? She'd come to Texas hoping to get a settlement that would take care of her daughter only to have that dream ripped away from her. But she'd also found a good friend and a place to start over and that made up for a lot.

"Your brother—"

"Which one?" Lucy interrupted.

"Jesse," Jillian said. "He's found a place for Mac and I—" There was nothing in Vegas for her. She had no family except for Mac. No ties to that neon city and

no real job prospects beyond being a cocktail waitress in one of the casinos. It was a good job and the
pay wasn't terrible, but spending hours a night walking around in high heels delivering drinks to people
who'd already had enough wasn't exactly her dream
job. Besides, she had to have a babysitter for Mac and
Jillian was starting to resent missing so much time
with her little girl.

"That's great, I'm so glad."

"Me, too." She sat back on the overstuffed couch.
"It'll be great to get out of that motel. Anyway, Will
and I were talking and then Jesse walked in and—"

"Really?" Lucy scowled a little. "I thought Will
wanted to talk to you alone. If I'd known it was a free-
for-all, I'd have been downstairs, too."

"I get the feeling Jesse wasn't invited," Jillian told
her. "He just…came."

Lucy nodded. "Sounds like him. What did he have
to say?"

"He told me about an apartment just outside town.
It's a small studio—"

"No way." Shaking her head, Lucy said, "Will can
do better than that."

Jillian stopped her cold. It had been hard enough
for her to accept any help at all. The thought of Will
setting her and Mac up in some luxury apartment was
just too much. She didn't want charity. She wanted
a chance.

Glancing around the quietly beautiful room she
sat in now, she acknowledged that a studio wasn't
going to be anything like this, but that was okay,
too. She was accustomed to making do and as long
as she could find a job, save some more money, Jil-

lian would be happy. She had plans and Royal seemed like as good a place as any to work on making those plans a reality.

"I don't want him to do better," Jillian said. "I can take care of myself and Mac. All I need is a place to start. Well, and a job."

"I can understand that, about the apartment I mean," Lucy said. "And as for the job, I might know of something if you're interested."

Surprised, Jillian fixed her gaze on her friend. "I'm interested."

Lucy laughed. "I haven't even told you what it is yet."

Kicking her long legs out in front of her, Jillian crossed her feet at the ankle. "Is it walking around in high heels wearing a Valkyrie outfit listening to drunken come-ons all night?"

"Sorry, nothing so exotic." Lucy grinned. "But now I want to see the Valkyrie outfit."

Jillian rolled her eyes. "I'd be happy to never see it again. So, what's the job?"

Shifting, Lucy pushed the stack of coloring books out of her way, then sat up cross-legged. "Okay, now understand, you don't have to take it or anything, this is just an idea. But I think it could work and you could be with Mac at the same time and—"

Jillian's lips twitched. "Just say it, Lucy."

"Okay," she pushed her dark hair back from her face, tucking it behind her ears. "They need help in the day care at the Texas Cattlemen's Club."

"Day care?" Jillian repeated, her mind already working through possibilities.

Lucy immediately started trying to convince her.

"It's really a great place, just a few years old, actually. Brody's been there a few times, when I've got clients to see and Mom's not available. But the thing is, Mac could be there when you're working. She can make friends, and you wouldn't have to worry about her and—"

Jillian held up one hand and laughed. "I don't need the sales pitch. It's a great idea."

"Fantastic," Lucy cried. "From what I hear, the pay's not bad and you wouldn't have to get a babysitter, since Mac could be with you, so you'd actually be making more money. I've already told Ginger Hanks all about you and she's excited to meet you. I thought if it's okay with you, we could go down there tomorrow. I'll introduce you and you can check the place out and see if you'll like it or not."

"Thank you." Jillian grabbed the other woman's hand and squeezed. "I really appreciate this, Lucy."

"Completely self-serving," she said, squeezing back. "I didn't want to lose you to Vegas."

She snorted. "No chance of that."

"Good. I'll find out where this apartment is from Will and take you by there tomorrow, too, if you want…"

"Not necessary."

Jillian's heart jumped into a gallop at the sound. That voice was so deep it seemed to roll through the room, demanding attention. Slowly, she slanted a look at the man standing in the open doorway. *What* was it about cowboys?

Just by looking at him, she could tell that Jesse Navarro was the kind of man who walked into a room and all eyes turned to him. Men wanted to be him and women just *wanted* him. Jillian had seen his type before, but Jesse took it to a whole new level. She'd never run into a man who simply *breathed* confidence and strength. It was a little unsettling, especially when you yourself were feeling just a little off balance anyway.

In a couple of quick seconds, her gaze swept him up and down and as she did, her heartbeat did a fluttery thing that she had zero business experiencing.

He just stood there, watching her. His eyes were like melted chocolate, his dark brown hair curled over the collar of his long-sleeved white shirt. The hem of faded black jeans stacked on the tops of his scuffed black boots and he held his black cowboy hat in one hand at his side. So still, she thought, and somehow *powerful* in that stillness. Enough that her heart did another wild series of beats that hammered in her ears and made her breathing just a little rough.

"Of course it's necessary, Jesse." Lucy spoke up. "It's not like Jillian knows her way around town yet."

He shifted his gaze briefly to his sister. "Lucy, you've got that meeting in the morning with the architect about your new breeding barn?"

Jillian tore her gaze from Jesse, because it was way safer to look at the other woman in the room. "Breeding barn?"

Lucy waved one hand. "Jesse likes to call it that. But I am building a new stable for the horses I'm—"

"Breeding?" Jesse asked.

"Fine. Yes. A breeding barn." She blew out a breath. "And he's right. I forgot about the meeting. Okay then, Jesse will take you to the apartment tomorrow and then I'll take you over to the TCC so you can find out about the job."

Jillian felt like she was being pushed downhill. She wanted to stop but she had the feeling the only way that was going to happen now was if she ran into a tree. Still, she had to try.

"Thank you," she said to Jesse, "but I've got GPS on my phone, so you really don't have to take me—"

"It's decided," he said, then gave both women a sharp nod. "I'll pick you up at your motel about ten, that all right?"

"Pointless to argue with him," Lucy gave a dramatic sigh. "He's got a head like solid concrete."

Jesse frowned at her, but there was no anger in the look, Jillian noted. Just brother-sister stuff, which was sort of entertaining to see. If she hadn't been right in the middle of it.

"If you'll just give me the address," she tried again.

"I will. Once we get there," Jesse told her. "See you then."

When he left, Jillian took a deep breath and let it slowly out again. "Your brother is—"

"Pushy? Opinionated? Arrogant?" Lucy provided with a grin. "My answer is D. All of the above."

And don't forget dangerously sexy.

Jillian swallowed hard. "Does anyone ever say no to him?"

"Many have tried, few have succeeded," Lucy admitted wryly. "You're okay with him taking you tomorrow, aren't you? I mean, he really is a good guy." She paused, gave Jillian a sly smile. "And he's single."

Jillian blinked. She'd seen that gleam in the eyes of other friends over the years and she knew that Lucy was trying her hand at a little matchmaking. Which just was not going to happen.

The whole setup thing always turned into a nightmare. Besides, she wasn't looking for a man. The last one she'd found had been the impostor who had swept her off her feet then left her pregnant and wondering who the heck her baby's father really was. No, she'd had enough of men. What she wanted now was to build a home for her baby girl. She wanted to make a future for the two of them and a man was a distraction she didn't want or need.

"No thanks," Jillian finally said, pushing up from the floor. Outside, the afternoon was slipping away and soon, a spectacular sunset would be staining the sky. "I'm not looking for a man. And I'm *really* not looking for one who likes to tell people what to do."

"Oh, he's not that bad. He's not a bully or anything, he's just… Jesse." Lucy shrugged and stood up, too.

"Uh-huh. And was your husband bossy?" The instant the words were out, Jillian wanted to drag them back into her mouth and lock her lips closed. Since she couldn't, she said, "I'm so sorry. I shouldn't have mentioned—"

"Relax," Lucy soothed, reaching out to give Jillian a quick hug. "I'm the one who told you I'm a widow, remember? I don't mind talking about Dane. I want Brody to hear about his daddy, so those of us who knew him *have* to talk about him."

Didn't make Jillian feel any better.

"But to answer your question, no, he wasn't bossy. After hanging around with Jesse and Will for a while, he tried to be, but he just couldn't pull it off." Lucy laughed a little in memory. "Dane was nothing like Jesse, really. Or Will, for that matter. But to be fair to my oldest brother, he's so used to taking charge I don't think it ever occurs to him to *not* do it, you know?"

No, she really didn't. Not one man Jillian had ever known had been the responsible type. They didn't want to take charge because they hadn't wanted to be blamed if things went wrong. Heck, her own father had walked out on his family when Jillian was just five because he hadn't wanted the responsibility of a family. So she didn't have any experience with men like Jesse. And maybe, she told herself, that was why he was bothering her so much. She couldn't pigeonhole him into any of the types she was most familiar with.

And maybe that was a good thing, since being a cocktail waitress in a casino gave her an up close and personal look at the worst kind of men. The takers. The whiners. The braggers. Now thanks to the impostor who'd convinced her he was crazy about her, she had another category. The liars. So far, Jesse Navarro seemed to be in a category all to himself.

"Well," she finally said, "I take care of myself and Mac and I don't take orders well."

"Then this should be interesting," Lucy murmured, and Jillian was pretty sure her friend was amused by the whole situation.

The apartment was clean.

That was the best Jesse could say about it the following morning. Hell, when he'd first suggested this place, he'd remembered the apartments being better than this. Bigger. Less...*institutional*. With Jillian and her daughter at his side, Jesse felt like apologizing for suggesting this apartment in the first place.

"It's perfect." Jillian walked farther into the numbingly boring, impersonal space.

"Put your glasses on," he muttered.

She whipped around to look at him. "I don't wear glasses. I see it clearly enough and this will be fine. It's got a lot of windows, so it's nice and bright."

"Which just makes me wonder why you're not seeing what I am when I look at this place. It's like a prison cell," he added, letting his gaze slide around the one big room.

At one end, there was a small, but complete kitchen, with a fridge, microwave, stove and dishwasher. The countertop was serviceable black, the cabinets were painted white and the sink was stainless steel. On the opposite side of the room was a double bed and against the front wall was a couch with a chair pulled up alongside and a tiny coffee table in front of it. There was a small bathroom with a tub/shower off the main room and he guessed the other doors were for the closet. Which pretty much described the whole place.

A beige, claustrophobic closet.

"Know a lot about prison cells, do you?" she asked.

He shot her a quick look. "Not personally, but I've seen movies. This would make a good set for one of them."

"There's nothing wrong with it," she argued. "A little paint, a few rugs and a bright quilt will make it shine."

"Shine?" he repeated dubiously. He walked toward

the kitchen—took him four steps—and turned around
at the sound of bedsprings squeaking. Mac was jumping up and down on the mattress, a gleeful look on
her little face. Leave it to a kid. Even in a cell, they'd
find a way to have fun.

"Mac, baby," Jillian cooed, "don't jump on the
bed…"

"Might fall apart," Jesse muttered, scowling as he
looked around the room again.

Jillian scooped Mac up in her arms, then turned
to face him. "It's perfectly fine for us."

"The whole place could fit inside my living room."
He shoved both hands into his jeans pockets.

She flushed at that and said, "Not all of us need
that much room."

"Not all of us want to live in a box, either," he
countered.

"Really?" She tipped her head to one side and
stared at him. "This was your idea, remember?"

"Don't remind me," he muttered darkly. When he
got back to the ranch, he was going to talk to Will
about this building. Get someone in here, a designer
or something to make these places less…depressing.

His gaze fixed on the woman watching him. Today,
she wore yoga pants that looked as though they'd been
painted onto her long, long legs and defined a figure
he'd only guessed at before. She had a dancer's body,
he thought, slim, but curvy in all the right places.
The long-sleeved red shirt she wore over those black
pants strained across breasts he'd really like to get his
hands on and that tail of wavy blond hair hung over
one shoulder as if drawing an arrow he didn't need
to the breasts he was thinking too much about. Her

hazel eyes were more green than blue today and he wondered what that said about her mood.

"Jesse!" Mac leaned out from her mother's grasp and held both arms out to him.

Dutifully, he stepped forward and plucked the girl off her mother's hip.

"You don't have to hold her," Jillian said, as if apologizing for her daughter.

"If I had to, I wouldn't want to," he said, and turned to look at the little girl clinging to him. She tugged at him, as completely as Brody did. But with Mac, he didn't feel the twin tug of guilt that he did with his nephew. "What do you think, Mac? You want to stay here or go back to the ranch?"

"Horsies!"

Grimly, he nodded. "That settles it. You can stay at the ranch until you find a better place. There's plenty of room there and—"

"No," Jillian told him.

"Excuse me?"

"Don't hear that word often, do you?" she asked. "Well, you'll have to deal with it. Mac isn't even two yet. Of course she wants to be with the horses, but she's not the one making decisions for our family. We'll be staying right here."

He saw the stubborn glint in her eyes and knew she'd dig her heels in on this, so he let it go. For now. But the damn truth was, she and Mac could stay at the ranch with no problem. There was the main house, his mother's cabin, a couple guest cottages...more than enough room for one woman and a tiny girl, and if they were there, Jesse wouldn't have to feel like he'd dropped them off in a dump.

"It's not a dump," she said, and he blinked. Had he said that last part aloud?

"You're not that hard to read," Jillian explained.

That made him frown. No man liked to be told he was clear as glass, and Jesse more than most had always prided himself on his poker face. Unless he wanted them to, no one knew what he was thinking. Well, until today.

"Dump!" Mac cried, clapping her hands.

He laughed shortly. "She agrees with me."

"Again," Jillian pointed out. "She's a baby." Then, turning around, she plopped both hands on her hips and gave the whole apartment a thorough look-see. Took her about ten seconds.

"I'll get a couple of rugs, but the hardwood floors are gorgeous."

"Not very big," he said.

"I'll paint the walls a pretty green, I think…"

"Won't need much."

"I'll get a crib for Mac and put it at the foot of the bed…"

"Don't get a big one."

She inhaled and sighed heavily, ignoring him. "Maybe a little table and two chairs…"

"*Very* little table."

"You know," she said, suddenly spinning around to face him, fire in her eyes and battle on her features. "You're not being helpful."

"I'm not trying to be," he said flatly. "This isn't much bigger than that motel you and Mac have been staying at."

"It's big enough. I'll get that job, take my time, look around and find something else when I'm ready."

"You should be ready now," he argued.

"I don't take orders from you."

"I'm not giving you an order. If I were, you'd follow it."

"Is that right?" She actually laughed and if he hadn't been so irritated, he'd have been charmed. That deep voice of hers sounded even sexier when she was laughing. Her eyes lit up and that incredible mouth of hers moved into a smile that was too damn seductive.

"You think a lot of yourself," she said, "but nobody tells me what to do."

"Somebody should," he countered, then huffed out an exasperated breath. "Look, I suggested this place, but now that I'm seeing it again, it's just not right. You and Mac, you deserve better."

Irritation slid off her face and she gave him another smile. This one warmer than the last. "Thank you. And you're right. We do. But I'm the one who's going to get it for us."

Hard to argue with pride since he had plenty of that himself. "Can't talk you out of this?"

She spun around again, taking another all-too-brief look. When she met his gaze, she said, "Nope. But you could drive us to the motel and help me move our things over here."

"Yeah," he said tightly. "Guess I could do that."

"Jesse! Horsies?" Mac asked, cupping her little hands on his cheeks to turn his eyes to her.

"Not right now, sweet girl," he said and frowned at the disappointment in the tiny girl's eyes.

Over the last couple of weeks, Mac and her mother had been at the ranch several times, and each time they were, the little girl had demanded time with the horses. He'd taken her up for her first ride himself and she hadn't been able to get enough. He knew what that felt like. He'd been about six the first time Roy Sanders had set him on a horse, and Jesse had known in that moment that he'd found where he belonged. Now little Mac had fallen for the same animals that had stolen Jesse's heart so many years ago.

So he tugged a lock of her hair gently and said, "We'll see the horses later, okay?"

"You shouldn't promise her something you might not be able to deliver on," Jillian warned. "She doesn't forget a thing."

He slanted his gaze to hers and locked on like a targeting system. "I always keep my promises."

Her eyes said she didn't believe him, and Jesse wondered what had made her so distrustful. Of course, the minute that thought entered his mind, he remembered why she was in Royal in the first place. A man had lied to her, used her and left her pregnant and alone. The kind of man who did that was no man at all to Jesse's way of thinking. And if he ever found the bastard, he'd make sure the son of a bitch paid for the pain he'd put so many people through.

But was it just the impostor who'd put that wary look in Jillian's eyes? Or was it more? And why did he give a flying damn?

He didn't.

"Come on," he said abruptly. "I'll take you back to the motel. We'll get your stuff."

"Stuff!" Mac laughed at the new word, and Jillian smiled.

Jesse met her eyes and he watched as her smile

faded. Probably best, he told himself. If that mouth of hers kept curving so temptingly, he wouldn't be able to resist tasting it.

And then where would they be?

Three

The Texas Cattleman's Club was impressive. A large, rambling single-story building, it was built from dark wood and stone, and had a tall slate roof. It looked just as a Texas men's club should look, Jillian thought. Historically, the TCC had been a rich man's private retreat. But all of that started changing several years ago, according to Lucy. Women became members, then took positions on the board and slowly but surely began to drag the TCC into the twenty-first century—with, no doubt, its oldest members kicking and screaming the whole way.

But Jillian could understand why the men had fought to hold on to one of their last bastions. Yes, she was a feminist. But there were times she wanted to be around only women. So why wouldn't men want the same thing occasionally?

Still, their loss was definitely her gain. One of the first things the female members of the club did was to open a day care center at the club. It was just to the left of the entrance in what had once been a billiards room. There were lots of windows and a set of French doors that opened out onto a shaded grassy area where the kids could play. The walls were white, but dotted with artwork provided by the children who spent the days there.

There were tiny tables and chairs and rugs in bright primary colors. Pint-sized easels were arranged on one side of the room where kids could paint and draw. Shelves filled with books and toys were neatly arranged along one wall. There was a small half kitchen with a fridge, a sink and a microwave that came in handy for preparing snacks and meals for the kids.

Ginger Hanks, about fifty with graying red hair, bright blue eyes and a knowing smile, was the manager, and there were two other women employed there, as well. If she got the job, Jillian would be the third helper, and as she was shown around, she realized she really did want the job.

She'd always loved kids, and being able to have her little girl with her while she was at work was a bonus she couldn't even imagine.

"The number of children we have every day differs," Ginger was saying as she led Lucy and Jillian around the room, taking a tour. "Sometimes it's twenty, other days it's five or six. Members of the club are welcome to leave their kids here while they use the facilities, or even if they're going out to lunch or shopping or something. We also have a few children who are here every day while their parents work."

"It's a great place," Jillian said and earned a wide smile of approval from Ginger.

"Thank you, we think so." Ginger bent down to scoop up a crying baby from one of the cribs pushed against the wall. The instant she did, the infant stopped crying. "Of course, you have to love children to work here."

"Oh, I do. I have a nearly two-year-old myself," she said and half wished she'd brought Mac with her. But a job interview hadn't seemed the right time to bring her daughter, so she'd left Mac at the Sanders ranch with Lucy's mother.

"Lucy told me, and you're welcome to bring her to work with you." Ginger looked around at the kids coloring, doing their numbers and letters, playing with dolls or trains.

"I told you," Lucy said, nudging Jillian.

"That's a relief to me." Jillian held out her hands toward Ginger and asked, "May I?"

The older woman gave her a long look before nodding and handing the baby over. Jillian cuddled the baby boy close and began an instinctive side-to-side sway. Ginger gave another approving smile.

"You've got a way with little ones, don't you?"

"Oh, I love babies," Jillian admitted. "I used to think I'd have a houseful of my own."

"You've got plenty of time for more babies."

Yes, she did. But she didn't have a man in her life and since that wasn't going to be changing anytime soon, Jillian could admit to herself that Mac would most likely be an only child. Just as she had been.

The difference was, Jillian would make sure her little girl never felt as though she weren't important. Mac would never know what it was like to listen to her parents shout at each other. Never know what it was to have those parents walk away from her without a backward glance. She would never have to doubt that she was loved.

Sighing a little, she told herself she could indulge her love for babies right here—if she got the job.

"That's little Danny Moses, isn't it?" Lucy asked, taking a peek at the baby's face.

"Sure is," Ginger confirmed. "He's good as gold, too. His mama's out on a lunch date with his daddy, so we're keeping him happy here."

Jillian's heart hurt a little as she held the baby and looked down into that tiny face. Days were going by so quickly it could make her head spin sometimes. It seemed like just yesterday Mac was this size and now she was talking and walking, and Jillian knew she had no time to lose—it was time to build that future she'd dreamed of.

"I'm glad Lucy brought you here today," Ginger said thoughtfully.

"Oh, so am I," Jillian told her, flashing a smile. "I don't want to put you on the spot or anything but I really would love to work here."

"That's plain to see," Ginger assured her and took the baby from Jillian. "I've got another woman coming in for an interview later this afternoon. Once that's done, I'll be in touch soon."

Jillian forced a smile, though she wanted to say, *Don't meet anyone else, hire me.* "Thank you."

When they turned to go, Jillian didn't see Ginger give Lucy a wink and a thumbs-up.

All right, Jesse kept his promise.

Jillian leaned on the corral fence and watched her daughter sitting atop what looked like a *gigantic* horse. The afternoon sun was bright, but the air was already warm. Early summer in Texas wasn't that different from Vegas weather. Of course, that was where the similarities ended.

In Las Vegas, the city was bright, crowded, noisy and jammed with locals and tourists. There was never a quiet moment unless you left the city and then you were in the middle of a desert, with no shade, no water, no trees. No nothing.

Here, though, there were oak trees, rivers, lakes, and there was quiet when you wanted it and plenty of noise to be found when you didn't. People were friendlier, less cynical. Jillian already knew more people in Royal after two weeks than she had known in Vegas after five years of living there. It was a different sort of feeling in small-town Texas and it was just what she wanted for her daughter. Mac would grow up in a place where people would know her, look out for her. She'd have friends and a home and a mother who would always be there for her.

It had been a big day so far. A new apartment—that would be fine once she fixed it up—and a job interview that she really hoped would work out. And now, she was back on a ranch staring at a cowboy who turned her insides to mush. Jillian's thoughts dissolved when a delighted squeal pierced the air. She fixed her gaze on the big man walking beside her baby and that horse. Jesse had one strong hand on her little girl's back, steadying her, while he held the horse's reins in the other hand, keeping the animal just as steady, Jillian hoped.

"Don't be worried. My kids are all great with horses."

Jillian turned to watch Cora Lee Sanders walk up to join her at the fence. In her sixties, Cora Lee was about five feet three inches tall, had thick, wavy, shoulder-length gray hair and sharp, grayish green eyes. Today she wore dark blue jeans, a yellow shirt beneath a black jacket and black flats. She also boasted a silver belt buckle at her waist that glinted in the afternoon sun. Cora Lee was every inch a matriarch. There were lines in her face, of course, but they were etched there by laughter, tears and years of living that had made her the woman she was today.

"It just makes me nervous," Jillian admitted. "That horse is so big compared to Mac."

Cora Lee smiled, laid her forearms on the top rail of the fence and watched her son walk slowly around the corral. "I can understand that. As mothers, we all will do whatever it is we have to to watch out for our children."

"True." She looked at Cora Lee and saw a woman who'd been through her own trials and had triumphed. Just as Jillian planned to.

"But in this case," the older woman said, "worry is unnecessary. That horse? That's Ivy. Sweet mare. She was one of Lucy's first rescues. Would you believe when the vet first brought her here, you could count her rib bones, poor thing. Someone tied her up in a barn and then moved, never telling anyone Ivy was there." Cora Lee's mouth turned into a tight frown. "If it hadn't been for one of the Stillwell boys cutting across the property taking a shortcut home from school and hearing her, she'd have died there, too."

"That's terrible."

"It really was. Nothing on this earth should be treated with such vicious neglect. But with a lot of love and good food and time, she's healthy now and even pregnant for the first time."

Jillian smiled, looking at the horse with new admiration. Ivy hadn't let her past get in the way, either.

"She's the most gentle animal on the face of the planet. And lazy with it, if truth be told. Likes nothing better than standing still under a shade tree and avoids running as if it would kill her."

Jillian's lips twitched. "Well, that's good then."

Cora gave her a quick look. "And not only that, but Jesse's a good hand with children. Patience. He got that from his father, not me."

Glancing at the woman beside her, Jillian waited, sure there was more. She wasn't disappointed.

"His biological father, I mean. That was the most patient man on the face of the planet." She chuckled, then added, "Now, Roy Sanders, the man who raised Jesse and Lucy and was their father in every possible way, was as impatient as I am." She laughed a little harder, gave a sigh and shook her head. "It's a wonder the two of us got along at all. But my, we had some good times. Some wonderful fights, too."

"Wonderful fights?" Even Jillian could hear the doubt in her voice. But she had too many memories of her own parents before they'd abandoned her, indulging in shouting matches that had terrified her.

"If you're arguing with the right man, yes." Resting her chin on her hands, Cora Lee said, "My own mother used to say, don't fight in front of your children. But Roy and I figured that wasn't healthy, either. Children grow up expecting everything to be sunshine and roses all the time and then they're never happy. But your kids see you arguing, then see you hugging and making up, they know you can disagree without the world crashing."

Jillian smiled. "I never thought of it like that, but I think you have a point."

Nodding, the older woman said, "You kids today don't know how much good a clearing-the-air fight can do for a marriage. Keeps things hopping, that's for sure."

The only fights Jillian had experienced were blurry memories of raised voices, tears and drama, with one or the other of her parents vowing to leave and never come back. There'd never been any hugging and making up. Maybe if there had been her parents wouldn't have left.

"There you are, Mom," Lucy called as she and Brody walked up to the fence to join the party. "We went to your cottage because Brody said you'd have cookies."

"You bet I do," Cora Lee said, scooping her grandson up onto her hip. "Who's my favorite four-year-old in the whole world?"

"I am!" Brody shouted and threw his arms around his grandmother's neck.

"Displaced by Grandma and her cookies," Lucy mused.

"Must be nice," Jillian said without really thinking about it, "to have your whole family right here on the ranch."

"Oh, it is," Lucy agreed. "But thank God we don't all live in the same house."

"Thank God," Brody parroted.

"That's enough of that, little man," Cora warned and shot her daughter a hard look.

Lucy just grinned. She pointed to where a small, English-style cottage sat amid a stand of oak trees. It had dormer windows, a stone chimney and a bright red door behind the snowy white porch railings. Roses, dormant now, climbed a trellised arch just in front of the porch.

"That's Mom's place. She moved in there once we were grown, said the big house should belong to Will."

"It was only right," Cora Lee said. "Time for my kids to build their own lives and they didn't need their mama watching their every move."

"There wasn't any point trying to talk her out of it, either." Lucy nodded and swung around to point toward another house not far away. "That's Jesse's place."

Jillian turned her head to study it for a long moment and decided it suited the man to a T. The building was low and long, with a stone front porch that seemed to run around the perimeter of the place. There were two stone chimneys jutting into the sky from a slate gray metal roof and a wide set of double front doors in the center. The house itself was wood and glass and managed to look masculine and cozy all at the same time. There were chairs, rockers and swings dotting that porch and she could imagine sitting there in the evening, watching a sunset. With that image came another of her and Jesse sitting on one of those swings together, and the instant she realized what her brain was up to, Jillian shut it down fast. Thankfully, no one else seemed to notice that her imagination was working against her.

"There are three guest cottages along the back of the big house," Lucy was saying, "so whoever's staying there has easy access to the pool and—"

"What's that house there?" Jillian pointed to what looked like an oversized bungalow with chimneys on each end of the house. Again, a wide front porch graced the building, but here, there was a balcony on the second floor, too.

"That was my house," Lucy admitted. "Mine and my husband's." Her voice dropped and a small sigh escaped her. "We were in the process of building it when Dane's accident happened. When he died, I just stayed at the main house. I didn't want to live there without him.

"The house was finished before I gave birth to Brody, but we never moved in. The big house works for us."

Jillian wondered if she could push her foot any further into her mouth or if even *she'd* already reached her limit. "I'm so sorry."

"Don't be," Cora Lee said, speaking up for her daughter. "Life happens whether we're ready or not, doesn't it, little man?" She turned her gaze on Brody.

"Can I have cookies?" he asked.

"You bet." Cora Lee hitched him higher on her hip and looked at her daughter. "Brody's with me." Then she added, "If you're going to be here a while, Jillian, why don't you bring Mackenzie by, too? We'll all have cookies together."

"Thank you," she replied without agreeing to anything.

When it was just she and Lucy again, Jillian said one more time, "I'm really sorry, Lucy. I didn't mean to bring up bad memories."

Lucy laid one hand on her forearm. "They're not *bad* memories at all. How could they be?" She shook her head and looked out at Jesse and the little girl squirming excitedly in the saddle.

"You said Dane had an accident?" Jillian asked quietly, since her friend seemed willing to talk about the past that no doubt still haunted her.

"He did. I loved Dane like crazy and he was eager to be here on the ranch. Of course he didn't know anything about horses, but he wanted to learn."

Lucy stared into the corral but Jillian knew she was looking at images much further away. Her gaze was fixed on the past and the memories brought a smile to her lips and a film of tears to her eyes.

"What happened?" Jillian's voice was a whisper.

"Just a freak twist of events that Dane was caught up in," Lucy said wistfully. "Jesse loves training horses. I mean, the ranch is his now and he loves that too, the cattle, the feed crops, all of it. But horses," Lucy said on a sigh, "hold his heart. Like they do mine. Dad left me in charge of the stud program, breeding exceptional saddle horses. And I'm also taking in rescue horses. Horses that have been abused or neglected—" Her features tightened and anger shone in her eyes. "I can't stand seeing animals hurt.

"But Jesse, his specialty is training the untrainable horse. He's got a good reputation, too. People from all over Texas bring their problem horses here and he finds a way."

Jillian wanted to say something, but damned if she could think of anything that would either stop Lucy now or make it easier to go on. Instead, all she could do was stay silent, stay close.

"A man from Waco brought Jesse a stallion to break and train." Smiling, Lucy added, "That was the meanest horse I'd ever seen. Hated everybody. But Jesse knew he could tame it. Jesse asked Dane if he wanted to help and he jumped at the chance."

Jillian's eyes closed briefly as she braced herself for what must be coming.

Lucy took a deep breath and blew it out. "The horse broke free and went a little crazy. Dane rushed in to help Jesse contain the stallion—and he was trampled."

Instantly, Jillian's gaze flicked to Mac astride that horse and she wanted to run out there and grab her girl, keep her safe. Yes, irrational, but the need was there.

"Nobody's fault, really," Lucy said quietly. "The horse wasn't to blame, either. He was just mad and scared and reacted the only way he could. Dane had a lot of broken bones, spinal injuries, but it was the head injury that killed him." She rested her chin on her joined hands on the rail fence. "He was in a coma a week before I finally accepted that he was gone. They pulled the plug that afternoon and the very next day I found out I was pregnant with Brody."

"Oh, my God." Jillian slumped against the fence, heart hurting. For all the troubles she'd had in her life, nothing could compare to what Lucy had already endured. Admiration filled her, because this woman was strong enough to get past her own grief and build a life for her son. She didn't hold on to bitterness or sit in a corner and scream *Why me?* She just went on with her life, taking care of Brody and focusing on the future. Jillian understood that.

"Wow." Lucy laughed shortly and slanted Jillian an apologetic glance. "That got grim fast. Sorry. Didn't mean to unload all of that on you."

"Don't apologize." She shook her head. "One of these days, I'll tell you my own sad stories and then we'll be even."

"Deal." Lucy's smile was wide and bright.

"I'm curious though," she said, shifting her gaze back to the man in the corral. "How did that accident affect Jesse?"

"It was bad for a long time," Lucy admitted. "He blamed himself. Still does, I think, in spite of how often I tell him there's no blame to be handed out."

Jillian thought Lucy was probably right. There was a darkness in Jesse's eyes; shadows that seemed to never lift. "What happened to the horse?"

"Oh, Jesse trained him. After that day, the stallion seemed to settle down. He went home a different animal."

Of course Jesse kept training the horse. He wasn't the kind of man to walk away from a job half-done, no matter the pain that surrounded the task. Funny that Jillian felt she knew Jesse so well after knowing him such a short time.

"Anyway, different subject entirely." Lucy turned to her and waited until Jillian was looking into her eyes to continue. "I actually came out here to tell you that I talked to Ginger at the day care—she forgot to get your cell number earlier—and she wants to know if you can start working on Monday."

Stunned, Jillian only stared at her. "Don't I have to be background-checked or…something?"

Tipping her head to one side, Lucy said softly, "Sweetie, when you showed up here claiming Will was Mac's father, every one of the Sanders lawyers went over your background with a dozen combs each."

"Oh." She swallowed hard. "Fabulous."

"I let Ginger know that everything had been checked already and that you're good." Lucy shrugged. "Told her if she had any specific questions, she should contact one of our lawyers. But the Sanders word goes a long way here."

Jillian wondered if the lawyers had enjoyed what they'd found? Silently, she ticked through her personal history. Father left the family when Jillian was a kid. Mother left two years later. Grandma Rhonda raised Jillian, taught her how to cook, instilled in her how to be loyal and strong and other lessons Rhonda's own daughter had never learned.

At nineteen, Jillian was engaged briefly to a rodeo cowboy who left because he decided he wasn't made to be a family man. Showgirl at a casino on the strip, then she met Will Sanders—or, she reminded herself, a reasonable facsimile—and he left her life without a backward glance.

Only this time, the man walking away from her had left her with something precious. Her daughter, Mac. And for that, she'd always be grateful to…whoever he was.

She wasn't a thief, had never been arrested or even gotten so much as a speeding ticket. But still, it wasn't much of a résumé.

"Stop looking so stricken." Lucy's elbow nudged Jillian's arm. "Ginger hired you, right?"

"True," she said, nodding to herself. Apparently, making bad choices and having every man you ever cared anything for walk out on you wasn't enough to keep her from getting the job. And that was what mattered, right?

If the people in Royal found out about her past, it shouldn't count at all. Because Jillian's past wasn't going to define her. It was her present she had to think about. And the future she was going to build. For herself. For Mac. And nobody was going to stop her.

"So, now that you're employed—"

And didn't that sound good?

"—let's talk about your apartment. Jesse tells me you're thinking of painting," Lucy said.

"Oh, absolutely." She grinned and sent another look at Mac, still laughing and squealing atop Ivy as Jesse walked them around the perimeter of the corral. Sighing, she added, "Beige walls are just so…boring."

"Agreed. Do you want some help?"

Jillian looked at the other woman and smiled. It was good to have a friend again. Good to feel like she was already carving a place for herself into Royal. "I really would."

"Great. Let's get Mac and hit the hardware store." Lucy's eyes were gleaming as she scrubbed her hands together in anticipation. "Oooh. Even better, we could leave Mac and Brody with Mom and not have to ride herd on kids in the paint department."

Thinking of Mac's adventurous nature and all the possibilities for getting into trouble in a hardware store gave Jillian cold chills. And yet. "Oh, I couldn't…"

"Sure you can." Lucy turned toward her brother. "Hey, Jesse, when you finish Mac's ride will you take her over to Mom's?"

"Not a problem," he said, never taking his eyes off the little girl in his charge.

That should make Jillian feel better. But leaving Mac behind with Cora again seemed like an imposition. She'd already watched Mac for a couple hours earlier today so Jillian could take the interview.

"Don't back out," Lucy said and tugged at Jillian's arm to get her moving. "If we get the paint right away, we can go by the Courtyard and check out the shops for furniture."

True, she'd have to buy a few things, anyway, but she didn't want to spend a lot of the money she had put away. Jillian had other plans for that. "No, I don't think I'll…"

"They have the cutest little consignment shop there. You'll love it. And oh, I'll look for a new desk for Brody. He's getting so big, I swear. He's going to kindergarten next year, can you believe it?" Lucy kept up a steady stream of conversation as she simply dragged Jillian in her wake all the way to a shiny red truck. Apparently, she was determined to not give Jillian a chance to change her mind.

Then she opened the passenger door and said, "Oh, when we're finished shopping, we can stop at the Sweets and Treats, bring Mom some of the fruit tarts they sell there. They're her favorite and it's the perfect way of saying thanks."

Jillian stopped dead and narrowed her eyes on Lucy. The innocence stamped on the woman's features didn't fool Jillian one bit. "That was pretty slick, telling me how to thank your mother for doing me a favor I didn't ask her to do."

Lucy's head tipped to one side and she grinned. "Wasn't it? Oh, come on. Admit it. You know you want to."

Jillian looked back over her shoulder to where her daughter was being swung up into the arms of a tall, gorgeous cowboy. Oh, what she was feeling for Jesse was dangerous. Especially because just for a second, she was envious of her baby girl.

Not a good sign.

Leaving was definitely the right thing to do.

Four

"Jillian's a lovely girl…"

Every instinct Jesse possessed went on high alert as he shot a wary look at his mother. Cora Lee was a strong woman who'd held her family together no matter what had come at them. She'd survived the loss of two husbands and had raised her three children while single-handedly running one of the biggest ranches in Texas until he and Will had come of age to take over.

Over the years, she hadn't slowed down much, either. She didn't run the ranch or the business end of the Sanders company anymore, but she kept up with what was happening both on the ranch and in Royal. Cora Lee wasn't a woman to sit back and watch life go by—she jumped in and did whatever the hell she wanted or needed to do. She'd never once in her life thought that being a woman somehow made her "less"—and she hadn't let anyone else believe it, either. She was strong, confident and impossible to ignore because she simply refused to allow her children to duck her interference.

She kept her fingers on the pulse of Royal, always knowing what was going on and why. Just as she somehow always seemed to know what her grown kids were up to. Jesse, Will and Lucy were her life and she didn't mind one little bit sticking her nose in if she thought any of them needed her "help."

"Yeah, she is," he said in as noncommittal a way as he could manage. Damn. Jesse'd thought that with Will back, their mother would be more focused on *him*. It seemed Cora Lee was the queen of multitasking.

"She's had a hard life," his mom mused thoughtfully.

"Imagine so." He hadn't looked at the background records the lawyers had dug up on Jillian. It had been enough for Jesse that they'd told him she'd checked out and wasn't trying to pull a fast one. Apparently, though, his mother had read the file.

Jesse took a gulp of coffee and told himself to run for it. He could take most anything and stand his ground. Hell, he'd faced flash floods and lightning storms on the open land without blinking. But when his mother started in on him, it was smarter to bolt.

Decision made, he set the screwdriver he still held down on the counter. "Thanks for the coffee. I think that cupboard door's good now, but if the hinge comes loose again, let me know."

"You're not fooling me, you know," Cora Lee said

softly. "I know a grown man trying to hide from his mother when I see one."

Well, that stopped him. Shooting her a look over his shoulder, he asked wryly, "Can you really blame me?"

Cora Lee considered that for a second or two, then smiled. "I guess not. Fine. You can relax. I won't say another word about Jillian."

"Thanks."

"For now."

He rolled his eyes. Jesse was beginning to suspect there'd been nothing wrong with the damn cabinet he'd just spent fifteen minutes fixing in the first place. His mother had probably loosened the hinge so she'd have an excuse to trap him in her kitchen.

Her cottage was quiet. The kids were gone, Brody with his mother to the main house and Mac with Jillian back to their new prison cell. He scowled at the thought. Still didn't like the idea of them living in that tiny, lifeless place, but the woman was as stubborn as she was beautiful.

His mind dredged up the image of Jillian laughing with Lucy when they came back from their spur-of-the-moment shopping trip. She'd looked... relaxed, like her guard was down, and a hot fist of need had grabbed Jesse by the balls and hadn't let go yet.

He didn't like his reactions to Jillian but hadn't been able to control them yet, either. It seemed that woman had the ability to turn him inside out just by looking at him. So, the last thing he needed was his mother's well-meant but unnecessary advice or opinion. Hell, he liked his life just fine the way it was. He wasn't looking for a family. He already *had* a family and a kid he would always be responsible for because Brody's father had died under Jesse's watch. So yeah. No changes to his life needed. When he wanted a woman he went out and got one. Drinks, dinner and sex filled out a single evening and then he was back to his real world. This ranch. His family.

What with Will coming back from the dead, Lucy a widow and Brody fatherless, he didn't need one more damn thing to think about. No more drama.

He opened the back door to leave, but stopped when his mother spoke up again. "Jesse."

The speculative, my-son-needs-a-wife gleam in her eyes had been replaced by a glimmer of the concern and worry etched into her features. "I need you to talk to Will."

He hadn't been expecting that. "About what?"

She dropped into a kitchen chair and held a thick white mug of coffee cupped between her palms. "About how he has to keep a low profile until the police and the FBI say he can come out of the shadows and get back to his life. About how he can't go off roaming into Royal like he tried to do just an hour ago."

Jesse's eyes went wide, and he shot a hard look at the main house behind him before looking back to his mother. "He can't go into town. What's he thinking? We already told him he's got to stay here on the ranch until things are figured out."

"Yes, I know." Her eyebrows arched. "I was there."

Sighing, he nodded. "Yes ma'am."

But Cora Lee wasn't finished. "Will's going stir-crazy I think. All he can talk about is getting out there and hunting down Richard Lowell himself. Will wants to reclaim his life."

Still furious, Jesse thought about Rich, a man who had duped them all. It was Will himself who'd figured out who the impostor was. When he heard that the man had claimed Rich had died in the boating accident, he'd known it was Rich himself who had stolen his life. Who but Will and Rich would have known the details? Now they were all trapped in this helplessness.

Jesse couldn't blame his younger brother for wanting to do something. Anything. He could understand the frustration and the fury. Hell, he shared it. Richard Lowell. Hard to believe that he was the man who'd impersonated Will for so long.

Rich and Will had met at college and become friends, but apparently that hadn't been enough for Rich. The man had been so eaten up by envy or whatever the hell it was that psychos got eaten up by, that eventually, he'd tried to kill Will and take over his life. And he'd come damn close to pulling it off forever.

"I know how Will feels," Jesse muttered. "I'd like to find that bastard—excuse me—too and let him know what a world of hurt really feels like."

"You think I don't?" Cora Lee's features were frozen into a mask of ice and steel. "Richard Lowell almost killed one of my sons. Stole from us. Used us. If I had him here in front of me right now, I can't say that I wouldn't reach back into time for a little frontier justice."

Jesse smiled grimly as he nodded in agreement. "But we can't. Will can't. Not yet anyway and he's just going to have to suck it up. Hell, for all we know, Rich is in that damn urn."

But even as he said it, Jesse hoped that wasn't true. He really wanted to make Rich Lowell pay for hurting his family.

"Agreed," Cora Lee snapped, taking a sip of her black coffee. "And it's pretty much what I told him an hour ago. Would have had better luck talking to a boulder. Maybe it'd help if *you* tell him."

"I can do that." Jesse left his mother's cottage and started for the main house. Moonlight lit his way, but he didn't need it. He could have found his way over any part of this ranch blindfolded. Jesse knew every stone, every tree, every damn speck of dirt on this land as well as he knew his own bedroom. It was his home. His life.

Already wired way too tight, Jesse felt like he was walking a fine line of control. Which meant he was in the perfect mood for a confrontation with his little brother.

Jillian glanced at baby Mac and smiled. The little girl had her very own paintbrush and was applying fresh green paint to the wall—though she was getting more on herself. What her daughter lacked in talent she made up for in enthusiasm.

Silly to start painting tonight and Jillian knew it. But she hadn't been able to stand it.

"Just one wall," she told herself. She'd do the rest of the work tomorrow, but for tonight, she really wanted to see how the color would look on the boring beige walls.

Already, the apartment was taking on a different

look. Of course that had a lot to do with the things Jillian had found while out shopping with Lucy. Not that she was spending tons of money—she'd found a few great items at the consignment shop and then had splurged at a discount store and bought a few pots and pans and a four-piece set of dishes, along with a new crib for Mac. Everything else they needed, Jillian figured she would buy a little at a time.

"The important thing here is," she said to Mac, "I have a job, we have a home and some wonderful new friends. Isn't that right, baby girl?"

Mac whipped her head around to look at her mother. A stray splash of green paint swiped across her little cheek and her green eyes danced with joy. "Jesse? And horsies?"

Jillian swallowed hard and told herself to distract her daughter. "And your friend Brody, remember?"

"Jesse!" Mac crowed the word and dragged her paintbrush against the wall again.

It looked like Jillian wasn't the only one in the family who was a little obsessed with Jesse Navarro. Now, she told herself, she had *two* hearts to protect.

Sighing, she set her brush down, walked to her daughter and swept the girl up into her arms. Staring into that beautiful little face, Jillian said, "Let's get you ready for sleep in your new bed, okay?"

Mac tipped her head to one side, her wispy blond hair waving with the movement. Touching her mother's cheek with her little hand, she smiled. "Jesse?"

"No, no Jesse tonight," Jillian answered and felt horrible when Mac's tiny mouth moved into a pout with a quivering bottom lip.

"Want Jesse." Mac's head dropped to her mother's shoulder in disappointment.

"Me, too, baby," Jillian whispered. "That's the problem."

Inside the main house, Jesse stalked across the entryway into the great room and stopped on the threshold, taking a long look at the familiar room.

Cora Lee had decorated this room as a family gathering place, so she'd made sure it was comfortable, welcoming and able to withstand dirty cowboy boots.

The overstuffed furniture, covered in dark red, deep blue and forest green fabrics, boasted deep, soft cushions. Hand-carved oak tables held books, magazines and a few of Brody's toys. Brass lamps with Tiffany glass shades threw puddles of golden light on the floor and the shadow of color on the walls. A man-height stone fireplace took up one wall and on the opposite side of the room a gigantic flat-screen TV took up most of the wall space. There were couches and chairs scattered all around the room, just waiting for a crowd to drop by and settle in.

Framed family photos dotted the tables and the walls, and colorful, braided rugs spread across the wood floor. There were bookshelves ringing the wide room and two cushioned window seats that during the day provided a wide view of the ranch yard. Tucked into one corner of the room was a bar where crystal decanters filled with whiskey, brandy and vodka glinted in the light. The hearth was empty and cold—about how his insides felt.

Will was slumped in a chair set close to the fireplace, a crystal tumbler of whiskey in one hand. Here in this room, the lamplight and the fire kept the darkness outside the windows at bay. The wind kicked up suddenly, wailing as it passed beneath the eaves, and Jesse made a mental note to have one of his men check the shingles on the barn roof tomorrow. When the wind was strong enough, sometimes he swore it could carry off the horses.

But for right now, he had a brother to confront. Will wore jeans, a blue T-shirt and his favorite brown boots—currently propped up on the coffee table in front of him. He looked at home. Where he belonged. Fake Will had moved off the ranch to Megan's house after their marriage and Jesse hadn't been able to figure that one out, blaming it on Will's grief and taking time to recover from the accident. Now, of course, it made sense.

Will lifted his glass, took a drink, then silently saluted Jesse's entrance.

"Welcome to my gilded cage," he said.

Jesse scowled at him and crossed the room, his steps muffled by the rugs strewn across the floor. "What the hell is wrong with you?"

Will studied the amber liquid in the glass as if searching for an answer to that question. Then he gave it up and shrugged. "Hell, what could be wrong? I'm alive. Back home. Married to a woman I hardly know. *Trapped.*"

"Trapped." Jesse walked closer, slapped Will's feet off the table and sat there himself, staring at his brother. "How are you trapped?"

"Are you kidding?" He took another drink and shook his head. "I can't even go into Royal for lunch at the diner. I'm stuck here on the ranch while that bastard Rich Lowell is off living God knows where. What about that seems right to you?"

"None of it. But you know why it's like this. Enough people already know what's going on," Jesse said, voice hard and tight. "Everyone who was at your funeral knows you're actually alive. We've got a lid on them, but you go strolling through Royal, the rest of the town finds out. With all the gossips around here, not to mention the media that loves to get the dirt on the top families in Royal—somehow word would reach Lowell before the cops can find him. Then he'd disappear and we'd never get his ass back to Texas."

"Right, so the thief who tried to kill me is free to go where he wants and I'm serving jail time." Will snorted and shook his head, taking another sip of his scotch. "He pushes me off my own damn boat in the middle of a storm and leaves me for dead. I'm in a damn coma in Mexico for months while he's here—"

He broke off, dragged in a breath and pushed one hand through his hair. "While he's *here* living *my* life and nobody—" he fixed a hard glare on Jesse "—not even my damn *family* notices that he's an *impostor*?"

That last bit Jesse knew he had coming. Hell, sometimes he couldn't believe himself that he hadn't known the impostor wasn't his brother. But Rich had done a damn good job of pretending to be Will. The man had not only fooled the Sanders, but the whole damn town of Royal.

"Yeah, well, I wasn't expecting a fake brother, was I?" he asked in his own defense. Pitiful and he knew it, but it was all he had. "Rich clearly had had surgery and he even explained away why his voice didn't sound like yours. He had excuses for everything, damn it." Jesse grabbed Will's scotch and took a long drink. "He even fooled Mom and that's not easy."

"Doesn't make me feel any better," Will muttered, grabbing his drink back. "When I finally woke up from that damn coma, I didn't know who I was. It took me forever to remember, all the while learning how to walk and move again and when I finally get home to my loving family, I find them burying me."

That had been a weird day for the ages.

"Glad we didn't. Bury you, that is."

"Who the hell is in that urn?" Will demanded.

That question had been bugging Jesse for the last couple of weeks at least and he was no closer to getting an answer than he had been the day Will had walked into the funeral. "Could be Rich."

"I wish," Will muttered. "I think."

"Could be *anybody*," Jesse continued. "With what he did to you, Lowell proved he's not afraid to murder someone. Could be one of his victims or a damn homeless man he thought no one would miss."

"None of this seems real."

"I know what you mean," Jesse said. "You know they sent the urn to the FBI for DNA testing."

"How're they going to test *ashes*?" Will demanded.

"Hell if I know," Jesse admitted. "But apparently there's usually enough bone and teeth left that we might get lucky. Get an identification."

Will sighed and took another sip of his drink. "Don't know if I hope it's Rich or not. Dead, I couldn't beat him with my fists. Which is something I really want to do."

"Get in line." Jesse grabbed the glass again and took another drink.

"Get your own," Will snarled and snatched the glass back. "You know, it won't be him in that urn. He's too slick to die. He's out there. *Somewhere.*" He stared into his drink again, then lifted his gaze to Jesse. "Not only did Rich steal from me and damn near kill me, but he screwed with my name. My reputation. Married Megan. He made me look like an ass."

Will looked tired, but more than that, he looked as though he'd been hanging on to a cliff's edge for too long and his grip was slipping. Jesse could sympathize. But he couldn't let his brother wallow, either. It was hard to accept any of this, but the sooner Will did, the sooner they could all get through this and back to normal. "What Rich did wasn't your fault."

"Feels like it is," Will muttered. "It was *my* name he was throwing around. He got Jillian pregnant pretending to be me, then walked out on her, leaving her to try emailing me for help—the *real* me, before the boating accident—" Will stopped and scrubbed one hand across his face. "Which is pretty much when Rich decided I was in his way. He hit me over the head and tossed me into the ocean right after I got Jillian's email. He must have known I'd figure it all out."

Jesse felt for his brother. He knew what it was to have pride in your name. Your honor. Their father had taught them that if a man couldn't be trusted, he wasn't a man at all. But Will hadn't actually done any of this. "And you were supposed to stop that how?"

"I don't know." Will shot him a hard look. "Stop using logic when I feel crappy."

Jesse nodded sagely. "Feeling sorry for yourself, you mean."

"Who has more right?" Will countered and jumped to his feet. Handing the scotch off to Jesse, he started pacing, shaking his head, muttering. "A man I thought was a friend stole my damn life."

Jesse finished off his brother's scotch in one deep swallow and relished the burn of the liquor on its way down. Setting the empty glass aside, he stared at Will and tried to get his own anger under control. Wouldn't do a damn bit of good for both of them to be furious and powerless to do anything about it.

But nothing stirred Jesse's temper like someone messing with his family.

"Yeah, he did," Jesse agreed. "But that's done now."

"Is it?" Will spun around to glare at him. "Hell, the ramifications keep tumbling down on me like somebody knocked over a domino and a whole long line of 'em are tipping over in succession—and they're all landing on my head."

"I know."

"I've even got a damn wife!" Will shouted, tossing both hands high. "I don't even know Megan Phillips Sanders, but we're married—"

"In name only," Jesse pointed out, knowing it didn't mean a thing because Will and Megan had to stay married—at least for the time being. They couldn't risk gossip no matter what it cost Will. He wished to hell he could do something to fix it.

"What difference does it make?" Will shoved both hands into his jeans pockets and let his head fall back until he was staring up at the beamed ceiling. "Rich married her using my name, so it's still a legal marriage to a woman I don't know."

"The lawyers are working on it."

"Well, that's comforting," he snarled. "And in the meantime, what the hell do I say to her?"

"Why don't you let her do the talking? Shut up long enough for her to tell you what happened." Jesse rattled the single ice cube in the glass. Standing up, he stared at his younger brother. "Making yourself nuts isn't going to solve a damn thing. You know that, right? So listen to what Megan has to say."

"Yeah, yeah, I can do that." Nodding, Will still looked furious as he suddenly snapped. "So, did you stand up for me at my wedding?"

"What?"

"I'm asking if you were best man to a stranger pretending to be me?" His eyes glinted with banked fury.

"No. You—*they* got married in Reno. The family wasn't invited."

Eyes wide, jaw dropped, Will asked, "And you didn't think that was weird?"

"Yeah, I did." Jesse met temper with temper. Damned if he'd take any more guilt heaped on him. Rich had fooled everyone. Did he like admitting that he'd been had? No. But the truth was, he hadn't been the only one fooled. "Hell, you'd been acting weird for a long time, so I wasn't surprised. Mom was hurt, but she wasn't shocked at the lack of an invitation, either. You cut the family out of your life, Will. You were never here. Flying all over the damn world, never showing up for work, drinking too much when you were here—"

"Yeah," Will interrupted, eyes flashing, "but that wasn't *me*."

"Well, we didn't know that, did we?" Jesse countered, glancing into the empty glass on the table, wishing it was full. "Rich was smart enough to make himself scarce. He didn't spend much time in Texas and almost no time at all at the ranch…"

Will pushed both hands through his hair. "This is like a nightmare I can't wake up from."

"What the hell do you want me to say?" The final threads of Jesse's patience unraveled. "Rich screwed all of us over. We'll get past it. I'm glad as hell you're back. Sorry if everything's not great, but you're alive. And thinking you were dead nearly killed Mom."

Will scowled as it looked like all the air left him.

Jesse took a breath and sighed. Voice softer, temper controlled, he said, "The whole family went through hell until you walked into your own damn funeral. If you expect me to feel sorry for you that you're alive and have a mess to fix, then you got a long wait coming."

Will's gaze met Jesse's. "Fine, but—"

"No." Jesse braced his feet wide apart and crossed his arms over his chest. He stared at his younger brother until Will shifted uncomfortably under his steady gaze. "You had your say and you've had time to pull it together."

"Yeah?" Will snorted.

"None of this is gonna be straightened out overnight."

"It's been two and a half weeks," he reminded Jesse.

"You were gone nearly two years. Might take more

than a few weeks to fix things." Jesse narrowed his gaze on his brother. "So stop whining."

Insulted, Will blurted, "I don't whine."

"Could've fooled me," Jesse said tightly. He knew his brother and sympathy wasn't what he needed. "You don't like being stuck on the ranch. I get it."

"Wow." Will nodded. "Thanks."

He ignored the sarcasm. "But you don't have a choice. You've got to keep a low profile. Don't let anyone beyond those who were at the funeral and saw you already know you're alive. Until we know if Rich is still alive and still pretending to be you— or if he's the one in that damn urn…the cops are on it and they'll find the bastard eventually."

"Eventually," Will repeated under his breath. "How long? A year? Two? *Ten?*"

Shaking his head, Jesse said, "Get over yourself. It's not going to be that long."

"Yeah. Hopefully not. It's just that I feel so damn helpless," Will admitted, his voice a low rumble. "That's the hardest part to swallow."

"I hear that," Jesse said. "Felt the same way myself when I thought you were dead. Felt it again when you came home and we realized we'd been taken in by a thief and liar. Feel it now when I'm trying to talk my little brother off a damn ledge."

A second or two passed before Will nodded. "I'm not on a ledge. I'm…okay, I'm *whining.* Fine. I get the message." He frowned then. "And what's this 'little' brother stuff? You're one inch taller than me."

"Don't you forget it," Jesse said with a grin. "Just like I'm the oldest."

"Yeah." Will nodded sagely and tipped his head

to one side, pretending to study Jesse carefully. "You've got five years on me, and brother, it's starting to show."

"What?"

"Yeah. You're getting old."

He knew Will was riding him and it felt good to have this dynamic back again. Damned if he hadn't missed ragging on his younger brother and having the insults tossed back at him. "I'm thirty-five, not sixty-five."

Will shrugged. "You know what they say, once you pass thirty, it's all downhill."

"Then hang on," Jesse told him, "your turn for the downhill slide starts this year."

"Some of us handle it better."

"Like you've been 'handling' everything else lately?" Jesse asked.

Will sighed. "Damn, you're like a dog with a bone. I already said you're right. I was wrong. I'll shut up and play along. I won't be happy about it, but I'll do it. I'll stop worrying Mom. I'll suck it up and be a good prisoner until we find Rich Lowell. Then," he said, features tightening, eyes narrowing, "I'm gonna beat that bastard so hard…"

"I'll help you," Jesse said.

"I know you will," his brother said. Will took a deep breath and said, "So. Change of subject. Even I can only talk about me for so long. I saw Jillian Norris was here again today."

"Yeah." Jesse turned for the wet bar against the far wall. Now that the storm was over, he could use his own drink.

"She get settled into the apartment all right?"

"Yeah, I took her and the little girl over there yesterday—" He poured two fingers of scotch then walked back to refill Will's glass, as well. "Speaking of those apartments, we've gotta do something there. Depressing as hell. I mean, small is one thing, but I swear it looks like every jail cell in every movie I've ever seen."

"That bad?"

"I thought so." Jesse took a drink. "I offered to get her something else, but she refused. Said it would do fine for her and Mac."

"Then it will."

Jesse snorted and took another drink. "You didn't see it."

"I'll take your word for it. We can hire someone to fix it. Hell, if it's that bad, we'll get all of the apartments in that building updated." Will walked across the room, refilled his own glass and then asked, "Back to Jillian though… Had a busy day. Interview at the TCC, new apartment, then back here to watch you give her daughter a riding lesson."

Jesse studied the scotch as he tipped the glass from side to side, making tiny, amber waves that sloshed against the crystal. "Lucy got her a job interview at the TCC day care."

"Uh-huh."

"And I promised Mac she could ride a horse."

"Uh-huh."

"Then Lucy and Jillian went shopping and left Mac here with Mom."

"Uh-huh."

Irritated now, Jesse snapped, "Is there something you want to say?"

Outside, the wind howled while Will affected an innocent pose that Jesse wasn't buying for an instant.

"No," his brother said, taking a sip of his scotch. "I just have plenty of extra time to study things now."

"Is that right? And just what are you studying?"

Will shrugged. "Not studying so much as noticing. Like the fact that Jillian Norris is really hot."

Jesse scowled at him. Like he needed Will to tell him about Jillian. Hadn't Jesse's dreams been full of her for the last few weeks? Didn't he wake up every damn morning with his body hard as stone and his blood steaming just under his skin? And just why the hell was Will "noticing" her anyway?

"That woman's legs must be a mile long," Will mused. "And that's just in her jeans. Can't help wondering what she'd look like in a dress…"

To hell with a dress. Jesse wanted to know what she looked like naked. Stretched across his bed, wrapping those long legs around his hips and pulling him deep inside her.

"Then there's her *hair*," Will said. "Always caught up in that ponytail. Makes you want to see how long it is when it's loose and hanging down her back…"

Or fisted in his hands, Jesse added silently. "Is there a point to this?" His hand tightened on the tumbler he held.

"No point." A half smile curved Will's mouth. "Just a couple of observations. But you know, maybe I should give her a call. Make sure she's happy with that apartment. If it's as bad as you say it is…"

Jesse stiffened. If anyone was going to be checking up on Jillian, it was going to be *him*. "Yeah, I'll take care of it. If you're so anxious to call a woman, call your *wife*. Let me worry about Jillian."

"Uh-huh." Will smothered a grin, but not fast enough to keep Jesse from noticing it.

"What's so damn funny?"

"Not a thing." His brother held up one hand in peace. "I'm just saying, she's a gorgeous woman is all."

"Am I blind suddenly?" Jesse demanded. "I can't see a beautiful woman so you and Mom have to point it out to me?"

"Mom, too, huh?" Will nodded. "Interesting."

Irritated with himself and his whole family, Jesse snapped, "No, it's not interesting. There's *nothing* interesting, damn it."

"Yeah, I'm convinced." Grinning now, Will walked back to his chair, sat down and propped his boots up on the coffee table again. Turning his gaze to Jesse, he said, "Beautiful woman, great kid who already likes you, yeah, nothing to see here."

Jesse's gaze shot to his brother's. Now he saw the same speculative gleam in Will's eyes that he'd seen on his mother's face just a little while ago.

Well, they could just get over it. He wasn't looking at Jillian any more than any other red-blooded male would. He could appreciate a hot woman with great legs, a wide mouth, full breasts and a first-class be-hind without it meaning anything. His insides fisted, and his groin went hard enough that his jeans felt like torture.

Fine. He wanted her. He could admit that—to himself. But want didn't mean anything. It was tempo-rary. Want could be eased by having. And that was what this was coming to. But being with Jillian wasn't going to turn out like his mother and brother were clearly hoping. He wasn't looking for a family.

Jesse already had Brody to look out for. He owed that boy because if it hadn't been for Jesse, Brody's daddy wouldn't have died. So his job now was to be there for Lucy. For her son. He didn't have the right to go looking for something just for himself. Selfish needs had to be buried for the sake of doing the right thing.

But knowing that didn't make this any easier. Tossing the rest of his scotch down his throat, he set the glass down and headed for the door.

"Where're you going?" Will called after him.

"Home." *To take a cold shower.*

Five

The first day at Jillian's new job went great.

She loved working with Ginger and the two other women, Patti and Teresa. The kids were terrific, with only a couple of tantrums thrown here and there, and best of all, Mac was with her during the day and making friends already. Jillian had a good feeling about how this was going.

When she'd first come to Royal she'd hoped only for a settlement from her baby's father. Instead, she'd found friends who had helped her get started on a whole new life—and she was eager to make the most of it. Already, her apartment felt like home as she and Mac decorated and made it their own. Not long ago, she'd worried about the future, and now, all she saw were possibilities.

She even enjoyed her new routine. People could

complain and say their daily chores were a rut, but to Jillian, a rut just meant "comfort zone." Every morning on the way to work, she stopped at the Royal diner to get herself a cup of coffee and some chocolate milk for Mac. And what really pleased Jillian was that already she was being treated like a regular. Now she and her baby girl were part of other people's routines.

Only that morning, Amanda Battle had called out a hello and said she had Jillian's order ready to go. It was a special kind of feeling, Jillian told herself, knowing that she was finally in a place where she and Mac could belong. Far from the neon and crowds of Vegas, in this small town, she could build something good and strong for her and her daughter.

Letting her gaze sweep around the bright room filled with young voices, she felt more confident about her life than she ever had before.

With one exception.

Her mind kept drifting to thoughts of Jesse Navarro.

She'd tried to stop, but her brain was working against her. And not just her brain. Her own body was traitorous, too. Every night, when she tried to sleep, her subconscious provided image after image of Jesse. His thick dark hair. Chocolate eyes. That cowboy hat pulled low on his forehead. The way faded jeans clung to muscular, long legs...

"Miss Jill!" Small hands tugging at her black slacks, an excitable voice calling a shortened version of her name since the tiny ones had too much trouble with *Jillian*. A little boy jumping up and down, looking at her with desperation in his eyes and just like that, her fantasies were dead, supplanted by reality.

"What is it, Cole?" she asked, crouching so she could look the three-year-old in the eye.

"Potty!" He danced in place as if to let her know he really meant it.

"Oh!" No time to waste. Jillian straightened quickly and started moving. Taking him by the hand, she said, "Okay, let's go," and headed for the bathroom. Then the front door opened, and she stopped dead as Jesse Navarro walked into the room.

A moment ago, she'd been thinking about him and now here he was. The universe was toying with her. Nerves hurtled through her stomach in a blink and her grasp tightened slightly on Cole's hand. "Jesse. What are you doing here?"

"Making a delivery," he said and stepped aside. Brody raced in, grinning. "Hi, Miss Jill! Surprise!"

"Hi, Brody, it's so nice to see you." She looked up at Jesse again as concern whipped through her suddenly. "We weren't expecting Brody today. Is Lucy all right?"

"She's fine. Got a meeting with an architect is all and can't really get the work done with—" he paused to give Brody a knowing look "—this little distraction running around. Mom's off to Dallas for the day, so…"

"I get to play," Brody explained and took off for the far corner where the train set was stored.

"Miss Jill…" Cole's voice, even more urgent.

Right. She'd forgotten. To Jesse, she said, "I'll, uh, be right back."

A slight smile curved his mouth. "You go ahead. I'll wait."

Heart racing, stomach spinning, Jillian hurried

Cole to the bathroom. By the time she returned, Jesse was perched uneasily on one of the kid-sized chairs sprinkled around the room. Mac sat on his lap, excitedly telling him a story. Her little hands waved, her eyes sparkled, and Jesse was giving her his complete attention.

Not fair, she thought. Not fair that a man that gorgeous, that dangerous, could be such a softie with her daughter. Most men she'd known put on a show of paying attention to Mac, just to get in good with Jillian. But it didn't take long before their eyes slid away, their patience dissolved, and soon, it was clear that they either didn't like children or simply didn't want to be bothered with them.

Jesse was different.

Damn it.

Not only did he affect Jillian on an almost cellular level, but he *cared* about Mac. Yes, he was good with Brody, too, but the little boy was his nephew. She would expect him to be kind and patient with family. The fact that he showed the same attention to her little girl really touched Jillian's heart. And that was dangerous.

As if he sensed her watching him, Jesse slowly turned his head and met her gaze. Even from across the room crowded with noisy children, Jillian felt the quick jolt of heat that raced from the center of her chest right down to the soles of her feet. A fire burned in her belly and just below, she felt the ache of need pulse into life.

Oh, don't do this, Jillian. She had a job, an apartment and the start of a brand-new life. *That's what you need to focus on. Not the gorgeous cowboy that makes you burn.* Her internal voice was stern, and she fervently hoped that this time, she'd listen to that voice rather than ignoring it.

"Horsies?"

Jillian heard her little girl and sighed. Mac had a serious crush on horses—and the cowboy who'd introduced her to them.

"When you come back to the ranch, you can ride the horse again, all right?"

Satisfied with that, Mac squirmed off Jesse's lap then ran to the corner to play with Brody. Not only was her daughter getting too attached to Jesse, but she was clearly starting to think of Brody as a big brother.

She turned back in time to see Jesse lever himself out of the child-sized chair. He headed right for her, and she could only think that watching him move was like seeing a lion slowly uncoil himself and get ready to— Okay, maybe not attack, but to stalk. Not that Jesse was a stalker or anything, it was just— Oh *stop*, Jillian.

When he was close enough, she took a breath and told herself to get a grip. She wasn't some timid virgin, for heaven's sake. But even as she reassured herself, she had to admit that she'd never dealt with a man who was so completely *male*.

"What's the matter?" Jesse watched her, a quizzical expression on his face.

"What? Nothing. Really." Jillian shook her head, took a breath and told her racing heart to slow the hell down.

"Okay." He didn't look as though he believed her, but he let it go. "Lucy will be here in a couple of hours to pick up Brody."

"Sure. That's fine." He was standing so close to her that she could see tiny gold flecks in his dark chocolate eyes. Why hadn't she noticed them before?

"Got a lot of kids in here today."

Safe subject. Good.

Jillian let her gaze sweep over the children in the big, bright room. "I know. Apparently there's some big dance here at the TCC in a couple days."

He nodded. "The black-tie gala."

She turned and glanced at him. "That's it. Well, some moms are out shopping for it and others are working here, getting ready for the big event." She shrugged and smiled. "So, we've got a full house. I don't mind, though. I love kids."

"It shows."

Jillian tipped her head to one side, looking at him.

He shrugged. "Most people would be dangling by the thread of their last nerve surrounded by this many hyper kids."

"They're not hyper," she corrected. "They're just excited to be with so many friends."

"Whichever," he said, shaking his head. "Seems like hard work to me."

"Harder than training wild horses?"

He laughed unexpectedly, and the deep sound of it rolled over her, lighting up every cell in her body. What a smile did for that handsome face of his should be illegal. Or at least come with a warning label.

"Oh, yeah. Give me a mean horse any day over this many kids all at once."

"You're terrific with Brody and Mac," she reminded him.

His smile slowly faded as he turned to look at those two children in the crowd. "They're different."

Before she could ask him what he meant, he set his hat on his head and said, "I've got to go. Things to do at the ranch."

"Okay…" She watched him turn for the door and wondered what had made him change so abruptly from teasing laughter to shadows in his eyes and a curtain dropping over his features.

"Jesse?"

He stopped and looked over his shoulder at her.

With his gaze on hers, Jillian couldn't think of anything to say. And since she felt like an idiot, she finally said, "Nothing. Goodbye."

"Yeah. Bye." He left then, and Jillian couldn't look away as he walked to his truck, climbed in and drove off.

Probably wasn't a good sign that her heart was still racing.

By the time Lucy came to pick up Brody, Jillian had had a long day. As much as she loved her darling daughter and every other child in the day care, she wanted half an hour of silence all to herself. It was all Jesse's fault, she told herself. She'd been doing fine until he showed up with his black cowboy hat, scuffed boots and whiskery jaws. After that, she'd had to work twice as hard to concentrate on the kids who needed her, because her mind kept dragging her back to Jesse.

"You look a little ragged," Lucy said, hugging her son to her side while she talked.

"It's been a day," Jillian admitted, though she

didn't tell Lucy that it was Jesse making her a little crazed. "The kids are great, don't get me wrong, but—"

"A break would be nice?" Lucy asked.

"Heaven," Jillian agreed, glancing around the room. Most of the kids had been picked up already. There were only four left now waiting for their parents. The noise level in the room had dropped dramatically, but still, Jillian longed for quiet.

"I can fix that," Lucy said.

"What?"

"I'll take Mac with me. I've got an extra car seat in the truck—" She grinned. "Sometimes Brody's friends need a ride. Like today for example."

Jillian shook her head, automatically refusing the generous offer. She just wasn't used to this level of friendship and though she liked it, it was going to take some getting accustomed to. "You don't have to do that."

Lucy smiled. "I know. But I just had three solid hours of a break. The least I can do is return the favor."

Jillian laughed. "You weren't on a break. Jesse told me you had a meeting."

"Yes, but I was talking horses! Trust me, that's a break."

Not surprising that the whole Sanders family seemed crazy about horses. They did live on one of the biggest ranches in Texas.

"Did you get your breeding/rescue barn all figured out?" Jillian knew absolutely nothing about horses or how to care for them, but she was interested in her friend.

"We did," Lucy said eagerly. "It's going to be gorgeous." She paused. "Bigger than I'd expected it to be, but that's okay. Just means I can rescue more horses."

"That's what's really motivating you, isn't it?" Jillian asked. "I noticed the other day when you were talking about this that you seemed more excited by the prospect of saving animals than you were by the breeding program."

"I'm that obvious, am I?" Lucy laughed a little. "I guess I am. It's so…satisfying—and that's not the right word, either—to help neglected animals get healthy and happy again. I just—"

"You don't have to explain."

"Good, because I don't think I can." Shaking her head, Lucy hugged Brody, still attached to her left leg. Looking down at him, she said, "Brody honey, why don't you go get Mac and we'll head home."

"Oh, Lucy—"

"No argument. We can have a drink when you come to pick her up later."

"That does sound good," Jillian said, sighing.

"Excellent. Hi, sweetie!" Mac and Brody raced up together, Brody in the lead and dragging the little girl behind him. "Do you want to go to the ranch for a little while?"

"Jesse!" Mac looked up at Jillian and grinned. "Horsies!"

Jillian sighed again. It seemed that despite knowing she should keep her distance from Jesse, she was destined to be thrown into his path.

"Sounds like someone's got a crush," Lucy mused, her gaze fixed on Jillian, not Mac.

"He's so good with her…"

"Handsome, too."

"Yeah, he really is—" Jillian broke off and glared at her friend.

Lucy was unashamed. "Hey, just wanted to see if there was anyone else with a crush and now I'm thinking there might be."

"Crush!" Mac yelled, and Jillian winced.

"I really like you, Lucy, but you're wrong."

"Sure I am. I can see that now."

"You're incorrigible."

"Isn't it great?" Lucy grinned, leaned down and scooped Mac up into her arms. "I don't plan to change, either. When I'm old and gray I'll be nosy, opinionated and people will run when they see me coming."

Jillian had to laugh. "I believe you."

"Mom, I want ice cream," Brody said, tugging on the hem of her black shirt.

"What a great idea! Mac, you want some ice cream, too?"

"Cream!"

"I think that's a yes," Jillian said, giving her daughter a smile.

"This is why I hang out with kids. They know what's good," Lucy mused. "We'll see you later, Jillian."

"I'll come to the ranch as soon as I'm off work and—"

"*That* is not a break," Lucy chided, shaking her head. "Take some time. Relax. Do nothing for a while. You are not allowed to show up at the ranch before at least seven."

Laughing, Jillian admitted, "I don't know if I remember *how* to do nothing."

"Give it a shot." She headed for the door, both kids in tow. "Say bye."

"Bye, Mama, bye!" Mac waved frantically, and Brody did the same. And when they were gone, Jillian felt a pang that was a mixture of relief and trepidation.

To pick up her little girl, she'd have to see Jesse again, and that was getting harder and harder. Because every time she saw him, her mind dredged up images that she had no business entertaining. She imagined his body covering hers, his big, callused hands sliding across her skin. His mouth on hers, tongues tangling in a wild, desperate dance. Her blood burned, her heartbeat quickened and her mouth went dry.

"Jillian?"

She jolted, dragging her completely aroused self out of her daydream and turned to face Ginger.

"You okay?" the older woman asked.

"Probably not," Jillian murmured.

"What?"

"Nothing, nothing." Taking a deep breath, she emptied her mind and hurried over to keep three-year-old Colton Jackson from eating a crayon.

Jesse and his ranch foreman, Carlos, were in a dead heat. Horses neck and neck as they raced back to the ranch after checking on the herd in the south pasture. The end-of-the-ride race was tradition, with pride and bragging rights the only rewards. Days like this reminded Jesse how lucky he was to live the life he loved. The ranch. The wide-open stretches of land.

The horses. Being outside as another storm rolled in with electricity alive in the air. The thunder of the horses' hooves against the earth sounded like drum beats. The wind in his face smelled of the coming rain. Sunset stained the sky red and purple and gold. And he loved it all.

He heard the cowboys cheer as they passed and Jesse grinned. He had this one. His horse was younger, stronger than Carlos's mount—and Jesse liked to win. Hell, he'd lost only one of these races in the last two months.

"Go boss, you got him."

"Come on, Carlos," someone else called, "don't let him win again!"

Laughing, feeling the rush of a fast horse and the wind in his face, Jesse beat Carlos into the ranch yard by a nose and pulled back on the reins to ease his horse into slowing down.

"You got me," Carlos said, laughing. "But tomorrow I take the stallion and you ride this lazy gelding."

"It's not the horse, Carlos." Jesse held out one hand. "It's the rider."

Still laughing, Carlos shook then warned, "Tomorrow it'll be different."

"Keep hope alive." Jesse swung down from his horse, handed the reins over to Carlos who would get the horses cooled down and stabled. Being out with the men, focusing on the work of keeping such a big ranch running well cleared his mind, gave him peace—however briefly. It wiped away worries about Will, guilt over Lucy and Brody and even numbed the thoughts of Jillian that were now almost constant. Now that he was back, work over for the day, he knew she would crowd his mind again and there was no way to stop it. No way to pretend he didn't enjoy it.

Scowling a little, he told Carlos, "I'll be by later to check on Dancer."

The mare was close to delivering her foal, and Jesse wanted to make sure everything was as it should be. He knew the local vet, Scarlett McKittrick, could be here in fifteen minutes if he needed her help, but chances were good Dancer would manage the labor and birth on her own as horses had been doing for millennia.

"I think it'll be much later, boss." Carlos looked past Jesse and nodded, a faint smile on his face. "Looks like you've got some company."

Jesse turned and felt a hard punch slam into his chest. A hell of a lot of good it did him trying to put her out of his mind when she could show up out of nowhere and knock him off his feet. Jillian stood there beside that beat-up Honda of hers, holding what looked to be a foil-covered plate. Not that he cared what she was holding. He just liked looking at her.

Jesse had seen Mac with Brody earlier and had known that sooner or later, the little girl's mother would be arriving to get her. And right now, he was glad as hell he'd come in from the pasture when he had. Otherwise he might have missed her.

When that thought settled in, Jesse frowned to himself. He didn't like that he cared whether or not he saw the woman, but the feeling was there whether he wanted to admit it or not. But now wasn't the time to worry about that. Instead, he filled his gaze with the woman who was driving him nuts lately.

Her long blond hair was in the ever-present ponytail that was beginning to really get to him. Nothing he wanted more than to free all that hair and run his fingers through it, watch it frame her face. He wanted to know how long it was, and how it looked lying against her bare skin.

She wore a dark red shirt, blue jeans, and stylish boots. With the hard wind blowing, the ends of her hair lifted and twisted as if dancing.

As he walked toward her, he watched her wide mouth curve into a smile that set a fire in the pit of his belly. It took everything he had to keep from giving in to the urge to grab hold of her and finally taste that mouth.

"You won." She shook a few windblown tendrils of hair out of her face and looked up into his eyes.

"Yeah." He grinned and tossed a look over his shoulder to where Carlos was leading the horses toward the barn. "This time anyway. You here to pick up Mac?"

"Yes," she said, "but I wanted to see you first."

Interesting. "Why's that?"

"I wanted to thank you," she said, holding out the foil-covered plate. "You've been so good to Mac, letting her ride the horses she loves. Helping me find that apartment—"

"Don't thank me for *that*." He shook his head. "Still can't believe you wanted to stay in that grim little place."

She laughed. "The apartment's fine and I appreciate it."

Frowning a little, he said, "Either way, you don't have to thank me."

"I already have." She was still holding the plate out, so Jesse took it.

"Heavy."

"Glass pie plate," she said.

"Pie?" Both eyebrows winged up. "You bought me a pie?"

"I didn't buy it," she told him, slightly insulted. "I made it. And I want that pie plate back when you're finished."

"Really?" He couldn't remember the last time a woman had given him anything, let alone something she'd taken the time and trouble to make herself. Pleasure shone in her eyes, and Jesse thought she just kept getting more beautiful. Then, pushing that stray thought aside, he lifted the edge of the foil and briefly looked at the golden crust before carefully covering the pie again. "What kind is it?"

She took a deep breath, tucked her hands into her pockets and said, "It's my specialty. Spiced cherry."

He looked into her eyes. "You have a specialty?"

"I do and you'll love it."

"Sounds good."

She met his gaze. "It's better than good."

Looking into those smoky green eyes of hers, Jesse felt another twist of heat down low in his gut. It wasn't pie he was thinking of now. He had a feeling that if he ever got his hands on her *she* would be better than good, too.

"Come on. We'll go to my place and I can taste this pie." When she glanced toward the main house as if deciding whether or not she should go and get Mac right away, he added, "Mac's playing with Brody. You can take a few minutes. See if I like this pie. I happen to be a pie-eating expert. I can tell you if it's any good or not."

"I'm not worried," she said proudly, lifting her chin slightly. "That's the best pie you've ever eaten."

He tipped the brim of his hat back. "That's a big statement since my mother makes the best apple pie on the planet."

"I really like Cora Lee," she said, "but I'll put my pies up against hers anytime."

"Well," Jesse said nodding, "now there's no choice. You have to come over so we can settle this."

She chewed at her bottom lip for a second before saying, "Okay. For a few minutes. Then I've got to get Mac and head home. I'm later than I thought I'd be, but I wanted to finish the pie so I could bring it to you."

The first raindrops plopped into the dirt as they climbed the steps to the stone porch. Jesse opened the heavily carved front door and stood back to allow Jillian to enter first.

He watched her as she looked around and Jesse saw his place through her eyes. Wide plank, golden oak floors, Native American paintings and family photos on the walls and Navajo rugs scattered across the floors. She wandered through the entryway, peeked into the main room, and he knew she saw a completely masculine space. Well, hell, he lived here alone, so why would there be feminine touches? The only women who ever came into his house were his mother and sister and the housekeeper, once a week. When Jesse wanted a woman he went to her place.

He never brought them to the ranch. To this house. He didn't want some woman to start feeling cozy in his place. Start leaving bits of clothing or makeup or whatever, trying to stake a claim both on him and his world.

This was different, though, he assured himself. Jillian wouldn't be here long. As much as he'd like to, he wouldn't be steering her down the hall to his room and laying her out across his bed. Gritting his teeth, he pushed that thought away and watched her. She looked around the main room and he saw it fresh, through her.

Burgundy-colored leather chairs and couches were grouped in front of a stone fireplace that was perfect when it was cold enough for a fire. Thank God he had a housekeeper, so the place wasn't covered in an inch of dust, but there were books stacked on tables, an abandoned coffee cup and invoices, records and bills scattered on the floor around the chair he usually sat in.

"It's a great place," she said, taking in the wide windows that overlooked the corral and the ranch yard. Then her gaze landed on the paperwork. "Interesting filing system."

"Yeah." He pulled his hat off and set it, crown down, on the closest table. "I was working when Carlos came to get me to ride out to the pasture and check on a few of the herd. We've got some pregnant cows out there and wanted to make sure they had enough water."

"I thought you had ponds and lakes."

"We do," he said, "but sometimes, the stock ponds get gummed up or start going dry."

"How do you keep track of so many animals?"

He shrugged. "The cowboys ride the land most

days, we keep a running head count of the cattle so if any wander off, we can go find 'em."

"So you're riding across the ranch every day?"

"I wish," he muttered, then glanced at the paperwork. "If I had my way, yeah. But there's a lot of that to be done, too. Plus there's more than the animals to care for. There are stock ponds to keep clean and clear, feed fields to manage and the pastures themselves."

She shook her head. "It sounds intimidating."

"Can be," he agreed, and realized this was the first time a woman had actually asked him about his work. And she looked as though she really was interested. "If you don't learn from the best. I did. My dad knew everything there was to know about ranching and he taught me."

"From everything Lucy and Cora Lee have told me about him, he sounds like a very special man."

"He was. In every way." Jesse stared out the front window at the ranch he'd loved from the first moment he'd set foot on the place. "He loved Lucy and me and raised us as if we were his own."

Nodding, she turned, too, to look out the window at the darkness creeping in as twilight ended. "That is special. Not everyone can accept a child other than their own."

"Yeah, well," he said, "Roy was one of a kind." To change the subject, he pulled the foil back from the pie and took a whiff. "Smells good."

"Tastes better." A couple of long, silent seconds ticked past, then she said abruptly, "Have you always wanted to be a rancher?"

"For as long as I can remember." He took her arm

and steered her down the long hall toward the back of the house. "Let's get to the kitchen so I can grab a fork."

They walked through the dining room, past a wide table long enough to seat twelve comfortably and through a door into the kitchen. Beside him, Jillian stopped dead, gasped in astonishment, then turned a slow circle, looking all around.

"What is it?"

She held up one hand for silence and murmured, "Just, wait. I'm having a moment here."

Her features told him she loved the room. The walls were a soft blue, cabinets were white and the countertops were black granite. In front of the bay window was a round pedestal table and matching chairs where Jesse usually ate since the dining room was too huge for a man alone. The appliances were all top-of-the-line stainless steel. Over the built-in gas stove was a copper range hood and in the middle island was a second sink and Jesse's favorite part of the kitchen, an indoor grill.

"This is…amazing." Her voice was low and breathy, as if she were in church. She took a step farther into the room, reached out one hand and stroked her fingertips across the black granite. Looking back at him, she said, "I have serious kitchen envy. What I could do with— It's a dream kitchen. Like something you'd see in a magazine."

He chuckled, moved past her and set the pie down on the center island. Yanking open a drawer, he pulled out two forks. "Glad you like it. And it's funny you should say that about a magazine kitchen. That's exactly what this was."

"What do you mean?"

He turned to a cupboard, took down two plates and then grabbed a pie slicer from another drawer. "When I was building this place, Lucy showed me a picture of this exact kitchen in a magazine. So I showed it to the architect and told him I wanted it."

She blinked at him and laughed a little. "I don't think I've ever known anyone who would—or could—do that."

He shrugged. "It's a kitchen. Don't really use it all that much, except to make coffee and to keep my beer cold."

"Oh, God…"

He looked up when she moaned. "The best part of the whole kitchen, to my mind, is the grill there. Most times when I come in at the end of the day I'm too tired to cook, but I can always grill. Toss a steak on there and I'm good."

"That's practically criminal," she said softly.

"What?" He looked at her.

"To have this fantastic kitchen and only use the island grill?" She shook her head again. "Criminal."

"Well, don't arrest me until I've tried the pie." He cut two slices, plated them, then carried both plates to the table. "Come on. If you don't have some I'll wonder if you poisoned it or something."

She followed and sat opposite him. Outside, twilight lay across the ranch and shimmered on the raindrops pelting the window. Within minutes, darkness would drop like a curtain. "I would never ruin one of my pies with poison."

He grinned. "Good to know."

It felt good, sitting there with her in the dying light.

Talking with her. Seeing her smile. Lust still clawed at his insides, but there was another part of him that was enjoying this moment. "Okay," he said, lifting his fork. "Moment of truth."

"I'm not worried."

"Confident," he said. "I like it."

He took a bite of the pie and the minute it hit his tongue, Jesse groaned quietly. Spices exploded in his mouth, combining into flavors like he'd never tasted before. He chewed, swallowed, then took another bite.

She grinned. "Told you."

When he could, Jesse said, "You're a witch or something, right? This is incredible. Seriously great."

She seemed to practically glow under his compliments and he had to wonder about that. "Thank you," she said, taking a bite of the pie herself. "It's my grandma Rhonda's recipe. She taught me."

"Like I said earlier, it's all about learning from the best."

Her smile widened. "She really was, too. The best, I mean."

"Got to see a lot of her when you were a kid?"

"She raised me," Jillian said simply in a tone that told him she wouldn't welcome questions.

He could live with that. "Well, she did a damn good job of it as far as I can see."

"Thanks."

"You should sell these," Jesse told her, wolfing down another bite of pie.

"That's the plan."

He stopped. "Is that right?"

Nodding, she said, "I love baking and I'm good at it."

"I can testify."

"I want to open a shop. Pies. Cookies. Cakes." She paused as if she'd heard the excitement in her own voice and was embarrassed by it. "Well, that's the dream anyway."

"With talent like this, it should be more than a dream."

She smiled and in the dim light, he thought he saw her eyes sparkling. Reaching back behind him, Jesse hit the switch for the overhead light. It was on a dimmer switch, so a soft glow settled over the table and the two people seated there.

"That's nice." She looked up at the rustic/industrial chandelier with glass spheres and curved iron arms.

"Yeah. Before dawn I don't like being stabbed in the eye with light while I drink my coffee."

She laughed a little and that low, throaty sound did some amazing things to his insides.

"So," he asked, "why're you working at the day care when you can cook like this?"

She shrugged. "I needed a job. Besides, I don't have enough money yet to get a pie shop going."

"How much do you have?" Jesse didn't know why he was asking, other than that he wanted to see that excited gleam in her eyes again.

She looked as if she was going to refuse to answer and he couldn't blame her. Kind of a rude question. But then she took a breath and sighed. "When I sold my grandmother's mobile home a few years ago, I got fifteen thousand, but I'll need more than that. So I've been saving and in a few years, I should be able to do it."

He took another bite of the truly great pie and

chewed thoughtfully. "We own half of Royal, you know."

"Congratulations."

"Not what I meant." He waved his fork at her. "I think I know a shop on Main Street that would work for you."

She gasped, clearly stunned, and he enjoyed the moment before she spoke. "Thanks, but like I said, I'll need more start-up capital to—"

"The shop's already set up with what you'd need. Used to be a bakery until the owner moved to Michigan for some reason…"

Her fingers tapped on the tabletop and he could see her thinking, wondering, worrying.

"But—"

"And if you need more capital, I can advance it to you."

"Absolutely not." She shook her head, squared her shoulders and sat so straight in her chair, it was as if she had a board stuffed down the back of her shirt. "The Sanders family has already set me up in an apartment. I took that because Mac needed it. But I don't do charity."

"Good," he said roughly, keeping his voice stern and businesslike. "Because that's not what I'm offering. I'll be your partner."

Six

Jillian just stared at him. She couldn't believe what she was hearing. How had she gone from bringing Jesse a pie to him offering to set her up in business? And why was she even considering this?

"Silent partner," he added quickly and took another bite of pie. "I'll back you and when the shop's up and going, you can pay me back. Buy me out."

Excitement shot through her, but she quickly stamped it out, as she would hot sparks before they could start a forest fire. She couldn't do this. Jesse as a *partner*? Hadn't she been telling herself to see *less* of him? Even if he was a silent partner, she would have to work with him. A lot.

Oh, why was she even considering this? It was crazy. Impossible. "It could take years to pay you back," she said, firmly shaking her head.

"Not if you're selling pies like this." Jesse waved the fork at her. "Once people taste what you can do, you'll be so busy it'll make your head spin. The solid truth here is, you make a hell of a pie."

That idea made her smile and everything in her yearned. Jillian had had this dream of her own shop for so many years now. And since Mac's birth, the dream had become more fierce. She wanted to have her own business, make her own rules, live her own life and show her baby girl that you could do anything if you were willing to work for it.

She hadn't expected this. Didn't have a response ready. Maybe she should have said "no" right off the bat. But the thought of making her dream a reality years sooner than she'd hoped was too tempting to dismiss offhand. Still, she had to know. Understand.

"I don't get it," she said softly, tipping her head to one side as she watched him, trying to gauge what he was thinking. "Why would you want to do this?"

"Do I need a reason?"

She laughed shortly. "Well, yes."

"Fine." He sat back in his chair and studied her in the golden glow of the overhead lamp. "I figure if you can bake a pie like *this* in that tiny excuse for a kitchen in the apartment—there's no telling what you could pull off with the room to grow."

"Hmm."

"This is a straight-up business deal," he said, and Jillian met his shadowed gaze. "We'll have the family lawyers draw up the paperwork—"

"I don't know…" She laid one hand against her belly in a futile attempt to ease the butterflies racing around inside. This was all happening so fast she couldn't be sure about what to do. But in the next instant, Jillian told herself that this was the chance she'd been waiting, hoping for. Did it matter that Jesse was helping her? Again? Once she paid him back, the business would be hers completely, and wasn't that what was really important?

As if sensing that she was waffling, Jesse looked into her eyes and said, "The shop on Main has most of what you'd need. Anything else required we can get. Have you set up and running inside a month if you want it."

"A month." She could have her own shop in a *month*. Jillian took a deep breath and held it, hoping to steady the nerves, the questions, rattling her. It didn't help. *A month*. All she had to do was forego her pride and accept Jesse's offer. But was it pride keeping her from accepting his help? Didn't other businesses have investors? Why shouldn't she?

"Or sooner," he tempted.

Sooner. She chewed at her bottom lip and mentally raced through the colliding thoughts in her mind. The pros. The cons. The temptations and dangers of being too close to Jesse Navarro. About giving up the very essence of herself—her self-reliance. Since she was a child when her parents disappeared from her life, Jillian had learned to count on *herself*. Her grandmother had taught her to go for what she wanted but to never expect someone else to get it for her.

She'd worked and saved and maybe in another year or two, she could pull off opening her own shop under her own power. Sure, she'd still have needed a business loan, but she would have taken as little as she could because the thought of being in debt was terrifying. But if she was willing to bend, she could have that dream much sooner than she could have imagined. All she had to do was get past the life lessons that had guided her for so long.

Really, what was wrong with his offer? She wasn't really giving anything up. She would still do the work and build the business on her own. It was as if she were getting a loan from a bank. Only this bank happened to be gorgeous and starring nightly in her dreams.

As Jillian considered everything, her mind a whirlwind of disjointed thoughts, she realized something. She wanted to do this. Why should she wait years to have what she could have now? Self-reliance would still be her mainstay as it would be up to *her* whether her shop was a success or not. She wouldn't lose anything by accepting Jesse's offer. Instead, she could take a stand and start building the future.

Then she considered Mac in all of this. Her baby girl. Jillian wanted so much for her. If she waited until she'd saved all the money she might need, it could be two or three more years before she could open a shop. And that meant it might be years before she could find a bigger apartment—or a house—and she wanted that for Mac. Her little girl deserved to have her own yard to play in. She'd seen Mac with Brody, here on the ranch where the kids had room to run and play and make all the noise they wanted to without worrying about upsetting the person in the next apartment.

If she accepted Jesse's help, she'd be able to put her dreams on the fast track and that meant a better life for Mac. Wasn't that what coming to Texas in the first place had been all about?

"I can practically hear you thinking," Jesse said wryly.

"It's a lot to think about," she admitted and watched him savor another bite of pie.

"Not so much really," he said and set his fork down. "You've got talent and a plan. I can help you with getting started on that plan. Pretty straightforward."

"When you put it like that, sure," she said.

"So is that a yes?"

Jillian looked into his eyes and knew she was going to say *yes*. If there was still some hesitation inside her, she could understand it, but she wouldn't let it sway her. Maybe it was just time to throw caution to the wind and take the chance being offered. She took a breath, held his gaze and took the plunge. "I think so."

"Good." A smile lit up his eyes as he reached one hand across the table. "Well, then. Before you can change your mind, shake on it."

Steadying herself, Jillian slipped her hand into his and tried not to notice how her skin sizzled and burned at the contact. Electricity hummed up her arm to bounce around her chest like a crazed ping-pong ball. He squeezed her hand. "I'll call the lawyers tomorrow morning."

Nodding, she took a breath and said, "Okay."

He let her go and for a second, Jillian really missed the feel of his much bigger hand wrapped around hers. That was probably not what she should be thinking about a business partner.

"You're not going to change your mind, are you?"

She looked at him and shook her head. "No. Decisions are hard, but once they're made, that's it."

"Good to know." He glanced at the piece of pie on her plate. "You going to finish that?"

Jillian laughed and felt the butterflies settle. She handed her plate over and said, "I only hope the rest of Royal likes my pies as much as you do."

His dark eyes locked onto hers. His voice dropped to a husky murmur. "You can count on it."

They were talking about the pie shop, but there was an undercurrent, as well. What else could she count on? Jillian wondered. And why were her insides jumping again?

"Mama!" An eager shout echoed through the house.

Jillian blew out a breath and smiled. The tension between them shattered completely and then another voice shouted and the shared moment was over.

"Uncle Jesse!" Brody's voice.

"Hey, you guys!" Lucy called out an instant later. "Mac saw your car here and we came to find you!"

Jesse sighed a little. "Guess we're done talking about this for now. Good thing we came to an agreement already." Then he yelled, "In the kitchen."

She smiled at the sound of both kids clattering down the hall toward them. "Let me know what the lawyers say."

"Absolutely."

An instant later, both kids ran into the kitchen in a burst of noise and color—they were laughing in delight at their race down the hall. Lucy was right behind them.

"Wow," she said with a knowing smile as she strolled into the kitchen, "this looks…cozy. Something tells me we showed up too early."

"Not at all," Jillian said, scooping her daughter into her arms as she got to her feet. "I was just about to come to your house to get Mac."

"Uh-huh." Lucy's smile didn't fade, but her eyebrows lifted as she studied first Jillian, then Jesse.

Jillian fired off a narrow-eyed look at her friend and wasn't surprised when Lucy unapologetically winked at her.

"Oh, what's this?" she crowed when she spotted the pie on the counter. "God, I love pie." Lucy grabbed a fork from the drawer and went for a bite. "This is amazing," she said, already dipping in for another bite. "Jillian, did you *make* this?"

"I wanted to thank Jesse for all of his help, so yes. I baked it this afternoon."

"Boy, when you want to thank *me* for something, my favorite is lemon meringue." Lucy went for another taste, but Jesse smacked her hand away.

"Get your own pie."

"Hmm. Territorial. Interesting." She shrugged, licked her fork, then looked from one to the other of them. "You know, I'm really glad you're both here together because I need to ask a favor."

Jillian was wary. It hadn't taken her long to know when her friend was up to something. "What?"

"Oh," Lucy said, reaching over to smooth Brody's hair back from his forehead, "you know the gala at the TCC? Well, I've got tickets to go, but I just don't feel right about it."

"Lucy…"

She ignored Jillian and focused on her brother. "I mean, Jillian's new in town and she's been working so hard, this would be a great way for her to meet people *and* have some fun for a change."

Jesse looked at Jillian and knew the woman was torn between wanting to go and wanting his sister to be quiet. Normally, he didn't do the formal get-togethers at the club. He was most at home in his jeans, a work shirt and worn boots, riding a horse, being out under the sky. Jesse didn't care much for spending an entire evening suffering through wearing a tux. But damned if he didn't want to see Jillian all dressed up. Watching her now, he could see how irritated she must be toward his sister. That he could completely sympathize with. But Lucy had a point, too.

"I don't need a night of fun," Jillian argued.

"Oh, please." His sister glanced back at her. "You proved how much you need one today. You were supposed to go and relax for a while and instead you made a pie. A great pie, but come on. Baking is not relaxing."

"It is for me," Jillian said.

Lucy sighed dramatically. "Jillian, everyone needs fun once in a while. Even the great Stone Face here, right Jesse?"

"What's a stone face?" Brody asked.

"Never mind," Jesse said, giving his sister a look that he gave her every time she was after something. It had never worked, but he kept trying.

"I really don't have anything to wear," Jillian was saying as a last-ditch attempt to make Lucy drop it.

Jesse could have told her the attempt was futile.

"Oh, this year it's called the Black and White Ball. We'll go shopping." Lucy whipped back around to look meaningfully at Jesse.

He got the message and for whatever reason, he found it didn't bother him at all to say, "So, Jillian. Want to go to the ball with me?"

Jillian kissed Mac, glared at Lucy, then shifted her gaze to Jesse again. He knew when he saw the shine in her eyes that she was going to agree, but he liked hearing her say, "I'd love to."

"Excellent," Lucy announced and immediately launched into plans for shopping, getting Jillian's hair and nails done, and while his sister talked, Jesse watched Jillian—the excitement in her eyes, the smile curving her mouth, the way her shirt clung to her breasts—and he fervently wished his sister was anywhere else.

The following day was Jillian's day off and true to her word, Lucy showed up at the apartment to pick up her and Mac. They dropped the kids off at the TCC day care for a few hours and hit the Courtyard shops. Most of the stores were no more than booths sectioned off inside a huge red barn that used to be part of a working ranch. But the land was sold, and some enterprising soul had turned the barn and several outbuildings into an eclectic shopping center.

Jillian normally guarded her bank account like a miser. But going to this black-tie gala, she couldn't exactly attend in jeans, so she was determined to treat herself. And the one dressy outfit she had with her had been fine for Will's memorial, but would be completely out of place at a gala. How long had it been since she had been on an actual date? Not that this was a date, really. Jesse was just doing his sister a favor and Jillian wasn't reading anything into it at all, but that didn't mean she couldn't look great, did it?

"It's a black-and-white ball this year," Lucy reminded her as they entered the boutique. "So no red dresses, which is a damn shame if you ask me, because you probably look great in red."

The shop was in one of the outbuildings near the barn itself and it was pretty without being intimidating. Beautiful clothes hung in groups of color and style. The walls were a pale yellow and there were baskets of live plants and vases of flowers scattered throughout the room.

"My Valkyrie uniform was red," Jillian told her, "so trust me when I say I'm okay with going for black or white."

Lucy shook her head and her layered brown hair swung around her face with the motion. "I really want to see that uniform. But for now... Ooh. Look at *that*."

Jillian followed in Lucy's wake and she felt both eyebrows arch at first sight of the dress. "I don't know," she said warily. "There's not a lot of fabric there."

Lucy sighed dramatically. "What are you, eighty? You've got a great figure, why not flaunt it? Knock Jesse off his feet."

Jillian eyed her friend suspiciously. "That's not what this is about."

"No, of course not," her friend cooed, lifting the hanger off the rack to further admire the really tiny dress. "But it couldn't hurt to make his eyeballs pop out, could it?"

Jillian thought about that for a second and if she was going to be honest with herself, she had to admit that it would be fun to make Jesse's jaw drop when he saw her. So far, he'd only seen her in jeans, with Mac or with the other kids at the day care.

"You could at least try it on after all the trouble I went to find it," Lucy urged, waving the dress back and forth as if trying to hypnotize her friend into submission.

Jillian laughed. "It's the first store we've been to and the first dress you saw."

"Oh, don't be logical." Lucy pushed the dress into Jillian's hands. "Just try it on while I look for more."

Sighing a little at the futility of actually winning an argument with her friend, Jillian carried the dress to the counter and a woman there opened a changing room for her. In a few minutes, she was wearing what little fabric there was and wondering if she could be arrested.

"Well?" Lucy asked from outside the door.

"My old uniform covered more."

Lucy laughed. "Come on, let me see."

Opening the door, Jillian stepped out and stopped in front of a full-length mirror. She tugged the hem of the slightly full skirt down, but it stopped midthigh no matter what she did. She pulled the bodice up, but it remained in place, displaying breasts that hadn't seen the light of day in more than a year.

She looked over her shoulder into the mirror and swore she could see the dimples at the top of her butt, the back was cut so low. "Oh, I don't think—"

"It's *perfect*," Lucy said breathlessly as she handed the three other dresses she'd brought just in case, over to the clerk. "We won't need these."

Jillian's head whipped up. "No, wait, I should—"

"Buy some sky-high black heels, wear your hair down and ooh, we should get you some black lingerie while we're out, too." Lucy slapped her hands together and scrubbed her palms. "Isn't this *fun*?"

"Lucy, I don't know about this…"

Her friend stepped up behind her and met Jillian's gaze in the mirror. "My brother's eyes are going to do more than pop. They'll probably jump out of his head and roll across the floor."

Jillian laughed, then tugged at the hem again. "There's an image."

Lucy slapped her hands down. "Stop tugging. You look amazing. Just enjoy it."

She half turned in front of the mirror, examining herself from every angle. The dress *did* look good on her. It was just that there was so little of it. Then she thought about what Lucy had said about Jesse's reaction. Jillian told herself that shouldn't matter, but she knew she was lying.

Of course it mattered. She might not want a permanent man—because so far, in her experience, men hadn't *been* permanent at all—but a temporary man might be just the thing. She'd spent so many nights dreaming about Jesse, wanting him, wouldn't it be better to just *have* him? Once the sexual tension was eased, she could get past this, right? Focus on her life, her daughter, her future.

They'd just reached an agreement. They were going to be partners. But if this incredible sexual tension remained between them, working together wouldn't be easy. So really, sleeping with Jesse would be the smart thing to do. *Oh, that was just a really sad attempt at justification.*

"Well?" Lucy asked from behind her. "What's the decision?"

Jillian looked her friend in the eye. "Where do we find me sky-high black heels?"

Lucy grinned.

Two hours later, they were both exhausted, and stopped at the Courtyard café for coffee and muffins. The sky was clear and sharply blue. The sun was shining and already warm, but in the shade, they didn't mind the growing heat as much.

Jillian should have been feeling guilty. She'd dropped a lot of money today on lingerie, shoes and a dress she couldn't imagine wearing more than once. And then there was the mani/pedi Lucy had talked her into. Still a little shocked, she whispered, "I can't believe I spent all that money."

"It's an investment," Lucy assured her and broke off a piece of blueberry muffin.

Laughing, Jillian asked, "In *what*?"

"Yourself, silly." Lucy leaned on the tabletop. "You're going to meet a lot of people at the gala. And when you've got your pie shop open, they'll all come and buy delicious goodies from you."

Wryly, Jillian said, "Because of the black dress."

Lucy grinned again. "Can't hurt. Besides, don't you deserve a treat once in a while, Jill? You don't mind if I call you Jill, do you?"

"No." She smiled. "My grandmother always did."

"Good. So anyway, Jill, you look fabulous and

Jesse will introduce you around and you'll make a big splash."

"Uh-huh."

"Oh," Lucy added as if an afterthought, "I was thinking that maybe the night of the dance, why don't we just have Mac spend the night at my place?"

"Why?" Suspicious, she watched her friend warily.

"Well, you'll be getting in late," Lucy said, lifting her coffee cup for a sip. "You don't want to wake her up just to take her home and put her to bed again, do you?"

"I guess not, but…" Cocking her head to one side, Jillian watched Lucy feign all innocence for a minute or two. "I get the feeling I'm being set up."

"That's because you're a very smart woman."

"Lucy…"

"Oh, relax already." The other woman took another bite of her muffin. "There's no big conspiracy or anything. We're friends. I'm just helping out."

"Uh-huh." Jillian wasn't convinced. "Lucy, this is really sweet of you, I think, but I don't want a man in my life."

"How about in your bed?"

"My— We're talking about your brother here."

"Yes and believe it or not," Lucy said in a whisper, "I know that my brothers have sex. The lucky bastards. I haven't had sex in too long to think about but that's not the point at the moment."

"What is the point?"

"That I've seen the way you and Jesse look at each other. Heck, the air between you practically sizzles."

Jillian took a breath. Lucy was right. She'd been feeling it for weeks now and there didn't seem any reason to deny it. "That doesn't mean—"

"It means, you're grown-ups. You clearly like each other. Obviously, you *want* each other. So, why not?"

"And this isn't about matchmaking?"

Lucy slapped one hand to her chest in mock outrage. "Would I do that?"

"Yes," Jillian said, laughing.

"Okay," Lucy admitted, unrepentant. "I would. But I'm not. I'm just paving the way to a little recreational sex." She sighed. "Just because I'm living like a vestal virgin doesn't mean you have to."

Jillian thought about it while Lucy went in to get them refills. This wasn't about love. She *did* like Jesse. A lot. And boy, did she want him. One night didn't have to lead to forever. Especially since forever just didn't exist outside novels. But one night could be something special she'd always remember.

When Lucy came back with fresh coffee, she asked, "So? Does Mac spend the night with me?"

"Yes." Nodding, Jillian said, "Just don't expect something to come of this because it's not going to."

"Jill, the truth is, I want to see my brother happy. I want to see my friend happy." Lucy shrugged. "Is that so bad?"

"No, it's not. And I really do appreciate the thought, Lucy, but I'm just not looking for love."

Lucy smiled. "Oh, sweetie, that's exactly when you usually find it."

Seven

The more Jesse thought about attending the gala with Jillian, the more he was worried she might get the wrong idea. She wasn't the kind of woman to be with for a night and then dismiss. She was a *mother*, for God's sake. His sister's friend. And now she was going to be his business partner.

No way he could be as cavalier with Jillian as he always had been with the other women who had come and gone from his life in a blur. But he couldn't offer her more, either. So what the hell was he doing?

Jesse walked into the main house, intending to dump all of this on his younger brother and see what Will thought about it all. Truth be told, he needed someone else's input. His own brain had been chewing on the problem of Jillian for weeks and he was still tied up in knots.

But at the threshold of the great room, Jesse

stopped dead. Will wasn't alone. If he'd been paying attention, Jesse would have seen the strange car parked outside the house. As it was, seeing Megan Phillips Sanders sitting on a couch beside Will caught Jesse off guard.

His brother and the woman he was legally married to were looking at a photo album and hadn't noticed his arrival.

"Looks like it was a nice wedding," Will said, flipping through pages.

"I thought so at the time," Megan said. "I thought it was romantic that you—I mean *he*—wanted the ceremony to be on a beach, just the two of us. Looking back, I feel like an idiot."

"You shouldn't," Will told her. "I'm the idiot who trusted Rich, gave him the room he needed to steal my life and to trick you."

Megan laughed shortly. "You notice how we're both blaming ourselves and *not* blaming the one person who deserves the blame?"

When Will smiled in response, Jesse was relieved to see it. There hadn't been many of those smiles since Will came home. Maybe Megan and Will could help each other through the mess that Rich had left in his wake.

"Oh, I blame Rich all right," Will assured her. "And I'm going to do everything I can to make sure he's caught and thrown into jail for a hundred years."

Megan took the photo album and closed it with a slap. "That'd be good."

Jesse was beginning to feel like some Peeping Tom, so he stepped into the room and said hello.

"Jesse, hello," Megan said. She was a pretty woman

with bright blue eyes, brown and gold hair, and she always looked like she'd stepped out of a magazine. Her clothes, shoes and purse always matched. Jesse had no idea how women did that.

"Didn't mean to interrupt," Jesse said.

"You're not," Will told him. "We were just talking. Megan was showing me pictures of her wedding to—well, *me*, I guess."

Megan sighed. "Not you. I know that now. Wish I had known then."

Jesse nodded. "We're all feeling that way, Megan."

"You're being very nice."

"None of this is your fault," Will told her.

Jesse thought that Will looked more relaxed than Jesse had seen him in the last several weeks and for that, the Sanders family owed Megan.

To Jesse, Will said, "I was just telling Megan that I have to put up with house arrest and she has to keep up the pretense of our marriage if we want to catch Rich and throw him into the deepest, dankest cell the law can find."

"I don't think that's a word, but I'm with you. And yeah," Jesse said, shifting to look at Megan. "I'm sorry about that. Got to be hard on you pretending to care about the man who lied to you."

She smoothed her palms over the black knee-length skirt she wore. "It's not, really. Rich is gone and I don't know if he even intends to come back this time. Don't know how he could, really, since everyone thinks Will Sanders is dead. But either way," she added, looking at Will, "everyone I know was used to you—I mean *him*—being gone on business a lot, so I just smile and nod when people ask about my husband."

"You're being really great about all of this," Will said.

"If I throw a fit, will it help?"

He grinned. "No."

"Well, then, why bother, right?" Megan rose and picked up her purse from the table. "I've really got to get going now. But if it's all right with you, I'd like to come back. Talk with you again, Will. About Rich and well…just all of it."

He stood up and took her hand. "I'd like that, too. Feels like the two of us are sharing a leaky canoe. I think teamwork is required."

Megan smiled at him. Jesse noticed the sparkle in her eyes and wondered if Will had seen it, too.

"If it's okay, I'll come back tomorrow and we can talk about what the plan is going forward."

"Sure. That's great." Will walked her to the door, the two of them passing close to Jesse.

"It was nice to see you," Megan said.

"You, too, Megan," Jesse answered.

"Be right back," Will said.

Jesse wandered toward the cold stone hearth and waited for his brother to see Megan off. So the two of them had been looking at a wedding album. Damn. That had to have hit Will like a truck. He couldn't even imagine what it was like for him to look at wedding pictures featuring the man who'd tried to kill him pretending to *be* him.

And what must Megan be feeling about all of this? She'd married a man who'd turned out to be nothing but smoke and mirrors. Now she was married to a *dif-*

ferent man with the same name. Jesse was beginning to think Royal, Texas, was the playground of some really annoying gods.

"Man, that was rough," Will said as he walked back into the room. He dropped down into a chair and stared up at Jesse. "I took your suggestion. This morning, I called Megan, invited her out to the ranch and when she got here, I shut up and let her talk. She told me everything from her point of view. I wouldn't have believed it possible, but now I want to beat Rich senseless even more than I did before."

Jesse perched on the arm of a chair opposite his brother. "How's she doing?"

"Oh, great." Sarcasm colored his tone. "She's married to a stranger, just like I am. What's that old TV show we used to watch in marathons?"

"Twilight Zone," Jesse provided.

"That's it. And that's where I'm living." Will shook his head, then scrubbed one hand across his eyes. "What's life like in the real world?"

"Confusing as hell."

Will's eyebrows arched. "Good. Tell me. Give me something to focus on that's *not* me."

Jesse snorted and pushed up from the chair. Stalking to the fireplace, he laid one hand on the mantel and leaned in, wishing it was cold enough to have a damn fire. There was something soothing about the snap and hiss of flames over logs. "Apparently, I'm not only going to back Jillian in a pie shop, but I'm taking her to the TCC gala."

Will shook his head. "Say again. Slower."

So Jesse told him everything and realized as he did

how much he'd missed being able to bounce things off Will. During that time when Rich was usurping Will's life, he'd pretty much cut himself off from the family. Of course now Jesse could look back and see exactly why. The impostor couldn't risk spending too much time with the Sanders family because they might have seen through the masquerade. At the time, he'd resented Will for putting their mother and sister through so much pain. Now, he was just grateful to have his brother back.

"So the pie was good, huh? Did you save me any?"

"Figures that's what you took out of everything I just said." Jesse shook his head. Had he just been thinking how good it was to be able to talk to the man?

"I'm hungry. Shoot me." Will grinned and gave his brother a long look. "I'm glad you're going to help Jillian out with the shop."

"Yeah?"

"Yeah. Rich pulled her into all of this then walked away. I figure the Sanders family owes her."

Nodding, Jesse said, "That's how I felt."

"But the gala thing…" Will's grin widened. "I've never known you to do something you didn't want to do. So—"

"I don't want to go to the damn dance," Jesse assured him. "What I want is *her* and that's not okay."

"Why the hell not?"

Jesse straightened up then scrubbed both hands across his face. "Because she's not the kind of woman for an uncomplicated affair and I'm not looking for anything else."

"Again I ask," Will said, "why not?"

"Seriously?" Jesse just stared at him. "You were here when Lucy's husband died, Will."

"What's Dane's death got to do with—" he broke off and sighed. "Guilt. Is that what this is about? You think you don't get something because you're not through paying your debt to some otherworldly fate?"

"Dane died because of me," Jesse ground out.

Will scowled at him and snapped, "He died because a horse trampled him."

"He was helping *me*."

"Because he asked you to teach him." Will stood up and faced his brother. "He wanted to fit in on the ranch. He wanted to be a part of it all and you obliged him. Not your damn fault that stallion went crazy."

He wished he could believe that, but Jesse knew different. He never should have allowed Dane into the corral with that horse. It was too wild, and he had been too inexperienced.

"I shouldn't have let him get so close."

"Hard to learn from a distance."

"Our nephew doesn't have a father because of decisions I made."

"Believe it or not, Jesse, you are *not* the center of the universe. Fate, Karma, whatever, doesn't revolve around whatever it is you're doing from day to day."

"Brody's father is *dead*. Nothing you say can change that."

Still scowling, Will reminded him, "Brody has two uncles, a grandmother and a mom who's nuts about him. That's more than a lot of kids have."

Facts didn't seem to ease the regret and guilt that could still rise up and choke him without a moment's warning. Just the other day, he'd watched Brody riding his first pony and thought that Dane should be there, seeing his son grow. Instead, the man had died, never even knowing that Lucy was pregnant.

"You're just determined to wear a hair shirt and beat yourself over the head with this, aren't you?"

Jesse shot his brother a hard glare. "For a while there, I was glad to have you to talk to again. Not so sure, now."

Will smiled. "If you're just looking for someone to agree with you, talk to yourself."

"Thanks. Helpful."

"You want helpful? Here it is." Will dropped into his chair again, stretched his legs out in front of him and crossed his feet at the ankle. "Go to the dance. Kiss that woman. Don't be an idiot, and take her to bed if she'll have you. Let yourself live again, Jesse. Because from where I'm sitting, it looks like I'm not the only one on house arrest."

The night of the gala, Jillian was as nervous as a teenager on her first date. "Silly." She looked at her reflection in the bathroom mirror and hardly recognized herself. She hadn't really bothered to fix her hair and take care with her makeup since Cora Lee had hosted that service for Will a few weeks ago. And that had really been more casual-dressy. This was something else entirely. And she hadn't worn anything so blatantly feminine since she quit her job and retired her Valkyrie uniform.

Anxious, she smoothed her hands down over the front of her dress and wondered *again* if she'd done the right thing buying it. Sure, it looked good on her, but maybe it would send the wrong signals to Jesse.

They were going to be business partners so they should keep things platonic.

"Yeah, this dress does not say 'Be my friend,'" she said, frowning. "It's screaming 'Take me, I'm yours.'"

At that thought she slapped both hands to her middle and forced deep breaths into her lungs. Mac was at Lucy's, and Jillian knew she didn't have to worry about her girl. Mac had been so excited to have a sleepover with Brody she'd forgotten to kiss her mommy goodbye.

"And that's a good thing," she assured her reflection.

Jillian made another adjustment to her hair, lying in soft waves down her back. Having her hair loose made her feel a little better about how much skin was displayed by the deeply cut back of the dress.

When the knock on the door sounded, she jumped, then laughed at herself. "Get a grip, Jillian." She checked the fall of the short, slightly full skirt, then resolutely left the bathroom.

Still nervous, she opened the door and simply stared. Jesse. Like he stepped out of a dream. Tall and gorgeous, the man had been born to wear a tuxedo. He might not be pleased about it, but Jesse was gorgeous. In his elegantly tailored tux, with a crisp white shirt and black bow tie, he looked as if he should be on the cover of *GQ*. Of course, you couldn't take the ranch out of the man completely. He wore shining black boots and a black cowboy hat that only added to the whole picture that was taking her breath away. "You look very handsome."

"I don't know about that," he said, "but you look beautiful."

The way he was looking at her—as if he could simply gobble her up—made her *feel* beautiful. And it made her feel other things, as well. Things she'd been trying desperately not to think about. But with the heat in his gaze as he looked at her, those thoughts roared into life and refused to be pushed aside. She took a breath to steady herself. "Thank you. Why don't you come in? I'll get my purse and wrap."

Stepping past her into the apartment, Jesse stopped and stared at the room in front of him. Jillian smiled at the stunned expression on his face.

"Look a little different in here?" she asked unnecessarily.

He glanced at her briefly and grinned. "I wouldn't have believed it."

Jillian looked at the apartment and gave a short sigh of satisfaction. The walls were now a soft green. There were framed photos from magazines of places she one day wanted to visit on the walls and a few brightly colored rugs she'd found at the consignment shop on the floor. She'd made a room divider from two old doors she'd found at a garage sale and used it to block her bed from the rest of the room. It was still small, of course, but now it had personality. It was home. Hers and Mac's.

"I can't believe you did all of this. It looks great."

"Thanks." She picked up her small, black bag and swung the rose-colored wrap Lucy had loaned her over her shoulders.

Jesse looked her up and down again and said, "You keep surprising me."

"Is that bad?" she asked, meeting his gaze.

"No. I like surprises."

The look in his eyes sent heat sizzling across her skin. Jillian took a breath and relished the burn. What he could do to her with his eyes was like nothing she'd ever experienced before. "Me, too."

His eyes flashed. "Good to know."

Oh, boy. She turned for the door. He grabbed her upper arm, spun her around and pulled her in tightly to him.

"Surprise," he whispered just before he bent his head and took her mouth with the kind of hunger that vanquished anything that stood in its way.

At the first touch of his mouth, Jillian gasped, then sighed, lifting her arms to hook them around his neck. He parted her lips with his tongue and she welcomed it, tangling her tongue with his in a seductive dance that had her heart hammering in her chest and her blood rushing through her veins.

She felt a burning ache awaken deep inside her and it throbbed in time with her heartbeat. Jesse's hands dropped from her waist to her hips, then swept beneath the short hem of her skirt to explore the curve of her behind with wide, callused palms. Jillian groaned in the back of her throat and held him more tightly.

He caressed her rear with long, sure strokes until she was quivering in his grasp. Jillian's breath staggered in her lungs. It was as if she were actually living one of the dreams she'd been having the last few weeks. Only better. *Much* better. He was so tall, so strong, so overwhelming to every one of her senses, she could hardly think straight.

When he tore his mouth from hers and looked down into her eyes, he blew out a breath. "I had to have that taste of you," he admitted, voice rough and low.

"I'm glad," she said, then stroked her fingertips along his jaw.

"Yeah. I hate to say it, but we've got to go to that damn party." He ran one hand through her hair, letting the silky strands slide through his fingers. "And if we don't go now…"

Jillian dropped her forehead to his chest and fought for air. Kissing him had opened up a whole new world of sensation for her and she was shaking in response. She wanted more. But she knew he was right.

"You're right," she said, lifting her gaze to his. "We should go. Besides, I think I need a drink."

He grinned briefly. "You are not alone."

The Texas Cattlemen's Club was crowded, noisy and decorated with black and white balloons and hundreds of strings of tiny white lights. Waiters moved through the mob of people like ballet dancers, balancing silver trays loaded with either canapés or flutes of champagne. Music streamed from the far end of the great room where a local five-piece band played on a stage.

Jesse supposed it was a good party, and he knew this one night would raise thousands of dollars for the Royal Health Clinic. Still, he thought, as he looked at the beautiful woman on his arm, he wished the evening were over so they could be alone again. That kiss still burned through him. His body felt tight and if he didn't keep his mind off the taste of Jillian, he wouldn't be able to walk.

"It looks beautiful," she said, looking up at him, eyes shining, wide, delicious mouth curved in a smile.

"No, it looks nice. You're beautiful." She just

stared at him, her eyes warm and soft, and Jesse had to tear his gaze from hers before he gave in to that nagging urge to taste her again. "How about some champagne?"

"Sure. Thank you."

He stopped a passing waiter, took two glasses from him and handed one to Jillian.

"It looks like half the town is here," she said, leaning in to make sure he could hear her over the crush of conversations and swell of music.

"That sounds about right," he said, letting his gaze slide over the gathered crowd. He nodded to old friends, then spotted someone he thought Jillian should meet. "Come on. I'll introduce you to Will's wife."

"His wife? Oh, that's right. She was at the service, too. Who's the other woman?"

"Allison Cartwright."

"Megan, Allison, good to see you both," he said. "I wanted you to meet my new business partner, Jillian Norris."

Beside him, Jillian jolted, clearly surprised at his introduction.

He looked at her and whispered, "The whole town will know soon enough."

"You're right." She nodded and shook hands with both women.

"So what kind of business are you in?" Megan asked.

"I'm opening a pie shop."

"Oh, lovely," Allison said on a deep sigh. "I do love a good pie."

"That's a great accent," Jillian said, focusing on the lovely redhead. "Ireland?"

Allison grinned. "You've a good ear. Most don't guess right first off."

"Well, I'm from Vegas and we got visitors from all over the world, so I recognize different accents." She took a sip of champagne. "Have you moved here permanently, Allison?"

"I wish I could, but sadly, my visa is soon to expire."

"Oh, I'm sorry."

"So am I," Megan said and dropped one arm around Allison's shoulders. "We're going to try to get it extended, though, right?"

"Worth a try." Allison flipped her long red hair back over her shoulder. "I'm having a lovely time in your country. There's so much to see and do and I'm not nearly ready to go home yet."

"Hopefully you won't have to," Jesse said.

He took hold of Jillian's hand and she curled her fingers around his. That simple connection with her, the feel of her warm, soft hand was enough to awaken barely banked embers inside him.

Allison beamed at their joined hands and Jesse made a mental note to talk to Rand Gibson at some point about the woman's visa. Rand was second in command to Will as CEO at Spark Energy Solutions. Will couldn't do it since he was still in hiding. So as much as Jesse hated getting involved in the business end of the family empire, it would be up to him to check on this.

But tonight wasn't about business. Tonight was to show Jillian around. He'd already noticed that every man in the room had watched her walking across the room. And he couldn't blame them. Hell, he could hardly take his eyes off her himself. That dress was designed to break a man. Her hair, long and wavy, was a golden blond temptation. Those heels she wore made her long legs look even longer than usual, and every time she took a breath, her breasts lifted beneath the deeply cut bodice and the view about stopped his heart.

And he couldn't get the taste of her out of his mind. The feel of her body pressed to his. The sigh of her breath against his cheek. Her eager response to his kiss. His body tightened, and Jesse silently wished they'd never left her tiny apartment.

He gave Jillian's hand a squeeze and held on. "I promised Jillian a dance, so if you ladies will excuse us…"

"Absolutely," Megan said, lifting her glass in a toast. "Enjoy yourselves."

The woman's smile was wistful, and Jesse understood why. He felt bad for Megan. She'd been sucked into the world's weirdest soap opera. But she was a standup, he'd give her that. She was sticking with Will and doing everything she could to help them find the bastard who had screwed with all of their lives.

But he wasn't going to think about any of that tonight, either. Jesse led Jillian through the crowd and idly noticed Rand Gibson standing in the shadows where he was close enough to have been listening in on the conversation he and Jillian had been having with Megan and Allison. Jesse frowned to himself. *Why the hell would Rand be eavesdropping?*

Shaking his head, Jesse took Jillian's champagne flute and together with his, left them on an empty table. Then keeping a firm grip on her hand, he threaded their way toward the dance floor. Several times he paused briefly along the way to introduce Jillian to different people. Everyone was excited by the idea of a pie shop opening on Main Street and that boded well for business. And, he told himself, once people tasted Jillian's pies, they'd be customers for life.

"Who's that?" Jillian poked his shoulder then discreetly pointed at a couple who were being toasted by a small crowd.

Jesse smiled briefly. "That's Knox McCoy and Selena Jacobs. They're just recently engaged, so that's a celebration."

"Aw, that's so nice." Jillian sighed a little, and he wondered what it was about talk of weddings that turned women into marshmallows.

On the dance floor, he swung her into his arms and began moving to the music, steering her smoothly into the steps.

"You're a good dancer," she said.

"Don't sound so surprised." Jesse slid his open palm up and down her bare back. "Cora Lee made sure both of her sons wouldn't stomp a girl's feet flat on the dance floor."

She laughed, tipping her head back to gaze up at him. "I knew I liked your mother."

He looked down into her eyes and fresh heat erupted between them. She took a breath and licked her lips, and Jesse nearly groaned. He was in a bad way here and fighting like hell to hold on to the few slippery threads of his control.

He trailed his fingers along her spine, and she shivered, her eyes going a little glassy. "I really like this dress," he said.

"Right now," she said softly, "I really like it, too."

"I don't think I even told you how beautiful you look tonight."

"You did. And just did again."

"It deserves repeating." He moved into a turn, holding her tightly, watching her long, silky hair fly out around her shoulders. "You puzzle me."

She grinned. "Isn't that a nice thing to say?"

"There it is again. Puzzlement."

"I'm an open book, Jesse."

He laughed. "Women always say that, but doesn't matter if the book's open if it's written in a language you can't read."

"You seem to do all right."

He shook his head and looked into eyes that haunted him day and night. "No. There isn't a man alive who can translate that book."

She smiled, laid her head on his shoulder and followed his lead. The music flowed on from one song to the next without breaking stride, and so Jesse continued to glide across the floor, holding her pressed to him.

"Thank you for bringing me here tonight," she said quietly, lifting her head to look up at him. "I know you didn't want to come, but you did anyway."

"It was worth it to see you in that dress." His gaze locked on hers.

"You look very handsome in that tux."

One corner of his mouth lifted briefly. "The tux is a small price to pay for dancing with the most beautiful woman here."

"You're pretty smooth when you want to be, aren't you?"

"You bring it out in me."

"Not until tonight," she said, laughing.

"Well, a lot of things changed tonight."

She sighed a little and again chewed at that bottom lip. He'd noticed she did that a lot when she was nervous, or unsteady about something, and he was glad to know she was as on edge as he was.

"I guess so," she said, and shivered. "That kiss…"

Instantly, his body fisted. He trailed his fingers up and down her spine, enjoying the sparks in her eyes as she reacted to his touch. "Yeah, I'm thinking about that, too."

"What're you thinking exactly?"

"I'm thinking we should do it again as soon as we get clear of this place." He waited to see her reaction.

"And I think that's a great idea." She slid her hand along his shoulder to the back of his neck and ran her fingers through his hair.

He gritted his teeth, glanced around the crowded room, then shifted his gaze back to hers. "Then let's do some fast introducing you to a few more of these people and get the hell outta Dodge."

That smile of hers was all the encouragement he needed. Leading her off the floor, Jesse made stops at several groups of people. If his friends wondered about why he stopped to say hello and then left again seconds later, it didn't matter to Jesse. Jillian charmed them all and he watched with a weird sense of pride. She'd been dropped into a new town, without knowing a soul, and she was handling it all with a lot more confidence and style than most would have. She was stronger than she thought and that appealed to him on multiple levels.

She was creative and kind and ambitious. She was a damn good mother and a hell of a kisser. Everything he discovered about Jillian Norris made him want to learn more.

A part of him was bothered by that realization. As he'd told Will, Jesse wasn't in a position to offer Jillian all the things a man should. He already had a family he had to look out for because of his own carelessness. How could he promise someone else forever when he already owed a debt to his sister and her son that he could never repay?

A sinking sensation opened up in his gut as he watched Jillian smile and laugh at something Sheriff Nathan Battle said. His wife, Amanda, slapped her husband's forearm playfully, then leaned in and whispered something he didn't catch to Jillian.

Still smiling, Jillian looked up at him and everything in Jesse turned over. Her eyes, her smile, the fall of her hair and the touch of her hand all combined to twist Jesse up into so many different knots he couldn't begin to untangle them. All he knew for sure was that he wanted her more than his next breath.

Eight

Twenty minutes later, they were headed for the door. Jesse got her wrap and his hat, then led her out into the cool summer night. The black sky glittered with stars that not even the streetlights could dim. A soft wind shot down the street, lifting the ends of Jillian's hair and flipping at the hem of her skirt.

She laughed and admitted, "I won't remember half of the people I just met."

"You'll meet 'em again," he told her. "When they come to buy our pies."

"*Our* pies?"

He winked. "Partners, remember? For now."

For now.

Jillian told herself she'd do well to remember those two words if nothing else from tonight. And she wondered if he wasn't trying to tell her that more than their business partnership was "for now." What they felt when they were together wasn't a declaration of love buzzing between them. This was plain old-fashioned lust. Nothing wrong with that—as long as you didn't try to convince yourself it was something more.

A pang of regret jangled her nerves before she could stop it and she shivered a little as she tried to let it go.

"You're not cold, are you?"

"No, it's nice tonight."

He studied her in the dim glow of a streetlight, and Jillian tried to read what he was thinking, feeling, and failed. "If you've changed your mind about this, just say so. I'll walk funny for a week, but it's all right."

Shaking her head, Jillian reached up, cupped his face between her palms and drew him down for a kiss that seared them both. Lust or love, this was too big to ignore. She had to have him with her even if it was only for this one night.

His arms came around her like steel bands. He lifted her off her feet and a part of her thrilled to it. In the glow of a streetlight, he kissed her deeply, letting her know without words that he wanted her as badly as she did him. That was powerful and for tonight, it was enough.

When he finally tore his mouth free of hers and drew in a deep breath, he said, "It's been killing me, waiting to get another taste of you."

A laughing couple burst through the door behind them and Jesse reluctantly set her on her feet. "But this isn't the place for it."

Last chance, she thought. Last chance to change her mind and turn away from what she was feeling before it overwhelmed her. But even as she thought it, Jillian knew it was already too late to go back. Maybe it had been too late since the first day she'd met him.

"My apartment's close," she said, locking her gaze with his.

"Not close enough." He grabbed her hand and hurried to his black Range Rover.

The drive was a short one, but two miles had never seemed so long to her before. Sitting beside him in the warm darkness, every nerve inside her lit up. It had been a long time since she'd been with a man and she'd *never* been with one like Jesse. He was the quintessential cowboy. Strong, mostly silent and a kindness underlying his strength that made him darn near irresistible. And she was done trying to resist him.

He parked the car in her building's lot and in a few minutes, they were up the elevator, and through her front door. He closed it behind them, threw the lock, then picked her up and slammed her against the door. "Have to touch you. Now."

"Yes," she said on a breathy sigh.

"You in this dress? Driving me crazy all night. Especially," he said, "since I've already had my hands under your skirt and I know you're not wearing much beneath it."

She lifted her chin and turned her head to the side, giving him access to her throat. He dragged his mouth along the column of her neck, and Jillian held tightly to his shoulders. "They're black."

"What?"

"My panties," she said. "They're black."

He groaned and lifted her legs to hook them around

his waist. Then he filled his hands with her bottom, squeezing, kneading until she whimpered as need whipped from a nagging ache to an overwhelming demand. Shifting his grip on her, he reached down to stroke the core of her and even through the silky fabric of her panties, Jillian shook with reaction. Spirals of pleasure and expectation coiled inside her, and she moved into his touch.

He dipped his head to the base of her throat, then lifted her higher against the door so he could taste the valley between her breasts.

"Jesse…" Breathless, she gasped for air and couldn't find any. Her heartbeat pounded in her ears and then he snapped the elastic band on her panties and she groaned.

He tossed the panties to the floor, then murmured, "Sorry about those."

"Don't care, don't care." Her head moved back and forth against the door. She hooked her legs tighter around him and arched into him, wanting, needing.

His thumb stroked that aching, throbbing core. She was wet for him and so hot she felt the fire inside spreading, threatening to incinerate them both. He pushed one finger, then two inside her, and Jillian cried out his name as she instantly splintered. Her body trembled with the waves of pleasure shaking through her and before they had ended, he withdrew his hand and worked at the button and zipper of his slacks.

Sighing, smiling, she looked into his eyes and said, "That was—"

"Just the beginning," Jesse promised and he pushed his hard length into hers with one sure stroke. Jillian moaned and took him in. He filled her so completely, so thoroughly, she couldn't have said where she ended and he began. And she didn't care. As long as he stayed inside her. Always. Higher, deeper, claimed her as no one else ever had.

She felt the cold of the door behind her back, but it meant nothing compared to the heat within. He was so big. So hard. His body locked into hers as if made to fit, and she wanted more. Her legs locked around his middle and her hips rocked furiously, keeping up with the rhythm he set.

"Take it all and let go," he whispered, fixing his gaze to hers.

She looked into his eyes, saw her own reflection there and was shocked by the naked desire etched into her face. Jillian had never known such wild desire. Such overpowering emotions and sensations crashing together inside her. Her body hummed, her blood rushed and as the tight tingle of expectation at her core expanded, she leaped into the fire.

Clutching his shoulders tightly, she called out his name and rode him hard as a climax bigger than anything she'd ever imagined roared through her. And still, he pounded himself into her, taking, giving, taking again until she couldn't think, couldn't speak, could hardly breathe and she didn't care.

His hands gripped her hips and she felt the impression of every one of his fingers against her skin. He held tight, looked into her eyes, then exploded into her body with a hoarse cry of release that shattered her every bit as much as her orgasm had.

They clung together like survivors of a shipwreck.

Jillian was still pinned to the door behind her and Jesse was still deep inside her. Where she would keep him, if she could. Breath staggered in and out of her lungs and she held him as he buried his face in the curve of her neck and fought for his own breath.

"Couldn't wait another minute," he said tightly. "Took you against a damn door."

"And I loved every second of it," she assured him.

He lifted his head, looked into her eyes and said, "Yeah, me, too. But like I said, I wasn't thinking. And now it's time to pay. Didn't use a condom."

Her eyes went wide and her mouth dropped open. Jillian's fuzzy brain fought to focus on the situation, but it was so far out of her scope, it wasn't easy. She hadn't given a single thought to protection and that had *never* happened to her before. Even the night she'd gotten pregnant with Mac, she'd insisted the Will impostor use a condom. It was Fate's little joke that she'd gotten pregnant anyway. But tonight— "Oh, God."

"That pretty much covers it." He pulled her into his arms, peeling her away from the door and disentangling their bodies.

Jillian didn't know which devastated her more—the knowledge that she'd been so completely reckless…or the loss of his body inside hers.

On her feet again, she pushed her hand through her hair and thought about where she was in her cycle, frantically figuring out if she was fertile or not. Finally, she said, "I think it'll be okay. I mean, I should be safe."

He scrubbed one hand across his face, then looked

her directly in the eye. "If you're not, I expect you to tell me."

"Absolutely." She wouldn't keep something like that from him. "And you should know, I'm healthy."

"So'm I," he said quickly. "So one worry off the table."

Her knees were a little wobbly, so she walked across the room to her bed and sat down. The bedsprings squealed and she laughed. "I can't believe—" she shook her head and looked up at him.

"Yeah, that's something I've never done before. I wouldn't take chances, Jillian."

"I know that," she said, looking up at him.

"I can only say I lost control." Then he added wryly, "I'm not sorry."

"Me, either," she admitted as a fresh, pulsing need erupted inside her.

"Good." He reached for his wallet and pulled out two condoms. Showing them to her, he said, "Because I'm not done with you yet."

"Oh, I'm so glad to hear that."

He peeled out of his clothes while she slipped out of her dress and in seconds they were naked, rolling across the mattress to the accompanying shrieks from the bedsprings.

"Should've gotten you a better bed," he murmured as he lowered his head to her breast. He took her nipple into his mouth and lips, teeth and tongue working that hard, pink bud until she twisted beneath him.

"If it gets too noisy, we can move to the floor," she insisted, reaching down to close her hand around the hard length of him. She ran her fingertips up and down his shaft, scraping gently with her nails until he lifted his head and groaned.

"You keep touching me like that I'll go wherever the hell you want me to."

Jillian grinned. "Don't plan to stop."

She slid her foot up and down one of his legs. She loved the strength of him. The hard solid body, the husky whispers, the gentle touch. In fact, everything about Jesse reached something inside her she hadn't known existed. Jillian didn't want to think about what that meant. Didn't want to think at all right now. She wanted to lose herself in what was happening to her body. Revel in what he made her feel.

"You're thinking," he ground out, then ordered, "stop it."

She laughed, and he rolled onto his back, dragging her on top of him. Her hair fell down on either side of his face like a blond curtain, closing the two of them off from the rest of the world.

He looked up at her and said, "You take my breath away."

Jillian's heart leaped as she looked into his eyes and saw the fire for her burning brightly. She kissed him slowly, lingering over the taste of him and beneath her, she felt his heartbeat jolt into a gallop. Lifting her head, she met his gaze again and whispered, "You make me feel…"

Reaching down, he stroked her center and made her gasp as fresh sensation rushed through her. "Jesse…"

"Can't get enough of you," he admitted. "Not sure I like admitting that."

She smiled in spite of the words because it was so

Jesse. She reached over to the small bedside table, grabbed one of the condoms and tore the foil packet open.

Jesse's gaze flashed, and she smiled. Going up on her knees, she straddled him, then curled her fingers around the hard length of him. She smoothed the latex on with a slow, deliberate motion designed to torture them both.

"You're killing me," he said, hands on her thighs, gripping tightly.

"I'm just getting started," she said and lowered herself onto him. Her head fell back and her spine bowed as she took him deep inside. Reaching up, his hands covered her breasts, his fingers tweaking and pulling at her hardened nipples. Her moans mingled with his as she moved on him, setting a rhythm that pushed them both into a race for completion.

He dropped his hands to her hips and rocked beneath her, pushing even higher into her depths. Jillian groaned with every slick slide of his body into hers. His hands tightened on her hips and he used his own strength to help her move, to keep up the sharp, fast pace leaving them both breathless.

Jillian met his gaze and never looked away as she began to move on him more quickly. She saw need burning in his eyes, felt it in the grip of his hands. That amazing chorus of sensations opened up inside her again and Jillian raced to meet it. To jump into that chasm filled with fire and light and explosions of pure pleasure.

Bedsprings shrieked and breathing sighed into the room as they moved as one, each of them striving to reach the conclusion they knew was coming. And when it did, Jillian shouted in surprise at the force of the climax slamming into her. She rocked wildly, drawing it out, making it last as long as possible and while her body was still trembling with release, Jesse leaped with her. The two of them tumbled into the abyss, holding tightly to each other to cushion their fall.

Jesse looked at the woman lying beside him on the loud, uncomfortable bed and knew he was in trouble. He'd thought that being with her would ease the need that had been clawing at him for weeks. Instead, all he could think about was having her again.

Before Jillian, the women in his life were like ghosts, appearing and disappearing from his world without leaving so much as a ripple in their wake. Jillian, though, had been causing nothing *but* ripples since the moment they met.

"Okay," she murmured, "now it's my turn to say I can hear you thinking."

His mouth twitched as he rolled to his side and propped himself up on one elbow to look down at her. God, she was beautiful. "All right, yes. I'm thinking."

She reached up and cupped his cheek in her palm. "You don't have to."

"Don't have to what?"

"Give me the speech." Her mouth curved and her beautiful eyes warmed.

There was a single light burning in the apartment and that soft, golden glow lay across her naked body like early-morning sunlight. "What speech is that?"

Smiling, she brushed her hair back from her forehead, then draped one arm across her belly. "You know the one. It starts off with *That was great, babe. But you know, I'm not the commitment kind of guy.*" She paused, then added, "And it always ends with *I'll call you.*"

Not much he could say to that since he'd given different versions of that speech too many times to count. This was the first time he didn't want to say any of it. And the one time it was most important to do exactly that.

"Jillian…"

"Relax, Jesse," she said, giving him another smile. "I don't need any promises from you. We both went into this knowing that it wasn't forever. I'm not going to beg you to stay."

Why the hell not?

And why did it irritate him that she was being so damn reasonable and understanding?

She laughed and shook her head. "You're insulted."

"What? No." He scowled. "Okay, maybe a little."

"We're business partners, right?" Jillian rolled out of bed, walked naked to the closet. He admired the view of that truly excellent butt and was disappointed when she reached into the closet, pulled out a short, pale blue robe and slipped into it.

She tied the belt at her waist, whipped her hair back over her shoulder and shrugged. "It's better for the business if we just forget all about tonight."

"Forget about it." He repeated it because he could hardly believe she was saying it. Jesse was pretty sure that tonight's festivities were burned into his brain. He'd have as much chance of forgetting what happened here as he would holding his breath for the next fifty years.

"Well, yeah." She walked to the bed, sat down on the edge and leaned in to kiss him. "This was great. I mean, really great. But I'm not expecting you to throw yourself at my feet pledging eternal love."

"Is that right?"

"Yes, it is." She tipped her head to one side and looked at him quizzically. "Do most women spend the night with you then start building wedding dreams?"

"No, but they're not usually in such a hurry to brush me off, either." And he didn't much care for the feeling of being discarded. He had a momentary regret for the women he'd dismissed so easily and a touch more respect for the *one* woman who had taught him what the others had felt.

Jillian gave him an understanding smile and one more soft, brief kiss. "It's better this way, Jesse. No promises made, so none broken. We'll be partners— for now," she reminded him and he didn't much care for having his own words tossed back at him.

"And then?"

She stood up. "Then, we'll be friends."

He gritted his teeth and said, "I don't normally want to bend my friends over a table and—"

She inhaled sharply and interrupted him. "That's not helping."

"Not trying to help."

"Why not?" she asked. "Isn't this just what you wanted? If I hadn't said it first, wouldn't you have given me the speech?"

"A man can't have this conversation naked," he muttered and swung out of the bed to snatch up his pants. Tugging them on, he zipped and buttoned them before talking to her again. "Once I give that speech, I'm not 'friends' with the woman I've given it to."

"First time for everything," she said.

"I don't want to be your *friend*, Jillian."

She threw her arms up and shook her head. "Then what do you want?"

He looked into those grayish-green eyes and realized that what he wanted was her. Sex hadn't eased that desire, it had only inflamed it. So no, he wouldn't be her friend. He wouldn't be her lover, either. Or any other damn thing. Once their partnership was over, they'd have nothing between them.

And he didn't like how empty that made him feel.

"You. Damn it, I want *you*."

"Then don't go yet," she said, untying her robe.

He didn't.

Nine

Jesse dressed to leave a couple of hours later and he thought he'd never done anything more difficult than walking away from this woman when she lay there naked and warm, a soft smile on her face. And *that* was the main reason he had to go.

He'd told himself that sex with Jillian would clear his head, get her out of his system. Sadly, the reality was that she was deeper inside him now than she had been before.

"I've got to get back to the ranch," he said. "Gotta be up at dawn to get a couple of the horses ready to be sent home."

She nodded, held the sheet to her breasts and sat up. Pushing that mass of blond hair back from her face, she murmured, "You don't owe me an explanation, Jesse. You don't owe me anything."

He scrubbed one hand across his face. "I don't want to hurt you."

"I know that. You won't."

Yes, he would, Jesse told himself. Because sooner or later, Jillian would start expecting more from him. She would start looking at what was between them as a relationship. Strong and smart, she was still female, and every woman he'd ever known eventually started looking for promises. And he couldn't do that.

Because when he made a promise, he kept it. So he was careful with what he said. He couldn't give Jillian and little Mac what he already owed to his sister's son and the memory of the father that little boy had lost.

With that thought firmly at the front of his mind, he picked up his hat and jammed it onto his head. "Guess I'll see you."

"Yes, you will. Tomorrow," she said. Then she laughed. "Don't look so panicked, Jesse. I'm not going to the ranch to hunt you down. Just to pick up Mac."

Idiot. "Right. I'll see you then." He walked to the door, opened it and looked back at her. "Lock this after me."

She was smiling as he left and Jesse told himself to make sure he was nowhere near the ranch when she arrived to pick up her little girl.

Two days later, Lucy and Jillian were outside the empty shop that would soon be filled with the scent of baking pies. She should be looking at the shop with Jesse, Jillian thought. He was her partner, after all. But she hadn't spoken to him since the night they'd been together.

If he was avoiding her, then he was doing an excellent job of it.

"I'm so glad Jesse helped you get this started," Lucy said as Jillian opened the door with the key provided by the real estate agent. "A little surprised, but glad."

"Surprised why?" Jillian asked, looking over her shoulder at her friend.

Shrugging, Lucy continued. "He's more of a stand-back-and-observe kind of guy. This is the first time I remember him doing anything like this."

Jillian thought about that for a moment and told herself it didn't signify anything. He was being kind, that was all. When she paid back his investment, the shop would be all hers and that would probably be the end of her time with Jesse.

Of course, since she hadn't heard from him in two days, maybe her time with him had already ended. There was no way to know and that was making her a little nuts even though she knew it shouldn't.

Jillian thought about that night with Jesse and everything she'd said to him. And how much it had cost to squeeze the words out past the knot in her throat. She'd told him it would be better if they both simply forgot that night, while her mind had been screaming at her that she would never forget. What she'd found in his arms was something she'd never thought to have. Knowing it wasn't hers to keep had torn at her even as she pretended to be untouched by it all.

She didn't want to love him, so she wouldn't allow herself to even consider the word. Hadn't she learned the hard way that men didn't stay? That love was something you found in a book but only rarely in life? Jillian had Mac to think about now and that was where she would put her focus—and not on the man who touched her heart, her soul, her mind.

Chewing at her bottom lip, Jillian reminded herself that *she* hadn't contacted Jesse in the last two days, either. Maybe she should have rather than wait for him. Was it cowardly to stand back and say nothing? But pride had to come into this at some point, right? Why should she be the one to go see him? To call him? He could have come to her. Talked to her. But he hadn't. And that meant what?

"So what do you think?"

"I think he could have called," Jillian grumbled. "Or said *something*."

Lucy's eyebrows shot up. "Well, blurted truths are always so interesting. But what I meant was, what do you think of the shop?"

Oh, God. Rolling her eyes, Jillian said, "Sure. I knew that." She looked around the interior of the shop and smiled. It was clean and had enough room for a few tables and chairs. There was a gleaming glass display case, an old-fashioned cash register and through the swinging door, she assumed, the kitchen. She walked around behind the counter, just to get a feel for the place.

Standing there, she could look out at Main Street and watch people hurrying down the sidewalks. In a few weeks, those people would be coming in here. To her shop. She took a breath and tried to focus on the moment.

"I think it's perfect," she said, more to herself really than Lucy. "Of course, I'll want to paint, make it sort of cheery, and I need to get some tables and chairs for the front here. Maybe tiny bistro size?"

"Okay, let's have it."

She looked at Lucy. "Have what?"

"Please." Lucy snickered. "The kids aren't here. Jesse's not here. So talk."

She didn't want to talk. If she started, she might not stop and the truth was, what *could* she say? That Jesse and she had had a few hours together that had completely shaken her to her bones and now it was over? How sad was that?

"Nothing to say, Lucy. Honestly."

Her friend just watched her. Seconds ticked past. Lucy continued to stare, never saying a word. And Jillian couldn't take it.

"Fine. Stop the torture." She sighed and admitted, "I just haven't seen Jesse in a couple of days and I thought he could have called or something and that sounds so junior high I'm embarrassed."

"He's in Houston."

"What?" Jillian stared at Lucy.

"Jesse had to drive a horse back to its owner. Most of our guys were out checking the herd and Carlos can't go because his wife is about to go into labor." Lucy shrugged. "So Jesse's been gone. I thought you knew."

"No," she mused, running her hand over the sparklingly clean white-and-gray marble counter. "He didn't tell me." But then why would he?

The more she thought about it, the more Jillian realized that Jesse was talking to her in his way. By *not* contacting her, he was sending a message. There was no real connection between them. What they had was attraction and some really great sex, but beyond that, they owed each other nothing.

"That's fine. That's good, really. Better." Jillian heard herself babbling and couldn't stop. "I mean, we're not a couple or anything. He doesn't have to check in with me and I don't have to call him or anything to report on the shop. Business partners. That's us. That's it. And I'm fine with this."

When she finally ran out of steam, the silence in the shop was overpowering. Shooting a look at Lucy, she asked, "You don't believe me, do you?"

"Nope."

"I'm not making any sense here, am I?"

"Nope."

"So I'm an idiot."

"Yep."

Jillian laughed and shook her head. "You're right. I am acting like an idiot. I keep swinging back and forth on what I'm thinking, feeling. I mean, I knew going in that Jesse and I didn't have a future, you know? That nothing serious was going to happen between us and yet…"

"You still hoped for it."

She looked at Lucy and sighed. "I guess so and that's ridiculous because I don't—"

Lucy snorted and held up one hand. "Don't even bother telling me you don't want or need love in your life." She shook her head and said, "It's the same sad song we all tell ourselves when we've been hurt too many times to want to take the risk again. But the real truth, is *everybody* wants love."

"You're a philosopher now?"

"I am a woman of many talents," Lucy said, smiling. "Like I can see that you had sex with my brother and that it was good."

Jillian sighed again.

"All details are happily accepted," Lucy said, then kept talking as she walked across the room and pushed through the door into the kitchen. "No, wait. On second thought, no details. This is my brother we're talking about and I don't want to throw up in your shiny new shop."

Jillian was right behind her. "Agreed. No details."

"Fine. But the point is the Amazing Lucy also sees that you're in love with my brother."

"No." Jillian instantly denied that charge. She didn't look at her friend because it was easier to talk about this without meeting her eyes. Instead, she looked around the small but efficient kitchen and smiled. "I mean, of course I care for him. Who wouldn't? Jesse's kind and gruff and funny and strong. He's wonderful with Mac and so patient, too, and—"

"Wow. Yeah I can hear how much you *don't* love him." Lucy opened one of the ovens, ran a finger over the door and inspected it. "Clean."

Oh, God, was Lucy right? Was it too late for her already? Jillian took a breath and asked, "Why are you so determined to have me love Jesse?"

"Because he deserves it," Lucy said, shutting the oven door. Turning around to face Jillian, she continued. "He deserves *you*. And Mac. I've never seen him as captivated by anyone as he is by you. He loves that little girl. He found this shop for you to help you with your dream. He's a good guy, Jill."

"I know that."

"And you deserve him." Lucy planted both hands on her hips. "For pity's sake, your eyes light up when you see him, you practically drool when he walks into the room…"

"I don't drool." Did she?

"That's metaphorical drool, but still…"

Even if she did feel more for Jesse than she was willing to admit, the bottom line was, "I can't risk it, Lucy. I've got Mac to think about."

Surprised, Lucy demanded, "You think he'd hurt that little girl?"

"Of course not." Jillian walked through the kitchen, too wound up to stand still. Too worried about what she was feeling to really take those emotions out and look hard at them. "He'd never do anything to deliberately hurt her. But—"

"I get it," Lucy said. "I've got Brody and I know what it is to worry about someone more than yourself. But what if you're just cheating Mac out of having a great father?"

As Lucy's question echoed in her mind, Jillian sighed, checked the cupboards, the cooling racks and the small bathroom at the back of the shop. It was perfect. And Jesse had arranged it for her. He'd had professionals in to clean the place top to bottom so she wouldn't have to worry about it. He'd become her *partner* so that she wouldn't have to wait years to make her dreams come true.

He'd said once that when he made a promise, he kept it. Did that mean she could trust him?

"You're overthinking this."

She looked at Lucy and said wryly, "I can't seem to stop."

"Well," her friend said, dropping one arm around Jillian's shoulders, "let me help. Jesse's in Houston so you can't do anything about any of this until he gets back. Right?"

"Yes…"

"So let's keep busy. We'll buy some paint and start working on the shop."

"I don't know." Truthfully, she had so much spinning through her mind, Jillian didn't know if she could be trusted with a paintbrush.

"Trust me." Lucy gave her shoulders a squeeze. "The kids are at the day care. We can probably get the whole front of the shop done in a couple of hours."

"I guess we could do that."

"Excellent." Lucy grinned. "You know I love shopping!"

Laughing, Jillian followed her friend out of the shop, locking it behind her. If it made her a coward to be grateful she could put off facing Jesse for another day, she was willing to accept the label.

The following day, Jesse was back from Houston and felt like he'd been dragged behind the truck the whole way. He hadn't had a decent hour's sleep since the night he'd left Jillian. No matter what he did, she was there, in his mind, refusing to be ignored.

He'd believed he could step back from her. But clearly it was going to take longer than he'd thought it would. What he needed to do was keep busy. Lose himself in the ranch, the work.

"Yeah, because that's working so well," he muttered as he walked across the ranch yard toward the main house. It took everything he had to not grab his damn cell phone and call Jillian. He could tell himself that he just wanted to check in, make sure everything was all right. But the truth was, he just wanted to hear her voice.

He was still muttering when he opened the front door and stepped inside. Instantly, his sister called out, "Jesse? Is that you?"

"Yeah."

"Well, thank God." She sounded irritated and impatient, but that wasn't anything new for Lucy.

"Jesse..." Mac's voice came as a plaintive wail that had him hurrying toward the great room.

"What's going on?"

"Hi, Uncle Jesse!"

"Hi, kid," he said, smiling at his nephew, playing with his trucks on the floor near his mother.

Lucy was sitting on the couch, a clearly unhappy Mac on her lap. His sister looked harried, Mac looked miserable and Jesse figured he looked confused.

"What's going on?"

"Mac's sick," Brody offered, never looking up from his trains.

"Sick?" he echoed.

"Sick," Mac whined.

"Come and take her," Lucy ordered, even as Mac held up both arms and wailed his name again.

"What's wrong with her? Where's Jillian?" He scooped the little girl into his arms while he looked around the room as if half expecting the woman to pop into existence. He was disappointed when that didn't happen.

"Jill had to work today," Lucy said, sweeping both hands through her hair. "Since she's quitting so soon after being hired, she felt bad about staying home with Mac and they were short-handed at the day care today, so she had to go in even though Mac's sick…"

"What kind of sick?" he asked, taking a quick look at the tiny girl in his arms.

"Sick, Jesse," Mac whined, laying her head on his shoulder.

Now that he was taking a good, hard look at her, he could see that her eyes were too bright and her cheeks were flushed. And a jolt of fear shot through him. "What's wrong with her? Did you take her to the doctor? Should I?"

Lucy grinned. "Calm down, oh, rational one. She's fine. She's just got a little fever and she's feeling pretty crappy."

"Crappy," Mac echoed.

"Oops," Lucy said with a grimace. "Anyway, I told Mac I'd keep her here, but she's been so restless, and all she wants is *you*."

Both pleasure and panic shot through Jesse in a split second. Pleased that the child had asked for him, even though he had no clue what to do for a sick kid. He patted Mac's back gently and felt his heart clench when she gave a tired sigh and snuggled in closer to him.

"You're panicking and it's not very attractive," Lucy told him.

Jesse ignored that. "What am I supposed to do for her?"

"Just hold her and keep her comfortable."

"Right." How hard could that be? God, he really wished he'd had a little sleep in the last couple of days. "Okay, I'm taking her over to my place. I've

got to get a shower and—" he broke off. How could
he do that when he had to take care of Mac?

Lucy read his mind again. "Go on. I'll ask one of
the guys to carry the crib to your house. Just lay her
down when you take a shower. Maybe she'll sleep for
you. She should be tired."

"Tired," Mac whimpered, and rubbed her eyes
with a tiny hand.

"Okay sweetie," he whispered, "we'll go lay down."

Lucy smiled at him. "Don't look now, but you're
sounding like a Daddy."

He fired a look at her. "Don't get any ideas, Lucy.
I mean it."

"Oooh, your stern expression." She held up both
hands. "Color me terrified. Go. Go home. One of the
guys will be there in a few minutes with the crib."

Jesse left the house with a sick child on his shoulder and a block of ice in the pit of his stomach. He
was being drawn deeper and deeper into the lives
of Jillian and Mac. Now he had a baby girl looking to him for comfort. How could he walk away
from that?

And what was it going to do to him when he finally had to?

By the time Jillian arrived at the ranch, she was
tired, on edge and worried about Mac. Lucy had
called her at work to say that Jesse was home and
taking care of the baby. It had made her feel better to
know that Jesse was with Mac because she knew how
much her daughter loved the man. But at the same
time, it was awkward because of the way things had
been left between she and Jesse.

Now, she wasn't sure what to expect when she walked into Jesse's house. Late afternoon sunlight poured through the door with her entry and lay across the wood floor like a path Fate wanted her to follow.

"Jesse?"

"In here," he answered, his voice quiet, soft.

She walked into the great room and dropped her purse onto the first chair she passed. The room was dim, but there was enough light for Jillian to see Jesse lying down on one of the couches, Mac asleep on his chest. He looked at her and held one finger to his lips for silence.

His hair lay across his forehead, he had one arm around her baby girl, keeping her steady. He smiled at Jillian and her heart turned over. Just like that, it was done. The final tumble.

She was in love.

Maybe she had been all along. Who could resist a man who not only turned your blood into lava but was strong enough to be gentle and sweet with a child? This wasn't good and she knew it. Jillian hadn't been looking for love and she knew Jesse wasn't interested in anything remotely resembling a relationship, so there was nothing ahead of her but pain.

Yet, she couldn't regret this feeling. There would be plenty of time for regrets in the future. For this moment alone, she was going to enjoy the sensation of having her heart stolen. All the years she'd spent protecting her heart now felt like she'd really only been waiting. For Jesse.

"She just fell asleep," he said, stroking Mac's back.

"I should get her home." And get herself away from Jesse before she revealed too much.

"There's a crib here. Let her sleep."

Jillian kept her gaze locked with his and she saw that he wanted her to stay. She wanted it, too, but how could she hide what she was feeling from him?

While she stood there, frozen with indecision, he stood up, moving carefully, holding Mac close. Looking at him, Jillian felt the last of her resolve drain away. She didn't want to leave. She'd missed him for days. She loved him. She wanted to be here. With him. For as long as she could.

"Will you stay?" he asked.

Looking into his chocolate-brown eyes, she knew there was only one possible answer. "Yes."

With Mac asleep in her crib, Jesse and Jillian went into his bedroom just across the hall.

"Can we hear her?" Jillian whispered as he unbuttoned her shirt. His fingers brushed her skin and she sucked in a gulp of air.

"Both doors are open," he whispered back, "we'll hear her."

Jesse's bedroom was a male bastion. Browns, beige and forest green were the colors, and Jillian thought it was almost like bringing the outside in. The bed was wide and covered in a dark brown duvet. There were two chairs pulled up in front of a small, green-tiled fireplace, bookcases on either side of the room and photos of the ranch framed and hanging on the walls. The bedside lamps were brass and there were French doors that led onto the stone porch.

And there was Jesse. Jillian stared up into his eyes and wondered how she could ever have tried to convince herself that she wasn't in love. She threaded her fingers through his hair as he backed her toward the bed. He laid her down on the mattress then stretched out beside her.

She laughed a little. "How did we get naked so fast?"

"It's a gift," he said and bent his head to kiss her.

Their first time together had been a feverish, desperate joining as they each reacted to the tension that had built between them for weeks. Tonight, there was no fever, just the swamping need. She saw desire in his eyes and wished she could see more.

"You're thinking," he chided when he lifted his head to look at her.

"Make me stop," she said and took his face between her palms. He kissed her again, and Jillian's mind blanked out. How could she possibly gather thoughts or worries when his mouth was on hers? When his hands were sliding up and down her body?

He touched her everywhere, as if burning every line of her body into his mind. She ran her hands over his chest, marveling at the muscled, bronze skin and the warm feel of it beneath her palms.

She watched him, wanting to remember every moment of this night. If she didn't have a tomorrow with him at least she would have this memory. Expectation coiled deep inside her as they moved together, skin to skin, hands stroking, mouths tasting. Her breath came fast and short when he moved over her and when he pushed himself home, Jillian gasped, arching her back, moving with him in a silent dance of desire.

Outside, the sun died and the darkness crept into the room, enfolding them in a deep, shadow-filled quiet. They moved as one, each of them pushing the other toward the edge and as she climbed, Jillian held on to him, arms around his neck, legs around his hips. When her body splintered into thousands of jagged shards, she had Jesse to anchor her. She held him as she trembled, then held him tighter as he joined her.

A few minutes later, Jesse lay on his back and held her to his side. "I missed you."

He didn't sound happy about admitting it, either. Still, she tipped her head back to look at him. "I wondered where you were."

"I meant to call..."

"No," she said, watching his eyes, "you didn't."

Now he stared down at her, frowning. "I didn't?"

"No." She trailed her fingers across his chest, feeling the solid thump of his heart. "You didn't want to miss me, Jesse. Didn't want to call me. You were trying to let me know that what we had that night was all there was going to be."

His frown deepened. "And how did I feel about you staying here tonight?"

He was irritated, and she couldn't have said why she found that a little entertaining, even under these circumstances. "You wanted me in your bed, but you don't want me getting comfortable."

"Well, I sound like a real dick, don't I?"

Surprising herself, Jillian laughed a little. "No, you don't. You just don't want to love me."

He eased up onto his elbow and looked down at her. Jillian touched his cheek, then let her hand fall back. "I know how you feel. I didn't want to love you, either. But I do."

He froze. It was the only word she could think of to describe what happened to him the minute the

L word was mentioned. It was as if he wasn't even breathing. His eyes flashed and those golden flecks shone in the dimness like spotlights.

"No, you don't."

"You don't get to tell me what I'm feeling," Jillian said.

"Why the hell not?" he demanded. "You just told me what I was thinking and feeling."

"Yes," she said sadly, "but I was right and you're wrong. I *do* love you."

"Stop saying that."

"Silence won't change anything. Even if I never say it again, you'll always know I feel it." She'd known it would go this way and still Jillian had had to tell him. Love, when it finally arrived, just shouldn't be ignored or dismissed.

"I don't want you to," he said, sitting up and dragging her up with him. "There's no future for us here, Jillian."

"I didn't ask for a future, Jesse," she reminded him. "I haven't asked you for anything. What I'm feeling—"

"Don't—"

"It's a gift." She shrugged and smiled in spite of everything. "I was afraid to love, too. Every man I've ever known has walked away from me."

"Jill…"

"I told you my grandmother raised me," she said and took one of his hands in hers. She rubbed her fingers across his palm, feeling the calluses and scars he'd earned through a lifetime of hard work. Jesse wasn't a quitter. Jesse gave his word and kept it. Jesse was the kind of man you could count on.

She wished he was hers. Looking up into his eyes she said, "My parents decided they didn't much like having a child, so they left."

"Jillian—"

"First my dad. I was really young and two years later, my mom left, too. Grandma Rhonda was my rock then."

"I'm sorry…"

"I don't need you to be sorry. I just want you to understand. I was engaged once, but he left, too. And then I met Rich, pretending to be Will, and I was so hungry to feel something, to love someone, I let him sweep me off my feet in spite of the fact I should have known better. Then he left, too."

He gritted his teeth and swallowed hard, but he didn't interrupt her again.

"So when I met you, I told myself that you would be just like every other man in the world." She smiled sadly. "But you weren't. You aren't. And Mac saw it in you before I did." Laughing a little, she said, "Mac loved you first. But I couldn't. I didn't trust myself. Or you. But Jesse…"

She reached out to cup his cheek and only flinched a little when he pulled his head back. Sighing, she let her hand drop to her lap. "Jesse, you're the one."

"I can't be, Jill—"

"I like you calling me that," she said. "And as for me loving you, it's too late. It just is. My love doesn't depend on you loving me back or even on us being together. It's just there."

He got up, walked to the fireplace and slapped one hand on the mantel to stare down at the cold, empty hearth. "I can't do this. Be what you want."

"You *are* what I want."

He shot a hard look at her over his shoulder. "I've got a debt to pay. To Lucy. To Brody. I can't claim a life for myself when their lives are broken because of *me*."

She scooted off the bed, walked to him and asked, "Are you talking about the accident? Lucy told me about it."

"Did she tell you it was my fault? That Dane died because I wasn't careful enough?"

"No, of course not." Jillian reached out to lay one hand on his shoulder and she could feel the tension in his body. "She doesn't think that, Jesse."

"Whether she does or not, I know it's true and that's enough."

"Jesse, it's crazy to blame yourself for a horrible accident."

"Yeah? What if something happened to Mac? Would you be so willing to forgive and forget then? What if I let her get hurt?"

He was so embroiled in his own guilt, there was no reaching him. No way to convince him that what had happened to Dane hadn't been his fault. He was too determined to punish himself for it.

And still, she tried.

"I would know," she said, "that you would always do everything in your power to protect those you love. You're not God, Jesse. You don't get to make the big decisions. The world is not a safe place. People get hurt. They die."

"Not because of me," he muttered thickly. "Not again."

Jillian's heart ached and she felt as if she'd been

wrapped in ice. She was cold, head to toe, and knew that she'd never really be warm again. Because loving Jesse wasn't enough. She wanted him to love her back. Wanted the whole dream.

And she wasn't going to get it.

"It's over between us, Jillian," he said and his voice was so tight, so deep, it seemed to reverberate in the air around her. "Best if we just don't see each other anymore."

She rocked on her heels, shocked at how quickly this night had gone from beautiful to awful. "What about our partnership?"

Nodding, he said, "That doesn't change. I'll help you get the shop and I wish you luck with it."

"Wow. Thanks."

His head whipped up and his gaze bored into hers. "What the hell do you want from me?"

"You already know the answer to that."

"And I told you why that's not going to happen."

"You gave me excuses, Jesse. Not a reason."

Even in the darkness, she saw his eyes glitter. "I gave you all I can."

"No, you didn't," she said, shaking her head. "But that's your decision and we'll both have to live with it, won't we?" She took a deep breath then added, "If it's okay with you, I'll spend the night in the guest room with Mac." She stepped back, putting some distance between them. He didn't notice because he hadn't looked at her again. "I'd rather not wake her up."

He nodded. "That's fine."

She gathered up her clothes and walked out of the room. But on the threshold she stopped for one more look at him. He was standing as he had been. Alone. In the dark.

"I was wrong, Jesse," she said softly. "I guess you are just like every man I've ever known. You're walking away, too."

Ten

The next couple of days passed in a blur of activity.

Jillian's heart was bruised and battered, but she buried her pain by focusing on Mac and on the shop she was about to open. If her thoughts wandered to Jesse a few dozen times a day, she pushed them aside as quickly as she could.

During the day, she could manage. It was her dreams at night that kept tripping her up. She dreamed of him holding her, smiling down at her, kissing her. She woke up with the taste of him in her mouth and had to choke down fresh pain every morning.

It didn't help that her baby girl kept asking for Jesse. Mac couldn't understand why her favorite person was gone from her life and trying to explain to a nearly two-year-old was a lesson in futility.

Just that morning, Jillian had been getting Mac

ready to go when the little girl put both hands on her mother's cheeks.

"See Jesse?"

Pain, sharp and fresh, stabbed at her heart as she said, "No, sweetie. We're going to the day care. You can play with your friends…"

"See Jesse. Horsies." Mac's little mouth turned mutinous.

"We can't, baby."

"Mama, Jesse."

"Jesse can't play today, baby, so we're just going to go to work, okay?" *Please be okay with this*, Jillian pleaded silently. She hoped Mac stopped looking for Jesse soon, because she hated the thought that her daughter was in as much pain as she herself was.

One tear rolled down Mac's cheek, and Jillian scooped her up for a tight hug meant to comfort them both.

Of course, it hadn't. How could it, when they were both missing the same man?

Sighing, Jillian went back to stacking the order of pie plates that had been delivered just that morning. For now, she was going with standard, aluminum pie plates. But one day, she wanted to invest in personalized pie tins with the name of the shop stamped on them. Then she could offer people a discount on their next pie if they brought in the used tins.

She could see just how the shop would be and Jillian really wished she was more excited about it. She'd thought about doing this for years and now that it was here, it was shadowed by the loss of Jesse.

"Stop it," she ordered grimly. "Stop wishing and thinking and start *doing*."

With that thought firmly in mind, Jillian continued stacking the plates and let her mind wander to everything else that still needed to be done. She had her tables and chairs—she'd found them at an outdoor living shop. Wrought-iron, the tables had glass tops and were just big enough for two or three people to share comfortably and the matching chairs were perfect. Getting them set up in the front of the shop had made everything feel immediate. Real. The walls were painted a cheerful pale yellow and there were baskets of flowers hanging from the ceiling in the corners of the room.

Her supplies were ordered along with the kitchen tools she'd need to make this dream a reality. Without Jesse's help, she wouldn't have been able to do this and she knew it. She only wished he were there to see it happen. But it seemed you could only have *part* of a dream.

Jillian made lists of her lists just to keep everything in order. She kept records of every penny spent on her laptop along with projections of what would need to come next. There was so much to buy, not to mention the employees she'd have to hire. But that was a worry for another day. Right now, she had to set up the kitchen just the way she wanted it.

Since Jillian was still working half days at the day care—at least until they found someone to replace her—she was able to leave Mac there while she worked at the shop.

"Thank God," she murmured, because trying to work while keeping Mac out of trouble would have been impossible.

As she finished with the last of the pie tins, Jillian

gave herself a mental pat on the back. And a second later, she heard the front door open and Lucy's voice call out, "Hey, Jill, are you in here?"

A sinking sensation opened up in Jillian's chest. She hadn't spoken to Lucy since the breakup with Jesse. Avoiding her friend hadn't been easy, but she hadn't wanted to put Lucy in the middle. And now, she didn't have a clue what she would say to her. But there was no way to elude Lucy today. "In the kitchen."

Lucy bustled in, carrying a cardboard tray with two cups of coffee and a bag from the diner. She wore jeans, boots and a dark red top. Her choppy brown hair was wind ruffled and her eyes pinned Jillian. "Hi, stranger! Thought you could use a break. I brought doughnuts."

"God, that sounds great," Jillian admitted. She hadn't had much of an appetite the last week, but a doughnut was always good.

"Good. Let's go try out the new chairs and table out front." Lucy turned around and headed out, talking as she went. "I love them, by the way. I'm devastated that I was not included in the shopping trip, but I can forgive—as long as you call me for the next excursion."

"I know I should have called you," Jillian admitted. "It's just—"

Lucy set the coffees down and spread some napkins on the table before laying out the doughnuts. "No problem. Well, of course there's a problem, but I know it's not me. It's undoubtedly my brother.

"Plus," Lucy added, breaking off a piece of rainbow sprinkle doughnut and popping it into her mouth, "said brother has spent the last two days with the lovely personality of a bear with a jagged thorn in its paw. He's infuriated so many people, all of the cowboys are avoiding him and Carlos is threatening a walkout if Jesse doesn't stay away from the stables."

Jillian smiled.

"Ah. This pleases you." Lucy nodded sagely. "Completely understandable because he's probably the one who caused whatever it is that happened. Since I haven't talked to you in forever, I brought doughnuts to bribe you into telling me what's going on. So spill."

Jillian slumped onto the chair opposite her friend. She could pretend otherwise, but why bother? For two days now, her heart had ached and she'd been walking in a fog of misery, so why not share it with the one woman she knew would understand? "It's a mess, Lucy. All of it."

She reached across the table and patted Jillian's hand. "Have a doughnut. Sugar is a cure-all. And then tell me."

Taking a sip of coffee, Jillian had a bite of doughnut and felt the sugar rush. Maybe Lucy had a point. "It's my fault."

"I doubt it."

Smiling sadly, Jillian said, "Oh, it is. I told him I love him and that's when everything went to hell."

Lucy sighed and took a sip of coffee. "It's so disappointing to find out my brother is a moron." Waving one hand in a "come on" motion, she prodded, "Tell me."

So Jillian did. She told her friend the whole story and in talking about it, she felt as if a blister on her soul had popped and she could take a breath easier than she had all week. Finally, she said, "He told me he can't be with me and Mac because he owes too much to you and Brody."

"What?" Clearly stunned, Lucy asked, "What the hell does that mean?"

"He blames himself for your husband's death."

"Of course he does," Lucy muttered, shaking her head. "You know, when our father died, Jesse was sixteen. As the oldest, he immediately appointed himself the 'man of the house' and started in on trying to manage all of us. Mom finally put a stop to that, but she couldn't make him see that the family and the ranch weren't solely his responsibility." She crumbled a piece of doughnut until it was crumbs and sprinkles, then stared at the mess.

Eventually, she lifted her gaze to Jillian's. "When Dane died, I was the one racked with guilt. If I hadn't gone along with his idea to be a part of the ranch, he'd still be alive. If I'd moved with him to Houston, he wouldn't have died. I drove myself crazy for a while until Mom stepped in and made me see that it was just an accident. If we'd lived somewhere else, maybe it would have been a car wreck that took Dane. We'll never know."

"Jesse believes he could have stopped it."

"That's because Jesse still believes he's the Grand Poo-bah of the Universe." Scowling, Lucy added, "I've told him and told him that Dane's death wasn't his fault, but he won't accept it. And still, I never thought he'd take this so far."

Now Jillian had guilt gnawing at her. "Lucy, I didn't mean to make you feel badly about this. It's not your fault."

"Oh," her friend said quickly, "no worries. I know *exactly* whose fault this mess is. Jesse is throwing himself on a pyre that only he can see. Idiot."

Jillian laughed a little and felt better than she had in days. She should have called Lucy sooner. Should have trusted her friend to help her through this.

"You really do love him, don't you?" Lucy's question sounded wistful.

"I do. It would be so much easier if I didn't."

"Who wants *easy*?" Lucy shook her head. "Mom used to tell me that nothing great comes easy. So I'll take hard if I can have great at the end of it."

Jillian thought about it for a second. "I guess I would, too."

"Good," Lucy said with a chuckle. "Because I guarantee that life with Jesse will be hard. The man has a head like concrete."

"Lucy... Jesse was very clear. He's not interested." And Jillian wasn't going to wait and hope that things would change only to have her heart broken again. How many times could she recover from that kind of pain?

"Of course he's interested. Otherwise he wouldn't be such a bear right now. So don't give up," Lucy said, picking up her doughnut for a bite. "He's not the easiest man on the planet, but I think you love him enough not to care about that."

"It doesn't matter."

"Oh, Jill, love is the only thing that *does* matter."

Jesse swung the hammer so hard that when it made contact with the post, the entire fence shuddered. Taking a breath, he released it slowly, trying to control the frustration that had been simmering inside him for more than a week. But it was no use.

Since that last night with Jillian, Jesse hadn't been able to get a moment's peace. He kept seeing her face. Hearing her say he was like every other man in her life—letting her down. Walking away.

"Well, hell, can't she see I didn't *want* her to go?" He pulled another nail from the box lying on the ground, straightened up and swung the hammer at it. Solid, hard work should be giving him a sense of satisfaction. At least fixing loose boards on the corral fence allowed him to take out his aggravation on innocent nails.

But it wasn't helping.

He yanked off his cowboy hat and wiped his forehead with his forearm. Summer was settling in and it promised to be a hot one. He jammed the hat back onto his head and braced his forearms on the top rail of the fence. He stared off at the ranch yard and then let his gaze slide to his house. For the first time since moving into that place, Jesse hadn't been able to find any peace in it.

Because Jillian was there. Her image. Her scent still clung to the pillow beside his. Mac was there, too, as he could remember holding the little girl while she cried and slept. The crib was still in the guest room and he felt a pang every time he walked past it down the hall.

Now he wondered what was happening with them. Was Jillian getting the shop put together? Was Mac still sick? And was he going to be doing this for the rest of his damn life? Wondering about the two people he loved because he wasn't with them to keep them safe?

Scowling, he went back to work. Lucy had left more than two hours ago and he knew his sister had gone into town to see Jillian. And he wished to hell he knew what they were talking about. "A hell of a thing, being jealous of your sister," he muttered and slammed the hammer home again.

He heard the car careening up the drive before he saw it. Lucy's truck was barreling toward the ranch house as if racing from a fire. Instantly, panic flared into life in the center of Jesse's chest. Was Jillian all right? Mac? Had something happened?

Jesse dropped everything and sprinted for the front of the house. Lucy jumped out of the truck, raced toward him and didn't have a chance to speak before he demanded, "Is Jillian okay? Mac?"

And just like that, Lucy's whole demeanor changed. Tension left her shoulders and a smirk twisted her mouth. "Well, that answers my question."

"What the hell are you talking about?" he demanded. "What question? Weren't you with Jill? Is she okay?"

"Jill's fine. So's Mac," she added, "not that you'd know since you haven't bothered to call her. Or to go see her."

"Damn it, Lucy," he ground out as his heart slowed from a gallop to a trot. "You had me thinking—"

"That they needed you and you weren't there?" Lucy finished for him. "Well, get used to that feeling because unless you wise up, you're going to be living with that."

"Why'd you drive in here like a bat out of hell? Just trying to scare ten years off my life?"

She leaned back against the side of her royal blue

truck, crossed her arms over her chest and glared at him. "I was pretty sure you were in love with Jillian, but I wanted to be sure. Seeing your panicked reaction convinced me."

"Well, good for you." He turned to go because at the rate his temper was building, he didn't trust himself not to use the kind of language his mother would still give him grief over.

Lucy grabbed his arm and held him in place. "Why are you ignoring your family, Jesse?"

"What the hell does that mean?" He waved one arm as if encompassing the ranch and said, "I've been right here, all week, spending time with my family."

"I'm not talking about *our* family," she said, irritation spiking the tone of her voice. "I'm talking about the family you built with Jillian."

"Butt out, little sister." The warning came out as a growl. Lucy wasn't impressed.

"Not a chance. You *love* Jill, and you love Mac." Lucy shook her head. "They love you, too, so what the hell are you doing?"

"I can't do this. Can't talk about this with you."

"Why not?" Lucy lifted her chin and fixed her gaze on his, and Jesse had to silently admit that his younger sister had become a fierce woman. "You're using me and Brody as an excuse to deny yourself a life, so I think you can discuss it with me."

"I'm not—"

"Dane died." Two words that shook both of them. Jesse heard the slight tremor in her voice before she covered it over in fury when she continued. "It wasn't your fault. It wasn't his fault. Or the damn horse's, either. It just happened. That's why they call things like that 'accidents.' You can't plan for it. You can't guard against it. It's just life, Jesse."

"I shouldn't have let him so close."

Lucy snorted a laugh. "Do you really believe Dane would have allowed you to keep him back? He was a city guy, but he was no coward."

"I didn't say he was."

"He was a good, kind, strong man who went after what he wanted." Lucy swallowed hard. "He died going after it, but it was important to him and he wouldn't have let you stop him."

Jesse thought back to his brother-in-law and conceded that she had a point. Dane had been just as hardheaded as the rest of them and determined to build a life on the ranch. He'd fought against Jesse's and Will's attempts to protect him and had goaded them and challenged himself in his quest to grab what he wanted most.

"Should I blame Dane, Jesse?" She looked up at him, shaking her head. "I could. I could say it was his fault for always pushing, doing too much. He shouldn't have rushed into things like he did, but he was so damn alive…"

"I'm sorry about Dane, Lucy. So damn sorry." Jesse shook his head, reached out and pulled his sister in for a hug. She wrapped her arms around him and squeezed.

"I know you are. So am I. But life keeps going, Jesse." She leaned her head back and looked up at him. "And if you don't wake up in time, life is going to pass you by."

He took a breath, easing the constriction in his chest. "But there's Brody to care for and—"

"Are you planning on moving off the ranch?" she asked.

"No."

"Then you'll be here for Brody. Just like you always are. And you can be here for Mac. And Jillian. And damn it, Jesse. Be there for yourself, too." She was frowning up at him and Jesse bent down to plant a kiss on her forehead.

"Since when did you get so damn bossy?"

"Since always and you know it."

"Yeah," he agreed. "But you didn't use to be right."

"Hah! I'm always right," Lucy teased. "You're just not willing to admit it very often."

He gave her another tight hug then let her go. Guilt would probably always be with him, Jesse silently acknowledged. But maybe for the first time since Dane's death, Jesse was coming to grips with it. Everything Lucy had said resonated with him and maybe if he'd really thought about it years ago, he'd have come to this conclusion sooner.

Dane had lived his life exactly as he'd wanted. Now, it was time for Jesse to go after what *he* wanted.

"I guess you're not the worst sister in the world…"

"High praise indeed." She hooked one arm around his waist as he turned toward the main house. "So, do you need some help picking out a ring?"

He pulled her hair. "Again, I say, butt out, little sister."

By late afternoon Jillian could admit that she was feeling a little better. She should have talked to Lucy sooner because that conversation with Jesse's sister had really done a lot to ease her pain. Maybe just being able to talk about the man she loved would be enough to help her transition into living without him.

Because no matter what Lucy said, Jillian couldn't afford to keep hope alive eternally.

"Jesse!"

Jillian sighed a little and looked at her daughter, sitting on the sidewalk beside her. Outside the pie shop, Jillian had been painting different designs on the display window, trying to figure out which one looked best. When she had it pinned down, she'd contact a professional sign painter to make it permanent.

"Not today, sweetie," she murmured automatically and looked up at the window. Miss Mac's Pie Shack. "There's your name, Mackenzie. You're on the window and maybe we could paint a little portrait of you, too. Use you as our logo, what do you think?"

"Jesse!"

Sighing, Jillian glanced at Mac again, noticed her daughter staring off down the sidewalk and lifted her gaze to see Jesse striding toward them.

Jillian's heartbeat clattered in her chest, making it almost impossible to breathe. He looked so good. Blue jeans, white button-down shirt, denim jacket and that black hat that never failed to set her pulse racing. "Oh, God…"

"Jesse!" Mac called it louder this time and took off down the sidewalk toward her hero.

"Mac!" Jillian started after her, but she needn't have bothered. Jesse swept the little girl up into his arms and then gave her the stuffed horse he'd brought for her.

"Mama, Jesse! Horsie!"

"I see that," she said softly, enjoying the flush of

pleasure on Mac's face and the bright light in her eyes as she stared at Jesse. Jillian's heart hurt. Jesse was only making this harder on Mac. The little girl had missed him so much that seeing him again would only freshen the pain when he disappeared again.

"Jill," he said, his gaze sweeping over her, up and down. "You look beautiful."

"No, I don't. I'm a mess." So of course he'd show up now. She wore jeans and a T-shirt and she had white paint on her cheek and her hair was pulled back in a ponytail threaded through the opening in a baseball cap.

"What're you doing here, Jesse?" Had Lucy talked to him? Had she made him see that sacrificing his own life as payment for something he thought was his fault was a waste? She wanted to hope but was too afraid to. She'd been hurt too many times.

He nodded, looked at the little girl in his arms, then back to Jillian. "Look, I understand that you might not be happy to see me right now, but I've got something I need to say to you. Then, if you want me to, I'll go and I'll stay away."

"Oh, Jesse, I think we've said it all."

"Not even close," he told her and took a step toward her. "When you told me you loved me, there was something I couldn't bring myself to say back to you. I want to do it now. I love you, Jillian. I love you so much it's a wonder to me."

She swayed in place as those three little words slammed home and took her breath away. "Jesse—"

"And I love Mac like she's my own."

"Jesse!" Mac hugged her horse, then laid her

head on Jesse's shoulder, patting his cheek with one tiny hand.

Jillian melted a little more. Her baby girl was happy. How could she not be?

"Without you, I can't eat. Can't sleep. My house is empty," he said, "and my heart's even emptier. Hell, Jill, until I met you, I was walking through life with my eyes closed. I swear, there was nothing but work and family.

"Then I met you and there was color and laughter and *life*, Jillian. There's life where you are and I want that life." He smoothed a strand of her hair back behind her ear. "I want it with you. And Mac. And however many more babies we can make together."

"Babies?" she echoed.

"Babies!" Mac crowed and clapped her little hands.

Jesse grinned at the girl, then dipped one hand into his jeans pocket, coming up with a dark red velvet ring box.

Jillian gasped and felt tears fill her eyes until the box, Mac and Jesse were nothing more than blurs in front of her. Frantically, she blinked her eyes clear because she didn't want to miss a moment of this. "You'll have to open it for me, since I don't want to put our girl down…"

Our girl. Those two words rippled through her mind and heart, and Jillian felt love rise up to wash over her like a warm blanket on a winter night. Hesitantly, she opened the ring box, took one look and gasped again.

"Oh, Jesse…"

"I wanted you to have something different," he whispered. "Something as special as you are."

She stared at the ring unblinkingly. A star sapphire, surrounded by diamonds, it winked in the sunlight and seemed to shine with a hundred different colors deep in its center stone. Finally, she looked up at Jesse and saw at last what she'd longed to see in his eyes.

Love.

"I uh, stopped at the jewelry store on my way here. Didn't want to show up empty-handed. I love you, Jill," he said simply. "I love Mac. I want to adopt her officially, if you'll let me—"

"Jesse." She slapped one hand across her mouth.

"My dad wanted to adopt me and Lucy, but Mom didn't think it was fair to our biological father. So, if you want Mac to keep—"

"I think Mackenzie Navarro sounds perfect."

He smiled even wider. "Me, too." He kept talking then as if he were on a roll and reluctant to stop. "And I want you both to marry me and be with me forever. Help me build a life, Jillian. Let me help you build that future you've always dreamed of."

Slowly, she took the ring from its velvet bed, then slid it onto her finger. Jesse looked deeply into her eyes and whispered, "I will never walk away, Jillian. I will be with you. Always."

Tears stung her eyes again and her heart lifted so high in her chest it was a wonder her feet didn't leave the ground.

Then he took her hand and kissed the ring as if sealing a promise between them.

"I love you, Jesse," she said. "I think I always have. I know I always will." She looked at her little girl, lying so trustingly in his arms, a pleased smile on her tiny face. "Mac loves you, too, and you are exactly the father she deserves."

"So that's a yes," he said, more statement than question.

"Oh, absolutely it's a yes," Jillian told him, moving into the circle of his arms. "We will marry you, Jesse. And we will love you forever."

"Thank God," Jesse whispered.

"Thank God," Mac echoed.

"Oh, Mac," Jillian chided.

Laughing, Jesse held on to them, linking the three of them into a unit. He kissed Mac's forehead, and when Jillian tipped her face up to his, he kissed her lips, lingering just long enough to tell her that he'd missed her as much as she had him.

"I love you," he said, his gaze locked with hers, willing her to see. To believe.

And Jillian did. She reached up, cupped his cheek in her palm and whispered, "I love you, too."

While Royal bustled around them, the three of them stood together in front of the pie shop where dreams were born.

Staring into her eyes, Jesse vowed, "I've got my girls back and I swear to you, I will never let either of you go."

* * * * *

BETWEEN
MARRIAGE
AND MERGER

KAREN BOOTH

One

Lily Foster delighted in the *idea* of a wedding—two people so in love they vow to be together forever. The *reality* of a wedding, even as an observer, made Lily break out in hives. There she stood in the New York City Clerk's Office, without the usual trappings of organ music or a minister or the bride in a flowing gown, and the nuptials still put her on edge. Her skin felt clammy. She couldn't stand still. Her instinct was to run out of the building as fast as her pumps would carry her. But she couldn't do that. She had to stay put. She'd been generously invited to the impromptu nuptials of her boss's sister. Lily would've done anything for her boss, Noah Locke. To her own detriment, she adored him.

Still, for Lily, watching anyone get married was like unpacking a dusty old steamer trunk of miserable memories of her dream day that never was. When a woman has been left at the altar, no matter the reasons for it, she doesn't forget it. Ever. And Lily's world seemed hell-bent on dredging up the memory today.

"By the powers vested in me by the state of New York, I now pronounce you husband and wife."

Tamping down her jealousy and choking back a sob of sentimentality, Lily watched as the bride and groom—Noah's sister, Charlotte, and her new hubby, ridiculously handsome Michael, got lost in a passionate kiss. For that instant, she could feel the love between them. It was a life force that hit her from five feet away. Tears silently streamed down Lily's cheeks. Charlotte, in a knee-length white dress that hugged her five-month baby bump, popped up on one foot, kicking the other into the air. It was like the cover of a fun contemporary romance. That was enough for Lily. She couldn't watch anymore.

She pulled a tissue from her bag and dared to look at Noah, who was standing up for the groom. Noah wasn't watching the kiss either. His hands were stuffed in the pants pockets of his slim-fitting gray suit. He was staring at his shoes, probably because they were beautiful and expensive, like everything in his life. Noah was a notorious playboy, so much so that the New York tabloids loved to play with him the way a cat bats about a mouse. Weddings were undoubtedly not Noah's scene. Lily didn't even need to ask.

It was no surprise that Noah chose to play the field. He was perfect—tall and trim, athletic but not muscle-bound, with expertly tousled sandy brown hair that was tidy around the ears and back, but a bit long on the top. His moss green eyes were hypnotic, or maybe it was the sum total of Noah that made Lily lose her words or her memory of what she was supposed to be doing. Noah was *that* guy. The one you can't stop looking at. The one you can't help but think about. Thankfully, Lily was beyond that for the most part. She'd spent the last two years training herself to ignore Noah's beguiling features. She'd had no choice. As her boss, Noah was off-limits. Her job was too important. She was good at it, and even better, Noah and his brother, Sawyer, knew it.

Charlotte turned to Lily and Noah. Her newlywed smile took up nearly all the real estate between her diamond stud earrings. "Thanks for being our witnesses. Michael and I really appreciate it. I don't know what to say. We just got a wild hair and decided today was the day."

Michael leaned down and kissed the top of Charlotte's head. These two were so adorable together it made Lily's cheeks hurt. It also bruised her heart a little bit. She'd had an impossibly romantic love like that once. Or so she'd thought, but it had slipped right through her fingers, groom and all.

"Happy to do it. Congratulations." Noah stepped in and kissed his sister on the cheek, then shook Michael's hand.

Charlotte's phone rang and she squealed, grabbing Michael's arm and rushing out into the hall. Probably some famous well-wishers. The Locke family was known for their extensive connections.

"Want to grab a drink? It's nearly five o'clock. No point in going back to the office." Noah extended the invitation to Lily as if it were no big deal, as if she were just one of the guys, a role she suspected she would always have in his mind. He and Lily had done a few social things together, and they were always fun, but they filled Lily with pointless notions like hope and left her with sexy dreams, the kind where she'd wake up at 4:00 a.m. drenched in sweat and gasping for air. The sort of dream where you couldn't bring yourself to open your eyes or get out of bed. You wanted to languish in it forever.

"It's sweet of you to ask, but I think I'm going to head home, get out of these shoes and maybe do some reading."

"Friday night. Headed to that bookstore you like? What's it called?"

Lily's favorite spot in the city was a bookstore specializing in romance novels. "Petticoats and Proposals. You know all my tricks, don't you?"

"I try. I pay attention. It's a long-lost art, you know."

Their gazes connected and Lily's heart took up residence in her throat, pounding like crazy. *Boom boom. Boom boom.* It was as if Noah's eyes were magnetized, pulling on her, not allowing her to look anywhere else. She wanted to put the world on Pause and simply stare into them for a few hours. In between kisses of course. If she was going to slip into a fantasy world, she might as well make it exactly what she wanted it to be.

"It's because I can't stop talking about it."

"I'm sure that's not the reason." Noah cleared his throat and looked away for a moment. "Thanks for coming today. Charlotte couldn't deal with the wedding and the baby on the way. I'm actually happy for her. I wouldn't want to deal with all of those plans either. It seems like such an ordeal and then it's all over."

"Yeah. Me neither." Noah didn't know the half of it. And no amount of paying attention was going to get Lily to talk about it. Some things were better left buried.

"Okay, then. See you Monday."

"Yep. Have a good weekend." Lily smiled and walked away. Exactly like it didn't hurt at all to distance herself from Noah Locke.

Working with Lily, Mondays were always the hardest. Noah had endured a few days away from her, and his ability to keep himself together had worn off. Today seemed like an especially difficult start to the week. He couldn't even look at her.

"You're in early for a Monday," she said, with her usual happy singsong. She was standing in his office doorway, undoubtedly stunning.

"Some emergency meeting about the Hannafort Hotels deal. Charlotte's coming in for it, too. Not sure if she told you, but we've cut her in since she made the initial introduction." Noah still hadn't raised his sights, but he could see in his periphery that Lily was wearing her blue sweater. *The* blue sweater. The one that not only showed off every beguiling curve she possessed, but the one that really brought out her mesmerizing sapphire eyes.

"Oh. Okay. Let me drop my things, check email and I'll be right in."

"Sounds good." As if the sweater weren't bad enough, he couldn't avoid her heavenly scent. The faintest trace of it floated in the air when she left the room—sweet and sunny, just like her. His iron will was going to have to work doubly hard today.

"Unless there's something you need right now," she added.

He could hear her drumming her fingers on the door casing. For a moment, he imagined those delicate hands unbuttoning his shirt, touching the bare skin of his chest. He had to stop that train of thought right there or he'd lose it. "I'm good. Take your time."

With that, Lily disappeared from view. Noah sat back in his chair and a heavy exhale rushed from his lungs. *This is becoming impossible.*

Even after two years, Noah's love/hate relationship when it came to working with Lily wasn't getting any easier. He loved seeing her face every day, the way she lit up the office and managed to diffuse tense situations, but he hated how she could turn him into a blithering idiot. He hated being in enclosed spaces with her, like the elevator, where it took superhuman strength to keep from telling her how badly he wanted to kiss her. He hated having this all bottled up inside him. It wasn't how he operated with women.

But if ever a woman was off-limits, Lily was. She was a dream employee, clever and capable, a quick learner who was also organized and meticulous. She was too valuable to Locke and Locke, the company Noah owned and operated with his brother, Sawyer. As Sawyer had said many times, Lily might be uncommonly lovely and smart and kind, but Noah needed to keep his tongue in his mouth and his eyes in his head. To compensate, he'd been letting his eyes and his mouth wander elsewhere. It helped, but only a little.

"Okay. I'm back." Lily waltzed into his office and started straightening papers on his desk. She knew exactly how he liked things, and he'd never even had to tell her. She'd simply picked up on his preferences.

"Good weekend?" he asked, making small talk and sneaking a single glance. Her golden blond hair in a low twist brought attention to her lithe and graceful neck. He loved the naughty librarian aspect of it. He wanted her to peer at him over reading glasses and tell him to be quiet.

"The usual."

"Friday night at the romance bookstore?"

"I can sit there for hours and get lost in love stories."

He found it adorable that Lily was a bookworm. He, too, loved to read, but preferred nonfiction—history and biographies. He was not an incurable romantic like Lily, which was probably a big part of his attraction to her. He longed to shed at least some of his pessimism about love. Case in point, Lily had teared up at Charlotte's wedding, even when the civil ceremony had none of the sappy buildup of a traditional wedding. Noah was happy for his sister, but he did not get choked up. The very notion of a wedding unnerved him.

Charlotte's voice rang out from the hall beyond Noah's office walls.

"Sounds like my sister is here." *Back to work*. Noah stepped out from behind his desk and only allowed himself the smallest of glimpses of Lily in her black skirt. Studying the sway of her hips was a luxury he couldn't afford.

"Morning." Noah greeted his sister in the reception area, aka Lily's domain. Charlotte came by the office now and then, especially since involving her in the Hannafort Hotels deal, but she usually only came at lunchtime. It wasn't normal for her to be here first thing. She was always too busy running around doing real estate agent things, and lately, mother-to-be things.

"Did Sawyer talk to you about the video?" Charlotte's voice had a frantic edge to it as she swished her long blond hair to the side and unbuttoned her wool coat.

"Sawyer's on a call with Mr. Hannafort," Lily chimed in, buzzing around the office, running the photocopier, answering phones. "He left a note on my desk and said he was not to be disturbed. I'm not sure when he'll be done."

Sawyer's door opened and out he marched. His suit coat was off and his shirtsleeves were already rolled up like he'd been working for hours. This was not a good sign. It was hardly ten minutes after nine. "Charlotte, did you tell Noah about the news story?"

"I haven't had a chance," Charlotte said.

"She just got here." Noah felt as out of the loop as could be. "Does somebody want to tell me what's going on?"

"Hannafort saw it. He's not happy," Sawyer said.

"Oh no." Charlotte bustled into Sawyer's office with

all the dramatic urgency of a lawyer about to declare "I object!"

"Do you want to sit in on this?" Noah asked Lily. He was unsure what "this" he was about to walk into, but he and Sawyer were making a point of including Lily in high-level discussions. She'd earned the opportunity and it made everything in the office run more smoothly.

"I do, but I'm almost done with the Hannafort projections. You guys will want those for the meeting." She smiled wide—a flash of bright white framed by full, pink lips. Noah savored that instant. He had a feeling the rest of his day was about to tumble sharply downhill. "You go ahead. I'll be there in a minute."

Noah wandered into Sawyer's office. "Does somebody want to tell me what's going on?" He took one of the two seats opposite Sawyer's desk. Charlotte was in the other. The morning sun streamed through the tall, leaded glass windows of their office in the Chelsea neighborhood of Manhattan. It was a bright late March day, a bit brisk for Noah's liking, although the mood in Sawyer's office was even colder.

"Charlotte called me early this morning," Sawyer started.

"I tried to reach you, Noah, but I got voice mail. Why do you never answer my calls?"

Noah hated his phone. He often turned it off or simply left it in another room. There was something about being available to everyone at all times that he detested. It made him feel trapped. "Sorry. So what?"

Charlotte pulled out her phone. "I have the link saved."

Sawyer held up a hand and turned his laptop around so Charlotte and Noah could see it. "Let me save you the time. I have it pulled up on my computer. Lyle Hannafort sent it to me."

The webpage Sawyer had opened looked to be a spot for online gossip. Not Sawyer's usual fare. If he was online, he was watching the markets or sports, particularly college basketball this time of year. "Now I'm really lost," Noah said.

"You won't be." Sawyer scrolled down and clicked on the icon in the center of the screen. The video began to play.

Noah only needed to hear his name, purred by a woman with a sultry voice, to feel like the ground had fallen out from under him.

Big Apple businessman, Noah Locke, of the Locke hotel family, has been busy with the ladies over the last several months. And do we mean busy.

All warmth drained from Noah's body. His hands went cold. He'd been in the tabloids before, but this was different. These were moving pictures—shot after shot of Noah walking into and out of bars, restaurants and apartment buildings all over the city. A different woman on his arm in every picture. With a number counting them off. One… two…three… They stopped at fifteen. Noah felt sick.

Although his brother, Sawyer, and sister, Charlotte, have both settled down, it seems Noah is rallying to keep that trademark Locke wild streak alive. His father, James Locke, has not only been married four times, he's been romantically linked to hundreds of New York socialites over the years. Perhaps the middle Locke child is patterning himself after dear old dad.

Noah had a real talent for shrugging things off, but right now, he wanted to put his fist through a brick wall. "I'm calling our lawyer. This is defamation of character."

"Is it? Did they lie about a single thing?" Sawyer turned his computer back around to Noah's great relief. That final voice-over line and slate in the video was already permanently burned into his brain. *Perhaps the middle Locke child is patterning himself after dear old dad.* That was absolutely *not* the case.

"Well?" Charlotte asked. "You didn't answer the question."

Noah sat back, kneading his forehead, trying to think of anything they'd said in the video that was untrue. He would've asked to see it again if it hadn't made him sound like such a miserable excuse for a human being. Was he terrible? He didn't want to think he was. "Well, no. I mean, yes, I dated all of those women. That's true. But the last time I checked, this is a free country and a single man is allowed to have dinner with a single woman."

"Or fifteen," Charlotte quipped.

"I don't really see the point of this. Is it the slowest news day in the history of the world?" Noah's jaw tightened. He hated this.

"People love gossip. Especially about rich men who like to spend time with pretty women," Charlotte said. "You should know that by now."

Noah did know that, but in the past, Sawyer had most often been the target if there was anything tawdry to be said about the three siblings. A few times Charlotte had been busted for her party girl ways, but that had been a while ago. Now that both Sawyer and Charlotte were hitched, and both sets of wedded couples had babies on the way, apparently Noah was left to be the top of the dubious Locke family heap.

Noah then remembered what Sawyer had said before they'd come into his office. "Hold on. Hannafort has seen this? How in the hell did that happen?"

"It's the internet, Noah. This stuff spreads like wildfire. He's not happy about it, either." The deal they were working on with Lyle Hannafort, founder and CEO of Hannafort

Hotels, was massive. A real game changer. There was a mountain of money to be made. "He's a straight shooter. He doesn't mince words. And he's already predisposed to thinking badly of anyone named Locke. You know how hard we've worked to convince him we're not like Dad." Lyle Hannafort hated Sawyer and Noah's father and the feeling was mutual. They were bitter competitors. As much as that might have been one of Lyle's reasons for doing this deal, it was also a reason for calling it off.

"I'm very aware of how hard we've worked."

"He said he's not sure he can do business with a man who doesn't treat women as they should be treated," Sawyer said.

Noah sprang from his seat and jabbed his finger into the top of his brother's desk. "Now, hold on a second. Taking a woman out to dinner does not equal treating her badly. I'm always a gentleman. Always."

"You're just a gentleman a *lot*." Charlotte cocked a judgmental eyebrow at him, bobbing her foot. Noah could've easily fought back—Charlotte had once dated half of the men in Manhattan—but he couldn't be mean to her. Plus, she was expecting, and if he was worried about being seen as an ass, lashing out at his pregnant sister would not be a good move.

"I know that you're a good guy, Noah," Sawyer said. "Charlotte knows that, too. But Hannafort has built an empire on being a family man. He has five grown daughters, so I'm sure he's seen his fair share of men behaving badly. He totally owns up to being old-fashioned. He and his wife were high school sweethearts."

Noah had been impressed to learn that little factoid about the Hannaforts. That was a long time with one person. How did they make it work? In Noah's family, they didn't. Their dad had burned through each of his marriages, and there had been many serious girlfriends in between. There was a difference between Noah and his dad, though, and it was plain as day—one man a serial monogamist, carrying relationships to a cherished place only to destroy them. The other man, Noah, knew his limitations. He never led a woman on. Never. He was always clear about where and when things were ending.

"So what is Hannafort saying?"

"Let's say that we've gone from a place where both parties were head over heels to a place where one side is thinking about leaving the dance."

This deal had been in serious discussion for only a month, so things were still fragile. After months of convincing Lyle to talk to them, they were just starting to get comfortable with each other. This was supposed to be the honeymoon phase, but that seemed to be over. "Seriously? It's that bad?"

"As he put it, he has no patience for negative publicity that could have been easily avoided." Sawyer rocked back in his seat.

"How was I supposed to avoid this? No one could've predicted this." Noah had been looking forward to a quiet day in the office. He had no meetings, only a few phone calls, and he and Lily were supposed to have a discussion about some new projects. He'd been looking forward to that, however hard he'd have to try to concentrate on work.

"I think his point was that it never would've happened if you weren't the guy who dates dozens of women."

"What he really means is that if I wasn't like Dad." *Which I'm not.* Noah grumbled under his breath, frustrated beyond belief. He would never admit it to anyone, but part of the reason he'd been going out so much was because of Lily. The nights when he went home alone were awful. He couldn't watch TV, he couldn't read a book. His mind kept drifting to Lily, everything she'd done or said at work that day, replaying in his head like a never-ending movie. There was something about her that stopped Noah dead in his tracks.

But Sawyer had been crystal clear about it—all of that was too bad. *Lily is the best employee we have ever had. She is perfect. Don't mess this up. We need her and all you do is break hearts.*

Noah got it. Lily was forbidden fruit.

"How do we convince Mr. Hannafort that Noah's not that kind of guy?" Charlotte asked.

Sawyer snickered. "By finding him a wife. Or a fiancée."

Charlotte stifled a grin. "But it would have to be right away. Preferably before we go to Hannafort's daughter's wedding."

"Ideally, yes." Sawyer stared off into space like he was brainstorming. Charlotte was doing the same. Noah wasn't about to contribute to their ludicrous meeting of the minds. There was no woman in his life he'd consider asking to marry him. No one was even close.

A knock came at the door. Noah turned as Lily walked in with four black binders in her arms. "I have the revenue projections from Mr. Hannafort's team. I cross-referenced them with our own, which are considerably more conservative."

"Great. Thank you," Sawyer said.

Lily doled out the presentations while Noah remained standing.

"Lily, you can take my seat. I'm happy right here."

She settled in, rocking her hips from side to side. "You got it all warmed up for me."

He sucked in a sharp breath. Good God, she was going to be the death of him.

Noah opened his binder. There was no time to absorb all of the information in this report, but one quick glance at a few spreadsheets told him one thing—they were going to make a lot of money if this deal went through. And his actions, which had been perfectly innocent at the time, could end up taking it all away. Charlotte, and Sawyer in particular, would never forgive him. Or if they did, it would take a very long time. There was already enough acrimony in his family from their dad. Noah refused to be the cause for this blowing up in their faces.

"Wow." Sawyer flipped through the pages. "These numbers are impressive."

"They are." Charlotte closed her folder and chewed on her nail. "Can't let this get out from under us."

"No, we can't." Noah racked his brain for a way to make himself seem less like a Lothario.

Charlotte narrowed her vision on him, then her sights drifted to Lily. She sat a little straighter and turned in her chair. "Lily, can I ask you a question?"

"Of course."

"Would you have any interest in going to a wedding with all of us? This weekend. I don't know what sort of personal obligations you have, and I know it's short notice."

As the words out of Charlotte's mouth found his ears, Noah quickly realized what she was doing. She was setting him up. With Lily. The woman who he'd been fighting to keep in the friend zone. Noah bugged his eyes at Charlotte, but she shot him a steely look right back.

"A wedding? Do you mean Annie Hannafort's wedding?"

Charlotte smiled effortlessly, like this all made perfect sense and would not cause a single problem. Noah already had a dozen reasons not to do what Charlotte was about to suggest. The reasons were already stacked up and waiting, and he'd only been living with this realization for less than a minute. "Exactly. It's just that we would need you to be Noah's date. Well, more than his date. We would need you to pretend to be his fiancée."

Two

Lily mustered the strength to hold her smile, but only because she was fairly certain her face was frozen. She managed to blink, so her eyes were working. That was good. Her mind, meanwhile, was frantically running around like a chicken with its head cut off. Had Charlotte Locke just said those words? Pretend to be Noah's fiancée? At a wedding, no less?

Lily's worst nightmare and her most closely held fantasy had decided to make sweet love to each other.

"Are you serious?" She realized how terrible the question must sound to Noah, but she needed clarification and she needed it now. This felt an awful lot like the moment her biggest high school crush asked her out in front of his friends, only to burst into peals of laughter. That was the day Lily learned how apt the word *crush* was when it came to love.

"I know it seems a little strange, but there's a reason behind it and you would be helping the company immensely."

Noah stepped closer and sat on the edge of Sawyer's desk, crossing his long legs, facing her with a look that could only be described as raw embarrassment. His expression was difficult to endure, which spoke volumes about how real it was. Noah was ridiculously easy on the eyes.

"You don't have to do this," Noah said. "This is not part of your job."

Lily couldn't decide if he was saying that because he desperately wanted his own out, or if he was simply being kind. She hoped for the latter, if only to save her pride.

"We would pay you, of course," Sawyer said. "We'll have to come up with a number. Maybe you should sit down and think about what you would need for three days away from home."

"Acting as Noah's fiancée." Lily wanted to be sure she'd heard that part right.

"Yes. There was a very unflattering video of Noah that turned up on a gossip website and we're trying to curb its effects. Mr. Hannafort wants to know that the Lockes aren't a liability when it comes to publicity."

"Unflattering video?" Lily could only imagine what Noah's sister was referring to.

"Do you want to see it?" Charlotte asked.

Noah grumbled. His straight shoulders dropped. "Don't show her the video. It's demeaning. Lily and I need to work together. I don't want her to think of me that way."

Charlotte leaned over the arm of her chair. "It's about the stable of women he's been dating lately."

Lily could feel her lips mold into a thin line. Oh, she knew plenty about Noah and his dates. A few women had come by the office, all intimidatingly beautiful. And she'd heard him talk to them, as smooth as could be. Lily would've done anything to have a man say one-tenth of what Noah regularly said to women he apparently hardly cared about. "I see."

"So as I said," Sawyer interjected. "We would need to come up with a number, but I promise we'll make it worth your while. This isn't normally something I'd consider, but desperate times call for creative measures."

Lily crossed her legs, her mind mired in the business of deciding whether or not this was a good idea. She loved working for Sawyer and Noah, so it would be next to impossible to say no. It wasn't in her DNA to let them down. But one downside of being employed by Locke and Locke was the limited opportunities for advancement. Lily had already worked her way well beyond the parameters of her title of Executive Admin. Sawyer and Noah had given her more and more responsibility, they'd even given her a few raises, but she was capable of even more. If the payoff was there. She was a hard worker, but she wasn't an idiot. She wasn't going to kill herself if they were just going to take advantage of her.

"If I do this, I don't want to be compensated with cash. I want a piece of the company." Lily was impressed with herself. She'd come out with it, no hemming or hawing. She sat straighter, fighting back any concern over how her proposal might be met. "A small piece, but a piece. I believe I've demonstrated that I'm a valuable asset to the company, but I want to do more."

Sawyer nodded slowly, as if he was still taking it all in.

"This isn't my call. I'm in on this Hannafort deal and that's it." Charlotte looked at her phone. "I'm also going to be late for my doctor's appointment if I don't leave now." She got up from her seat and shot both of her brothers a very pointed glance. "Don't screw this up. And Lily, don't let them screw this up."

Lily grinned as Charlotte excused herself and left. She did love the way Charlotte put her brothers on notice.

"What do you think?" Sawyer asked Noah.

"You've said it yourself a thousand times. Lily is by far the best employee we've had. She's irreplaceable. If she's willing to put up with me for a weekend, we should give her what she wants."

Sawyer chuckled quietly, and that made Noah laugh, which filled Lily with happy flutters in her chest. She was overcome with pride, knowing that she'd been a frequent subject of conversation between the brothers and in such a positive light, no less. It reaffirmed her decision two years ago to focus on her career and let romance and her personal life take a back seat. This might actually end up paying off.

"I think one percent is fair," Noah said.

"Agreed," Sawyer quickly added. "It might not sound like a lot, but if the Hannafort deal goes through, it will be sizable. And it should be income that comes in for years and years. Not bad for three days' work."

Lily was a bit of a whiz with numbers, so she knew exactly how big 1 percent of Locke and Locke could end up being, especially after having worked on the Hannafort projections. A nest egg to last her a lifetime? All for one weekend pretending to be enamored with gorgeous, unattainable Noah? This was a no-brainer if ever there was one. Even if the part about Noah did make her stomach flip-flop. Yes, she struggled at weddings, but she'd just endured one. What difference could another one possibly make? "I'll do it."

"That's great news. Thank you." Sawyer's eyebrows drew together. "I hope you know this is not something we would normally ask you to do."

"I've been here two years. I know this is not the way

things work around here. Sometimes things have to be done for appearances."

"Exactly."

"I should probably get back to my desk. I have lots of other stuff to do. Emails to answer." Lily rose from her seat, but something about this was still leaving her unsettled. Was this the right thing to do? Would it ruin her working relationship with Noah? They got along so well. She didn't want it to be awkward later. "I do want to clarify that this is for show, right? We're pretending. That's it."

Noah's eyes found hers and she felt naked, like he was looking right through her. "That goes without saying."

She smiled and nodded, like the loyal employee she was. But inside, all she could think was *of course*. Noah Locke was *that* guy and he always would be.

Noah closed the door when Lily walked out of Sawyer's office. "I don't think you've fully thought this out." He paced back and forth, between the chairs and the window. "We're talking about pretending to be engaged to each other. Do you know what engaged people do?"

"Um, I'm pretty sure, but why don't you fill me in." Sawyer was still poring over the Hannafort reports, dismissing this conversation as if it was nothing.

"Hugging. Holding hands. Kissing."

"Sounds about right. I know you remember how to do all of those things." Sawyer flipped to another page.

"But am I not supposed to be staying away from Lily? You were the one who wouldn't stop going on and on about how I needed to pretend that she was my sister. Don't mess things up, Noah. Stop making up excuses to be around her, Noah." He planted both hands on Sawyer's desk and stared him down. "This could easily mess things up with her. Then what? We lose our best employee because of some stupid stunt?"

"Now you see the validity of my original argument? When we're being forced to set it aside?" Sawyer closed the binder and looked him square in the eye. "I think the one thing that video proved is that you have no problem with walking away, so I'm certainly not worried about your feelings. As for Lily, she's being rewarded handsomely and she seems completely comfortable with the idea. She's a very strong person. I'm a little concerned, but I'm not overly concerned. How confused can two people get over the course of three days?"

"Honestly? I have no idea. I've never been fake engaged before."

"And that's the important thing to remember. This is fake. It's not real. It's not the same as if you had actually pursued her. That would have hurt her feelings when you decided to end it. Or…"

"Or what?"

"Or maybe she would've ended up ending it. Maybe she would've turned you down. I'm sure it's hard for you to imagine, but it could've gone down that way."

"You think I don't worry about that every time I ask a woman out? Because I do." Noah had thought about that a lot when it came to Lily, if only when he was trying to convince himself that going there in the first place would be a huge mistake.

Surely Lily dated a lot. She simply never mentioned it. In fact, she rarely talked about herself. He could only assume that she didn't have a serious boyfriend right now. She never complained about working late and she was always doing her Friday night visit to the bookstore she liked so much. It was silly, but a few weeks ago, Noah had been dateless and bored on a Friday night, so he'd gone for a run and accidentally on purpose ended up there. He'd peeked in the window, but couldn't see the corner she'd talked about. He'd also been too embarrassed to walk in. So he'd pretended his shoelace was untied and jogged back to his apartment, realizing how stupid the whole thing had been in the first place. What would he have said if she'd seen him? *I always go for runs in neighborhoods that are totally out of the way from where I live.*

"And don't forget, Lily's a tough cookie," Sawyer said. "I'm not as concerned about it as I was when we first started working on the Grand Legacy project and you couldn't keep your eyes off her or your tongue off the floor."

"You act like I'm the horniest guy you've ever met. Have you not noticed how stunning she is?"

"I noticed. Believe me. I've noticed. As have lots of our clients."

The worst part…or the best part, Noah couldn't decide, was that Lily didn't seem to know it. Or if she did, she didn't seem driven by it or obsessed by it. She simply seemed comfortable in her own skin, which Noah found very sexy.

"Okay. Well, I guess I'm going to go back to work with my fake fiancée. This is officially the craziest thing I've ever done, just so you know."

"I don't want to be a jerk about it, but this was your own doing. I appreciate your willingness to make it right. It'll all be fine. We'll do the deal with Hannafort and you and Lily can quietly break up. I doubt it'll even be on his radar at that point. But we need to remove any doubt he has now."

"Got it." Noah reached for the door.

"Wait. There's more. We need word of the engagement out before we leave and Lily is also going to need a ring. Everyone will want to see the ring."

Noah groaned in frustration. "How do we go about announcing an engagement? Do we call the society page?"

"I don't think we have time for that. I'll talk to Kendall. We'll figure out a way to leak it to the press." Sawyer's wife, Kendall, was a PR master. She'd done a brilliant job on the reopening of the family's historic hotel, the Grand Legacy.

Noah stifled another sigh. "Let me know." As he walked down the hall, he noticed that Lily was not at her desk. He rounded into his office. She was putting things away in his filing cabinet. He came to a dead stop. He didn't say a thing. Lily had this habit when she was standing, but concentrating on something—she'd step out of one pump and balance on her opposite leg, rubbing the back of her calf with her bare foot. Up and down, over and over until she was finished with the task. It was one of the many inexplicably sexy things she did.

Maybe this fake engagement had a bright side. Maybe this was the chance to get Lily out of his system. His brother couldn't say a thing about holding hands, long embraces, or kisses now. And if those things continued behind closed doors, and Lily wanted him, too, clothes could come off and he could finally know what it was like to make love to her, to have her hands all over him, and at the end of the weekend, they could part ways on the romantic front. It was perfect.

A little too perfect.

Noah couldn't escape the notion that his plan sounded like something his dad would do. He was not his father, and he would do anything he could to prove it. That meant he would have to be doubly careful and keep things especially chaste between them, all while trying to create the illusion that they were hopelessly in love. He had no idea how he was going to pull this off.

Lily whipped around, surprise in her eyes. She dropped down onto her bare foot and pressed her hand to her chest. "You scared me."

"I'm sorry. I didn't want to startle you, but you were so deep in concentration."

Lily worked her foot back into her black pump. "You could tell?"

"Yeah. You do that thing with your foot when you're focused."

Her cheeks turned the most gorgeous shade of pink, like cherry blossoms in spring, except brighter and more vibrant. It made him want to embarrass her more often. "I do?"

Noah swallowed hard. He hadn't had time to get used to the fact that it would be okay for him to say something about this now. Before, a topic like this was best avoided. "I did. I've noticed it for a while now. I'm sorry if that bothers you."

She shook her head. "No. Of course not. It doesn't bother me at all." Was that a hint of flirtation in her voice? If so, he liked being fake engaged to her, even if the clock hadn't yet started ticking on their charade.

"So, are you okay with our arrangement? There's still time to back out if you want." He didn't want to come off as unsure, but it was important to him that she not feel as though she'd been cornered. There had been three Lockes in that room and only one Lily Foster. It wasn't entirely fair.

"I'd be lying if I said that I was completely comfortable with the idea. I'm not much for faking something."

"Yeah. Me neither."

"But I'm also smart enough to know that people do all sorts of things in business to make a deal happen. And maybe if you aren't willing to be daring with something, you'll miss out. This would be a big thing to miss out on."

"The Hannafort deal."

"Of course."

It was good to have clarification, if only to keep things straight. "Well, our next step is for me to take you shopping for a ring."

"Wow. A ring." Lily looked down at her own hand as if she were trying to picture it. "I guess that's a must-have, isn't it?"

"Can't be fake engaged without a ring." He smiled when she shot him a knowing glance. "Except the ring will be real. I'm not putting a fake ring on your hand." Lily absolutely deserved a real ring, but he did have to wonder if this harebrained plan was going to end up ruining any fantasies she'd had about getting engaged. He didn't want to make assumptions based on her gender, but she did prefer books with happy endings.

Noah had zero fantasies about marriage. Or engagement. He'd never imagined the moment when he'd get down on one knee. He'd never thought about what it would feel like to love someone so much that the only thing that made sense was to be with them forever. It had always seemed, at best, unlikely and, at worst, doomed. Would he ever be in love? Would he ever feel as though he couldn't live without someone? Seventy-two hours or so and he usually knew that the woman of the moment wasn't the one. Or, admittedly, he'd gone into it with the assumption he would not find love. It wasn't the best attitude, but time and again, things played out that way. It was hard not to assume that the common denominator—his heart—wasn't built for love.

"Good to know that you're not going to force me to be excited about a cubic zirconia. Not that I wouldn't be happy with whatever you gave me. But, you know. A girl wants a diamond if she can get it."

"The only thing about the ring shopping is that we have to plan it out in advance. Sawyer's going to have Kendall leak it to the press so it will hopefully make its way back to Hannafort. And if not, we will at least have countered the bad publicity with good."

She nodded. "So the video was that bad?"

The thought of it made his stomach sink yet again. He hoped Lily never saw it. He hoped she never looked it up on the internet, although if the roles were reversed, he definitely would have done some due diligence. He truly didn't want her seeing him in that light. Even if it was biased, and pulpy, it wasn't a lie. There was a whole lot of truth in it. "It wasn't my best showing, that's for sure."

Lily patted him on the shoulder. When she moved her hand, it felt as though she'd marked him for life with her touch. "Hopefully we can make it go away. We should probably start tomorrow."

"Do I have a hole in my schedule?"

"No meetings from eleven to three. A nice big window."

"Perfect. Tomorrow at eleven we have a date to buy that ring." Noah could hardly believe the words after they'd left his lips. For a guy who'd sworn he'd never get engaged, he'd said it like it was no big deal, when he knew for a fact that it was.

Three

Lily did her best to stay busy at work the next morning, but knowing where she and Noah were going at eleven made it tough to focus. A mere twenty-four hours into their fake engagement and Noah was about to take her to buy the ring. She'd be lying if she said she'd never thought about stepping into a fancy jewelry store with a sweet, handsome, romantic guy. Her broken engagement had come with a ring that was a family heirloom, no shopping required. She'd had no idea that Peter wouldn't be able to go through with the promise that accompanied that ring, but returning it had been a simple process. She'd thrown it at him in a quiet room just outside the nave. He'd cursed her, scrambled on his hands and knees for it, nearly ruining his tuxedo pants. She'd cried and braced herself for what followed—telling a church full of invited guests that they were welcome to enjoy the reception, but there would be no wedding.

The events of that dreadful day were precisely why her fake engagement to Noah, although fun in premise, was about business and nothing else. She'd never had financial security in her life and that became her top priority after the love part went south. She had to take her chance to secure her future. It would be one fewer thing to fret about, in a world fraught with things that could make a woman worry, like whether or not Mr. Right would ever come along.

Out walked Noah from the confines of Sawyer's office. "So we're all set with the photographer or whoever is supposed to be outside the jewelry store?"

Sawyer followed his brother. "According to Kendall, yes. As to who it is and where they'll be, I have no idea. You'll have to be as convincing as possible. These people are very good at sniffing out a fake. And, honestly, you need to act like someone is watching, even when you don't know for certain that they are. The video should have taught you that much."

Noah cast his sights at Lily. It was as if he was saying *Can you believe what we're doing?* To which Lily would have replied *No*.

"I don't want any obvious signs that this is a Locke and Locke purchase, so put the ring on one of your personal cards instead of the company's. We'll find a way to reimburse you for it," Sawyer said. "I don't know if they'll let us return it when it's all said and done, but I suppose we could always sell it if we had to."

This was all too strange, an unromantic transaction. Lily dug around in her purse for a piece of gum, just to distract herself from this deeply uncomfortable subject.

"Sawyer, listen to yourself. We're not doing that." Noah grabbed his coat and slipped it on. The man had incredible shoulders, but the black wool brought out the strong line of them, enough to make her stifle a sigh. "If I give Lily a ring, she gets to keep it. I'm not asking for it back, even if this is fake."

Lily's heart broke out in a gallop, fierce and strong, like a young horse discovering it could run for as long and as far as it wanted to. That might have been the most romantic thing a man had ever said about her.

Even when his sweet sentiment was tied up with a satin bow called "fake."

Sawyer stuffed his hands into his pockets. "You're right. You're absolutely right. Lily, whatever you choose today, it's yours to keep."

"Oh. Well, thank you. I guess we'll call it combat pay?"

Sawyer laughed. Noah did, too, but it was far less convincing and came only after his brother had started it. He seemed so tortured over this whole thing, it was impossible to feel good about it.

"I'm kidding. Of course. If I wanted combat pay, I'd ask for cash." She smiled sweetly and got up from her desk, wishing there was a protocol somewhere for interactions with your fake fiancée and your fake future brother-in-law. She felt a bit like she was failing right now.

"You two have fun. Try not to get into too much trouble," Sawyer said, heading back into his office.

"No promises," Noah muttered. "And we're going out to lunch afterward."

"On the company dime?" Lily asked.

Noah unleashed a devilish smile. "Of course." He then offered her his arm, which he held in midair while Lily struggled to keep up with what she was supposed to do. "Remember what Sawyer said. We need to act like someone is watching at all times."

"Right." She hooked hers in his and he snugged her against his body, sending a lovely shock right through her.

One touch, through layers of coats no less, and she felt like her shoes might shoot right off her feet.

They took the stairs down to the street. Noah's driver was waiting for them, standing outside the sleek black town car. He opened the door as they approached and Lily struggled to stay in the moment, to not let her consciousness become too detached from what was happening. This was a fantasy brought to life, and she should embrace the good parts. There would surely be bad moments when she would end up with flickers of regret over doing this crazy thing. For now, Noah Locke, Mr. Unattainable, was taking her to buy an engagement ring. She wanted to soak up every minute.

They got settled in the back seat. "Warm enough?" Noah asked.

She nodded. "Yes."

"Good."

"Yes." *Wow. So this is what the world's worst small talk is like.*

"I was thinking..." He looked out the window and shook his head.

"What? You were thinking what?"

He turned back and looked at her so earnestly she thought she might disappear into his green eyes. "What do people do after they buy an engagement ring?"

Have sex? Lily thought for a second about putting it out there, but decided there were only so many inappropriate jokes she could make. That would not be professional. "I don't know. Kiss?"

"Yes. Exactly." He nodded a little too fast, almost as if he was nervous, which seemed impossible. She'd witnessed more human moments out of Noah in the last day than she'd ever seen before. It was nice. "And, obviously, we haven't done that yet. I don't think it should be awkward. It should seem natural, especially if anyone is taking a picture."

She put her hand on his. "Right. Like Sawyer said."

"Following orders."

"He needs us to put on a good show. We should practice. At least once." The instant she said it, the air crackled with electricity. She'd pushed things to the next level. With the help of some convenient excuses, of course.

Noah's clever half smile crossed his lips, and his eyes swirled to a darker shade. The city whizzed by outside the window. Lily was overcome with the freeing feeling of being given permission to do something you shouldn't. Kissing Noah was such a bad idea, but when you'd thought about a bad idea for two whole years, it was hard not to be excited by it. His hand slipped under her hair and around her neck. She sat straighter. She angled herself closer. Every nerve ending in her body was cheering him on. His thumb settled in the soft spot under her ear. His touch was more than warm. It was a superhuman zap of heat. It might turn her into something she'd never been before.

His lips parted ever so slightly and she raised her chin as he lowered his head. His hair slumped forward. She loved that. She'd fantasized a million times about running her hands through it, feeling the thick strands between her fingers and smoothing it back. She wanted to stare at him forever, but she also wanted to savor every delicious heartbeat of anticipation. Her eyes fluttered shut. When his mouth met hers, she waited for it to change her life, but it was a soft brush of a kiss. A first date kiss. An *oh hi nice to meet you* kiss. It was nice. So nice. But nice wasn't going to cut it. Her body didn't merely tell her so, it was screaming it in both ears. She slanted her head and pushed up from the seat, aiming her shoulders straight for his. He pulled back. Her eyes flew open. Their gazes connected, both of them searching. It was an entire deliberation about their next kiss, wrapped up in two seconds. He smiled. She swallowed. He was coming in for the real thing.

The next thing she knew, she had all ten fingers working into his hair. Her arms landed on his shoulders. His hand was molded around her hip, squeezing like he was trying to get down to the bone. Their lips were in a mad scramble, parted, making way for tongues to roam. In under two seconds, they'd gone from zero to sexy sixty. The kiss was flat-out reckless now, like neither of them cared about ramifications. She was a woman and he was the hottest man she'd ever set her eyes on. One well-placed rub and they might as well be dry tinder. A fire was inevitable.

Lily dropped one hand and worked her way inside Noah's coat, which he'd been kind enough to leave unbuttoned. She palmed his firm chest, and even through layers of clothes—his suit coat, his shirt—she could feel the frantic pounding of his heart. She wanted nothing more than to experience that with bare skin against bare skin. Noah's hand traveled down to her knee and under the hem of her skirt. Lily felt like she might burst into full flame. He didn't waste a second, heading north, his palm caressing her stocking. Her heart was beating like a kid dragging a stick across a picket fence. He came to a dead stop when his thumb reached the top of her thigh-highs. Noah pulled back, breaking their kiss, breathless. Thankfully, his hand hadn't moved.

"Are those?" His eyes were dark with a brew of lust and curiosity.

She nodded, her lips floating back to meet his and steal one more kiss. "I can't stand regular panty hose," she murmured against his mouth. She took a soft nip of his lower lip.

A low groan escaped his throat.

The divider between the driver and the back seat started to lower. Lily scrambled to find a more demure position. The driver, most likely accustomed to this scene, didn't look at them. "Mr. Locke. We're here at Tiffany."

Noah gawked at Lily. Maybe he hadn't expected her to go for it. *Carpe diem, Mr. Locke. Carpe diem.* "Um. Ready?" he asked.

For what? she almost answered. *For you to tear off my clothes?* "Hold on a sec." She reached out and combed her fingers through his silky hair, which was just as tangled as her thoughts right now. "Your hair." It was even softer than it had been a minute ago. Maybe it was because she wasn't wholly distracted by his lips and chest.

"Thanks for looking out for me." He then scrutinized her hair and smoothed back one strand that was grazing her cheek. "You weren't nearly as disheveled."

Embarrassment crept over her, shrouding her from head to toe. She hadn't merely gone overboard, she'd behaved like a teenager who'd spent her adolescence locked up in an all-girls school. Lily made a mental note: *practice some damn decorum.* At least this was probably the norm for Noah, women going crazy for him. He didn't seem particularly fazed by it at all.

Noah was quite frankly shocked that he could climb out of the back seat and straighten to his full height. It felt like his pants had shrunk two sizes and *not* in the waist. Thank goodness for unseasonably cool weather, as well as his long wool coat. It could hide a multitude of sins. And stiffness.

He took Lily's hand as she stepped out of the car. The flush in her cheeks filled him with an unavoidable sense of accomplishment. He liked knowing that had been her response to him, but even better was having experienced it firsthand. She'd gone for far more than a practice kiss, which had honestly surprised him. She was always so businesslike in the office, never showing any interest in him outside the professional. Which was fine, and as it should have been. But it had disappointed him from time to time, for sure. Was there more there? Or was she amped up because her whole financial future was about to become so much sunnier?

Either way, it didn't matter. He wasn't going to be his father. He couldn't go overboard like that again. He had a professional relationship to maintain with Lily. Kissing like they just had was a one-way ticket to ruin.

They stepped inside Tiffany & Co., the beautifully appointed showroom with a maze of glass cases filled with jewelry, towering displays of crystal bowls and the ever-present flashes of their signature blue. Lily squeezed his hand a little tighter, which only made him want to reassure her that they were in this together. As unorthodox as their arrangement was, they had each other. For a few days.

An older gentleman at the first counter stepped out from behind it. "Mr. Locke?" His British accent made him even more distinguished than his appearance. His silvery hair was impeccably groomed.

"Yes. You must be Mr. Russell." Noah turned to Lily. "I made an appointment. I didn't want us to have to wait."

"Absolutely not. I understand you are a very busy man, Mr. Locke." He then turned his attention to Lily. A warm grin crossed his face and he stood even straighter. "And this must be the future Mrs. Locke." He reached out his hand and shook hers, regarding her as if she were made of fine china.

"Yes. That's me. Won't be long and I'll be Lily Locke." Mr. Russell let go and Lily smiled nervously at Noah. He got it. He hadn't thought about it in terms of her married name yet either.

They followed Mr. Russell to a counter in the middle of the store. He pulled out a velvet-covered board with at least a dozen engagement rings on it. "I took the liberty of picking out a few things to start. You had said platinum, right? And something larger than a carat? But you also wanted something ready-made. Not a custom ring, correct?"

Noah nodded. He didn't much like the idea of something right off the sales floor, but thus was their timeline. "Yes. Correct. We don't want to wait." He put his hand on the small of Lily's back. "What do you think?"

Lily leaned down, perusing them, but didn't touch a thing. When she turned back to Noah, there was a decidedly panicked edge to her expression. "These all seem really big."

"Yes…" His mind went blank as he tried to decide what sort of pet name Lily might like. "Honey. We talked about this before. Remember? I want you to have a beautiful ring. A ring that's just as gorgeous and amazing as you." That was the sort of thing a romantic guy would say, wasn't it?

"But aren't these a little extravagant?"

He shook his head as sweetly as possible. "No. I don't think so."

Mr. Russell cleared his throat. "Oh, dear. A few of these aren't quite as clean as they should be. Let me polish them up and I'll give you two a chance to chat." He'd obviously been doing this for a very long time. He seemed quite practiced in the art of ducking away when a couple was about to have an argument. "I'll be right back."

As soon as Mr. Russell was gone with the rings, Lily started in. "They're too much, Noah. It doesn't seem right that I would get that on top of the one percent. I want to be compensated, but I also don't want to take advantage of you or Sawyer."

"I hear what you're saying. And it's sweet, but you need

to think about me and my family. People are going to expect Noah Locke's fiancée to have a huge hulking ring. Did you see the rock that Sawyer gave Kendall?"

"It all seems very superficial. A man's love should not be demonstrated by the size of an engagement ring."

"And it isn't. The size of a man's wallet is demonstrated by the ring. The love part people will have to figure out on their own." That last thought gave him a sour stomach. He and Lily both deserved better than to be picking out engagement rings with someone they weren't head over heels for. "You're going to have to trust me on this one. When we get to the wedding this weekend and you show off that ring, we want people to be blinded by it. If it's small, it'll just cast suspicion on the engagement and that's one thing we can't afford."

Lily blew out a long breath through her nose and looked around the store, shaking her head the whole time. "You know, I'm surprised the grand Locke family doesn't have a cache of heirloom engagement rings tucked away somewhere. Surely you guys have been handing down jewelry from generation to generation. Maybe that would be easier. Then I could give it back when we're done."

He didn't like that she was making assumptions about his family or their history. There might have been many Locke fortunes made over the last century, but there had been a lot of sadness and heartache, too. They weren't all spending their days rolling around on piles of money. "There's no cache of rings. There is one family ring in the mix, and that's all I know of. It was my mother's. The sapphire engagement ring my father gave her. He gave it to me when I turned eighteen."

"It sounds pretty."

"It's beautiful. A big oval surrounded by diamonds." Noah almost choked on the words. More than twenty years later and he still missed his mom. Plus, all he could think about was what his dad had said when he'd given him the ring. *If you ever manage to find the right woman, you should give this to her when you ask her to marry you. I'm just not sure you have it in you to be like me.* "I didn't really think that was appropriate for today."

The expression on Lily's face fell. "Oh. Of course. I'm so sorry. I wasn't thinking."

Noah understood how bad it sounded, but Mr. Russell was only a few feet away. "Wait. I didn't mean it that way."

She waved him off, not looking at him. "No. It's fine. I get it, Noah. Really."

"Right, then," Mr. Russell started. "Have we had a chance to have the 'size matters' discussion?" He winked at Lily and she laughed quietly. Thank God for Mr. Russell.

"Yes. We have." She leaned down, her thumb resting on her lower lip. "I think I'd like to try that one."

Mr. Russell picked up the ring and placed it gently on Lily's left ring finger. She slid it into place and held out her hand so Noah could see. "What do you think?"

The ring was stunning. And it looked lovely on Lily's hand.

"It's a square solitaire, just under two and a half carats. Platinum setting, of course, and approximately another two carats of small diamonds in the band." Mr. Russell watched Lily closely. "I'll get you the exact carat weight if this is the one you decide to take."

"It's a gorgeous ring. No question about that," Noah said. This was Lily's decision. Not his.

"Okay, then. We'll take this one."

"Are you sure? You don't want to try any others?" Mr. Russell asked. "How does the size of the band feel?"

Lily shrugged. "No. I'm good. I like this one. It seems like it fits fine."

"Okay, then. You have to appreciate a woman who knows what she wants." He smiled wide at Lily. "Truly. Some couples are here for hours."

"I bet." *At least we're efficient.*

"I'll get the paperwork together." Mr. Russell didn't leave, though. He seemed to be waiting, perhaps for the moment he'd undoubtedly witnessed many times with countless other couples.

Lily leaned into Noah and showed him the ring again. "I love it, darling. Truly."

Noah then remembered the show they were supposed to be putting on. He gazed into her eyes, but it wasn't the same as things had been when they were in the car together. Alone. This version of Lily was all business. "Good. I'm so glad." He leaned closer and they kissed. It was sweet and soft, but only an echo of the passion they'd shared mere minutes ago.

Mr. Russell smiled, seeming satisfied. He left for a moment, and returned with a packet of paperwork certifying the diamonds, along with a blue Tiffany box for Lily to keep the ring in, and the final bill. Noah pulled out his credit card, hoping that at some point, this might all start to seem at least a little more normal. Mr. Russell presented him with the receipt, Noah signed on the dotted line.

And just like that, it was done.

They bid their farewell and walked out of the store, hand in hand. As soon as they were in the car, he had to say something. "I'm sorry about what I said about my mom's ring. It didn't come out in a particularly kind way."

"No. It's fine, Noah. I get it. Our arrangement isn't real. We both knew that going into it." She held out her hand and wiggled her fingers. The chunky diamond sparkled. "And now I have the ring to prove it."

Four

It didn't take long for the photos of the Tiffany & Co. engagement ring kiss to end up online. In fact, it took less than an hour.

Noah's phone beeped with a text soon after they ordered their lunch at a restaurant he'd suggested. "It's Sawyer. Kendall just sent him a link to the photo of us picking out your ring. I'm not sure whether I should be happy or not, but we are now officially tabloid fodder."

Lily scooted closer to him in the half-round booth. It would be so easy to become accustomed to being near him, breathing in his citrusy cologne and putting her hands on him anytime. He showed her the evidence of their dubious newfound fame. There they were on a gossip website, locking lips in the most famous jewelry store in the world. It was so surreal. That was Lily Foster from an average family in Philadelphia, doing something distinctly not run-of-the-mill. "Yikes."

"Are you not happy with this?"

"It just…" Lily's stomach was filled with all sorts of uncomfortable feelings. She did not like the loss of control. She disliked the scrutiny of her private life. She hated feeling as though other people's opinions of her could boil down to this. For the first time, she understood how deeply upsetting it must have been to Noah when the tabloid video was released.

"Just what?"

"It's strange. Why would anyone care about this?" She winced at how unworldly her words might make her seem. She didn't want to be naive, but she couldn't escape the feeling that a person's love life should not be entertainment for perfect strangers.

"Now you know how I felt when that video ran. At least we knew this was going to happen. That's a big improvement over the way things happened for me."

Lily sighed and looked at the pixelated photograph again. This was the new cost of doing business, the price she'd be paying for securing her future with her small piece of Locke and Locke. This was the new normal. "Do you think this will be the extent of being in the tabloids? We won't have to keep doing this, will we?"

Noah took a sizable gulp of the Old-Fashioned he'd ordered to go alongside his steak sandwich and fries. "This should be enough to do the trick. We just needed Hannafort to buy the idea of us as an engaged couple before we show up at his daughter's wedding."

She smiled thinly and nodded. His words pointed to one truth—the notion of Lily and Noah as a couple was indeed something that needed to be sold. It needed the help of smoke and mirrors. "Okay."

The expression on Noah's face softened. "Are you just

saying okay? I have the feeling this is really bothering you."

She didn't want to make a stink. She wasn't someone to complain, but it did bother her. At least Noah was being thoughtful about it. That she appreciated. "I don't want to sound like a hopeless romantic, but it's a big deal to get engaged. It feels like we're tempting fate by doing it for show."

Worry crossed his face, a look she disliked. Noah was too perfect to stress. "Think of it this way, it's helping you build a nest egg, right?"

"Yes. That's important."

"And, hopefully, there are worse people you could be fake engaged to."

I'm not sure there's anyone better to be fake engaged to. "Of course. Don't be silly."

"More than anything, do you have any idea how many people get stuck with super unflattering pictures of themselves in the tabloids? This photo of us is pretty hot. We look good together." He smiled, seeming like he was desperate to reassure her everything would be okay. It was so endearing.

"True." Lily gnawed on her lower lip. She *had* noticed that. "Can you get Kendall to email me that link? So I have it?" She might be upset by the newspaper story, but she might also have that photo blown up and framed. She could hang it on the wall in her bedroom. Oddly enough, the kiss in the jewelry store hadn't been particularly hot. It had been sweet and nice. She hadn't noticed when it was happening that Noah had not only rested his hand on her hip, he'd curled his fingers into her coat. Even with the graininess of the photograph, she could see him pulling on her. Like he wanted her. Like that moment in the car when his hand slipped under her skirt and he'd discovered her stockings. There was a good deal of feminine pride wrapped up in being able to surprise a man like Noah. Very few women had likely made such an impression.

Noah's phone rang. "I'm so sorry. I should get this. It's Charlotte." He pressed the button on the screen and jabbed his finger into his ear. "Hey. What's up?" He nodded and popped a French fry into his mouth. "Okay. Hold on." He handed the phone to Lily. "She wants to talk to you."

"About?"

"Something about shopping."

"Hello?"

"Lily, it's Charlotte. I'm wondering, and I'm not totally sure how to ask this, but do you have the right clothes for this trip?"

Lily had no clue what that might entail. Did she have nice clothes? Of course. She made a point of being impeccably dressed at work. Did she have fancy, expensive clothes? No. "I'm not sure. Noah hasn't told me anything about what we're going to be doing."

"I'm not surprised. I'm sure it's the last thing on his mind. Thankfully, it's the first thing on mine. I do not want you feeling unprepared. You should feel comfortable in the Hannaforts' world of big money and luxury. I'll take you shopping to be safe. Plus, Noah's paying."

"Does he know that?"

"Not yet."

Lily snickered. "Okay. When?"

"Now? I had a client cancel on me this afternoon and Michael is working late."

Lily glanced over at Noah. How anyone could look so smoking hot eating a sandwich was beyond her. And the way his lips curved around the glass? She'd never wished so badly to be an ice cube, to slide down and crash into his mouth. "You sure? You don't have to do this."

"Are you kidding? I live for stuff like this. Meet me at the Saks in midtown in thirty minutes?"

"I'll have to clear it with Noah first, I guess."

"I'm clearing it. If my brother says a peep, remind him that he's on thin ice with me right now. Plus, if you're going to be my pretend sister-in-law, we should spend more time together, don't you think?"

"Good idea." It was nice to think that Charlotte could be Lily's ally in this. She needed someone on her side who wasn't an impossibly handsome man. Noah wielded too much power as it was. "I'll see you in a bit." Lily returned Noah's phone. "Your sister's taking me shopping for clothes for the wedding, but she wants me to meet her in a little bit. Can you and Sawyer manage if I'm out of the office this afternoon?"

"I don't have much choice. When Charlotte decides something is going to happen, it does. Case in point, our engagement."

"She does seem like a force of nature."

"She's always been like that. Even when we were kids."

Lily had often wondered what it must've been like to grow up on the sprawling Locke estate out on Long Island. "What about you? What were you like?"

"Quiet. Uncoordinated."

"You're lying."

"I'm not. I was always the one in the background. Sawyer was the star. He was the better athlete. He had more girlfriends. He did better in school. Charlotte was the one who was in crisis or kicking up trouble." Noah sat back and draped his long arm across the back of the booth. Lily hadn't moved back after scooting closer, so they were only inches apart.

Lily sat there and stared at Noah, his admission still

plain on his face. "I can't even imagine you like that. It seems impossible."

"I assure you it's more than possible, it happened that way."

Lily was seeing Noah in an all-new way and she wasn't sure what to make of it. Noah always seemed like the cocky golden boy of the Locke family, while Sawyer was the strong type A oldest sibling. Maybe she'd read it all wrong.

Noah got yet another text. "This is why I hate my phone." He picked it up from the table, shaking his head when he read the message. "Sawyer needs me to get back to the office. You should take the car to meet Charlotte and I'll hop in a taxi." He flagged down the waiter and handed over his credit card to pay the check.

"You don't have to do that. It's only eight or nine blocks for me."

"What kind of fiancé would I be if I let you walk in those shoes?"

Lily had strong thoughts on the answer. Peter had once left her to walk to a gas station two miles away when her car broke down. She'd called and asked for his help, but he'd been at the gym and wanted to finish his workout first. Noah probably had no idea how impossibly sweet he was being right now. "I want to walk. But I sincerely appreciate the offer."

"Okay, but I'll pay for a cab if you change your mind." He signed the bill when the waiter returned it, then plucked the card from the leather folio and handed it to Lily. "Shopping is on me, too."

"You don't have to do that either. I have money."

"You never would've been in this situation if it wasn't for me."

Lily couldn't forget it. It was omnipresent in her brain. It would be interesting to see where exactly the idea resided once she was back from the Hannafort wedding and all was back to normal.

Noah walked Lily out to the car and opened the door before the driver had the chance. "Tell you what. I'll send my driver to Saks after he drops me at the office. Then you won't need to worry about getting back."

Again, he was being so sweet. "That would be great. I'll try to be quick."

"As much as Charlotte likes shopping, she does not dawdle. I predict you'll be done pretty fast."

"Good to know." Lily was about to head up Fifth Avenue when Noah grasped her elbow and pulled her closer. Her heart sprang into action, beating double time.

"I need to kiss you goodbye," he whispered. "Or else it will seem strange."

She nodded, her brain as fuzzy as could be. His words were saying one thing, while his lips were telling her yet another. The kiss was soft and sensuous. Much hotter than the first acquaintance kiss in the car or even the one at Tiffany. Had that really been that morning? So much had happened today and it was only two o'clock.

"Bye." She wished the tone of her voice didn't contain such longing.

"Bye, honey." Noah cocked an eyebrow and climbed into the back seat of the car.

Lily stood on the sidewalk for a moment, processing. She'd kissed Noah four times today. Not bad for a day's work.

She began her short trek up to Saks, winding her way through the continuous stream of pedestrians. The air was crisp and cool, but the promise of spring was in the air. It filled Lily with sunny optimism. Despite her strange arrangement with Noah, things weren't bad.

She approached Saks Fifth Avenue, with its stony facade

and procession of American flags flapping high above the famous windows. The displays, like the weather, were harkening the start of spring with flashes of pretty pastels and flowers. Lily marched through the door and nearly walked straight into Charlotte. "You're here already."

"I don't like to be late."

Lily pulled back the sleeve of her coat to consult her watch. She was still five minutes early. "Where to first?"

"Follow me." Through the sprawling cosmetics department, avoiding salespeople threatening spritzes of expensive perfume, up the escalators they went.

Lily had never even been in this store before, although she had been to the outlet a block or two away. It wasn't that Lily was averse to spending a lot of money on clothes. It was more the product of growing up in a very middle-class family. It wasn't something that was done. And she'd always acted accordingly.

Lily followed as Charlotte got off on one floor and started tooling around like this was a time trial. Even more than five months pregnant, Charlotte was hell on wheels. "For the record, we should not be doing this on such short notice. We leave in three days."

Lily hadn't thought of it in those terms, but Charlotte was right. They'd be leaving for the Florida Keys Friday morning, flying on the Locke private jet, no less. Talk about being plucked from one world and landing in another.

Lily trailed along as garments flew off the racks in the department of every classic high-end designer you could imagine. Escada. Chanel. Louis Vuitton. Each item was handed to a salesclerk named Delia, whom they'd acquired along the way. Delia smiled, but she was definitely struggling to keep up. It would've been hard for most people to stay on pace with Charlotte, even without being loaded down with an armful of clothes. Lily herself was testimony to that fact, shuffling along as Charlotte explained her thinking behind each wardrobe choice she made. A dress for this, a skirt and blouse for that.

"Are you sure you don't want to pick anything out?" Charlotte asked. "I don't want to take over your fashion life."

"I'll let you know if I see anything I love. I trust that you know what you're doing."

"I've been to weddings like this before, and you will end up needing several outfits each day. Plus, I don't know about you, but I feel better when I travel if I have a lot to choose from."

Lily nodded. She'd had a modest upbringing, but her parents had loved to schlep her and her brother on weekend trips when she was growing up. "Yeah. I get that. It seems like a lot of clothes. I don't want to go overboard when I'm not paying."

Charlotte's eyebrows popped up into high peaks. "For what you're doing, you deserve to be compensated well. Noah backed us into this corner in the first place."

"The video itself wasn't really his fault. How could he have known that would happen?"

"He couldn't. The tabloids aren't known for giving their prey a heads-up. But still. He's the one who decided he needed to date half of the women in the city."

"I suppose he wasn't doing himself any favors." Lily sighed. What exactly was Noah looking for? A good time? If so, it was working. He always seemed very content— lots of women, and plenty happy about it.

Charlotte took another gander at the department she'd upended. "Anything else?"

"I trust you. Completely." Charlotte had classic taste. Everything was fresh and modern, but not overly trendy.

Lily went into the dressing room while Charlotte waited in an adjacent lounge, chatting away on the phone while Lily tried on outfit after outfit, parading about and seeking Charlotte's two cents.

"That is gorgeous on you," Charlotte said when Lily stepped out in a flowing royal blue gown with skinny straps and a bit of a plunging neckline. "That's perfect for the wedding. A definite yes."

Lily turned in front of the large dressing mirror. "You think it works?"

"Yes. Just be careful when you're wearing it around Noah."

Lily felt good in this dress, but thinking about it in the context of Noah seeing her in it made her extremely nervous. "You think he won't like it?"

"I think he'll like it a little too much, but that's his problem." Charlotte shooed Lily back into the dressing room.

A half hour later, Lily had five new dresses, three pairs of pants, six or seven blouses, and a raging headache from being under fluorescent lights for too long. Delia took everything to the register. "Now what?" Lily asked.

"Shoes," Charlotte answered flatly.

"Seriously?"

"I promise it'll be quick."

Sure enough, as soon as they arrived in the shoe department, an enthusiastic salesman named Roger was waiting for them. Charlotte kissed him on both cheeks and introduced Lily. Charlotte had apparently called him ahead of time, because he presented Lily with some carefully curated options. "These are for travel. Can't go wrong with classic black pumps."

Talk about an undersell. Lily had never imagined she'd own a pair of Christian Louboutin shoes. "Gorgeous."

"These are some fun beachcomber sandals you can wear

with a sundress or going to the beach." He set aside the first two boxes and pulled out a third pair—sky-high, sparkly and strappy. Two-thousand-dollar Jimmy Choo heels. "Absolutely gorgeous."

"Well? I'm thinking you can wear them for the wedding," Charlotte said. "And before you say a thing about the price, that's not the question. I want to know if you like them."

"I love them. All of them. But especially the silver ones."

"Perfect. Let's get your size and we'll get out of here. Roger, can you bring these to Delia?"

"Absolutely."

Five minutes later, it was time to pay. Lily nearly fell over when she saw the total. "I still feel weird about this." She pulled Noah's credit card out of her purse and presented it to the clerk.

"Don't. This is part and parcel of your job this weekend. Not that you couldn't with your own clothes, but I think you'll have more fun if you have some new things."

"Okay. Thanks." Lily might have to wait for her guilt to subside. She wasn't an extravagant person.

They took Lily's packages and hopped on the escalator. As they rode down, Lily couldn't help but notice that Charlotte was studying her. "Is something wrong?" Lily asked.

"I think I should warn you ahead of time that my brother is almost guaranteed to try something this weekend."

"Try something?"

"Make a move. When you're alone."

"I'll be fine. I can handle Noah." Or so she hoped. The one time they'd been truly alone, in the back of his car, things got very hot and she'd lost her mind in no time at all.

"I'm sure you can. And I'm not saying he won't be a

gentleman, because I know he will. But I also know that he's the king of smooth. He'll be all smiles and kind gestures and compliments."

"Isn't that what all women want?"

"Precisely why he's so good at getting them. I don't see any way he passes up the chance to be with you, especially when you're staying in the same hotel room. I want you to be prepared."

Lily imagined herself as the most willing sitting duck in history. "It'll be fine. I'm not worried about it. We've been alone lots of times in the office and he's never been anything but professional."

Charlotte nodded, but there was skepticism behind her eyes. "I know. He's handsome and all that. It's fine if that's what you want. But know that whatever happens, it won't last. I don't want to see you get hurt."

They stepped off the escalator and rounded to descend to the ground floor. Lily was torn. There were a million reasons why Noah making a pass would be a bad thing—the sanctity of their working relationship, closely followed by the fragility of her own heart. She only wanted to believe in happy endings, and since she'd never had her own, it made her more gushy than most when it came to romance. A guy who only skirted it? He was a terrible idea.

But there was this part of her that was so drawn to Noah and his magic—his smile, the way he made her pulse race when he walked into a room. It was impossible not to want more of that. She couldn't help but want him, even when all logic said he wasn't attainable. The thought of one night with him was incredibly tempting. And after their one passionate kiss? When he'd run his hand up her skirt and they'd both lost all sense of decorum? Her most base impulse was to throw caution to the wind when it came to Noah.

But ultimately, she had to preserve not just her job, but her stake in Locke and Locke. Another job she could get. But if she wanted to make the most of that 1 percent? She needed to keep a very close eye on it. Anything less would be reckless and irresponsible.

Five

Ever organized, Lily was packed and ready to go thirty minutes early on Friday morning. She was dressed in a brand-new outfit, a wrap dress in coral pink, the new black pumps with the signature Louboutin red bottom and a sparkly necklace, bought on Noah's dime. If ever there'd been a time when she looked confident and felt nothing of the sort, today was the day. Expectations galore had been foisted upon her for this trip. She had to appear as if she were a woman befitting the handsome and wealthy Noah Locke. And good God it made her nervous.

After her chat with Charlotte at Saks, she forced herself to reframe her expectations. At that point on Tuesday, a day into her role of fake fiancée, she'd started relishing the part where she got to kiss and touch Noah a little too much. She needed to remind herself why she had no business getting her hopes up about Noah, but she hadn't figured out how to shock herself into the right frame of mind. Then it came to her that morning in the shower. She needed to watch the video. She needed to see firsthand what was not only horribly embarrassing, but painfully true.

With twenty more minutes until she had to leave, she sat down at her home computer. An internet search quickly produced what she needed. Since it had first run, the video had been picked up by a spate of gossipy websites. Noah's dirty laundry was everywhere.

She pushed Play, sat back in her chair and crossed her arms over her chest. The voice-over started right away. *Big Apple businessman, Noah Locke, of the Locke hotel family, has been busy with the ladies over the last several months. And do we mean busy.* Then came the barrage of images. Noah's taste in women was hard to pin down— she'd give him that much, but there was no question that he was indeed a ladies' man. Some were curvy, some were rail-thin. Some were statuesque, others petite.

Lily took each image as it came. She was tough. The women in Noah's life were a fact. She'd known this about him all along. Still, being confronted with the visual evidence created a stabbing sensation in her chest. It's one thing to hear about a disaster, like a tornado ripping its way through a town, and quite another to see the footage of the actual devastation.

The worst of it was everything they said about him— that he was just as much of a womanizer as his dad and that he treated women as if they meant nothing. Lily was certain the former wasn't true, but she wasn't so sure about the latter. Judging by the breadth of Noah's female companions, it seemed safe to say that he saw no point in settling down.

Lily powered off her computer. Why should Noah have to decide anything? Handsome, single and wealthy afforded him the freedom to do whatever he wanted. Why should anyone deny him what was his to have if he so chose? The women in Noah's rotation had to have known what they were walking into when they agreed to go out with him. The rumor mill in the city was fierce. They had to know that Noah Locke was not the guy you get serious with. He was a fantasy, and a stunning one at that, but he wasn't for keeps.

Lily's phone beeped with a text.

We're here. Do you need help with your bags?

She replied to Noah.

I'm good. I'll be right down.

However rattled she might be by having watched the video, she was glad she'd done it. It was a solid reminder of what this weekend was about—a business transaction designed to convince Lyle Hannafort that Noah could be trusted. Lily was a prop, and nothing more.

She opened the door and reached for the handle on her roller bag when Noah appeared.

"Morning." Everything about him—his deep voice, his penetrating gaze and his casual confidence—stopped her dead in her tracks.

Prop, meet your date for the next three days, Mr. Tall, Suave and Smoking Hot. "How'd you get into the building?"

"One of your neighbors was coming out. I didn't want you to have to carry down your own bag." Noah reached for her suitcase, his arm brushing her shoulder. "Ready?"

Was she ready? An entire weekend of getting to look at him, hold hands with him, kiss him in front of other people, all while knowing it wasn't real? There was no way this wasn't going to leave a dent in her sense of self. "Yes."

"Got your ring?"

She presented her hand, which seemed like the normal response, but he had to go and cup her fingers, lifting them for further inspection. "It really is stunning. It suits you."

As to whether he was inferring that she was also stunning or merely that it did its job in giving her the appearance of a woman of substance, Lily was unable to determine. She knew only that her heart pinged around in her chest. "It's gorgeous." *You're gorgeous.* "Thank you."

Noah took her bag, Lily locked up and they made their way downstairs. His driver rushed over to them, taking Lily's suitcase and placing it in the back of the car. She climbed inside, followed by Noah.

"Won't take us long to get out to Teterboro," Noah said, referring to the small airport in New Jersey popular for private and corporate planes. "I hope it's okay, but I need to make some work calls."

"Please. Go ahead." This was perfect—he'd work and so could she. Lily sat back in her seat and opened her email on her phone. Her job was her ace in the hole. She didn't question herself when it came to that.

She responded to messages about several Locke and Locke projects, all commercial properties, one a renovation and the others new construction. One of Lily's primary responsibilities was to communicate with the general contractors and make sure they were on schedule and on budget. It was the nuts and bolts of the entire operation and freed up Noah and Sawyer to focus on long-term strategy, including deals like Hannafort Hotels.

She didn't take Noah's and Sawyer's trust lightly. Crucial and sometimes sensitive information came across her desk every day. She appreciated that they had no qualms about trusting her with it. Now that she had a stake in the company, her job was even more important to her. If ever there was a reason to stay on the straight and narrow this weekend, that was it. Being Noah's fake fiancée was simply another part of her job. Unconventional for sure, but if she looked at it like that, in three days, she'd have her nest egg, and an even bigger chunk of Noah's and Sawyer's confidence. As long as she kept her heart and her libido out of it, she'd be fine.

They arrived at Teterboro and the driver pulled through the security gate back to where the Locke private jet was waiting. Charlotte and Michael were climbing the stairs to board. Lily had arranged for the jet a few times, but she had yet to go anywhere on it. Scenes like this had never been part of her life, although she'd sure read about them in books. As much as most stories came alive in her mind, living it was surreal. Everything was moving in slow motion.

"Anything we need to go over before we get on the plane?" she asked, if only to keep herself wedged in reality.

"About?"

"You know. Us. We never had a conversation about getting our stories straight. You got called to that meeting after we bought my ring and I went shopping with Charlotte. Things in the office have been crazy the last few days. We haven't talked about it at all."

"It's pretty straightforward, isn't it? You came to work for us and we became close and there was an attraction and one thing led to another."

This was *not* helping Lily keep her head in the game. Her mind was too drawn to the many memories of times she and Noah had flirted at work. He'd flash his green eyes at her and make a joke. She'd laugh and smack his arm. And then next thing she knew, she was fantasizing about ripping his shirt off. "That works."

"We know each other so well, I think we can fake our way through it pretty easily."

"Of course."

The driver opened the door and Noah climbed out. Lily scooted across the seat and looked up to see Noah put on his sunglasses. He turned and offered his hand. Her skin touching his instantly put her off her game. It led her mind in too many hopeful and delusional directions, but she would've been lying if she'd said she didn't enjoy it. They walked across the tarmac, a stiff breeze blowing her hair from her face and rustling her coat. It was run-of-the-mill brisk weather for early April in New York, but she was glad for it. The crisp blast helped keep her wits about her. Noah kept rubbing the back of her hand with his thumb. He stopped at the bottom of the airplane stairs, letting her go first. Taking each step, she reminded herself to relax. She'd be fine once she was settled in her seat.

The interior of the plane was straight out of a movie— pure luxury with white leather seats, white carpet and chrome accents. A flight attendant was hanging coats in a closet. The chairs were clustered in fours, pairs facing each other with a table in between. Charlotte and her husband, Michael, were seated across from Sawyer and Kendall. They all waved and said hi, but they quickly returned to their conversation. That left Lily and Noah to sit together across the aisle.

The flight attendant breezed over. "Please, let me take your coats." The woman hardly looked at Lily, her eyes were so trained on Noah. Lily was used to his effect on women. She endured it every day, although before they'd become fake engaged, she'd tried to think of it as a perk, not a test.

"Want the window?" Noah asked.

"Oh, sure."

Lily took her seat and Noah settled in next to her. Charlotte leaned across the aisle. "How's the happy couple this morning?"

"Great," Noah responded. "Couldn't be better."

Charlotte smiled. "Perfect. You look amazing in that dress, Lily."

Noah turned to Lily and in the light streaming in from the window, his eyes were especially entrancing. "Better than amazing. You look perfect."

Out of the corner of her eye, Lily could see the look on Charlotte's face. It was exactly the same one she'd given her on the escalator at Saks. Noah was doing everything she'd said he would and Lily needed to prepare herself. At some point this weekend, Noah was going to make his move.

The flight time from New York to Key West was just under three hours—long enough for Noah to gain a full understanding of exactly how challenging this weekend was going to be. He not only had a front row seat to Lily in that mind-blowing dress, he had his siblings and their spouses watching. He could tell they were scrutinizing everything he and Lily did—talking and drinking champagne, chatting about work, Noah leaning closer to Lily when looking out the window on their approach into Key West. He hated it. They were all in love, they'd all found their soul mates, and they all knew he was faking it.

The instant Noah stepped off the plane in Florida, the humidity and tropical breezes wrapped around him, and he had the most unexpected response. He relaxed. His spine got a little looser, and as he put on his sunglasses, he warmed his face in the sun. They weren't in New York anymore. Noah hadn't realized how much he'd been hating the city until the salt air filled his nose and his view became nothing more than palm trees rustling in the wind. He took Lily's hand as they walked down the stairs, an action that had already become second nature. The timing was perfect. It was showtime.

A black stretch SUV emblazoned with the Hannafort Hotels logo was waiting on the tarmac to take them for the hour-long drive to Key Marly, the private island where the newest Hannafort resort was located. Lily and Noah sat next to each other on one of the long cushy black leather seats.

"I can't wait to see Key Marly. It's supposed to be incredible." Charlotte folded up her sunglasses and placed them in their case. "Private cabanas with plunge pools and everything."

Sawyer eagerly nodded in agreement. "This wedding is a prime example of why we need to be working with Lyle. The man is a marketing genius. He rolls out his brand-new resort with a private sneak preview weekend for his closest friends and business associates."

"All while his daughter gets married on the company dime, I'm guessing." Michael put his arm around Charlotte and tugged her closer.

"Exactly," Sawyer added.

All Noah could think as he looked over his shoulder at an outside landscape of funky shops and restaurants, with peeks of pristine ocean stretches, was that Lyle might be a genius for an entirely different reason. This was paradise.

When they arrived on Little Torch Key, they were taken to a gated dock where a gleaming white cabin cruiser was waiting. Luggage and passengers transferred, they skimmed through the calm crystal-blue water inside a luxury cabin with 360-degree views. The air-conditioning was a nice break from the heat and they were offered all manner of drinks and snacks by the attentive staff, but Noah was itching for a less contained experience.

"Do you want to go stand out on the deck and look at the ocean?" he asked Lily.

She nearly sprang out of her seat. "Yes."

As soon as they walked through the cabin doors, the sights, sounds and smells of untamed ocean took over, and Noah couldn't have been any happier. "It was driving me crazy in there."

"Me, too. It's way too beautiful to be sitting inside. I don't know how anyone could stand to sit in there and listen to that horrible elevator music they were playing anyway."

"Yes. The music. Terrible." Lyle might be a genius, but some aspects of his operation could stand some refining.

Noah and Lily both leaned against the railing, wind and sun in their faces as the boat approached Key Marly, a dot of an island straight ahead, a thick stand of tropical trees and foliage atop a sliver of silvery sand. Noah couldn't help but fantasize about Locke and Locke moving away from high-rises and into resorts. He could imagine an office on the beach, where he could take his laptop outside whenever he wanted, curl his toes into the sand and set up shop on a lounge chair. The best of both worlds. Of course, if he was working, he could only imagine it with Lily there, perhaps sitting right next to him, where they could discuss work and they could enjoy each other's company as much as they did now.

But could there be more between them? Could that dream scenario include things like love and romance? In his head, he wasn't sure. He wanted to see himself like that, but his mind refused to make the leap. The whole thing seemed like nothing more than a fantasy. The risk of their romantic involvement was too great. Forget that his own brother and sister didn't trust him not to break her heart, Noah didn't trust himself. He knew that panicky feeling he got when things started to get serious. He had no idea how to ever ward it off and Lily deserved better.

"It's so ridiculously beautiful." Lily peered down at the water as it rushed by.

Noah watched her instead, unable to keep from noticing how sexy it was when she tucked her hair behind her ear to tame it. *You're so beautiful.* He wanted to say it. He should say it. But he couldn't toy with her heart. He couldn't explain later that yes, he'd meant it, but he wasn't capable of following through. "It really is, isn't it?"

"I can't wait until we get there and I can take off these shoes and run around in my bare feet and stick my toes in the water."

"We're supposed to have our own plunge pool if you want to cool off." He suspected how ill equipped he was for the moment when he'd first see Lily in a bathing suit, but he couldn't take the suggestion back now.

"I vote for both ocean and pool if we can."

"I couldn't agree more."

A few minutes later, the boat pulled up to the Key Marly Resort dock. A line of uniformed bellmen were on hand to take their bags. At the end of the gangway, Mr. and Mrs. Hannafort were waiting. Even from a distance, Lyle Hannafort was an imposing man. He was about as tall as Noah, who was six feet three inches, but Lyle's broad frame was nearly twice as wide. He had a bowling ball bald head and a dark mustache. Lyle's wife, Marcy, was hardly five feet tall, and slim. With a thick mane of raven hair and her signature bright red lipstick, in many ways Marcy made just as much of an impression as her husband.

Noah and Lily were so excited to get to their cabana that they were first off the boat. He took her hand as they traversed the wood-planked surface, but her enthusiasm had turned to trembling. He leaned closer and whispered in her ear, inhaling a heady mix of her sweet perfume and ocean air. "We're in this together. It'll be okay."

She smiled up at him, sunglasses glinting in the sunshine, and squeezed his hand a little harder. "The dynamic duo."

Lyle Hannafort held out his hand to shake Noah's. "Nice to see you, Noah. Is this the young lady I've heard about?"

Noah didn't particularly like the idea of presenting Lily as if she were some sort of prize, but that seemed to be what was warranted. "Yes, Lyle, I'd like you to meet Lily Foster, my fiancée."

"Good to meet you, Lily. This is my wife, Marcy."

Marcy glommed right on to Lily, grabbing both of her hands and craning her neck to make eye contact. "Lily, darling, I am so happy to meet you. Let me see that ring. I heard about it in the newspapers, you know. Lyle showed me the picture. We were so glad to hear your happy news. I told Lyle that I really hoped that awful tabloid story about Noah wasn't true. I'm so glad to know they were just spreading rumors."

Noah wanted to hate that this had all started over a misunderstanding, but the truth was that if it hadn't happened, Lily would be home right now and he'd be attending this wedding stag while he watched his siblings carry on with their happy coupled lives. Every time he looked at Sawyer and Charlotte, he wanted to think that it meant he could find that kind of partner someday, too, but it felt too much like confirmation that two of the three Locke kids had cheated their family's marital curse and he'd better not press his luck.

"Mrs. Hannafort, that was not the real Noah. I hope you know that."

Lily's voice was as emphatic as could be, but Noah was stuck on her words. He *was* the guy in that video. They hadn't said a single untrue thing. And maybe he was like his father, which he didn't want to be. That left him even more convinced that he must be an absolute gentleman with Lily this weekend. They would put on the show of doting couple when they were in public, but in private? He would keep his hands to himself. He would sleep on the couch. On the floor, if needed. Lily would know exactly how much he respected her as a partner in Locke and Locke. She would know he revered her as a business-person and a friend. He would suppress his more lustful feelings. He wouldn't think about what it was like to kiss those petal-soft lips. He would try very hard to erase all memory of his hand on her thigh and his thumb rubbing across the lacy top of her stockings.

Marcy patted Lily's hand. "Of course that's not the real Noah. And it doesn't even matter, does it? You're getting married. That's all you need to think about right now."

Lily smiled thinly. "Yes. I know."

Married. Funny, but Noah had only thought about their arrangement in terms of being engaged. After this weekend and the deal was done, they'd quietly call it off.

"I want you both to know that we've taken extra good care of our newly engaged couple for this weekend," Marcy said.

"Indeed we have," Lyle added. "The staff knows to give you two the royal treatment. We don't want you to miss out on a single romantic moment."

"That really isn't necessary." Noah cleared his throat when he realized how quickly he'd blurted his response. "I mean, thank you, but don't go out of your way."

Lily elbowed him in the stomach. "It sounds truly lovely. Thank you so much."

Sawyer and Kendall walked up behind them and Noah took the chance to get away. They followed a bellman along a circular wood-planked walkway, which had paths spoking off to the individual thatch-roofed bungalows. Off in the distance, in a clearing, was the larger main building of the resort, which was presumably where much of the wedding would take place.

Noah and Lily were in bungalow eight. They entered a stone-tiled foyer that opened up into an expansive sitting room with high wood-beamed ceilings and a fan whirring overhead. On the coffee table in front of the sofa was a bottle of champagne on ice and a beautiful arrangement of tropical flowers in purple, orange and pink. There was even a note.

Don't forgot to put out the Do Not Disturb sign!
Love, Marcy.

"What does it say?" Lily plucked the card from his hand.

It says that I'm in deep trouble. He only wished that he could put out the Do Not Disturb sign and leave it there for days. *That* would be a vacation.

She smiled and put it next to the champagne bucket. "That was very thoughtful of her."

"Yes."

"Let's check out the rest." Lily led the way into the master bedroom. They both gasped when they stepped inside—through a full wall of accordion doors open to the ocean air was a small black-bottomed plunge pool surrounded by a lush garden. Beyond it was a full view of the stunning turquoise sea. The bedroom had a sprawling king bed with crisp white linens and mosquito netting draped overhead. "It looks like something out of a magazine or a movie. We can sleep with the windows open."

Noah nearly laughed. This place was perfect. If he were to take Lily somewhere to seduce her, this would be the ideal place. They wouldn't even still be wearing clothes right now. The special allure of hotel sex was too great and in a setting like this? It would be impossible to not be in the mood. Too bad that wasn't going to happen.

"I can sleep on the couch out in the living room." He stared at the bed, trying not to imagine Lily lying on it, waiting for him.

"No. It's too small. I'll sleep there."

"I'm not letting you sleep on the couch. That hardly seems fair. I'm the one who got us into this."

"We can't call the front desk and ask them to bring in a rollaway. Then they'll know the jig is up."

Noah sat down at the foot of the bed. Lily sat right next to him. They were inches apart, both staring out at the water. He glanced over at her, noticing for the one hundredth time that day how exquisite she was in that dress. He would have emptied his entire bank account to kiss her. He racked his brain for any lame excuse to revisit the notion of practicing.

"Compromise," Lily said. "We're both adults. It's a big bed. We sleep together. I will keep to my side. You won't need to worry about me."

Why was fate being so delightfully cruel to Noah? "Are you sure?"

"Absolutely." She patted him on the thigh, sending a sizzle straight to his groin. "Now let's change into our swimsuits and get into the water."

Six

In her aqua-blue bikini, Lily stretched out on the chaise lounge next to the plunge pool. She soaked up the day's fading rays, running her hand back and forth across her bare stomach. From behind her sunglasses she kept one eye peeled on Noah. He was floating in the plunge pool, resting his arms on the side with his back turned to her. She was pretty convinced by now. Something was up. There was no way she was the one woman on the planet Noah did not find attractive.

Still, he'd had a zillion opportunities to make a move and he hadn't taken the bait. Not when she'd asked him to put sunscreen on her back, not when she'd splashed him playfully in the pool, not when she'd made a comment about how good he looked in his black board shorts. If anything, it felt like he was trying to keep her away, which made no sense. Charlotte had said he was guaranteed to make a pass. And Lily would never forget the curl of his fingers in the paparazzi photo of them at Tiffany. He'd wanted her in that picture. She'd seen the evidence.

She propped up on her elbows and watched him. This view of his shoulders was nothing short of spectacular— every sexy contour and rounded muscle you could imagine. Noah was not overly built, but he was in excellent shape. "You're going to prune if you don't get out soon," she said, invoking a seductive inflection. This was the perfect opportunity for him to turn and get an eyeful, but he only made a cursory glance before diving under the water. That was it. He was practically daring her to make the first move. But he was her boss. If only she wasn't so concerned with keeping her job.

He broke the water's surface, planted his hands on the edge of the pool and hoisted himself out. He was a dripping wet Adonis. Every firm inch of him was glistening in the sun. They'd been in Florida for only a few hours and he was already tan. He grabbed a towel from a stack near the patio doors to their room and ruffled his hair. Lily had an irrational desire to walk over and help him with everything else that was in need of drying, especially that spot on his lower stomach, right below his belly button, where the narrow trail of hair led beneath the waistband of his board shorts. There were only two words to describe that part of him: *Yum. Oh.*

"We should probably get ready for dinner, don't you think?" he asked. "I'll hop in the shower first if you want a few more minutes out here." He wouldn't even look at her. And it was driving Lily up the wall.

"You go ahead. I need to figure out what I'm wearing anyway."

"Sounds like a plan." With that, he disappeared.

Lily flopped back onto the chair and groaned. This frustration was impossible. She wanted Noah so bad she could spit. But it was a terrible idea. She'd thought this trip might give her an out—he could make a pass, she could enthusiastically acquiesce, they could give each other a few amazing memories, and then they'd go back to the way things had been before. She already knew Noah was capable of that. As for herself, she wasn't certain she could pull it off, but she'd lived with far worse heartbreak. She'd been dumped at her own wedding. Nothing would ever be as horrendous as that.

Lily got up from her chair, put on her cover-up, traipsed back inside and flipped through the dresses in the closet, choosing a gauzy black maxi dress with skinny straps. It was the perfect sexy beach dress and she could wear flats with it, which would be nice and comfy.

Noah came out of the bathroom, wearing one of the white waffle-weave towels the resort provided. Lily was far too aware of what else he was wearing. Nothing. "The bathroom is all yours."

Lily decided another test was in order. She pulled her cover-up over her head and walked right up to Noah, planting her hand on his cheek. His stubble scratched her palm as she peered up into his eyes. He was so beautiful it made her chest ache. "I think your scruff could use some neatening up. It's getting a bit scraggly."

"Really?" His eyebrows drew together.

"You want to look your best for the Hannaforts. You can use the bathroom while I shower." Maybe a trial like this would be enough to push him over the edge.

"I really don't think that's appropriate. The shower has glass walls."

Sure enough, he flunked the test. Or passed with flying colors, depending on which side you were on. "Fine. Go ahead and finish up. I'll wait."

She plopped down on the end of the bed, resigned to

her fate. There would be no fun between her and Noah. At least she could triumphantly tell Charlotte she was wrong.

A moment later, Noah was done, looking as perfect as could be. "Better?"

No. "Much." She snatched up her dress and the rest of her clothes, and breezed past him into the bathroom. She took her shower, deciding to focus on the night ahead. It was better to worry about impressing the Hannaforts, rather than the endless cycle of Noah sex thoughts rifling through her brain.

Hair up in a towel, she slipped into her dress and turned in front of the mirror. Like Noah, she'd gotten a good amount of sun today. Quite frankly, she looked amazing in this dress. Such a waste. Noah wasn't even going to notice.

Noah put on a pair of black dress pants and a French blue dress shirt. *Keep it together, buddy. You can do this.* Only he was sure he couldn't do this. Being around Lily wasn't merely a test of his willpower, it was the Iditarod of chastity. Spending the morning with her on the plane was one thing, but he had not been prepared for the moment she'd stepped out onto the patio in her bikini and he'd had no choice but to jump straight into the plunge pool with no warning.

"Really wanted to go swimming, huh?" she'd asked.

"It's way too hot out here." He'd looked at her for a few seconds too long, his eyes traveling the length of her body, up from her feet to the swell of her hips and the gentle nip of her waist, to the round lusciousness of her breasts. He would've given up a year of his life to have had the chance to kiss her and press against her while she was wearing that bathing suit, but he knew where that ended—both of them naked in that beautiful bed under the mosquito netting. If he was going to ruin everything, he might as well go down in a blaze of glory, but no. He had a lot to prove to himself. He wasn't like his dad. He had to be strong.

"Noah?" Lily called from the bathroom. "I need help. I can't get this necklace clasp."

"Sure thing. Two secs." Maybe she'd be wearing a frumpy Hawaiian muumuu to dinner. *Please be frumpy. Please be frumpy.* He stepped into the bathroom and got his answer. Her dress was flowing and delicate, with a low back and a slit up one leg. She had her hair pulled to one side, and was holding the ends of the necklace at the nape of her neck.

"I hope you can get it. The clasp is tiny and so is the link it's supposed to go into. Your fingers might be too big."

He stepped behind her, taking the silvery chain, fumbling like a fool as he drew in her sweet smell and wished they didn't have to go anywhere tonight. Again and again, he missed with the hook of the clasp. His hands were slick with sweat. His pulse was thumping in his ears. His knuckles grazed the velvety skin of her neck, drilling electricity right into him. Finally, he hooked the clasp. He dropped the necklace like it was on fire, stepping back abruptly.

"Thanks," she said, shooting him a quizzical look via the mirror.

"No problem." He ducked out of the bathroom, thinking of icebergs and blizzards. That was the only way he'd make it through his evening with Lily.

They left their room and headed down the walkway, under the canopy of palm trees down to the main resort building. This was no high-rise hotel but rather three sprawling stories of exclusivity, containing a mere eight suites. Along with only twenty individual cabanas on the island, guests could enjoy a quiet and tranquil stay.

Noah and Lily followed the signs for the rehearsal dinner, which led them down a crushed stone path through a lush tropical garden to the pool area behind the hotel. The multilevel expanse of stone, water and plants seemed to go on forever, with waterfalls, spas and places to swim. A few folks were still partaking of the pool. Everyone else was milling about, enjoying a cocktail and the balmy night air. Noah took Lily's hand and they walked over to where Lyle and Marcy were chatting with a small group of people. Still no sign of Charlotte, Michael, Sawyer or Kendall.

"There's my favorite newly engaged couple." Marcy practically squealed with delight. "Did you enjoy the champagne I sent to your room?"

"We haven't had a chance to drink it yet," Noah answered. It had been his call to stick the bottle in the fridge. Popping that cork could've led to any number of poor choices. "But thank you so much. It was very thoughtful."

"Anything to make you all feel comfortable and welcome. I hope you enjoy what the staff has for you when you get back to your room tonight. I think you'll find it very romantic." Marcy nodded with a conspiratorial grin.

Lily looked at Noah, her eyes sweeping across his face as if she were trying to gauge his reaction. He had no idea how to respond to this revelation. He could only imagine what Marcy had in store, but one thing was certain—everything about their circumstances was made to sexually frustrate the hell out of him. "I can't wait to see it."

"I'd ask you to report back tomorrow, but I don't think I need to know the details." Marcy smiled wide. "Now if you'll excuse me, I need to visit with some of my other guests."

"I wonder what the surprise is," Lily said. "Chocolate-covered strawberries?"

"Probably. The usual clichéd trappings of engagement."

Lily's mouth formed a thin line. "You might think it's clichéd, but I think it sounds quite nice. Plus, there are worse things than someone leaving chocolate-covered fruit in your room."

"I know. You're right." *It's just that I'm going to want to feed it to you and take off your clothes and that was not part of my plan for this wedding.* "Let's go mingle."

Over the course of the next several hours, Noah and Lily met nearly every member of the extended Hannafort family. Lyle's parents, then Marcy's, as well as cousins and aunts and uncles. They had a lovely tropical-themed meal served poolside. Lily was a big hit, making sparkling conversation with the other guests and impressing everyone with her knowledge of everything from real estate development to romance novels. She even told Lyle's uncle a few off-color jokes that made him belly laugh and declare Noah the luckiest son of a bitch he'd ever met.

As the sun set and the sky turned darker, torches blazed and flickered. The waterfalls were lit with dramatic effect. The ocean breezes blew, and although the air cooled, it never lost that warm and humid feeling.

"I'm really tired. Let's go back to the room," Lily said.

It was ten o'clock and most of the guests had left. Noah had been putting off their departure, going back for seconds on key lime pie and ordering one last drink. He couldn't stomach the thought of what their romantic surprise might be. Surely something that was only going to make his charge that much more difficult. "You sure you're ready? It's so beautiful out tonight."

"Fine. You stay. I'll go back by myself." Lily got up from her chair.

"No. No. I don't want you walking by yourself." He reached for her hand, and she turned back, stealing his breath from his chest. She was so breathtakingly beautiful in this light, with the wind blowing her hair across her shoulders and her skin glowing with a gorgeous peachy tan.

"I couldn't possibly be in a safer place. And it's pretty obvious that you'd rather be here and not alone with me."

His stalling had been transparent, probably a little too much so. There was a very hurt edge to her voice that he disliked greatly. "I was enjoying myself with you tonight. That's all." He smiled. However much he wanted to create distance between them, he didn't want her to think he didn't enjoy her company. He did. He simply enjoyed it too much. He got up from his chair and took her hand. "Come on. Let's go see what over-the-top thing Marcy has waiting for us."

They took their time on their walk, listening to the birds in the trees and the gentle lap of the ocean off in the distance. Lily dropped his hand and traced her fingers along the inside of his arm, snugging him closer. He knew he should've ignored it, but he didn't want to. He put his arm around her shoulder and let her lean into him as they took the final steps to the front door.

When they walked inside, there was no sign of romance in the seating area where the bottle of champagne had been left earlier. "Huh. I wonder if they forgot."

Lily walked ahead of him into the bedroom. "Oh my God, Noah. In here. It's unbelievable."

He braced himself and followed her. The lights in their bedroom were off, but a warm glow came from the glass doors to outside. Hundreds of candles were lit out on the patio around the plunge pool. Even more were floating in the water. The bed had been turned down, and purple orchid blossoms were strewn all over the duvet. Another bottle of champagne was on ice next to the bed, and a tray was next to it with coconut massage oil. He couldn't have arranged a more romantic, sexy setting if he'd wanted to.

"Marcy wasn't kidding," Lily said.

"It's going to take forever to clean this up." He felt like

such an ass the instant the words left his mouth. Lily deserved every romantic delight before them and he was raining on her parade.

She cast a disappointed look at him. "We can't really call housekeeping and ask them to take care of it. Anyone who knows this is here thinks that our clothes are off by now. They think I'm giving you a sensuous massage. They think we're making love."

As imagined visions of Lily naked, her hands all over him, wound through his consciousness, desire and determination battled inside him. He wanted her more than he'd wanted any woman. She was right there. Mere inches from him. What if he took her in his arms right now and kissed her? What if they did everything that logically came out of this quixotic setting? Would it really hurt anything?

"You know," Lily started.

Noah held his breath. Was she about to give him an out? Tell him that they had to go through with it, lest housekeeping rat them out?

"Charlotte would be laughing her butt off if she saw this right now. She told me you were going to make a pass at me. She said you couldn't help yourself. This whole thing with the candles and the flowers and the champagne seems like they're practically daring you to do it."

And there he had his answer. Charlotte expected him to do that because he'd always done that, and their father had always done it, as well. He wanted no more assumptions made about him. His thirst for Lily only felt so potent because he'd been tortured for two years. What was another night or two? "My sister thinks she knows me, but she doesn't. You said it yourself that I'm not the guy in that video. I am not only capable of being a gentleman, it is my full intention to be exactly that."

Lily walked over to the head of the bed and lifted a corner of the duvet. "Fine. But we still have to make it look like you aren't." She grabbed the edge of the duvet and with a dramatic flick of her wrists, the orchid blossoms popped into the air, most of which fluttered to the floor. "I'm going to wash my face and brush my teeth. It's been a long day and I'm tired." She sauntered into the bathroom, leaving Noah to wonder how this all got even more messed up than it had seemed in New York.

He flopped back on the bed, staring up at the ceiling. Lily was going to be back soon. To sleep in the same bed with him. And he had to make sure absolutely nothing happened. Even if it killed him.

Seven

Lily made it through the night. She made it through waking up next to Noah, and having breakfast with him. She'd lived through an entire morning and part of the afternoon together, ignoring his good looks and the lack of passes made. She'd taken it all in stride, but now that she was dressed for the wedding, in the royal blue dress that Noah probably wouldn't even notice, she needed to take the edge off. She simply had too much baggage when it came to "I do."

There were three bottles of champagne in their fridge—one from yesterday, one from last night after the rehearsal dinner and a third that had shown up with that morning's room service alongside a beautiful tropical fruit platter and some omelets. They hadn't ordered the bubbly, but Marcy and Lyle had sent it anyway. They were apparently highly invested in Noah and Lily's engagement. At least someone was. Noah had shown no interest in at least enjoying their odd predicament in paradise.

And Lily was sick of it.

Pop. She waited until the wispy mist had trailed out of the bottle before pouring herself a glass of glorious golden bubbles.

"Oh. You decided to open one," Noah said, walking into the room all dressed for the wedding. He looked perfect, of course. Whomever had designed the modern-day men's suit had clearly had Noah in mind when they'd come up with the idea. He was straight out of the pages of a magazine.

"Can't let all this champagne go to waste."

"We could pour it out before we leave."

Lily took a sip. The effervescent sweetness was delightful on her lips and tongue. It was quite frankly the first blip of pleasure she'd had in the last several hours. Being around Noah was killing her. "We are not pouring this out. It's way too good. In fact, I'm pouring you a glass right now." She didn't bother to wait for his response. Maybe it would loosen him up a little bit.

"Fair enough." He took a sip and nodded. "Okay. You're right. It's delicious. We should drink every drop."

"That's the spirit." Lily felt so much better. This was the Noah she adored. If he was going to make her crazy, at least he could be a little more fun about it. Still, his strange attitude yesterday and that morning was eating at her. "Can I ask you a question? Did I do something to make you mad? You haven't been yourself at all since we got here. We're in paradise, but you don't seem like you're having any fun."

He took another sip and stared down at his shoes, his hair slumping forward. "I'm stressed about the Hannafort deal. I feel like so much of it rests on our shoulders and it doesn't really seem fair. It also doesn't seem right. He wants to do business with us because he thinks I'm the sort of guy who wants to get married. How messed up is that?"

"It's very messed up, but it's his call. So we go with it. But the part I don't understand is that you said we were in this together. It doesn't feel like that anymore. You're avoiding me and it's really starting to hurt my feelings." It felt so much better to get that off her chest. Even if Noah told her she was overreacting, at least she'd said her piece. "If there's something else going on, please tell me."

He downed the last of his champagne and bunched his lips together. He was clearly deep in thought. "It's hard to be around you sometimes, Lily. You're a very beautiful woman. I like you a lot. But you're also extremely important to our company. Sawyer would have my head if I touched you. And quite frankly, I'd be more than a little disappointed in myself. So, yeah. There have been a few moments in the last twenty-four hours that were more than I'd bargained on."

Lily wasn't sure she was still breathing anymore. Her brain was sucking up all the oxygen her body needed. That wasn't quite the response she'd been expecting. "Wow."

He shook his head. "I shouldn't have said anything. I'm sorry."

Lily reached out and grasped his hand. Touching his skin felt as though she'd completed a circuit and electricity was now free to zip back and forth between their bodies. "No. Noah. I'm glad you said something. I'm just taking it all in. I was starting to wonder if you found me unattractive."

"No. Quite the opposite."

Heat rose in her cheeks. "If it makes you feel any better, I'm just as frustrated. You're way too hot to be fake engaged to."

He laughed, and unleashed his megawatt smile. "You're funny."

She would've done anything to kiss him right then and there, but she knew she wouldn't be able to stop if she started something. "Not really what I was going for, but thanks."

Noah's phone beeped with a text, pulling them both out of the moment. He fished his cell from his pocket. "It's Charlotte. She and Michael are saving us seats. We should probably go."

Lily slugged down the last of her champagne, jammed the cork back into the bottle and put it in the fridge. "No matter what, you and I are sharing the rest of that bottle later tonight. Out on the beach."

The surprise on Noah's face was priceless. She should catch him off guard more often. "Yes, ma'am."

They held hands during the short walk to the ceremony, which was in the garden on the far side of the pool area. White chairs were set up in orderly rows with sprays of tropical flowers hanging from the back of each seat. A satin runner ran up the aisle between the two sections, nearly filled with guests, and at the very end sat a beautiful bamboo archway covered in orchids and lilies with a waterfall behind as the crowning touch. It was a gorgeous sight, picture-perfect, and everything a bride could ever want. Lily decided to start pricing everything out in her head, to keep her mind from wandering to bad memories. She'd planned her own wedding right down to the guest favors and the fondant icing. She knew exactly how much all of this cost or at least she knew the ballpark. Lyle and Marcy Hannafort were sparing no expense.

Noah and Lily found Charlotte and Michael. "Where are Sawyer and Kendall?" Noah asked.

"Kendall hasn't been feeling well since dinner last

night. I don't know if they're even going to make it for the ceremony."

"I hope everything's okay," Lily said.

"I think so. She said the baby is kicking like crazy and Mr. Hannafort had a doctor friend check on her this morning. They're making sure she gets lots of fluids and some rest," Charlotte said.

Noah grumbled and crossed his legs.

"Everything okay?" Lily muttered into his ear, taking her chance to inhale his cologne.

"Yeah. It just irks me when Sawyer doesn't let me know what's going on. I hate that Kendall is sick and I didn't know anything about it. What if it's something serious?"

There was the evidence of how close the three siblings were and just how easily they could set each other off. Lily took his hand and laced her fingers in with his. "It's okay. I'm sure he didn't mean anything by it. And maybe it was a guy thing. You know, like he didn't want you to see how upset he was. It's probably easier for him to be vulnerable with Charlotte."

Noah looked at her and smiled softly. "Yeah. You might be right. Thank you."

"Anytime."

The music started and the groom and his groomsmen took their places up near the archway. The minister stood at center stage, hands folded in front of him. Lily tried to ignore the way it felt to hear the strains of Pachelbel's Canon in D. Like a zillion other brides, she'd chosen this song for her own wedding as a prelude to her big moment. She'd stood at the back of the church and listened to it, a little bit nervous, a little excited, a whole lot of ready to get her show on the road.

Today, every note grated. They picked at the memory of standing in the back of the church and having her cousin run out and proclaim that there was no groom. Peter had not come into the church with his groomsmen. This exact music had sent Lily scrambling to find him. Later, she would find out from the church organist that he'd played it seven times before Lily made her way into the chapel and announced to everyone that there would be no wedding that day.

The music changed to Wagner's "Bridal Chorus" and the guests all stood. When Lily turned and looked at Annie Hannafort on her father's arm, her heart plummeted to her stomach. Annie was wearing almost the exact same dress Lily had worn on her day from hell. Matte satin in winter white, strapless, empire waist with a full tulle skirt. Lily watched in shock and awe as they marched past. Noah put his hand on Lily's shoulder and she panicked for his fingers, squeezing them as the tears began to stream down her face. She closed her eyes, willing herself to keep it together. Her broken engagement was in the past. It didn't hurt anymore. The trouble was Annie Hannafort was living her dream day right now. And it made Lily want to run away.

Lily forced her eyes open and faced the altar. Annie had joined her husband-to-be and Lyle had taken his place with Marcy. Everything was as it should be. But Lily felt queasy. And uneasy. Why couldn't they have been invited to a Hannafort funeral? At this point, it would've been better. As the guests all sat, Lily sucked in a deep breath, trying to ward off persistent images threatening to make her cry again. Her father's anger with Peter over dumping his baby girl and causing him to waste a pile of money. Her mother's face as she tried to be brave for Lily, all while she was obviously crumbling on the inside. The worst was her grandmother, who had never seen such a spectacle in all her life. She passed away two months later. It had been the last time Lily ever saw her.

"You okay?" Noah whispered into her ear.

She could only nod, looking straight ahead. She didn't want Noah to see how badly this hurt. Let him think she was the girl who choked up at weddings.

He then did something for which Lily was ill equipped. He put his arm around her and pulled her close. He stroked her arm with the backs of his fingers. He leaned closer and kissed her on the temple. "It's a wedding, Lil. It's okay to cry if you want to."

A small smile broke through her tears. What would she do without sweet Noah right now? Sweet, sexy Noah was going to make her lose her mind by the time they left Florida and their fake engagement was over. "I'm fine." She trained her vision straight ahead.

The minister spoke his first words. "Dearly beloved, we are gathered today to join this man and this woman in holy matrimony."

Lily choked back the tears. She didn't want to think about how much she had once hoped to be standing up there listening to those words.

Two hours later, Lily was doing much better, but it was all because of Noah. She pushed the remaining bites of wedding cake—vanilla layers with a sublime mango mousse filling—around her plate. She didn't care about food right now. Noah was too entertaining, a few yards away, crouching down and letting two of the flower girls put a flower crown on his head. He stood straighter and the girls giggled, then took his hand, and they turned in a circle in time to the music. Noah was being so charming and adorable right now, it hardly seemed fair.

Lily eyed him as he returned the crown and said goodbye to the little girls, making his way back to her. He was a vision to be sure—all long limbs and swagger. The smile on his face showed nothing but complete relaxation, a glorious change from the previous twenty-four hours. Lily was sure that every single woman at this wedding was jealous of her engagement to him. She hardly cared that it was all a charade. She could count the number of times she'd been in such an enviable position on one hand.

Still standing, Noah reached for his glass of wine and took a long drink, looking down at Lily while he did it.

"Thirsty?" She was unable to disguise the flirtation in her voice. Between enduring the buildup of the last two years, and the sheer exhaustion from keeping her hands off him over the past two days, she wanted him more than she ever had. Logic said that they might as well give in to it while in a setting where it was called for, but as Lily had learned, their arrangement made little sense. Soon they would head back to their room where the kissing and hand-holding would be cast aside in favor of their chaste and platonic real-life dynamic.

"Dancing with flower girls is exhausting."

"I bet. Probably all tuckered out, huh?"

He crinkled his forehead in that adorable Noah way. "Doesn't matter. I have yet to take my fiancée out on the dance floor for a spin. That needs to be rectified right away."

His fiancée. If only.

Noah held out his hand. He even winked at her, but Lily reminded herself this was all about appearances. This wasn't about wanting to dance with her. It was because Lyle and Marcy Hannafort were out on the dance floor. Noah and Lily needed to finish selling the idea of the two of them as a couple. It was yet another instance where these odd circumstances at least afforded Lily the fulfillment of a fantasy. Dancing with Noah, being in his arms, was one thing Lily had dreamed about more than once.

She slipped her hand into his and he quickly wrapped the comforting warmth of his fingers around hers. She rose to standing and he held his hand at the small of her back as they walked out to the dance floor. It was like stepping into another world, where white lights twinkled, soft breezes blew and romance was unavoidable. There was no tension, only happiness and celebration of love all around them. Noah pulled her into his arms and tugged her closer. Her breath left her lips in a rush. An arrogant off-kilter smile crossed his lips. If Lily could've done anything, it would've been to trap the magic of that moment in a box and keep it forever.

Marcy glanced over at them and smiled. Lily returned the expression, watching Marcy with Lyle. They were in love. You could see it in the way they clung to each other, the way they gazed into each other's eyes.

"What are you looking at?" Noah didn't look to see what had her attention. He remained focused on her.

"The Hannaforts. They're so in love."

"How could you possibly know that?"

"I can tell by looking at them. You can feel it."

"Whatever you're seeing is probably just as much of an act as we are."

The statement hurt. She hated the pessimism in his voice, made even worse by the reminder of their arrangement. "How can you can say that with such conviction?"

"I've seen my dad look at lots of women the way Lyle looks at Marcy. Trust me. It doesn't last."

"My parents look at each other like that and they're still in love. Happily married for nearly thirty years." She didn't like the pleading nature of her voice, but if she believed in anything, she did believe that some people found true love.

"I don't even see how it's possible to keep a spark for that long. It has to die out. Then what do you have to look forward to?"

Lily shook her head. "That's the excuse every affirmed bachelor uses. You don't have to rationalize your life choices. There's nothing wrong with being single. Look at me. I'm single, too. And I'm basically happy being that way."

"Why is that, exactly?" His eyes swept across her face. "Or more precisely *how* is that, exactly?"

"I don't understand the question."

"Well, you clearly believe in love and romance. You got all choked up at the wedding today. And at Charlotte's wedding. So why wouldn't you find some guy and jump in feetfirst?"

If only he knew it wasn't as simple as that. She wasn't about to tell him now. "Maybe the right guy never came along."

"Ah, the elusive right guy. The guy who doesn't worry about things like the spark dying out. He doesn't date dozens of women. Am I right?"

"The guy who was in that tabloid video is the wrong guy." She hoped that he would draw the logical conclusion from that. He wasn't like the Noah in the video. Not really. She refused to believe this story he kept telling himself about how he wasn't capable of more.

"So you watched it." His entire body tensed.

"I did. Yesterday morning."

"And now you know I'm a total ass."

She shook her head. "I've never thought that about you, ever. The guy in that video skims the surface. He doesn't care about anything deep or meaningful. I don't believe you're that guy. I know you're capable of more."

He scanned her face, but it was difficult to gauge his

reaction. Was he upset? It didn't seem that way. "What makes you think that?"

"I see how much you care about your job. I see how close you are to Sawyer and Charlotte. It really made you mad that Sawyer didn't tell you Kendall wasn't feeling well. Anyone who cares that deeply about anything is capable of love and commitment. I'm thinking that in your case it comes down to you not wanting to be like your dad."

His lips molded into a thin line. "It's more complicated than that."

"It always is. Emotions are tricky. You're not the only one who struggles with them, Noah. That's part of why I worry about what we're doing."

"Our arrangement?" he whispered.

There was so little reward in the admission she wanted to make, but at least it would be off her chest. Tomorrow, they'd fly back to New York and she could disguise her embarrassment for a few months and it would hopefully fade away. "Walking around holding hands and kissing all the time, I can feel myself getting attached to you. And I know I'm not what you want."

A low groan left his throat, and even though the song changed, Noah kept them moving on the dance floor. "Why would you say that? Why would you ever say that?" There was an angry and restless edge to his voice.

"And why are you acting so frustrated?" Lily looked up into Noah's face. His eyes darkened.

"Frustrated doesn't begin to cover it."

"Is it something I did or said?"

"It's not your fault. You're being honest. You're just being you. Which has been the source of my frustration over the last few days."

It felt as though Lily's breath had been stolen from her chest. Her mind raced, especially through the last few hours. "I don't understand. I've done everything you wanted me to do."

He looked away for a moment, surveying the crowd on the dance floor, then returned his attention to her. His gaze put her on notice, but as to what she was supposed to glean from it, she had no idea. He pulled her closer. The arm he had around her waist was tight. If she'd done something wrong, and this was what she got as punishment, she hoped he would tell her so she could keep doing it. He lowered his head. He was coming in for a kiss. Was this another part of their charade? Or was there something more? Here they were in this romantic setting, swaying on the dance floor at an extravagant wedding. If ever there was a time to kiss one's fake fiancée, this was it.

Lily tilted her chin up, making her lips into as seductive a pucker as she could. She closed her eyes and locked her knees—every time he kissed her, it was a challenge to remain standing.

The next thing she knew, Noah's lips were at her ear. "It's this. It's impossible to be around you and not want more. I thought I could make it through this trip without admitting it, but I can't."

Lily's pulse was pounding in her throat. She opened her eyes and looked at him, hoping for clarification. Was this the inevitable move that Charlotte had warned her of? Or was this something different? "More?" Lily had spent a whole lot of time wanting not only Noah's kiss, but the more part, as well. She had to be sure of what he was saying.

"You're so sexy, Lil. I don't know how I could not want more. I want you. If you want me."

Goose bumps popped up on her skin. She looked around at the other guests on the dance floor. No one was paying a lick of attention to them. Toasts had been made. Cake had been served. She returned her sights to Noah. He was so adorable right now, tentative and unsure. She'd never seen him like this before. "Do you want to get out of here?"

"Seriously?"

"Yes, seriously."

"Yes. A million times, yes." He took her hand and they beelined off the dance floor as stealthily as they could. Out of the reception hall, through the pool area they raced. Noah set the pace with his long legs, but even in heels, Lily had no trouble keeping up. She was highly motivated.

Noah pulled his key card from his wallet and swiped it to get them through the gate to the private cabanas. The wind always picked up the instant they were out of the safe confines of the pool area, where high walls helped to keep the two worlds separate. The night air was warm and soft against her skin, but it was nothing compared to Noah's hand as he pulled her along eagerly. He was a man on a mission and she loved that about him. It made her feel good. He wanted her.

They wound along the walkway to their cabana. The heel of Lily's shoe dropped between two planks. She stopped. Noah yanked on her arm, then rounded back.

"I'm stuck." She tugged on her leg, twisting her foot back and forth, but it wasn't going anywhere.

Noah dropped to his knee and wrapped both hands around her ankle, tugging on her leg.

"Ouch. Ow. Stop it."

"Sorry. I can't pull you loose." He looked up at her. The wind blew his floppy hair all over the place, making it an even sexier mess than usual.

"Damn. And I love these shoes. Charlotte convinced me to get them."

"Don't worry. We'll save your shoe. Let me figure this

out." Noah looked down at her foot again, but as he was assessing her plight, he started caressing her calf.

Lily sucked in a breath sharply. His fingers on her bare skin felt impossibly good. How was she going to handle it when there was even more touching? She might never recover. Which, right now, was perfectly okay with her. "Unbuckle it."

"Good idea." He freed her foot, then tried to pull the shoe out. "If I pull too hard, it's going to ruin the heel. Are you okay with that?"

"No. Don't do that. You paid a fortune for these shoes."

"Then what do you want me to do? Call maintenance and get them to remove the board?" Noah dropped his shoulders. He was frustrated again.

"Leave it. We'll get it later."

He straightened to his full height. "Really?"

Lily loved those shoes, but she'd waited an awful long time to be with Noah. This might be her only chance. "Yes." She stooped down and unbuckled her other shoe. Before she could take a single step in her bare feet, she was no longer standing. She was in Noah's arms.

"I'm taking zero chances. You get a splinter out here and it'll ruin everything."

She wrapped her hands around his neck and he headed straight for their cabana. This was a much faster way to travel. They arrived at their door in under a minute, easy. Noah put Lily down and swiped his key card. They both hustled inside. Lily dropped her saved shoe to the floor, rose to her tiptoes and wrapped her arms around Noah's neck. He kissed her with such force, she was glad she was holding on to him.

It was like he was sending a message. *I want you.* She not only received it loud and clear, she returned it with the same raw enthusiasm with which Noah had delivered it. Their tongues were a mad frenzy. Noah's hands were everywhere—her waist, her hips, her butt. He scrambled to pull up the voluminous fabric of her skirt, but Lily had no patience for that. He could be searching for her legs for days.

She turned her back to him and pulled her hair to the side. He cupped one of her bare shoulders and pressed his hips against her bottom. She felt his gentle breath at her nape as he skimmed his lips over her skin. She dropped her head to the side as he trailed openmouthed kisses along the slope of her neck. Luckily, he was also drawing down the zipper at the same time. The cool air on her skin was such a delicious contrast to Noah's velvety, red-hot kisses.

He slipped the straps from her shoulders and they both let the dress flounce to the floor. Lily fought the urge to cover herself, standing in nothing more than a bra and panties in front of the man she'd fantasized about countless times. Noah was accustomed to such flawless beauty it was hard not to worry about every little imperfection.

He cupped her shoulders with his hands, drew his fingers down her arms, twining his hands with her own. He pulled her closer, her back against his chest.

"I want to make sure you're okay with this," he muttered into her hair. "This was never part of our arrangement and I respect that, no matter my frustration. Just say no and I'll jump in the pool."

She giggled. "Does that really work?"

"It did yesterday when I first saw you in your bikini."

"You're joking."

"Nope. Boner city."

She closed her eyes, realizing that things might not have been the way she'd thought they were over the last few days. She wasn't the only woman he didn't want. He'd been resisting. She turned in his arms and raised her hands to his handsome face, forcing him to look right at her. She wanted her words understood. She wanted them to make an impression. Then she wanted to forget about them and take off his clothes. "I am more than okay with this. I want you. And I'm more than a little excited by the fact that you want me."

A smile crept across his face and he took his jacket off so fast that she was surprised he didn't tear the sleeves off.

"Careful," she said. "I'm sure that suit cost a fortune."

He unbuttoned his shirt and she helped. "Like the shoes, that's the exact last thing on my mind right now."

As soon as his chest and torso were naked, she took a moment to admire the carved contours of his body, but she also didn't waste any time unhooking his belt and unzipping his pants. Noah shucked them nearly as fast as he'd dispatched the jacket.

Finally, they were on a more even footing, Noah in dark gray boxers, Lily in something that seemed to be making an impression—thank goodness for the power of lace and satin. He grasped her rib cage and squeezed, making her breasts plump inside her strapless bra. She never imagined Noah would see her lovely underpinnings, except perhaps by accident, and she was so glad she'd been judicious with her selection.

His hands slid to her back and he unhooked the bra. Lily flung it across the room and it connected with the flat-screen TV. Noah slid his palms to her breasts, molding his hands around them, then rubbing her nipples in small circles with his thumbs. Lily gasped at the pleasure. Noah was a master.

He dropped his head and drew one tight bud into his mouth, drawing circles with his tongue and sending Lily into near oblivion when she dared to watch him. His lips against her skin, his thick hair slumping to the side—each inviting detail was almost too much to take. This was happening. With Noah. She wanted him with every ounce of desire she had built up inside. Everything between her legs yearned for his touch, longed to have him make love to her.

She reached down and took his hand, rushing into the bedroom. She kissed him, hard, cupping her fingers around his stiff erection. She pressed into him with the heel of her hand, which brought a sexy rumble from his throat. Then she wiggled his boxers past his hips and took his length in her hand, stroking intently, watching his face as his eyes shut and his tempting mouth went slack. Having Noah Locke at her command was an awfully embolden-ing experience. She had to wonder if once would ever be enough. She worried that it wouldn't.

"Do you have a condom?" she asked, trying to hide the desperation in her voice. If the answer was no, she might explode.

"I do. In my shaving kit. One second." He ran off to the bathroom. Lily loved watching the defined muscles of his frame in motion, especially his butt. Noah had an espe-cially amazing butt, complete with heartbreaking dimples right above it.

Lily sat on the bed, swishing her hands against the silky linens as the seconds ticked by and anticipation bubbled up inside her. Noah appeared in the doorway, tall and mus-cled and ready for her. She thought she might faint. The only thing that kept her from doing exactly that was the fight inside her. She'd waited for a long time to have sex with Noah Locke. She wasn't going to let anything ruin it.

That first glimpse of Lily perched on the bed, wearing nothing more than maddening black panties and a smile, stole Noah's breath right from his lungs. She was so much more beautiful than he'd ever imagined, just as she'd been more heavenly to kiss than he'd ever fantasized. He wanted her with every inch of his body, but some parts of him were more insistent and begging for attention. He was glad he'd opted to put on the condom in the bathroom. He was sure he'd never been so hard, was sure he'd never ached for a woman the way he did for Lily. He couldn't wait much longer.

He dropped his knee on the bed and stretched out on his side, smoothing his hand over Lily's bare stomach and urging her to her back. He caressed her breasts, cupped her cheek and brought her lips to his. They fell into a kiss that had no logical end. He could've kissed her forever then, their tongues winding in a perpetual loop. He could've dug his hands into her silky hair forever, rubbed her soft skin with his fingers. He breathed in her sweet scent, which seemed even headier in the sticky tropical air.

His fingers slowly trailed along her spine, building the anticipation when he honestly didn't want to wait another minute. Lily arched her back, and a smile interrupted their kiss. They exchanged a breathless laugh, their lips softly brushing together, then things got serious again when his hand slipped into the back of her panties. He cupped her bottom and pushed them past her hips, removing that final barrier between them. Lily hitched her leg up over his hip, grinding her center against him. She needed him and he loved her urgency, the way she told him everything he wanted to hear with an insistent rotation of her hips. He slipped his hand between their bodies and found her apex. Lily groaned so fiercely that he wasn't sure at first that the sound had actually come from her. She nipped at his lower lip. He moved his fingers in rhythmic circles, listening for the changes in her breath as they were drawn back into another perfect kiss.

Lily nudged him gently to his back and she straddled his

hips. In a move he never expected, she sat back for a moment, lazily drawing a single finger back and forth across his chest, then trailing it down his midline. Noah watched in utter fascination. She was so beautiful it boggled the mind, but he was drawn to some features in particular—her deep rose lips, the swell of her hips, those beguiling blue eyes.

She shifted and raised one leg, taking him in her hand and guiding his erection between her legs. As she sank down onto him, a torrent of heat and pleasure rushed through him. She molded around him. Warm. Hot. Soft and hard all at the same time. Being inside Lily was so much more than he'd hoped for. They moved together, Lily lowering her chest to his, but not resting her body weight on his. Instead, she rubbed her nipples gently against his bare chest. That vision alone was enough to send him over the edge.

Her breaths were already rough and short. Her eyes drifted shut, then opened, and closed again. She rolled her head to the side, shoulders rising up around her ears over and over again. He loved the way she surrendered to the pleasure. It was such a turn-on.

Finally, she pressed her chest against his and he was able to kiss her deeply, the way he wanted to. Things were different now—frenzied and fitful, like neither of them could settle down. Noah thrust more forcefully, lifting Lily from the bed. The need coiled in his hips. It was like a cat about to pounce. He pulled her flat against him and flipped her to her back. He might have been a bit too forceful, judging by the way it sent her hair up in a flurry, but she seemed to like that, a lot.

"I'm so close," she mumbled, digging her fingers into his shoulders, her heels into the backs of his thighs, and bucked against him with her hips. He was soaking up her raw beauty, the way the color had rushed to her cheeks, when her chin rose, her mouth fell open, and the orgasm hit her, causing her to gather tight around him.

His own pleasure felt like it was torn from the depths of his belly, relentless waves of tension letting go. Lily gasped and pulled him close, kissing his cheek and neck over and over again. He rolled to his side and they were in each others' arms, breathless with contentment. He could hardly believe he'd finally had a taste of this woman he'd desired for so long.

She turned to him and nuzzled his chest with her nose. When she lifted her head to look at him, the vivid blue of her eyes kept him in the moment like a jolt of caffeine from a potent cup of coffee. They'd given in. This had really happened.

"That was wonderful," she murmured, kissing him softly.

"I couldn't agree more." He wanted to tell her how long he'd waited for this, for her, and that he'd spent so much time thinking that it would never happen. But that would ruin everything when they had to return to work. Better she think that this was just another Noah tryst. Hopefully she already knew that she meant a lot to him on other levels, most important was friendship.

"I'm wiped, though. I hardly slept last night. It was tough being in the same bed with you, knowing I was supposed to keep my hands to myself."

"Really?" He was surprised by her admission. He'd assumed that his frustration with physically staying away from each other had been one-sided.

"Yes, Noah. Really. Have you looked at you? I'd be a fool to not want to try something."

He smiled and pulled her closer. "And why didn't you?"

"I was waiting for you to give me a sign."

A sign. Had it been as simple as that all along? If he

had met Lily in a bar or at a party, yes. But they'd met at work, she'd become indispensable before he could figure out a way around it and the rest was already determined. Tomorrow, they'd go home, the charade of their fake engagement would be far less necessary, and it would end as soon as the Hannafort deal was signed.

Lily's breaths were already soft and even. She was falling asleep in his arms and it was a surprisingly pleasant feeling. He kissed her temple, wondering if he should let her sleep for long. Now that he'd done the thing he'd sworn he wouldn't, he refused to live with regrets. He wanted more of her. If he was going to get her out of his system, and he really wanted to, tonight was his only chance.

Eight

Lily woke up to two things—the amazing landscape of Noah's naked back and a knock at their cabana door.

"Did you order room service?" She was half-awake and more than half-tempted to tell whomever it was to go away. Forget food. She wanted to press up against Noah and get him to go for one last round before they had to leave for New York.

"No. I hope it's not more champagne. We still have another bottle to drink before we leave." He rolled toward her, now flat on his back. He absentmindedly scratched his stomach, eyes still sleepy. The sheet was barely covering him. He was so hot she was surprised the bed wasn't on fire.

Another knock came at the door, this one more insistent. "Do you want me to get it?" he asked.

"I'll get it. Maybe they have the wrong room. Or it's housekeeping." Lily scrambled for some clothes, but all she could find was Noah's shirt from last night. She threaded her arms into the sleeves and buttoned up lightning fast, then bolted for the door.

Lily was greeted by Charlotte, wagging her fingers.

Oh crap.

"Morning. I think you lost something." Charlotte held up Lily's sparkly shoe.

Lily felt the blood drain from her face. So much for keeping this quiet. In the flurry of rushing to bed with Noah, she'd completely forgotten about sending him out again to retrieve her beloved shoe. "Thanks. I was wondering where that went."

Charlotte bounced her all-knowing eyebrows at Lily. "There are only three things that make a woman leave behind a brand-new designer shoe. A flood, a fire, or a man. So which is it?"

Lily wedged herself into the door opening. "Unless I missed something, I don't think there were any natural disasters last night." *Woman-made disasters, yes.*

"Nice shirt, by the way. It looks better on you than Noah."

That was impossible, but there was no use arguing the point. Plus, if there had been any doubt that Charlotte knew exactly what had happened last night, it was gone now. "Somebody was pounding on the door. I had to answer it wearing something."

"Where is my brother, anyway?"

Lily cleared her throat. "In bed."

Charlotte handed over the shoe. "Look. I'm all for a woman taking whatever she wants. I just want to be sure that you're watching out for Lily. I love my brother to pieces, but I guarantee you that he isn't worrying about your career or your feelings. It's not on his radar at all. Honestly, I don't know that he's capable."

Lily didn't want to believe that either. Noah had been

the most attentive man she'd ever gone to bed with, by a long shot. Simply thinking about it was enough to send Lily grabbing the wall to steady herself. But Charlotte was probably right. Noah had a horrible track record, one he did not try to hide. Plus, he was her boss and this was technically the last day of their fake engagement. Tomorrow, they would be back in the office working together. No more kisses. No more holding hands. Certainly no sex. *Bummer.* "Okay. I'll take that under advisement. Thanks."

"See you out at the dock in an hour? The boat will be there to take us to the car." Charlotte turned away for a second. "Oh, Lily. Can you let Noah know that Sawyer and Kendall ended up leaving late last night? She still wasn't feeling well and the doctor thought it best she get home and see her own physician. Everything's fine, though. I got a text from him thirty minutes ago."

"Oh, sure. I'm glad everything is okay." Noah was going to be so mad he didn't get that call. "We'll see you at the dock." Lily closed the door and padded back into the bedroom.

Noah was on his side, head propped up on his hand, the silky white sheets covering very little of his sun-kissed skin—just everything between his waist and knees. No question about it—Noah was a slice of heaven. That long torso, narrow waist and the alluring trail of hair under his belly button was enough to make her choke on the words she had to say. His come-hither smile and the flicker in his eyes made it so much worse.

"Coming back to bed?" he asked.

Yes. I am. Forever and ever and ever. "No. Sorry. That was your sister. She knows what happened last night." Lily held up the shoe as proof.

Noah shrugged and patted the mattress. "Charlotte likes you. She won't say anything to anyone. I promise."

Lily plucked her dress from the floor, turned it right side out and draped it over her arm. "I'm not worried about discretion, although I definitely do not want Sawyer to know about this."

"Why not?"

"Because I have to work with your brother and it's going to be bad enough going into work every day and seeing you, knowing that you know what I look like naked. It's not professional, Noah, and that's really important to me." Every word out of her mouth was a potent reminder of what she was really supposed to be doing at this wedding—securing her professional future, not sleeping with the boss. There was only one future for Lily and it was wrapped up in her 1 percent of Locke and Locke, not with Noah the serial dater. "Last night was fun, but I think we both know that we're better off if we pretend like it didn't happen and just move forward."

He pursed his lips and looked back over his shoulder, out at the gorgeous ocean vista. "You're right. It wasn't a good idea. I was serious when I asked if you really wanted to cross that line last night."

Why did he have to swing so far in the opposite direction? "No. It was my choice and I refuse to regret it. We're both consenting adults. But I think..." Her voice tapered off as she searched for the right words to say. It was as if the devil was on her shoulder, urging her to ask Noah for one more roll in the proverbial hay. She wanted his hands all over her, his kiss on her lips, his body weighing her down. She wanted him to make her fall apart at the seams again and again.

Noah turned back to her. "Let me guess. What happens in the Florida Keys, stays in the Florida Keys?"

Lily didn't even bother holding back her sigh. "Trite, but yes. That's the perfect way to put it."

He knocked his head to the side and threw back the covers with zero regard for the fact that she now had a full view of everything she wanted so desperately. "Okay, then. I'm taking a shower." He hopped up from the bed and traipsed into the bathroom. Lily stole her final chance to watch Noah's perfect butt in motion. She was going to miss that view. She'd rather look at him than the ocean.

"Just start packing," she told herself. "You had your fun, now it's time to go back to work." Lily did exactly that, wondering if she'd ever again wear some of these beautiful designer clothes she now owned. There was no telling when she'd be invited to another event as fancy as this wedding, but now was not the time for pessimism. Knowing she'd never sleep with Noah again was depressing enough.

An hour later, she and Noah made their trek out to the dock, ready to go. Charlotte and Michael were chatting with Lyle and Marcy. Lily could only hope that Noah's claim that his sister was discreet ended up holding water. Loose lips sink ships, as her mother used to say.

"Where are Kendall and Sawyer?"

"Oh, shoot. I forgot to tell you they headed back early because Kendall still wasn't feeling well."

"You'd think my brother would want to share these things with me, but apparently not."

"I'm sure he was just worried about Kendall and figured Charlotte would tell you."

"Yeah. I guess you're right."

Marcy Hannafort turned and caught sight of Lily and Noah. She beelined over to them, looking like a woman on top of the world. "Honestly. What a handsome couple you are," she said.

"Thank you. That's sweet of you to say." Lily shifted

her weight uncomfortably. They *were* a handsome couple. What a waste of two perfectly good people.

"We're very happy." Noah pressed a dutiful kiss to Lily's cheek that nearly knocked her off her feet. "Thank you so much for including us this weekend."

"I know it was my daughter getting married, but I just love weddings so much." Marcy Hannafort smiled and stared off wistfully, as if she were reliving the last forty-eight hours.

"It was a lovely event. You and Lyle must be relieved it went so well." Lily shifted her weight again, glancing at Noah, wishing he knew to change the subject to anything other than weddings. Unfortunately, memories of last night, the ones seared into her memory, were dug up every time she looked at him. She was starting to realize exactly how difficult it was going to be to work with him. She would never be able to forget what his touch was like. She'd probably spend at least the next month avoiding eye contact completely. She never should've crossed that line, but she couldn't have helped herself last night if she'd wanted to. Noah was too irresistible and the wait had been too long.

"Honestly, weddings are like a drug for me, so I'd gladly redo the whole thing over again," Marcy continued.

Lily merely nodded. Considering her history with weddings, she was proud of herself for having lived through this one. As for drugs, she might prefer a horse tranquilizer to witnessing more marriage vows anytime soon.

"You know, I was a wedding planner for years and years. Before the hotel business really took off and Lyle needed my help."

"Oh, I didn't realize that." Noah acted as though he were genuinely interested.

"I helped Annie quite a bit with planning this weekend,

although she's such a Daddy's girl. She wanted Lyle's help much more than mine. Even when it came to things like picking out the flowers and tasting cake. You know, normal mother-of-the-bride things."

"That's sweet, though. She loves her daddy very much." Lily desperately wanted to get out of this conversation. Simply thinking about picking out flowers and cake made it feel like someone was jabbing a knife in her side. The mere mention of it made her feel ill. But she couldn't be even the slightest bit rude to Marcy Hannafort. The big deal wasn't even close to being signed.

"To be fair, Lyle didn't have to do much. Once he came up with the idea of using Key Marly, and she agreed to it, the staff took over most of the planning."

"That's wonderful." Lily tried to send psychic messages to Noah to get his gorgeous mouth working harder so he could charm Marcy into a different topic of discussion. "And now you don't have to worry about it at all."

"I know. It makes me so sad." Marcy flashed her eyes at Lily and rubbed her hands together like she was scheming. "So, tell me what you two have planned for your big day. I understand that yours is the next big wedding on the horizon since Michael and Charlotte opted to get married at City Hall."

"Oh, I guess you're right. Well, we haven't really had a chance to get to the meat of it yet." Lily laughed nervously. Where was she going with this? Lily and Noah were fake engaged, not fake getting married.

"Noah, you mentioned that you and Lily have been discussing how big of a wedding to have. What's the date?"

Lily was struck with panic unlike anything she'd ever experienced. She was the prepared one. She was the person who was always on top of things, but she was out of her depth and Noah had apparently thrown them both under the bus by delivering factoids about their non-wedding. Lily had to be very careful here, or everything could go up in smoke. "Oh. Uh. June. I know it's a cliché, but we liked the idea of it." She shrugged it off.

Mrs. Hannafort gripped her elbow, her face showing deep concern. "But what's the actual date? Where are you having it? Have you sent out the save-the-date cards? Have you put together the guest list?"

Lily found herself glaring at Noah like she was drowning and he was the life preserver. She didn't even know when the Saturdays in June were. "Oh, I forget. So many dates swirling around in my head right now."

"It's whatever that last Saturday in June is." Right then and there, Noah upped the ante. Lily bugged her eyes at him, but the look on his face said he was winging it as much as she was.

"Neither of you knows the actual date?" Enough confusion crossed Marcy's face to cause Lily more than a little worry. Surely she and Noah were sending mixed signals right now.

Lily grabbed Noah's arm and cozied up to him, digging her fingernails into his biceps for good measure. If she was going to suffer, he could, too. "You mean June 28. Remember?"

"We haven't settled on a location yet because we haven't decided how big the guest list should be. We're still making up our minds. Lily has been so busy at work," Noah said.

This is my fault? "Noah won't admit it, but he's the real reason we haven't made any decisions. He's very hard to pin down." *Although he had no problem pinning me down last night.*

Marcy's face appeared positively horrified. "No. No. No. Lily, darling. This will not do. You hardly know the date of your own wedding? And you haven't picked a venue yet? We need to straighten this out right away." She turned to Noah and stuck her finger in his face. "And you need to stop being so indecisive. No bride wants to deal with that. If she wants your two cents, you give it to her."

"Right. Of course." Noah looked as though he'd never been scolded so harshly in all his life.

Marcy shook her head. "I swear you two are exactly like Annie and Brad. You need to take this more seriously. Chop-chop." She popped up onto her tiptoes and waved down her husband, who headed right over. "Luckily, I have an idea."

Lyle set his hand on Marcy's shoulder when he reached them. "Looks like we're having a real confab over here."

"I was talking to Lily and Noah about their wedding. It's June 28 and they don't have a venue yet. What if they did it at the Grand Legacy? And we could use the wedding as part of a publicity plan in conjunction with announcing the joint venture between Hannafort and Locke? Sort of like we used this weekend to have our soft opening of Key Marly."

Lily could see the gears turning in Lyle Hannafort's head and that scared her right down to her bones. "My darling, you are a genius. I love it. We're going to have to light a fire under the lawyers if we're going to get the deal done that quickly, but you know me. I don't like to sit around and wait. Plus, I can just see it. A big, fancy Locke family wedding at the newest beauty in the Hannafort Hotels stable. I think it's a fabulous idea. Lily? Noah? Would you be up for that? It'll get the deal going on a quicker timetable."

"Yes," Noah blurted. "Absolutely. It's a wonderful idea."

"Maybe we should talk about it first?" Lily asked, giving Noah's arm an extra hard squeeze.

Marcy shook her head at Lily while a sweet but condescending smile spread across her face. "I know you're nervous, darling, but trust me. You need to make these decisions now or you won't have your dream wedding. You only get one shot at this."

Or two, if you're me. Lily did not like this scenario at all. Pretending for a weekend was one thing. This was an entirely new level of deception and lying, all tied up in a bow called mental anguish. Could she do this? Noah shot her a look that said he was sorry, but she'd better fall in line. She hated it when he looked at her like that. She had no good answer for it. She scanned Marcy's and Lyle's faces and forced herself to see her nest egg. Her secure future. Everything she'd worked so hard for over the last two years. If this meant the deal happened faster, she and Noah could break things off before the actual wedding happened, and hopefully it wouldn't have to be that big of a deal since everything would be easily canceled with the Grand Legacy.

"I'm sure Sawyer will be pleased." Lyle reached over and patted Noah on the shoulder. "And to think I almost pulled out of it after seeing that silly video. Now I know what a good guy you are."

"Then it's settled," Marcy said. "And I want to donate my services as wedding planner. Lyle and I will be back in New York in a few days and we can start working on it then."

Lily's heart sprang into a full-on panic. "Oh, no, Mrs. Hannafort. That's totally not necessary. I'm sure that Noah and I can handle it on our own."

"But you don't have my experience. And Noah just told me how busy you are at work. This will save you more time than you can possibly imagine. And you won't have to worry about making any big mistakes. I'll make sure that doesn't happen."

Lily looked at Noah's handsome face, colored by an expression she could describe only as surrender. He was on board. Lyle and Marcy were on board. Lily needed to concede and figure out the rest later. "Okay. That sounds great."

Except Lily was sure of one thing—the only thing about this that would be great would be her regret.

Nine

Lily was the first to arrive in the office Monday morning. After being away on Friday, she'd have a ton of email to catch up on, as well as faxes, mail and voice mail messages. She wanted Sawyer and Noah to come in to their usual well-oiled machine. She also wanted to be capable, on-top-of-it Lily when Noah arrived. She wanted to avoid the sense that he was imagining her flat on her back and at his mercy.

One thing she could not avoid today. Sawyer was about to learn that Lily and Noah were now planning a fake wedding. Hopefully, he'd appreciate the business side of what had happened—Marcy Hannafort had backed them into a corner, and they'd done the only thing they could to keep moving forward with the deal. Lily also hoped Sawyer wouldn't give Noah a hard time about it. Until Lily had been folded more fully into the inner workings of Locke and Locke, she hadn't been quite so aware of the friction between Sawyer and Noah. Noah clearly looked up to his brother very much, and felt dismissed or ignored at least some of the time.

Sawyer arrived fifteen minutes after Lily. "Sorry we missed you and Noah yesterday. I trust Charlotte told you we had to leave early?"

"She did. Is everything okay with Kendall?" Lily got up from her desk.

"Yes, thankfully," he answered. "The doctor thinks it was a mild case of food poisoning. A bad shrimp or something. Don't say anything to the Hannaforts. I'm sure they'd be horrified."

"Yikes. I didn't hear anything about the other guests getting sick, so hopefully it was a blip on the map." The mention of the Hannaforts made Lily jittery.

"Any sign of Noah yet?"

Lily was able to assuage her paranoia over whether or not Sawyer might know about recent developments. It was apparent he didn't. "No. But I'm guessing he'll be here soon."

"Did I miss anything important yesterday?"

"Noah can fill you in on everything." Lily was torn over her answer, but if she told Sawyer now and Noah walked in on them discussing it, he would once again feel out of the loop.

"Were you happy with the way everything went with you and Noah this weekend?" Sawyer took a seat in reception. "I hope it wasn't too awkward."

Lily fumbled for her mug and took a swig of lukewarm coffee. She needed a second to think. A million different answers sat on her lips, none of which she'd ever share with Sawyer. "It was fine. I had a nice time."

The office door opened and in walked Noah. He stopped

dead in his tracks, sights sweeping between Sawyer and Lily. "What's up?"

"Just chatting about the weekend."

"Did Lily tell you what happened right before we left?"

She shook her head. "I thought it was better if we were both here for it."

"Good. I agree."

"Whoa. That does not sound good. Do you want to tell me what's going on?" The tone of Sawyer's voice was unmistakable. The Hannafort deal meant too much for there to be any new problems.

Noah took off his coat and Lily had to ignore the memories that flooded her mind. That moment when she first saw him take off his shirt and she was able to have her hands all over him. "Well, the easiest answer is we have news. Mr. and Mrs. Hannafort want to have the wedding at the Grand Legacy. They want to use it for publicity as part of the official deal announcement."

Sawyer's eyes narrowed. "What wedding? Is one of their other daughters engaged?"

"Our wedding. Mine and Lily's."

The words *our wedding* made Lily flinch. Any hope that the state of affairs might appear better in the light of a new day was gone. It only looked worse.

"A wedding? You're actually getting married? How in the hell did this happen? And why didn't one of you call me last night?"

"It's my fault," Lily blurted. She was prepared to do anything to get Sawyer to stop using words like *wedding* and *married*.

"No. Lily. That's not fair." Noah was quick to step in. "Marcy had you in a corner. Who knew the woman was so obsessed with weddings?" He turned to his brother. "She asked Lily about the date and kept asking until she finally had to give her an answer. I figured that we had to do everything we could to keep the deal together. We didn't really have a choice."

Sawyer raked his hands through his hair. "I'm so sorry, Lily. If I would've known it was going to get this out of control, I never would've allowed this in the first place."

"Hold on a minute." The anger in Noah's voice was so unfamiliar Lily wouldn't have believed it had come from his mouth if she hadn't seen him utter the words. "You *allowed* this? I seem to remember that this was ultimately my call, along with Lily. We knew what we were getting into. No, it's not what either of us would've planned, and it's certainly less than ideal, but we have it under control."

Seeing and hearing Noah be firm with Sawyer created a pleasant flutter in her chest. She loved the idea of them as a unified front. He'd been so right two days ago on the dock. They were in this together. "Sawyer, it's fine. We did what we had to do to make the deal work. We're a team."

Sawyer shook his head in dismay. "I hope you two know what you're doing."

"We do."

The fax machine on Lily's desk sprang to life. She only needed to see a few inches of the letterhead to know who it was from. "We're getting something from Lyle."

Noah and Sawyer stepped closer. They all watched the machine chug out the first page. Lily swiped it from the paper tray. *Subject: Deal Memo.*

"This is it." Noah leaned into Lily, subtly enough that Sawyer would never notice, but close enough for his body heat to make her tingly from head to toe. Between Noah and the anticipation of the official offer, this was almost too much to take. "We don't look until every page comes out."

"Fine," Sawyer said. "I'll be in my office. Let me know when it's all here."

Lily and Noah stood sentry over the fax machine until all twelve pages arrived. She collected them in her hands and handed them over to Noah. This was his deal now as far as she was concerned. He'd been in it from the beginning, he'd yanked it back from the precipice every time it was in danger of falling apart.

Noah took a step away from her desk and turned back to her. "Coming?" That flash of his eyes turned her knees to rubber.

Lily was so excited and scared she didn't know what to think. She swiped her notepad from her desk. "Yep. Coming."

A short ten minutes later, they were all still in shock. Sawyer looked out the window. Noah sat back in his chair, staring up at the ceiling. Lily was unsure of the appropriate reaction from her, so she sat perfectly still. This was her first time in on a big deal. She had to tamp down her desire to leap out of her seat and dance around the room. Her nest egg was about to be a lot bigger than first thought.

"We still need to have the lawyers look everything over," Noah said. "And run everything by Charlotte. She should be able to come by the office this afternoon."

"Yes. Of course." Sawyer pinched the bridge of his nose. "I just… I knew Lyle was excited about this deal. But I'll be honest, I never thought the offer would end up being two times the number we started at."

"It's amazing," Lily offered, still feeling out of her element.

"It really is."

"We should go out and celebrate, don't you think?" Noah asked.

Sawyer dropped down into his seat. "Sure. A drink after work? Kendall is still feeling a bit under the weather, so I'm probably not good for much else."

"Six o'clock?" Noah asked.

"Perfect." Sawyer picked up his phone.

Noah and Lily took that as their cue to leave. As they reached her desk, Noah put his hand on her shoulder. "This wouldn't have been possible without you. I want you to know that. And it's more than the stuff that's happened over the last week. It's everything you've done for us over two years. We're both happy to have you here, but I'm especially happy about it."

Lily didn't want his words to make her feel the way she was feeling right now—soft and mushy on the inside. It contradicted the strength she needed to convey in business situations. Still, she so appreciated the kind words. "Thank you very much."

"No problem." He patted her on the shoulder, almost as confirmation that their relationship had returned to being only about business, exactly what she'd wanted. "Now let's get to work."

Lily sat at her desk, a ridiculous smile on her face, and got busy on the hundreds of things that had been pushed aside on Friday. They ordered lunch in and Lily devoured a Cobb salad while poring over spreadsheets and construction schedules. She had calls with two contractors, scheduled meetings for Noah and Sawyer. Six o'clock arrived in no time.

Noah had reserved a corner booth and had champagne waiting at a bar a few blocks from the office. It was a hot spot on weeknights for the after-work crowd, and the place was bustling with people. Lily, Noah and Sawyer were getting settled just as Charlotte joined them.

"I'm only here for a minute." She plopped down her enormous handbag and took the seat next to Lily, who was left shoulder-to-shoulder with Noah. "It's too depressing for me to be around people drinking right now. I would kill for a glass of wine."

Lily laughed. "I bet. Only a few more months to go, though, right?" Pregnancy was a life event that seemed so far off for Lily that it might as well be her retirement.

Charlotte smoothed her hands over her belly. "Yes. And it's all worth it. Doesn't mean I don't enjoy making others pity me."

"Not gonna happen tonight, Charlotte. There's too much to be happy about. We ordered you a glass of ginger ale. Hopefully the thought of all that money will make it tolerable," Noah said.

Right on time, the waiter delivered Charlotte's drink. She raised the champagne flute. "To Locke and Locke. And Lily. And Lyle Hannafort. That's entirely too many *L* names for one toast, but I couldn't care less." She grinned as glasses clinked and they took their celebratory sips.

"Well, that's it for me." Charlotte pushed her drink to the center of the table.

"I thought you were kidding," Noah replied.

"I have a super-hot husband waiting for me at home and he's ordering a pizza. No offense to you guys, but that's way more tempting." Charlotte popped up from her seat and hooked her handbag on her arm.

Sawyer finished his drink. "Hold on. I'll see you out. I need to go meet Kendall."

"Bye," Noah said, seeming annoyed.

Charlotte leaned over the table, looking both Noah and Lily directly in the eye. "If you're staying, be sure to put on the Lily-and-Noah show. You're out in public, and it's only a matter of time before news of the big wedding gets out. If anyone has loose lips, it's Marcy Hannafort."

"Yep. Of course." Lily watched as Noah slipped his hand on top of hers. Lord help her, she would never get accustomed to his touch. His skin against hers would always awaken every nerve ending in her body.

"We're big kids, Charlotte. We've got it under control. You can go now." Noah took another sip of his drink.

Charlotte rolled her eyes. "Bye."

"Do you ever get tired of taking orders?" Noah asked. "Because I do."

"Your sister has a very defined idea of the way things should be done. I get that. I'm the same way."

"It's not just Charlotte. Sawyer does it to me all the time."

"So tell them to stop."

Noah shrugged. "The thing is, most of the time they aren't wrong. And if I had told them to stop when they suggested our engagement..." He cleared his throat. "I wouldn't have had nearly as much fun at the wedding."

Fun. Was that what Lily was to him? It was hard to imagine she was anything more. Not that she had any right to be disappointed about it. She'd eagerly grabbed her chance to be with Noah, to have that heavenly taste of him, no strings attached. "It was fun, wasn't it?" She drew her finger around the rim of her glass. She knew her voice shouldn't be so flirtatious, but now that she'd finished her first glass of champagne, she had no need for defenses. Not with Noah. They'd had major good news today. He was in a great mood. She had her nest egg secured.

"My favorite kind of fun." He put his hand on hers again. His fingers slipped between hers, gently spreading them apart. Down and back he rubbed, going deeper with his touch on every pass. Lily stared at their hands and nearly gasped from ecstasy. "I know we said Florida was the end of it, but maybe we should try to get everything we can out of our arrangement." He turned toward her, dropped his chin and nuzzled the spot behind her ear with his nose. His warm breath skimmed the length of her neck. The scruff on his cheek scratched at her skin.

"What did you have in mind?" she asked.

He laughed quietly in response, but she didn't think it was that funny. She wanted to hear him say the words. "This." He kissed the delicate skin beneath her ear. It took every ounce of self-control not to push him back against the booth, straddle his lap and pop the buttons off his shirt. He kissed her cheek, then moved to the corner of her mouth. The anticipation was killing her. "And this."

His lips brushed hers and she went in for one of Noah's mind-bending kisses—where constructs like time and place mean nothing. They pressed against each other, her hand dug into his hair. She was only vaguely aware of what was going on around them. People milled about, but she didn't care. They were engaged, dammit, and if people couldn't handle a public display of affection, that was too bad.

Noah pulled back, his mouth sexily slack. "We need to slow down or I won't be able to walk out of here without embarrassing myself."

She loved having that effect on him. It was not only a total turn-on, it made her want to give him the night of his life. "Why don't you get your driver to bring your car around? So we can go to your place."

Noah had never heard sweeter words. He'd been certain she was determined to keep things as they'd been before Florida, but apparently not. Unfortunately, he saw trouble out of the corner of his eye—tall and gorgeous and for the life of him, he couldn't remember her name. Whatever it was, she was definitely a woman he'd dated and she was zeroing in on him like a heat-seeking missile.

"Noah Locke, you are a royal jerk." The woman swished her long brown hair over her shoulder.

"I'm sorry?" It was the only thing he could think to say. The look of horror on Lily's face was making it hard to think straight.

"Was I not clear? You're a jerk. I saw the pictures in the tabloids. We went out two weeks ago and now you're engaged to be married? So what was I? A little something on the side?" The woman directed her sights at Lily. "I hope that ring is worth it, because I'm not sure he is. Unless you want to be treated as if you're disposable."

Lily sat a little straighter, but didn't say a thing. She merely cocked an eyebrow at Noah.

Noah scooted out of the booth and stood. "I'm sorry, but I'm going to have to ask you to leave. My fiancée and I are trying to enjoy ourselves."

"I'm sure you're not used to women calling you out on your crap, but somebody needs to do it. I hope the marriage works out, because I think you've run out of single women in Manhattan anyway." With that, she stormed off.

Noah plopped down, unsure of what had just happened, but certain that was his pride she'd ground into the floor. "I'm so sorry. That has never happened. Well, almost never."

"You certainly increase your odds when you go out with enough women to warrant a tabloid video."

"You know that's not me."

"I do know that. It still doesn't make what just happened any better."

"She was terrible, wasn't she?"

Lily squinted at him. "What? No. That's not what I was saying. She felt used, Noah. No woman should feel like that. Do you have any idea how many times I've been that woman?"

"Approaching a former boyfriend in a bar and making a scene?"

"No. The spurned lover. The woman who gets dumped by the handsome guy who can have whatever and whomever he wants. I've been in her shoes and it's not fun. I nearly made room for her to sit and offered to buy her a drink. Or at least tell her that our engagement isn't what it appears to be."

"It's not my fault if other guys treated you badly."

"This is not about me. But for the record, I have several of those. It's not fun to be yanked around."

"Hey. I didn't yank her around. I don't do that. I'm always up-front. I'm always clear it's not serious. Sawyer practically drilled that into my head."

A breathy laugh left Lily's lips. "And you're going to keep walking in Sawyer's footsteps? He managed to figure out that wasn't the way to live his life."

Noah felt as though Lily had plunged a dagger into his heart. Yes, he looked up to Sawyer. How could he not? Sawyer was the one positive male role model in his life. So, yes, they'd shared the same attitude toward women—don't get involved, don't buy into that moment when everything is new and it's easy to get swept away. Their dad had made an embarrassing habit of that, leaving a trail of broken hearts in his wake.

"I don't need you to psychoanalyze me, especially not on this topic. There's plenty you don't know."

"Seriously? I've had to spend the last two years hearing you sweet-talk women over the phone or even worse, bring them by the office. I know exactly what your modus operandi is." She grabbed her purse and coat and scooted out of the booth. "I'm just going to take a cab home. Good night, Noah."

He was still catching up with what she'd said. Had he

hurt her by letting her witness glimpses of his love life? "Lily, wait. My driver can drop you off at your place. We can talk about this."

She took off and Noah had no choice but to wind his way through the throng of people in the bustling bar. He followed her out onto the busy sidewalk. Dozens of people walked past, some filing in and out of the bar. The sun had set and the air held a chill.

"You and I both know what happens the minute we get in the back of that car, Noah," Lily muttered while tugging on her coat. "We can't keep our hands off each other. But we have to. That's the only way I get out of this ridiculous situation with my pride and job intact. Those are both supremely important to me."

"So you've said."

Anger blazed in her blue eyes. "Don't you dare fault me for putting my career first. A man does that and nobody bats an eye. I'm going now. See you tomorrow. At *work*."

Noah looked around. There were people everywhere and Charlotte had been clear that they had to remember the show they were putting on. They were so close with the Hannafort deal. "No kiss goodbye? We're supposed to be getting married."

Lily sidestepped to the curb and thrust her hand up in the air. A cab zipped right over. "Nobody's watching. We're fine." She opened the door and climbed inside without another word.

Noah stood there feeling like an idiot. He'd been so stupid to think that a little role-play with Lily would be harmless. He felt as if his entire sense of self was dissolving, and he knew he'd played a huge role in that. Why did it have to be that the allure of Lily was so great, and she was the one person who could send this all tumbling down?

Ten

At the office the next morning, a number came up on Noah's caller ID that made his stomach lurch—his dad. He picked up, slumping back in his office chair and preemptively kneading his forehead. "Dad. Hi."

"You don't have to sound so excited to talk to me."

Last night at the bar had nearly killed Noah, kissing Lily's neck and having it all blow up in his face. Now this. It was going to be a brutal day. "Trust me. I'm thrilled."

"I was hoping this would be a happy phone call, but after seeing the papers this morning, it looks as though this engagement of yours isn't going to stick. I'm sorry to see that."

Papers? Noah had no idea what his dad was talking about. He cradled the phone between his shoulder and cheek, typing his own name into the search bar on his computer. It only took a fraction of a second for the story to come up. Trouble in Locke Paradise. Beneath the headline was the photographic evidence of his argument with

Lily in front of the bar. This would've been a very different article if she had just listened to him.

"It's the tabloids. This is what they do. It's nothing." His words might have sounded cool and collected, but Noah was feeling anything but that on the inside.

"Pictures don't lie. I really was hoping you'd finally get your act together. You can't always let Sawyer be the perfect son."

The perfect son. This was a classic example of their father's cruel ways. He'd never seen Sawyer as the perfect son. If anything, their dad put more effort and attention into sabotaging Sawyer than he did Noah. But he liked to tell Noah that his older brother was the perfect son merely to get under his skin.

"My engagement to Lily is great. Thanks for calling to congratulate us, by the way."

"Thank you for calling to tell me about it."

Touché. "I would've gotten around to it eventually. Work has been incredibly busy." The instant the words were out of his mouth, he regretted them. Giving his dad any inkling of what was going on with their business was always a bad idea.

"So I gather. I understand that you attended Lyle Hannafort's daughter's wedding. There isn't something brewing between your little company and Hannafort, is there? That would be a real slap in the face to everything I've worked so hard for. You know I despise Lyle. The man is a self-righteous blowhard and a terrible businessman."

Noah's pulse thundered in his ears. He and Sawyer had long suspected that somebody was feeding their dad information on the Locke and Locke business dealings. Noah couldn't take the chance that his dad would get wind of the Hannafort deal. He and Sawyer had taken great pains to keep everything under wraps. "For a terrible business-man, he's got quite the empire."

"And looking to add to it, from what I understand."

That one hit a little too close to home. Noah had to end this, now. "We went to a wedding. Charlotte used to work on weddings with Lyle's wife. Stop reading so much into it."

"You and your brother can be as coy as you like. I just want you to know that I'm watching."

Noah sat up in his chair and plopped his elbow down onto the desk. "Is there something else you wanted? I have some work I need to get to."

"No. Merely calling to make sure everything is okay. I worry about you and your siblings."

No, you don't. "Everything's great."

"Okay, then. I'd like to meet my future daughter-in-law at some point if that's possible. That's a courtesy your brother wasn't willing to extend to me. I had to meet Kendall on my own."

Another lie. Dad had met Kendall weeks before she and Sawyer were engaged, and only because he'd tried to buy off Kendall to spy on Sawyer or at the very least sabotage the reopening of the Grand Legacy. "We'll see. I'll let you know."

"Have a good day, son."

A low grumble fought to leave Noah's lips. "You, too." As soon as he hung up, he tossed his phone aside onto a stack of paperwork. He didn't want to look at it again anytime soon.

Just then, Lily marched into Noah's office and tossed a copy of one of the most infamous New York tabloids on his desk. "Page five." She jabbed her finger into the headline then dropped down into the chair and crossed her legs. Even when she was obviously mad, she was ridiculously hot. Last night had been torture. He'd been so close to taking her home.

"I've already seen it. I told you we should've kissed each other goodbye."

Lily dropped her chin and shot him a pointed glance. "Don't make this my fault. We wouldn't have had that argument in the first place if it hadn't been for your former lady friend stopping by for a visit."

Noah took one more look at the paper. He and Lily were both attractive people, but it was amazing the unflattering angles the paparazzi were able to capture. He hated the tabloids. That much was official. It didn't even matter anymore that they were what had brought Lily closer to him. Now they were driving her further away.

"I hate this, Noah." Lily sat back in her chair, staring out the window, her head wagging slowly back and forth. "It's too much. This is way more than we ever talked about."

"What do you want me to say? It's not like I can control this."

"My neighbor saw this. The little old lady who lives down the hall from me. She was so upset and I had to convince her that we were still together, when the reality is that it's all fake."

Don't remind me. This was getting to Noah, too. Being around Lily while she tried so hard to keep him at arm's length was much worse than the misery he'd been experiencing before.

Sawyer poked his head into Noah's office. "Did you guys see the story in the paper? Kendall showed it to me. Not good." He stepped inside and leaned against the doorframe.

Noah didn't get headaches often, but today was already an exception. "It gets worse. Dad saw it. And he knows we went to the wedding. He suspects something is going on with Hannafort. It's only a matter of time until he finds out. My worry is that it's going to happen before everything is signed and he finds some way to interfere. For all we know, Dad was behind the tabloid video in the first place."

Sawyer sucked in a deep breath, adopting his trademark look of concern. "It could happen, especially considering everything he did to mess with the Grand Legacy."

"I also think Dad suspects there's something off about my engagement to Lily. He could out us, easily."

Lily's gaze flew back and forth between Noah and Sawyer. "Do you think he could put the deal in true jeopardy? I haven't done all of this extra work for that to all go south."

Noah couldn't for the life of him figure out what Lily wanted from him anymore, but he was starting to get a better idea. Between sticking up for the woman in the bar and now treating their fake engagement as nothing but work, it was clear that everything that had happened between them in Florida had meant very little to her. Noah was getting a taste of his own medicine and he didn't like it at all.

"We have to do something," Sawyer said. "Any suggestions?"

"I have one," Noah said. "How about we not give the tabloids any more free material?"

Lily shot him a look so fast it could've sliced his head off. "That's not fair. We can't exactly control that."

"Or can we? I mean, at least circle the wagons and keep you two away from negative publicity." Sawyer nodded, clearly calculating. "I think we need to double-down on the engagement. Lily, I think you need to move in with Noah."

Lily's eyes grew as big as saucers. "Move in with him. As in pack up all of my stuff and move into his condo in the Grand Legacy. You do realize this is far more than I was originally asked to do. Way more." Her voice was reaching a pitch that would soon only be audible to dogs.

"Don't forget, I have to go meet Marcy Hannafort in a few days and plan a fake wedding."

There was no mistaking what Lily was saying. She wanted more money. Noah knew it. "Fine. Then we up your percentage." If ever there was a message that everything was back to being business, that was it. Part of Noah hated that it had come to this, but it was unavoidable. It was a tangled mess and Lily was not wrong. They were asking her to go well beyond the call of duty.

"Three percent?" Sawyer asked. "That seems fair to me."

Lily took in a deep breath through her nose and nodded. "Yes. That sounds fair."

"Great. Done." Noah shuffled some papers on his desk, wondering what in the hell he'd just proposed and agreed to. He and his brother were buying off the woman Noah couldn't get out of his head, all so she could move in with him. This was all kinds of wrong.

"In the meantime, we need to double our efforts into figuring out where Dad is getting his information. I read an article about a security company specializing in corporate espionage. I don't like that word when we're talking about our own dad, but it's pretty much come to this." Sawyer rapped on the door casing two times and walked away.

Painful silence hung in the air with Sawyer's departure. Lily sat in the chair, arms crossed, her foot bobbing. Noah vacillated between staring at papers he couldn't care less about and trying not to look at Lily's legs. He really needed to get his act together.

"So. When do you want me to move in?" Her tone said she was resigned to this new reality. That extra 2 percent apparently made the idea tolerable.

"Whenever. Tomorrow?"

"Okay. Sounds good. I'm going to get back to work. I

have a ton of emails to answer." She rose from her chair and headed for the door.

Noah wanted to let the events of the last half hour go, but he couldn't. "Extra work, Lily? Is that what this has been to you?"

"Excuse me?"

"I realize we've had some uncomfortable moments, but it's not like you weren't taken care of. We went to an amazing destination wedding together. And I guess more than anything, I thought we had fun in Florida."

"We did have fun, Noah. We talked about that last night. But that still doesn't mean that I wanted all of this other stuff to happen."

He didn't believe for a minute that she was so naive. "What do you want from me? You had to know what you were getting yourself into when you agreed to this in the first place."

"Like I had a choice, sitting there in Sawyer's office while everyone basically laid the entire future of Locke and Locke on my shoulders. Plus, I agreed to a weekend. That was it. Now we're moving in together. This was the last thing I planned on."

"Yeah. You and me both."

In case the tabloids were watching, Lily moved into Noah's brand new condo on the seventeenth floor of the Grand Legacy in broad daylight, around noon the next day. They made a show of the movers hauling her things into the building, but more than half of the boxes were empty. This was a temporary measure and Lily was, quite honestly, tired of the act.

"Is that the final load?" Noah came out of his home office as the movers marched by with more boxes.

"I think so." Lily was doing her best to remain upbeat,

but this was yet another life event she hated faking. She'd never moved in with Peter, which ultimately ended up being a blessing, but that made this a first for her, unlike getting engaged. And it put her in whisper-thin proximity to Noah, when every warning sign imaginable was going off in her head.

One of the movers had Noah sign some paperwork while the rest of them filed out of the apartment. Once he was gone, Lily was alone with the man she couldn't resist, who held her professional future in his hands.

"I guess I should get myself set up in the guest room."

"Sounds like a plan. I have some more work to do." Noah went down the hall to his home office and Lily decided that distance was the best. Things were still chilly between them after the argument yesterday.

Lily unpacked her clothes. She hung dresses, skirts and blouses in the closet and put everything else away into the bureau. Noah's apartment was straight out of *Bachelor Pad Monthly*, lots of expensive modern furniture and not a single soft touch anywhere. Her bed was a platform style in dark wood with built-in floating bedside tables. The bedding was dark gray. She would've called it austere if it wasn't such a high thread count. Lily had no idea how long she'd be living here, but if it ended up being more than a few weeks, she might need to go shopping for cute throw pillows or a scented candle. A few weeks? Her nerves would be rubbed raw by then. It was that difficult to be around Noah and pretend like everything was fine and that nothing had happened.

Still, he had not only agreed to the 3 percent, he'd suggested the increase. And there was an argument to be made that their predicament was exactly that—theirs. They were in the same boat, for better or worse, and perhaps Lily needed to stop being so hard on Noah.

She headed down the hall to his office. "I was thinking that I'd make dinner. If you're up for that."

Noah looked up and his green eyes worked their way into her soul. The part of her that had been mad at him was a distant memory now. "You don't have to do that. I order in most nights."

"May I?" She gestured for the brown leather chair opposite his desk. Noah's office was by far the most comfortable room in the house. Beautiful antique desk, soft lighting and an array of cool art on the wall—black-and-white photographs and some old playbills from jazz shows at the Village Vanguard.

"Yes. Please." He got up from his seat and walked over to a turntable in the corner and flipped the record. When he moved the stylus over to the spinning vinyl, some familiar jazz began to play.

"Oh, wow. I haven't heard this since I was a kid. Art Tatum?"

Noah nodded. "The one and only."

Lily looked behind her. There was an entire wall of records at the far side of the room. She got up to peruse the spines. "My grandfather used to play this all the time."

"Are you calling me an old man?"

"No, but you are the man with a record player. I don't think I know anyone else who has one."

"Vinyl's making a big resurgence. It sounds so much better than anything else, especially if you're into music recorded in the '50s and '60s. That music was engineered for this medium. It's not really meant to be listened to any other way."

He might not be wrong about that. The record sounded amazing. "I also don't know anyone who has this many records. You must've been collecting forever."

"Not forever, but I did go through a big audiophile stage

when I was a teenager. I took my dad's record collection since he never listened to it and I built on that. I would take the train into the city on the weekends and spend hours in record stores."

"Interesting. Were you just bored?"

"I don't know. Aren't all teenagers bored? I know that for me, Sawyer had moved out and Charlotte was off doing her own thing. Partying, mostly. I was a nerd. I was not out partying."

Lily could hardly believe the words out of Noah's mouth, but he had hinted at this the day they went out to lunch after he bought her the engagement ring. "I really have a hard time believing that."

He held his hands up in surrender. "True story. I didn't have my first girlfriend until I was a senior in high school. I went through a very unfortunate pudgy stage."

"Okay. Now I really know you're lying. You're so trim." Remarking on Noah's physique was bringing back the memories of their tryst at the Hannafort wedding. Noah wasn't just slim, he was all lean muscle. Yes, a bit lanky, but she had a big weakness for that.

He held up a finger. "Hold on one minute. Allow me to dig up some very embarrassing photographic evidence." He crouched down and slid open a panel in a midcentury oak credenza. He rummaged around and eventually pulled out a photo album. He flipped through several pages, finally showing it to her. "There."

Lily sat on the Persian rug, hardly believing what she was seeing. Sure enough, there was Noah's hair, and definitely his straight nose, and what appeared to be his beautiful green eyes, but they were in a decidedly rounder and much shorter package. "You were still cute." Her voice broke a bit and she wasn't quite sure why. Maybe because she so often saw Noah as superhuman. The golden boy with the world at his feet. This made him seem more real, which was a ridiculous concept. She worked with him every day. She'd seen him get angry and upset. She knew that he was human. But still, this was not something she'd ever expected to see.

"I really wasn't cute, but thank you for saying that."

"How old are you in this picture?"

"Fifteen. I grew about a foot and a half the next year."

"And Sawyer was out of the house at that point?"

"Yeah. He left as soon as he could. Went into the military, which really pissed off my dad. He'd wanted him to go to business school and work for him, but it didn't happen that way. Plus, I think my dad felt like Sawyer was always making him look bad. Dad went to a military school as a boy, but didn't have the nerve to do what Sawyer did."

Lily lifted the page to look at more. "May I?"

"Yeah. Of course."

She flipped to the next set of photographs, some more formal-looking portraits around a Christmas tree. "Who's in this one?"

Noah went straight down the line. "That's my dad, my dad's second wife, Charlotte, me, Sawyer and then my stepsiblings, Todd and Beth."

"Did you like them?"

"I did. A lot. We were actually quite close. But then my dad divorced their mom, they moved out and I had another set of siblings to get used to."

"Not exactly your normal upbringing."

"No. Not really." Noah took the photo album from her hands. "What about you?"

"Hey. I wanted to look some more." She let her voice express her true disappointment. She loved looking at old photos, especially of Noah.

"I promise it's more of the same."

"No baby pictures?"

He laughed. "Hold on one second." He put the photo album back and pulled out a small leather box. Inside it was a tidy stack of old photos. "Here you go. No laughing. This was the origin of chubby Noah."

Lily couldn't help but smile as she looked at the photograph. There was a very happy baby in the arms of a beautiful woman. "All babies are chubby. And you were adorable with your big bald head and thigh rolls."

"Exactly what every guy wants to hear."

"Is that your mom? She's beautiful."

"Yep. She really was beautiful. I miss her a lot. You know how they say some people are the glue that holds a family together? Well, my mom was the glue. Things were never the same after she died."

"I'm so sorry, Noah. I'm sure that was hard for you." Lily noticed that there was a blue Tiffany box inside the leather box. "Made more than one trip to Tiffany?"

He shook his head. "Actually, no. This is my mom's ring. Remember I told you about it the day we went to get yours?"

"Right. Of course." Lily didn't ask to see it. It was just a reminder of their arrangement.

"You didn't answer my question. What about you and your family? For as much as we've worked together, I don't know much."

"I'm boring. My parents are happily married. I have one brother. He's two years younger than me. Grew up outside Philadelphia. My mom and dad managed a small hotel. That's how I ended up in hospitality."

"That doesn't sound boring at all. That sounds really nice."

"It definitely wasn't bad."

"And then what brought you to New York?"

"Honestly, I just needed to get out of Philadelphia. I figured all of the best hotels were Tiffany in the city, so I moved here to get a job. I switched around a few times, trying to get a position as a general manager, but I wasn't getting anywhere. But then I read in a hospitality magazine that you and Sawyer were going to renovate the Grand Legacy and I wanted to be a part of it." She picked at a spot on her jeans. At the root of that story was Peter and the failed engagement.

"Hold on. Back up. Why did you feel like you needed to get out of Philadelphia?"

Lily could've easily talked her way out of this, but Noah had shown her some pretty embarrassing things about himself. Maybe it was time to let him know at least a little bit about her past. "Yeah, that. A bad ex."

He turned to her, his eyes saying he was eager for more. "One of the guys who yanked you around?"

"Yeah. You could say that." The words were like a rock lodged in her throat. "He broke off our engagement."

Noah's shoulders visibly dropped. "Lil. Why didn't you tell me about this?"

"It's not exactly something that comes up during a job interview or in normal office chitchat."

"Well, yeah, but I took you to Tiffany and bought you an engagement ring. Now I feel like an ass. I mean, even more of an ass than I felt like before. I'm so sorry."

She hated hearing the pity in his voice. "Don't be. It's not your fault. And I dodged the proverbial bullet. He got married and divorced since then."

"Yeah, but that day at the jewelry store had to have been uncomfortable for you. I never would've even known it."

She shrugged. "I guess I'm really good at hiding things."

"I don't want you to feel like you have to hide things from me. You know, no matter what happens, our friendship has become really important to me. It's funny, I always used to think of Sawyer as my best friend, but it might actually be you."

Lily felt like she needed to hold her breath, if only to hold on to this moment. Tears misted her eyes. "Now you're going to make me cry."

"Don't do that. Come here."

Noah pulled her into a hug and she sank into his embrace. Right or wrong, Noah's arms were the only place she wanted to be. She felt safe, like nothing could ever hurt her. That was saying a lot considering the chaos in which they were currently living. He caressed her back and rocked her back and forth. It felt so good. Impossibly good.

"It's okay to cry if you need to. You've been under a lot of stress. I'm sorry for that. I know my brother and I have been the source of a lot of it."

She clung to him, not wanting to let go. If only he knew that this hug was about so much more than her painful past or a bad boyfriend—it was about having what you want within your reach and not being able to take it. She wanted him even more now than she had at the wedding. She wanted things to be uncomplicated. She wanted a chance at Lily and Noah. But everything seemed to be standing in their way—the business, her career, his reluctant heart.

It was difficult, but she extracted herself from the hug. Giving herself false hope was a one-way ticket to misery. "So? Dinner?" She discreetly wiped a tear away from her cheek.

"I have no clue what it's in my fridge, but there's definitely wine."

"Good. I'm going to need that. Maybe a permanent IV drip."

"Moving got you that stressed out?" He got up from the floor and extended his hand to help her.

"Among other things." Now that she was standing, it took everything she had not to hug him again, but she didn't need to tell him that he was most of the reason she needed wine. "I get to meet Marcy in the grand ballroom downstairs tomorrow afternoon to start planning our wedding."

"Can we have a chocolate cake? I hate those plain vanilla ones."

"You can have whatever you want." She laughed, but her heart ached at the thought of what her words really meant. This wasn't a joke. They were spinning a fictional web and it was messing with her head and her heart. She didn't want to be pretending anymore. It hurt too much. "We both know the wedding's not going to happen."

Eleven

Lily liked spending time with Marcy Hannafort just fine, but she had been dreading their wedding planning meeting. She hated everything about this—pretending to have a life that she'd never have, with a man she could easily end up wanting forever, and now they were planning the one thing Lily couldn't stomach the idea of—a wedding.

She did like spending time in the other parts of the Grand Legacy, though, so she tried to focus on the positives of that. She and Marcy walked around the grand ballroom, Marcy discussing seating and flow while Lily admired the glorious art deco glass ceiling and other historic details Noah and Sawyer had so painstakingly restored.

"Lily, darling. I feel like you aren't really here with me. Is everything okay?"

Apparently, Lily wasn't as good at faking some things as she'd thought she was. "There's so much to think about. It's overwhelming." The truth was that it wasn't overwhelming at all. If this were her real wedding, Lily would be organizing the heck out of it, exactly as she had the first time. No detail would be overlooked. The groom would have whatever flavor of cake he wanted. The guest list would've been set weeks ago. Lily would have her perfect dress, just like before. It would be a different gown the second time, though. The first had landed at a thrift store. Hopefully a bride-in-need had found it *and* her happy-ever-after.

"I don't know, Marcy. This is stressing me out. I have a million things I need to do back at the office and we're trying to make all of these decisions. This isn't really my sort of thing."

"Do you want me to take over? Because I can. I can promise you a beautiful wedding. It'll be your dream day. Just like you've probably imagined since you were a little girl."

Lily was instead stuck with the indelible vision of her nightmare day, of standing in the back of the church and never getting to walk up the aisle. Brides don't get left at the altar. There's no reason to even go into the chapel if the groom-to-be isn't standing there, waiting. Brides get left in the lobby.

As Lily learned, canceling a wedding at the last minute was a horrific task. She'd had to break the news to her guests, standing at the front of the church about to fall apart and saying that she was so sorry they'd come for nothing. Lily had to suggest that everyone take their wedding gifts with them when they left. All the while, she was crumbling on the inside because the man she'd thought she would spend her life with had decided that wasn't going to happen.

Never mind that Lily had never been convinced that Peter loved her. That was a realization that had taken a long time to reach. She was a solid choice, and he was, too. But there was no fire between them. Zero spark. Just safety and security. In many ways, their wedding had been a game of chicken. And Peter had the guts to end it first. Lily could be thankful for that now, since she couldn't imagine a life with him, but it didn't mean that it still didn't hurt. She'd spent a lifetime as the girl who made a habit of seeking un-attainable guys and it never working out. Just when she'd resigned herself to something more realistic, a man who wasn't quite a romance novel hero, she'd managed to fail at keeping him, too.

"Maybe we should postpone the wedding," Lily blurted. She was ready to try anything at this point. "You said it yourself. We have so little time."

"Lyle seems awfully set on the publicity we can get out of the event. I'd hate to disappoint him."

"Yeah. Me, too." Never mind that Marcy's reason was no reason at all to have a wedding.

Marcy shook her head and took Lily's hand. "Do you have cold feet? Are you questioning your love for Noah?"

Lily almost laughed. She didn't question her attraction to Noah, at all. She didn't question her affection for him either. But love? She wasn't there. Her heart and her head kept telling her those were treacherous waters. She would not fall in love with Noah, however much she had zero problem imagining it. Her pride and her future depended on staying wedged in practicality.

"No," Lily answered. "I just don't want to make a mistake." That much was not a ruse.

"Do you mean the wrong man? Was that video about Noah really the truth?" Marcy shook her head. "I had a feeling there was something off about this. I told Lyle I had misgivings, but he didn't want to hear it."

Lily had to squash Marcy's misgivings. "No. No. That

video was not the real Noah. That much I can promise you. He's a very sweet and caring person. He's taken good care of me." Financially, that was true, as well. "Maybe I need a night to sleep on it. Think over everything we talked about today."

Marcy nodded. "Sure, hon. That makes sense. Let me give you this list of the things we need to decide on. The guest list, the cake, the menu, the place settings and tableware, the chairs, the color scheme. Good God, yes. We haven't even chosen a color scheme."

Lily felt like Marcy was trying to drown her in details. "I have the list. I promise I will go through it and make some decisions."

"Don't take too long. We've got to get this show on the road."

Noah had left work early. He couldn't concentrate without Lily in the office, knowing that she was at her meeting with Marcy. Normally, it was Lily's presence that was distracting. Today, it was her absence.

He tracked down Marcy and Lily just as they were leaving the grand ballroom. "There you are. How'd everything go? Did I get my chocolate cake?" The minute he started asking questions, he could tell from Lily's face that things had not gone well.

"Chocolate has been decided. Everything else is up in the air, I'm afraid," Marcy said.

"I wasn't much help today. Maybe you and I can talk about it upstairs," Lily said.

Noah took her hand and kissed her cheek. "Don't worry. We'll get it all done."

The three of them wound their way through the back hall to the elevator. The lobby was straight ahead. "You know where you're going, right?" Noah asked Marcy.

"I do, thank you. Lily, we'll talk tomorrow? Maybe a good night's sleep will help." Marcy smiled at Noah. "Or no sleep might help, too."

Noah laughed, wishing that was an option available to him. "Thank you for your help, Marcy. Lily and I both appreciate it." As Marcy walked away, he punched the button for the elevator, which opened right away. He and Lily stepped on board. "Do you want to talk about it?"

She stared up at the numbers above the door and shook her head. "Not right now. Upstairs."

Noah took her hand and her cue, staying quiet. He sensed she needed him right now, and he'd be lying if he said it didn't feel good. Having her move in yesterday had been the best and the worst thing that had happened to him in a long time. Last night had been amazing, the two of them staying up late and talking. He'd never done that with a woman. He'd never felt comfortable enough to open up. Lily was his safe place. Those two years of frustration over working together and not being able to touch her or kiss her or tell her everything going through his head had not been for nothing. It had built a solid friendship. It had established trust, and Noah understood just how important that was.

The elevator stopped on his floor, seventeen, and he and Lily ambled down to his end of the hall. As soon as he opened the door and they stepped into his foyer, she let loose. "That was a disaster."

"That bad?"

"It's a nightmare." She marched right down the hall, past the kitchen and into the living room, and he had no choice but to follow. "There's the cake that will never be baked and the dress I'll never buy and the guests we'll never invite." She turned back to him, her face strained in a way he'd never seen before. "I can't do it, Noah. I can't.

The lies, the standing there and chatting about place settings and DJs. It's impossible. We have to say or do something to put her off."

He went to her and held her hands, rubbing his thumbs over her fingers to reassure her that everything would be okay. She looked so stunning today in a simple black dress she'd worn to the office at least one hundred times. Her eyes were stormy and sad right now. He hated seeing her so upset. "Okay. We'll come up with an excuse of some sort. I don't know what. Come on and sit down with me and we'll have a drink and we can brainstorm some reasons why people cancel weddings."

Noah went to lead her to the couch, but Lily was frozen. "Lil. What's wrong?"

"I…" A single tear rolled down her cheek. "I can't."

"Just tell me." He wasn't sure what the awful sensation in his chest was, but it felt like his heart was being torn in two.

"I'll tell you why people cancel weddings. They do it when they decide they don't love the bride. When they decide that she isn't special enough or smart enough or kind enough or pretty enough to spend an entire lifetime with. That's why people cancel weddings."

Noah swallowed hard. *The broken engagement.* "Hold on a second. Are you talking about…"

Lily nodded frantically, her lips pressed tightly together, her eyes welling with tears. "He dumped me in the church, Noah. He didn't want to marry me and it was the worst day of my life. And now I feel like I'm reliving every stupid minute I spent planning it. Only this time, the groom is you, which might be amazing if it were real, but it's not. This wedding isn't going to happen either."

Noah struggled for breath as her words tumbled around in his head. Did Lily have feelings for him? It sounded like she did. If ever there was a time to come out with his own feelings for her, this was it.

"I have something I need to tell you."

"I can't take any more bad news."

Just say it. "I've wanted you for a long time. A really long time, Lily. Probably since the moment you walked into our office that first day." It was such a relief to finally come out with it. How foolish he'd been to keep it bottled up all this time. "So when I admitted at the wedding that I was frustrated, it was about far more than seeing you in a bathing suit or because we'd been holding hands and kissing. It was because I finally had a taste of what I'd wanted for so long, but I couldn't have you for real. All because you were too good at your job to let me screw it up. I couldn't let my brother down like that, but it's been killing me. Slowly. Every day."

She looked up at him, her eyes wide, traveling back and forth and searching his face. Her lower lip dropped. A puff of breath left her lips, but no words came out. It was torture to come out with his truth and have it met this way. Was she about to tell him once again that her job was too important?

"Talk to me, Lily. If you're going to hurt me, it's okay. I can take it. Nothing could be worse than the last two years. And if you need to forget that we ever had this conversation, we can do that, too. We can pretend like it never happened. By now, I think we both know we have a talent for putting on a show."

"Will you just shut up and kiss me? For real. No more pretending."

The words echoed in his head. "Are you saying that this is a good thing?"

The sweetest, sexiest smile broke across her face. "You aren't very good at following directions, are you? I told

you I wanted you to kiss me. For real, Noah. Kiss me like
you want me."

"But I do want you."

"So show me."

Everything in his body went tight as he pulled her close,
lifting her to her tiptoes. Her lips met his, soft and giving.
It felt like a second try at their first kiss. It was all new
between them now that he was no longer burdened with
the secret he'd been carrying around so long. He had so
much to say to her now, every word crammed into a kiss.
*I think about this every day. I wonder about you. Do you
want me? Could you want me?* Her lips parted and he
hoped like hell that was the answer. She bowed into him.
Their tongues met and tangled, a return to that moment
of bliss at the wedding when she'd wanted him the way
he wanted her.

But it meant more to him now, and he had to know that
she felt the same way. He could've kept going, he could've
made his move and unzipped her dress, but he wasn't sure
he deserved to have her if she didn't feel the same way. As
much as he didn't want their kiss to end, he broke it and
settled his forehead against hers. "See? Do you get it now?"

She nodded slightly, her eyes only part open. "I have
my own confession to make."

"Tell me."

"I've wanted you from that first day, too. I have fantasized a million times about you backing me up against the
filing cabinet and kissing me. When I'm standing there
rubbing the back of my leg with my foot? I'm thinking
about you."

Noah's heart was about to punch a hole through the center of his chest. "Tell me more." Every muscle in his body
flooded with white-hot need.

"When you sit on the edge of your desk? I want to walk

up to you and stand between your knees and unbutton your shirt." She popped one of his buttons. "Like this."

Noah had never been more turned on. "That afternoon in the car, the day we went to buy your ring? I thought I was going to explode I wanted you so bad."

"You can have me, Noah. Right now. For real. No more pretending."

"There's no going back if we say it's for real."

"I know." She untucked his shirt and went to work on the rest of the buttons. He watched as she rolled the garment from his shoulders, spread her hands across his chest. "Your skin. It's so warm."

"It's you, Lily. You make it like this."

Lily had never had such a reversal of fortune in all her life. An hour ago, she'd been miserable. Now she was on cloud nine. Her fingers scrambled through the buttons on Noah's shirt. She made quick work of his pants, too. He unzipped her dress and they let it drop to the floor right there in the living room. Of course, today, she was wearing stockings—black ones from France, with a seam up the back and a wide band of lace at the top. Noah groaned when he saw them, his eyes now half-closed with desire.

"Is it possible to keep those on?" He reached around with both hands and grabbed her bottom.

Lily laughed as her lips trailed over his cheek. "Anything is possible if you believe in yourself."

"Good."

He took her hand and tugged her over to the couch. He sat down, his legs spread, his glorious chest and shoulders on full display. She could also see exactly how ready he was for her and it made her absolutely ache for him. It had been only a few days since they'd made love, but even that had been far too long. There were also quite a few things they'd never gotten around to in Florida, and she was keenly focused on pleasing him right now. He'd been so sweet to her the last few days. Lily dropped to her knees and caressed his erection through his black boxer briefs. She smiled up at him and he returned the expression, but it was clearly hard for him to keep it together. His head was bobbing. He was floating between pleasure and paying attention.

"Touch me, Lily. Please."

Noah raised his hips off the couch as she teased his boxers past his hips and down his legs. She wasted no time taking him in her hand and stroking firmly, then wrapping her lips around him gently, sucking and grazing his taut skin with her tongue. Noah dug both hands into her hair, softly massaging her head, gathering the strands in a handful at the nape of her neck. He piled her hair on top of her head, holding it in place as he moaned with every pass. She felt so damn sexy and wanted right now, she wasn't sure which way was up.

"Come here, Lil. I need to kiss you."

She released the grip of her lips and stood before him. He sat forward and wrapped his hands around her waist, kissing her belly, then slipping his fingers into the waistband of her panties and shimmying them past her hips.

She gazed down into Noah's gorgeous green eyes and knew she was with exactly the right guy. "Make love to me, Noah. I want you. I need you."

He stood and took her hand. "Not here. The bedroom." They rushed down the hall and Noah ducked into the bathroom, returning quickly with a condom.

"Come here. I'll put it on." Lily was standing next to the bed, waiting for him.

He walked up to her and they fell into another deep kiss as she took his length in her hands and took care of him.

He reached behind her and finally unhooked her bra, taking her breasts into both hands and nearly sending her into oblivion with flicks of his tongue against her nipples. Heat rushed to the surface of her skin. Her center ached for him. She stretched out on the bed, wearing only her stockings.

"I'd say that the ensemble is super sexy, but in reality, it's you." He took her foot and planted it in the center of his chest, trailing his fingers from her ankle to her knee. He bent her leg and kept going with his hand, down the inside of her thigh, making her need for him that much more pronounced. When he reached her center, she thought she might burst into flames. He remained standing, towering over her, caressing her apex with teasing, delicate circles. With every pass, she was closer to her climax, but that restless need for him wouldn't go away.

"Don't make me wait any longer, Noah. It's not nice."

He smiled and put his knee on the bed, spreading her legs wider with his hands. He positioned himself at her entrance and drove inside so slowly she thought she might pass out. Lily's mind swirled with the pleasure, especially when she heard the primal moan that came from Noah's sexy lips. He felt so perfect inside her, she didn't want it to end. But the peak was already bearing down on her, just like Noah's body weight against the ideal spot to send her over the edge. Every thrust he made was purposeful and strong. His breaths were hard and fast now, and his actions matched them.

Her peak was coming at her so quick, she could almost see it in her mind. The pressure coiled inside her, it fought to wind in on itself further. She thought she couldn't take it anymore right when the pleasure slammed into her and Noah followed almost immediately. He let his full weight rest on her as they kissed, their bodies damp with perspiration. She wrapped her arms and legs around him, pulling him closer when there was nowhere else for him to go, all while his body gave her relentless pulses of beautiful bliss.

They collapsed on the bed together in a lovely, breathless tangle. The beauty of that moment didn't fade, it only created an imagined glow around them. "That was amazing," Lily muttered into Noah's chest.

"Amazing, yes, but I can do better. Give me ten minutes and a drink of water and I'm ready for more."

"Better?" Lily could hardly speak, let alone open her eyes. She instead breathed in Noah's masculine scent and reveled in having made her way into his actual bed. Next, she'd have to focus on working her way into his heart. "I don't know how you can possibly top that."

"You have no idea, darling." He skimmed his fingers from her knee to her thigh, past her hip and up to her breast. He cupped it with his hand and pressed a hot, wet kiss against it.

Lily arched her back. Everything Noah did when he touched her was exquisite. "I think you're trying to unduly influence me."

"Absolutely. I intend to do nothing else all night."

Twelve

Noah wasn't sure he'd ever been so happy to wake up with a woman in his bed. He never wanted Lily to leave it, ever. He never wanted either of them to bother with clothes again, or work for that matter. He wondered if Sawyer would be okay with it if they both called in sick for the next month or two.

Lily rolled over and opened one eye. "What time is it?"

Noah stroked her arm gently. "A little after six. We have time to sleep if you want." Touching her bare skin was bringing every nerve ending in his body to life. "Or we could do something else to spend the time."

A smile rolled across her lips. She'd closed her one open eye. "You're a terrible influence on me. You realize that if we start, we're going to have an awfully difficult time stopping, which will only end up making us late to work. As my boss, I would think that would be the last thing you would want."

He scooted closer until his naked skin was touching hers. The blood began to rush through his body, spreading heat, narrowing his ability to think about anything more than sex. "As the boss, I think I can approve any activity I deem appropriate, regardless of whether or not it makes us late to work."

"What if we can have the best of both worlds?" Her voice was still sleepy and sexy.

"I'm not sure I know what you mean."

"Well, we both need to take a shower, right?"

Bingo. Noah was ready to launch himself out of bed. "I'll start the water."

Lily laughed and threw his pillow across the room.

Even after a long stay in the shower and a quick breakfast, Lily and Noah were only five minutes late for work. It felt a bit like they were conspiring when they stepped off the elevator, especially when they ran square into Sawyer.

"Good morning," he said, but there was nothing good-sounding about it.

"What's wrong?" Noah asked. Whatever it was, it couldn't bring him down. His brother could hurl one hundred problems at him today and it wouldn't matter. Noah reached for the door to their office.

"No. Noah. Out here. We can't talk in there."

"What the hell? Why not?"

Sawyer ushered Noah and Lily to the far corner of the hall, next to an empty office. "Dad called me about an hour ago. He knows about the Hannafort deal. He knows the details of the term sheet and everything. He knows that we lied to Lyle about your engagement and he's threatening to out us unless we meet his demands."

"Demands? What demands? He can't do this. It's blackmail."

"He wants the Grand Legacy back. I think this is what

all of this BS has been about. He just couldn't get over the fact that I inherited the hotel and not him."

"He can't do this. It's blackmail. We should call the police."

"And tell them what, exactly? He made the threat over a phone call. It's not like I had a tape recorder going. And I dislike him as much as you do, but he's our father. I don't want him in jail."

I do. Noah forced himself to take deep breaths. There was a war being waged inside of him right now. He was furious with his father, but not just for what he was doing and what he was after. He was mad because he'd gone to Sawyer first. Everything always boiled down to Sawyer. "Why didn't you call me the minute this happened?"

"Have you even looked at your phone, Noah? I left you a voice mail."

Noah dug it out of his pocket. Sure enough, there was a notification for a missed call from his brother. "We have to call that security company. The one that specializes in corporate espionage."

"Already done. They'll be here any minute."

Of course. Sawyer had everything under control, as he always did. "What can we do in the meantime?"

"Nothing. They told us to touch nothing. They don't even want us going into the office."

The elevator dinged and the doors slid open. A handful of men and women wearing black pants and matching black shirts, all carrying armfuls of equipment stepped into the hall. Sawyer rushed over and introduced himself to one of the women, then waved over Noah.

"We'll do a full sweep of the office for listening devices and cameras," the woman said. "We'll also run diagnostics on every computer, looking for spyware." She glanced down at Noah's hand. "Is that a work laptop?"

"Yes."

She reached down and took it from him. "I'll need that, too."

"How long will this take?" Sawyer asked. At least he had enough sense to ask the question. Noah was still reeling. Lily was standing over in the corner, seeming equally confused.

"Not long for an office of your size. A few hours. I'd go get a cup of coffee or something."

The woman opened the door to their office and her team followed her inside.

"As if today couldn't get any crazier, I'm supposed to meet Kendall at the obstetrician's office in a half hour. You two should find some way to keep yourselves busy."

Now you tell me. Noah would've much preferred to be at home with Lily, back in the shower. "Okay."

"Call me if you find out anything. I hope to be back before they're done." Sawyer jabbed the button for the elevator. "Then we start strategizing on what to do about Dad." He stepped on board and the doors closed behind him.

Noah ran his hands through his hair as Lily approached him. "This is so weird."

She took his hand. "I'm sure it'll all be fine. You and Sawyer have faced bigger challenges."

"Aren't you the least bit worried about this? Your nest egg is on the line if the Hannafort deal falls through."

She nodded. "I know. I just don't want to get all stressed out about something that might end up being nothing." She popped up onto her toes and kissed his cheek. "Now come on. Let's go get that cup of coffee."

They took the stairs and strolled a block down to a corner coffee shop that had killer pastries. After ordering two lattes, a lemon poppy seed muffin and an almond scone, they grabbed one of the café tables in front of the window. "Are you worried?" Lily asked. "I don't want you to be worried. You're too handsome to worry."

Noah laughed, but it was born of exasperation. When would everything go right at once? He and Lily had made a big breakthrough last night, one that he'd never thought he would ever make. He'd never professed his feelings to any other woman. He'd not only never wanted to, he'd never had the feelings he had for Lily.

"How are you so together right now?"

She looked down at her coffee and gave it a stir. "You need me right now. I don't know how else to be. I guess that's what makes me a good employee."

He reached across the table and took her hand. "It's also what makes you an amazing friend." *And what makes me love you.* The words were right there in his head, but they were as foreign as a language he could neither read nor speak. He wanted to say them to her, but he was as unsure right now as he'd ever been. He knew he couldn't take them back if he'd said them only out of weakness and ultimately couldn't live up to them. Lily deserved better.

She rubbed her thumb back and forth across the back of his hand. "You're an amazing friend, too. And my favorite person to take a shower with."

He smiled and raised her hand. Her engagement ring hit his lips when he kissed her fingers. Could that ring ultimately end up meaning something? "I feel the same way."

Several moments of silence played out between them as they sipped coffee, ate and watched the other patrons in the café. Still, neither let go of the other's hand. Once again, they were in this together. In so many ways, Lily was more important to their surviving this ordeal. Just like his mom had been the glue that kept the family together,

Lily was the glue of the business. It all started and ended with her. And Noah was starting to think the same thing about his life. He couldn't fathom the idea of not having Lily around.

"We should probably head back, don't you think?" he asked.

"Feeling antsy?" Lily got up and put on her coat.

"I want this resolved. That's all. I'm tired of the turmoil."

"You and me both."

The office looked like a war zone when Lily and Noah returned. The security team had taken everything apart, even going so far as to cut holes in walls, looking for listening devices. It was like something out of a spy movie. Sawyer was already back, and called Noah into his office.

A burly, bearded man from the security team cornered Lily. "I'm going to need you to stay right here." He pointed to one of the chairs in the reception area.

"But I have work to do."

"I understand, but we're still sorting things out. I can't allow you to touch your computer or answer the phones, either."

Lily plopped down into the seat. What in the world was going on? She racked her brain, wondering if she somehow knew the source of the leak. A member of the cleaning crew? The guy who came in to fix the copier? At least she knew it wasn't her, even if she had a very stern man fifteen feet away from her, staring her down, that made her feel as though she might have been responsible.

The entire premise of Sawyer and Noah's father having an inside source was so ridiculous to begin with. How could a parent go around purposely sabotaging his own children? Because of professional jealousy? Because they demanded their independence? It was terrible.

Sawyer's office door opened. "Lily. We need you to come in now."

She stood, but with every step, her heart beat a little more fiercely. It was hard not to feel like this was a walk to the gallows.

"Please, Lily. Sit down," Sawyer said when she'd stepped inside.

She did as instructed, which meant she was sitting right next to Noah. He turned and looked at her, his expression inexplicable. "Please tell me you didn't do it."

"Noah. Stop." Sawyer's tone made Lily jump.

"No, Sawyer. I can't. I can't even stomach what you're about to say to her."

"We have our evidence. We have to move forward."

"Does somebody want to tell me what's going on?" Lily asked, wishing it was appropriate for her to hold hands with Noah. She needed him right now.

Sawyer looked right at her. "We need you to be completely honest with everything we're about to ask you. If you can't be forthcoming with the facts, we'll have no choice but to press charges and talk to the police."

"The police?" It felt as if the ground beneath her had cracked open and she was plummeting through space. "Whatever it is that you're about to ask me, I will of course tell you everything I know. I would never hide anything from either of you."

"I told you, Sawyer. Lily would never do what you're about to accuse her of." The desperation in Noah's voice only made Lily feel worse.

"Will you let me get through this?" Sawyer asked. "Lily, we need you to tell us everything about your involvement with our father."

"I don't understand. I don't even know him."

A dismissive breath left Noah's lips. "Sawyer. This is absurd." Noah turned to her and the look in his eyes was full of remorse. Lily had never seen that expression. He was too laid-back to get worked up about much, which was part of why the entire morning had been so hard to deal with. "Your computer is the source of the leak."

"What? No. How is that possible?"

"Every night, the contents of your email folders are uploaded to a server owned by one of our dad's businesses. That's how he's been one step ahead of us this whole time, going all the way back to the renovation of the Grand Legacy."

Lily didn't know what to say. She was in shock. "I honestly have no idea what you're talking about. I would never do that. You have to believe me."

Sawyer crossed his arms over his chest and sat back in his chair. "Well, I don't know what to say. Until we straighten this out, you're on leave. I can't even allow you to look at your computer or touch anything before you leave the office. Noah will walk you out."

Lily stood and did as she was told, but she was on autopilot. As soon as they were out of Sawyer's office, she grabbed Noah's arm. "Please. You have to believe me. Do you honestly think I could do such a thing?"

"I do believe you, but this is an impossible situation right now. All evidence points to you. Sawyer seems convinced."

All she could think about was everything that had happened in the office for the last two years. She'd feared that things would end badly if she got involved with Noah, and that had come to fruition, but not in the way she'd thought it would. "Doesn't everything I've done for Locke and Locke count for anything?"

"Of course it does. But it also incriminates you. The transmissions started the week you began working here. And you made yourself indispensable, which put you right in the thick of some very high-level meetings."

Lily's brain was working double time to find some bit of information that could exonerate her. "If I was working for your dad, why would I have agreed to move in with you to save the deal? I could've let the Hannafort deal fall apart right then and there."

"But that's not his true motive. He doesn't want the story to come out. He wants the Grand Legacy. He always has. He tried to make our lives miserable through that project in the hopes that we would abandon it."

Lily looked up at the ceiling, in utter despair. She loved her job more than anything. Except Noah. She loved him. She knew it. And she definitely loved him more than her job. But what if she ended up losing both of the things she loved? And her nest egg? She couldn't bear the thought. The tears started to come and they weren't about to stop anytime soon.

"Mr. Locke." The security guy with the beard was standing right next to Noah. "Ms. Foster should not be in the office right now. We need to ask her to collect her things and leave."

Of the many things Lily had worried about, leaving this office she loved so much in utter disgrace was not one of them. "Okay. I'll go."

"I'll help you. And I'll call my driver and get him to bring the car around to take you back to the Grand Legacy."

Lily watched as Noah retrieved her bag and coat. She wasn't even allowed to touch her desk. Sawyer didn't even say goodbye. He was still holed up in his office. Noah walked her down to the street. It was starting to rain and she had no idea where her umbrella was. Somewhere in a box, back at Noah's.

He pulled her into a hug while the driver stood, waiting, the car idling. "We'll figure this out. There has to be some other explanation. I'll convince Sawyer somehow that he's wrong."

"Okay." She looked up into Noah's face, making a point of remembering every perfect angle, his amazing lips, his unforgettable eyes. She'd suspected all along that he wasn't meant for her and right now, it felt like every circumstance in the world was pointing to that very fact. If she wasn't proven innocent, Sawyer would fire her. He would bring criminal charges. If anything was going to make Christmas morning awkward, it would be spending time with your former boss and boyfriend's brother, the guy who'd tried to send you to jail.

The words she wanted to say were on her lips, but they would do no one any good now. They would only complicate things, make them worse when they were already impossibly bad. *I love you* was not going to fix anything today.

"Will I see you at home?" Noah's question dripped with the same doubt Lily was carrying around in her heart.

"Maybe. We'll see."

"Thinking about going to the bookstore? What's it called?"

"Petticoats and Proposals."

"Right. How could I forget?" He laughed quietly.

"And it's only Thursday. I go there on Fridays." Even the promise of a romance novel couldn't lift her spirits right now.

Noah pressed another kiss to her forehead. "I'll see you soon. It'll be okay. Somehow."

She nodded, even though she wasn't sure what she was

agreeing to. "Okay." She climbed into the car and the tears rolled down her cheeks.

"Are we headed to the Grand Legacy, ma'am?"

"For now, yes."

Thirteen

Noah got home early that night. He couldn't stand being around Sawyer or the office anymore. "Lily?" he asked. "You home?" He dropped his keys on the foyer table, but the sound echoed through his apartment in a way it never had before. He felt her absence in his bones. Coming home to an apartment that had no Lily was a whole new level of empty. Warmth and happiness were gone, and in their place was the clatter of metal keys on hollow wood. "Lily?" he called one more time, but there was no response. Noah had never felt more alone.

He still refused to believe that Lily had betrayed Sawyer and him. It didn't seem plausible, but the evidence was damning. After she'd left, he and Sawyer had talked over the timeline and it all made her look that much more guilty. Had she pulled the wool over their eyes? Was there a cold and calculating woman under that guise of perfect employee? She was no ordinary employee, either. She had the paperwork to claim her 3 percent of Locke and Locke forever, which was awfully convenient. The thought of Lily conspiring with their dad, undermining them, sabotaging their hard work was unthinkable, but the evidence was there and Sawyer was pushing him hard to believe every shred of it. *Use your brain, Noah. It's right here in black-and-white. She screwed us over.*

This was the price he'd avoided paying for so long. If you don't get close to people, they can't hurt you. Noah had never had to worry about money. He'd never had to worry about his career or the roof over his head or whether or not his future was secure. The only thing he'd ever had to worry about was whether anyone would not only love him, but whether they would actually stick around. He was the unlovable one—the guy who only skimmed the surface and was, thus, easy to walk away from. He'd feared that for half of his life and been sure of it for the other. And Lily had only proven his theory. She'd walked away from him today.

He wandered into the kitchen. She'd cleaned up. So much so that it was as if she'd never been there. Her tin of tea bags was gone. The flowers she'd put on the center island were, as well. He opened the refrigerator and everything was neat and tidy, and exactly the way it had been before she moved in. No nonfat yogurt. No bowl of strawberries. Just milk for cereal, orange juice and beer. Bachelor staples. And that was about to be his life again.

He closed the refrigerator door. He couldn't fathom deriving pleasure from food ever again. Instead, he headed for the home bar, loosened his tie, poured himself a double tequila and downed it. He stared straight up at the ceiling and focused on the burn. It hurt all right. Everything hurt right now and he'd better get used to it. There would be no more covering up pain with meaningless hookups or laughing it off with a joke he'd made one hundred times. He couldn't live like that anymore. He needed to embrace the pain of his existence, wrap his head around the reality and find a way to get up tomorrow morning, go back to work and hope that he and Sawyer could hold on to the Grand Legacy and keep the Hannafort deal together.

But first, one more drink. The second one burned as badly as the first. So much for numbing himself to anything at all right now. He replaced the stopper on the bottle and shuffled down the hall and straight back to his bedroom. He took one look at the bed and was smacked in the face with a memory he'd been so eager to cling to. Twenty-four measly hours ago, he'd been as happy as he'd ever been. He'd climbed out from under the secret he'd kept for two years, confessed that Lily had always had his number and her reaction had been everything he'd been so terrified to hope for.

Last night put their night at the wedding to shame. It was no longer lust and forbidden fruit—delectable and worth having, but not on a par with what had happened when he'd dared to bare his soul. The things they'd done to each other in that bed, the pleasure they'd given and taken, was unrivaled. He'd planned to hold on to it forever. Now he couldn't wait to be rid of it, although he couldn't imagine how he was ever supposed to go about doing that. Lily was seared in his memory. No woman would ever make him feel like that again.

He dropped down to a crouch, buried his head in his hands, then screamed right into his palms. The air tore from his lungs, but he felt no better after he'd done it. If anything, he only craved the release that much more. There was no way he was going to be able to sleep in that bed tonight. He couldn't sleep in the guest room either. It undoubtedly smelled exactly like Lily. Maybe he should move out of the Grand Legacy. Hell, he'd have no choice if his dad got his hands on the hotel. Maybe he should change his entire existence. Grow a beard and buy a cabin in Maine and spend his days chopping wood for the winter and learning to fish. He would look terrible with a beard. Good. It would keep women away.

Noah straightened and opened his eyes. That was when things got even worse. There on the nightstand was Lily's engagement ring, resting on top of a note. It felt as if his heart was being ripped from his chest for the third or fourth time since that morning. There'd be nothing left of him when this was over. Forget the beard and the cabin. He'd disappear.

He perched on the edge of the bed, picked up the ring and held it in the palm of his hand. He'd known that day at Tiffany that what they were doing was wrong, but he'd wanted to do it anyway. Even when he feared it would mess with her head and his. He would've done anything to be close to her. What a sap he'd been.

He flipped open the paper and Lily's sweet voice filled his ears.

Dear Noah,

Despite the deal we made, I can't keep the ring. It's too painful to keep. Without you, it means nothing.

For that same reason, I can't keep my 3 percent of the company. Even though I worked my ass off for that share, I don't want it if Sawyer doesn't trust me. I don't need it if there's even a chance that you doubt me. It will just be a reminder of everything we had and the way it all went away.

For the record, what we had never felt fake to me.

*Even when I was keeping my distance. I was only
protecting my heart. You were the guy in the ivory
tower and I was the girl standing on the ground,
peering up at you, desperately hoping you'd take a
minute to look at me. And notice. That part had always been important to me. I always wanted you to
notice. Even if it was only for a few minutes or days.
I guess I got my wish. It's just that nobody tells you
that when you get your wish, you might not get to
keep it. That's a life lesson I'm still not comfortable
with. I wish it wasn't true.*

*I hope you know with every bone in your body
that I would never, ever betray you. After today, it's
pretty clear to me that Sawyer doesn't know that. I
guess I'd allowed myself to believe that I was part of
the inner circle, but I never truly was. That's okay.
I understand how strong your bond is with your
brother. He's your rock. I had hoped to be that person in your life, but some things just aren't meant
to be.*

*Lastly, I want you to know that I harbor no ill
will. It's just not part of who I am. I will never understand vengeance or an anger that never dies. I can
only understand loyalty, friendship, love and good
intentions. Those are the only things that make any
sense to me. I hope you saw that in me, for however
long it lasted.*

*Love,
Lily.*

Noah ran his fingers over her name, while visions of
her wouldn't stop playing in his head. How was it that the
one time he actually had his act together with a woman,

it all had to blow up in his face? It didn't seem fair, but it did seem like confirmation from the universe that Noah and love were not meant to be. Yes, he'd fallen in love with Lily, but she and her apparent actions were now standing between him and the only other thing he could count on in life—Sawyer.

Sleep had not come easily that night, especially since Noah had opted for the couch. He tossed and turned, mulling over everything that had happened in the office yesterday. None of it added up. The supposed evidence was too obvious, too easy. Almost like it was being spoon-fed to them by a person with ulterior motives—their father.

But who else had access to Lily's computer? Nobody other than Noah and Sawyer.

He turned off his alarm before it sounded, got in the shower and then headed to the office. The sun was still coming up when he arrived. He went straight to his old planners, stored in the bottom drawer of a filing cabinet. The one from two years ago prompted a strange feeling when he saw it. The cover was burgundy leather, not his normal black. That year, his favorite color had sold out early and he'd been stuck with one he wasn't crazy about. But that wasn't the thing that struck him about it. It was that he had such vivid memories of closing it at the end of every work day that year—the year he started to fall for Lily.

He flipped through the calendar until he got to March. Lily had started on March 12. He would always remember the date. It was the first time he'd laid eyes on her. Sawyer had conducted her only in-person interview. Noah had only spoken to her on the phone. Noah then went back one week to find the name he was looking for—Robert Anderson. His phone number was right beneath it. Robert had been the guy who came in the week before Lily started work to deliver and set up her new computer. Noah and Sawyer had decided that they would use the one week of downtime between administrative assistants to get a few things in line—they bought a new desk, had the reception area painted and even put in all new furniture. But it was the computer that Noah was fixated on.

Noah glanced at the clock. It was only 8:00 a.m. But he decided to try the number anyway. He got voice mail for a nail salon in Queens. He double-checked the number and called again. Same message. Something was definitely up. The realization made the hair on the back of Noah's neck stand up. Robert Anderson was a mole. Noah knew it with every fiber of his being. He pulled up the website for his dad's development company and began doing image searches for every one of his father's employees he could find.

After about an hour, Sawyer came in. "You look like I feel."

Noah ran his hand through his hair, beyond exhausted. "I feel like hell. I didn't sleep. At all."

"The Lily thing really got to you, didn't it?"

Noah shook his head and got up from his desk. He loved his brother, but damn, he was being dense. "Yes, Sawyer, it did. It bothered me a lot. Do you want to know why? Because I let you mow me down yesterday."

"I was acting on the facts we had. What else was I supposed to do? Our business is the most important thing we have."

"No, Sawyer. Kendall and the baby are the most important thing you have. The business is what you *do* all day. I know it's your passion, but you have more in your life and I'm tired of believing that only you and Charlotte get to have that. I want it, too."

Sawyer set his laptop bag down in a chair. "I never said that I didn't want you to have that. Your track record never suggested anything else."

Noah was ready to scream again, but that wasn't going to accomplish anything. "Look. Stop digging up the past. I'm tired of it. The only thing that matters right now is that I don't believe Lily is capable of the things we have accused her of. She's our partner, she's an amazing employee and, most important, she's the woman I love."

"Hold on a minute. You love her? Did you two sleep together?"

"It's more than that. A lot more."

"You can't let your libido get between your own brother and the truth."

"I'm not. I'm going to find the real truth. I have to find a way to fix this."

The look of pity on Sawyer's face made Noah want to knock it right off, and Noah had never hit his brother. Not even when they were kids. "You're wasting your time."

"Think about it, Sawyer. If Lily was working for Dad, why be such a flawless employee?"

"That put her further into the inner circle."

Noah hated that his brother had an answer for everything. "I don't buy it. I also don't think Dad would've kept her on after the Grand Legacy was finally open. He would've had her disappear. The hotel is Dad's real obsession."

"Okay, then. Prove to me that Lily is innocent."

"I will. And then I will say I told you so when I'm done."

Sawyer left and Noah got back to work. After what seemed like hundreds of searches, he finally stumbled across what he was looking for, but Robert Anderson went by an entirely different name—Dan Lewis. The man worked for their father's IT department out of his main office in New Jersey. Aside from the name change, he was practically hiding in plain sight. Noah printed the page from the website and walked into Sawyer's office.

"I found the guy who sabotaged Lily's computer."

"What? Is that what you think happened?"

Noah explained his theory. Now that he was going through everything a second time, it made perfect sense. "And now I'm going out to Long Island to make things right."

"If you're going to talk to Dad, I'll go with you."

Sawyer wasn't going to lead the charge on this one. This was much more about saving Lily than rescuing the business. Only Noah could do that. "I need to do this on my own. I need to end this."

Sawyer nodded. "Okay. You do what you gotta do."

Noah grabbed the printout from the website and reached for the door. He turned back to his brother one more time. "Oh, and Sawyer. I told you so."

In the car on the way out to the Locke estate on Long Island, Noah did the unthinkable. He called Lyle Hannafort and told him everything. It was not a pleasant phone call, but Noah smoothed the ruffled feathers by the end. A man like Lyle Hannafort doesn't make a deal solely based on a man's reputation. Plus, Lyle seemed to appreciate that Noah would do anything for his business. In the end, it came down to zeroes and dollar signs. And the promise of an in-person apology to Marcy. That much Noah could do.

When he arrived at the stone-and-iron gate, he got the usual runaround from Tom, the guard stationed at the estate entrance.

"I'm not supposed to let any of you kids onto the property. You know that."

"Tom, I'm thirty and you've known me since I was ten. Maybe longer."

Tom grudgingly pressed the button opening the gate. "If I lose my job, I'm coming to work for you and your brother."

"Do it anyway. I promise you'll be much happier."

The car started down the crushed stone driveway, along the manicured hedges. The sprawling and stately white house with the black slate roof rose from the stand of trees starting to leaf out. What was it like for other people to return to their childhood home? For Noah and his siblings, the mixed feelings were too numerous to count. There had been more unhappy moments than happy in the house, but this was the only place they had known their mom. As far as Noah was concerned, this house was where love had once had a chance, but was squashed under the weight of their father's ego. Everyone around him—children, spouse and employees—existed only to serve him. To laud him. To shower him with affection he never deserved.

A member of his dad's security detail was standing outside when Noah arrived at the front door. Noah had to once again talk his way in. Since the kids had left home, their dad had practically turned the house into a fortress. As the guard radioed for approval, Noah stood with his hands stuffed into his pockets, noticing how the grounds and house were starting to look dilapidated. There were browned-out sections in the hedges and green algae bloomed near the foundation. Maybe his dad was losing touch with reality. Or maybe this deluded attempt to grab the Grand Legacy was about money and a man desperate to maintain a level of success beyond that of his own children.

"You can go in now. Mr. Locke is waiting for you in his study."

"Thanks." Noah saw no point in being rude to the guard. He was doing his job.

Noah strode through the familiar marble-floored foyer, under the antique crystal chandelier and to the left, down the long hall that led to the private quarters. Even this space, which could have easily been more humbly decorated, had a fine Persian runner and museum-quality paintings in gilt gold frames. The house was deadly quiet. A library had more life.

His father's study door was open and Noah didn't wait to go in. This would not be a long visit.

"Noah." Like a king who has no time for commoners, his dad didn't bother rising from his seat behind the tank of a desk to greet his youngest son. "I was hoping you'd bring your lovely fiancée. Or is there trouble in paradise? Perhaps you should've stayed in Florida with your friends, the Hannaforts."

Noah stood dead center in front of his dad's desk. "Honestly, things could be better. That's for sure."

His dad was smugly fighting a smile, but Noah noticed how much he'd aged. His salt-and-pepper hair was thinning more, his wrinkles were more pronounced. "Sit. Let's catch up."

"I'm good. I'm not staying."

"If things could be better, I take it your brother is having a hard time after we had our conversation?"

"It's not just Sawyer. I'm having a hard time with it, too. You can't have the hotel, Dad. It rightfully belongs to us."

"You mean it belongs to your brother."

Noah shook his head. "No. It belongs to all three of us now. Sawyer cut both Charlotte and me in on it."

"He'll bring you two on board, but he won't give his own father what is rightfully his?"

His father's sense of entitlement had always bothered

Noah. "I like how you care about fatherhood when there's something in it for you. Sawyer brought us in to protect the hotel from you. The Hannafort deal is part of that."

"So you admit that you're cutting a deal with one of my oldest business rivals, on a property that should belong to me? Do you have any idea how insulting this is?" The anger in his dad's voice was clear, but Noah preferred it that way. No hiding his true feelings.

"You treat everyone like they only exist to do your bidding and this is what you get."

His father's nostrils flared. "This is not what I get. I want the damn hotel." He pounded both fists on the desk. The sound reverberated through the room, but Noah stood firm. He didn't let it faze him.

Noah planted both hands on his father's desk and looked him square in the eye. His pulse pounded in his ears. Rage coursed through his veins. "You don't get the damn hotel. Great-Grandfather saw you for what you are. You never cared about it. You cared about appearances. Your own flesh and blood cut you out of the will and you can't stand the way it made you look." Now that he was on a roll, he couldn't stop. Noah reached into his pants pocket. He fished out the printed page he'd brought from the office, placing it on his father's desk. "We know about Dan Lewis and what he did to Lily's computer."

His dad hardly glanced at the picture. "I'm impressed. Dan's one of the best in the business."

"I don't really care what he is. The reality is that you tried to sabotage our company and we have the evidence. We'll bring charges of corporate espionage against you, but I'm hoping it won't get that far. I'm hoping you can finally learn to let your children live their lives." It felt so good to get that off his chest. Avoiding a brass-tacks talk with his dad had left a huge weight on his shoulders.

"Fine. I'll just give Lyle Hannafort a call after you leave. We have a lot of catching up to do."

"Tell Lyle whatever you want. I called him from the car a half hour ago and explained everything."

As that bit of news settled in the room, his dad's eyes reflected the defeat Noah had come for, but didn't relish. He didn't want things to be like this. But his dad had insisted on stirring the pot. Hopefully this could be the end. "So you told him the engagement was fake?"

"Was, as in past tense. Today, I ask Lily to marry me for real."

Fourteen

Even from across the street, Noah could see that Lily's favorite bookstore, Petticoats and Proposals, was packed. A steady stream of people was filing inside. More were out chatting on the sidewalk in front of it. This was not what he'd expected. Lily had always said she liked Fridays because the store was especially quiet and she could sit in the back corner and read in peace. Would she even be there? There was only one way to find out. Even when turning up at a busy romance bookstore with a bouquet of roses and a ring in your pocket was a sure way to look like you were trying too hard.

The signal turned green and Noah marched across the street, his heart pulsing at a rate he wasn't sure he'd ever reached when running. He spotted the sign on the door as soon as he got closer. An author was doing a reading and signing tonight. Judging by the crowd inside and out, this author was extremely popular. Noah really hoped Lily was a fan.

Noah pulled the door open. A bell jingled against the glass. A gray-muzzled beagle sauntered past him, winding between the people gathered, not noticing Noah at all, exactly as Lily had once described him. The bookstore had that familiar aroma of paper and coffee and ink. Lily loved it here. She'd talked about it many times. The stories contained on these pages represented the part of her that refused to believe anything other than love conquers all. Even when real life had shown her that loving someone only hurts, she still clung to the notion that it simply wasn't the right love. She'd taught him that. And now it was time to show her that their love was the right one, the one they'd both been waiting for.

He walked past the front counter, where the clerk was busy ringing out a customer. Noah walked down the center aisle between the bookshelves. This was the moment when everything would either come together or fall apart. He had spent a lifetime avoiding scenarios like this, never pushing things to their limit to test how strong they were. Whether he'd realized he was doing that or not didn't matter. He couldn't allow it to happen anymore.

He reached the back of the store and looked left, seeing only more books and customers. He turned right, and down at the end of the aisle was exactly the picture Lily had painted for him—a comfortable red chair and a reading lamp next to it. Noah's heart sank. The chair was empty.

A young woman approached him. "Can I help you find a book? Or did you get lost on the way to a photo shoot for a romance novel cover?" She nodded at the bouquet in his hands.

Noah felt foolish, but he was determined. "I'm hoping you can help me find one of your customers. Her name is Lily and she comes here almost every Friday night. She reads in this chair. She told me all about it."

A look of recognition crossed her face. "Pretty blonde?"

Noah nodded eagerly. "Yes. The most beautiful blue eyes you've ever seen."

"I know exactly who you're talking about. Come on." She waved Noah to the center of the store, near the back room where the reading was taking place. When they arrived at the door, she pointed to the front of the jam-packed room. "She's right there," she whispered.

Noah scanned the rows and rows of people, and the instant his eyes landed on Lily, his heart flip-flopped in his chest. There she was, as gorgeous as ever, listening intently to the author's reading. "How do I get in there?"

Several people standing in the doorway turned around and shushed him.

The clerk pulled him aside. "You can wait until she's done with the reading. It should only take another twenty minutes or so."

He considered this option, but it didn't feel right. "I don't want to wait. I feel like I've been waiting my whole life for her."

A look of charity and pity crossed the woman's face. "Maybe text her?"

Noah hated his phone, but it might work. Otherwise, he'd be forced to walk into that room. Talk about scrutiny—getting down on bended knee and popping the question was likely to get healthy critiques from romance readers. He fished his phone from his pocket. Turn around. I'm here.

He watched as she scrambled for her purse. He'd never studied a person's facial expressions more than at that very moment. When a smile crossed her face, the relief he felt was immense. She turned and their gazes connected. The room of hundreds of people seemed to fade away.

"Come here," he mouthed.

She got up, but it was no easy task to make her way through this room. Noah watched as Lily had to sneak her way out, crouching down and tiptoeing past row after row of people. By the time she reached him, she practically stumbled out of the room. "What are you doing here?"

The women who'd shushed him turned around again. He knew he had to redeem himself. "I'm here to hopefully make everything better." He held up the bouquet as evidence.

A wide smile crossed Lily's face and she took the roses from him and smelled them. "Thank you. They're lovely."

"You're welcome. Can we talk?"

Lily looked around. "Outside? There's no privacy in here."

Noah was so relieved. "Yes."

Out they went onto the street. Lily tugged on her coat and Noah helped her, but every second he had to put this off was grating on him. "Did something happen with the computer and Sawyer and your dad?" Lily asked. "It doesn't seem like you'd bring roses if there was more bad news."

Noah told her the whole story, complete with the admission that even Sawyer didn't know about yet, that he'd called Lyle Hannafort and told him everything.

Lily clasped her hand over her mouth. "I can't believe you spilled the beans."

"I had no choice. I didn't want us to live under the shadow of that anymore. It wasn't right."

"And it didn't jeopardize the deal?"

Noah shook his head. "In the end, the almighty dollar was stronger than a silly story in a tabloid or a fake engagement."

A contented smile crossed Lily's face. "If flowers are your way of inviting me back to work, I would've come back anyway. I love working for you and Sawyer. I'm so relieved it all got worked out."

He took Lily's hand and knew this was his moment. This was his chance to go for everything he thought he'd never have, his one shot to get the girl. Right there on the sidewalk, he dropped to one knee. Lily's eyes were bigger and more beautiful than he'd ever seen. Her smile grew, too. "Lily, I love you. I love you more than anything in the whole world and I can't even conceive of a life where you aren't at the center of everything." He reached into his pocket and pulled out the blue Tiffany bundle, hoping this was the right thing to do. "Will you be my wife?"

When he popped open the box, Lily gasped. She reached for the ring, her hand trembling. She didn't even take it. She only looked at it in awe. "Noah. The sapphire. Your mom's ring."

"The right ring. The only ring. The one you were meant to wear."

She gazed down at him, her eyes watery, but it was unlike the other times he'd seen her cry. He saw happiness and joy. He saw everything he'd ever wanted. "Yes, I will marry you, Noah. Yes, I will be your wife."

Noah rose to his feet and pulled the ring from the box, slipping it onto Lily's finger. "That other ring looked pretty good on your hand, but this one is perfect." He took another look at her and didn't wait, pulling her into his arms and planting a suitably hot kiss on her lips. He couldn't wait to get her stuff back from her apartment and move her in, again. This time, for real.

Lily ended the kiss and grinned. "I'm so happy, it's ridiculous." From inside the store, the muffled sound of applause came. A customer opened the door and hoots and hollers erupted from the store entrance. The window was lined with customers who must have seen the proposal. Lily laughed. "It appears we've attracted a crowd."

Noah wanted one more kiss. "This is one time I don't mind anyone watching."

Lily's second visit to the New York City Clerk's Office for a wedding was much more romantic than the first. She gazed at Noah, knowing now that he was hers. The years of longing for him were nothing more than part of their journey, the story they could tell their children someday. She'd done her time with unrequited love. Now she had it—Noah's affection, his devotion and his glorious self. She couldn't have been any happier if one of her favorite authors had written this happy ending. It was the one she never saw coming.

"By the power vested in me by the state of New York, I now pronounce you husband and wife."

Noah grinned like a goof, but there was that sexy edge to it, the one that said he couldn't wait to get her home and take off her clothes. Of course, there would be no tearing off the wedding dress. There would be careful and judicious removal of said garment, followed by hours of hot sex. She was going to get everything that Lily Locke was entitled to. Or Lily Foster-Locke. She still wasn't sure which was better.

"Do I get to kiss her?" he asked the clerk, suddenly seeming unsure of himself.

"Come here." Lily popped up onto her tiptoes and wrapped her arms around his waist, pulling him closer. The kiss was steamier than was probably warranted for a government building on a Tuesday, but Lily didn't really care.

They both lingered for a moment, lips still a whisper away from each other. Their breaths were in perfect sync.

The spark between them, the magnetic pull that made it impossible to stay away from Noah, was making its presence known. It took everything Lily had not to kiss him again. Lily heard a woman in the office speak. *I want a man to kiss me like that.*

Lily sighed, contented, and landed back on her heels, still grasping Noah's arms. She not only had a man to kiss her like that, she got to keep him. This was so much better than the first time she tried to get married, aside from the obvious upside of the desired outcome. Today felt like a happy dream, the kind you never want to wake up from, rather than an unthinkable nightmare. But even better, the pain she had gone through the first time was now a good thing. If she hadn't been dumped, she never would've moved to New York. If she hadn't moved to New York, she never would've found Noah.

She slipped back into her lovely new reality when Noah spoke. "Can we get out of here? I'm starving."

Charlotte was the first to congratulate them. Sort of. "Don't you dare screw this up, Noah. Or I will hunt you down and slap you silly."

Lily laughed, but Noah's forehead crinkled with annoyance. "Don't worry. I'm not about to let Lily out of my sight." He took her hand and squeezed it three times.

Sawyer appeared and held his arms wide for Lily. "I need to give my new sister-in-law a hug." When they were cheek to cheek, he said one more thing. "I hope you know how sorry I am that I ever doubted you."

Lily waved it off. "Water under the bridge. I don't believe in grudges."

"So I've been told," Sawyer said.

Kendall was right behind him. "Welcome to the family, Lily. I hope we can become good friends."

"Absolutely," Lily replied.

"Now let's eat." Noah kissed Lily's temple. "On to the Grand Legacy."

With a wave of his hand, Sawyer made way for Lily and Noah to lead the procession out of the building. A stretch SUV was waiting to take them to lunch at the hotel. Noah and Lily sat in the back, holding hands.

"I can't even believe today, Noah. It all feels like a dream. Pinch me."

"That sounds like something for later tonight." He nuzzled her neck and kissed that delicate spot beneath her ear, making her go weak in the knees, even though she was sitting.

"I can't wait."

The car pulled up in front of the hotel and they all climbed out. Sawyer, Kendall, Michael and Charlotte filed straight into the revolving door, but Noah held Lily's hand and kept her back.

"Is everything okay?" she asked.

"Everything is perfect. I just want to make sure you're okay with not having the wedding here at the Grand Legacy. Of not going through with the things you started planning with Marcy. I hope you know that I only made this suggestion because I didn't want to wait, but if you want to have a more formal ceremony, we can still do that. I don't want you to feel cheated out of your perfect wedding."

Lily raised her hand and dug her fingers into Noah's hair, admiring his fine face that she now got to kiss as much as she wanted. It was so sweet that he was concerned about this, but it was time and effort wasted. "I don't need the perfect wedding, Noah. I got the perfect guy."

* * * * *

LET'S TALK
Romance

For exclusive extracts, competitions
and special offers, find us online:

Or get in touch on 0844 844 1351*

For all the latest titles coming soon, visit
millsandboon.co.uk/nextmonth